THE YOUNG VICTORIA

Tyler Whittle was born in 1927, served for two years in the Royal Marines and began his writing career in 1955. Since then he has broadcast many radio talks and features and television programmes, written children's books, novels, books of essays on botany and gardening, a history of plant hunting and biographical novels on Richard III and Queen Victoria; some of his work has been translated into German, French, Polish and Japanese. He lives in Norfolk, his favourite part of England, and also has a home in the South of Italy. His greatest pleasures are collecting and cultivating plants, reading and bathing. *The Young Victoria* is the first of three novels on the life of Britain's longest reigning sovereign. The two later books are *Albert's Victoria* and *The Widow of Windsor*.

CONDITIONS OF SALE

THE YOUNG VICTORIA

TYLER WHITTLE

Unabridged

PAN BOOKS LTD : LONDON

First published 1971 by William Heinemann Ltd
This edition published 1973 by Pan Books Ltd,
33 Tothill Street, London SW1

ISBN 0 330 23656 3

Made and printed in Great Britain by
Cox & Wyman Ltd, London, Reading and Fakenham

TO ARTHUR AND DORIS GAMBLE

AUTHOR'S NOTE

Though a fictional treatment, *The Young Victoria* is entirely faithful to the known facts. Nothing has been deliberately distorted or omitted simply to make the writing easier or to suit a preconceived idea. No character has been invented save those who are representative of people who must have existed. The few small liberties taken to bridge gaps in the documentary evidence lie always within the seemliness of historical probability.

T.W.

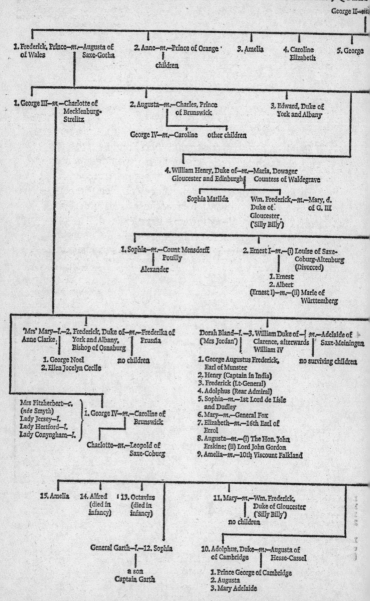

1. Frederick, Prince—m.—Augusta of
of Wales   Saxe-Gotha

2. Anne—m.—Prince of Orange

children

3. Amelia

4. Caroline
Elizabeth

5. George

1. George III—m.—Charlotte of
Mecklenburg-
Strelitz

2. Augusta—m.—Charles, Prince
of Brunswick

George IV—m.—Caroline   other children

3. Edward, Duke of
York and Albany

4. William Henry, Duke of—m.—Maria, Dowager
Gloucester and Edinburgh   Countess of Waldegrave

Sophia Matilda

Wm. Frederick,—m.—Mary, d.
Duke of   of G. III
Gloucester
('Silly Billy')

1. Sophia—m.—Count Mensdorff
Pouilly

Alexander

2. Ernest I—m.—(i) Louise of Saxe-
Coburg-Altenburg
(Divorced)

1. Ernest
2. Albert

(Ernest I)—m.—(ii) Marie of
Württemberg

'Mrs' Mary—l.—2. Frederick, Duke of—m.—Frederika of
Anne Clarke.   York and Albany,   Prussia
Bishop of Osnaburg

1. George Noel
2. Ellen Jocelyn Cecile

no children

Dorah Bland—l.—3. William Duke of—| m.—Adelaide of
('Mrs Jordan')   Clarence, afterwards   Saxe-Meiningen
William IV

1. George Augustus Frederick,
Earl of Munster
2. Henry (Captain in India)
3. Frederick (Lt-General)
4. Adolphus (Rear Admiral)
5. Sophia—m.—1st Lord de Lisle
and Dudley
6. Mary—m.—General Fox
7. Elizabeth—m.—16th Earl of
Errol
8. Augusta—m.—(i) The Hon. John
Erskine; (ii) Lord John Gordon
9. Amelia—m.—10th Viscount Falkland

no surviving children

Mrs Fitzherbert—c.
(née Smyth)
Lady Jersey—l.
Lady Hertford—l.
Lady Conyngham—l.

1. George IV—m.—Caroline of
Brunswick

Charlotte—m.—Leopold of
Saxe-Coburg

15. Amelia

14. Alfred
(died in
infancy)

13. Octavius
(died in
infancy)

11. Mary—m.—Wm. Frederick,
Duke of Gloucester
('Silly Billy')
no children

General Garth—l.—12. Sophia

a son
Captain Garth

10. Adolphus, Duke—m.—Augusta of
of Cambridge   Hesse-Cassel

1. Prince George of Cambridge
2. Augusta
3. Mary Adelaide

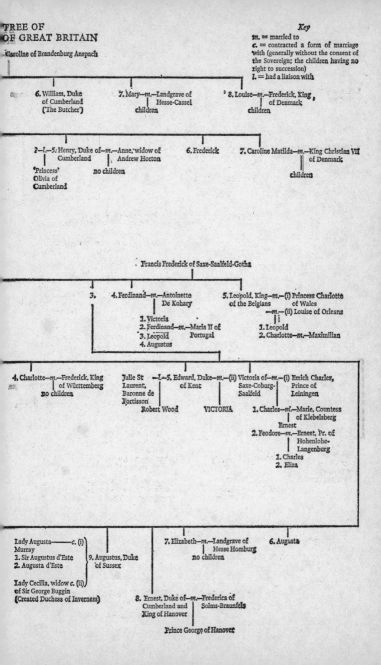

TREE OF
OF GREAT BRITAIN

Caroline of Brandenburg Anspach

Key
m. = married to
c. = contracted a form of marriage with (generally without the consent of the Sovereign; the children having no right to succession)
l. = had a liaison with

6. William, Duke of Cumberland ('The Butcher')

7. Mary—*m.*—Landgrave of Hesse-Cassel
children

8. Louise—*m.*—Frederick, King of Denmark
children

?—*l.*—5. Henry, Duke of—*m.*—Anne, widow of Cumberland / Andrew Horton
'Princess' Olivia of Cumberland — no children

6. Frederick

7. Caroline Matilda—*m.*—King Christian VII of Denmark
children

Francis Frederick of Saxe-Saalfeld-Gotha

3.

4. Ferdinand—*m.*—Antoinette De Kohary
1. Victoria
2. Ferdinand—*m.*—Maria II of Portugal
3. Leopold
4. Augustus

5. Leopold, King—*m.*—(i) Princess Charlotte of the Belgians / of Wales
—*m.*—(ii) Louise of Orleans
1. Leopold
2. Charlotte—*m.*—Maximilian

4. Charlotte—*m.*—Frederick, King of Württemberg
no children

Julie St Laurent, Baronne de Fortisson
Robert Wood

—*l.*—5. Edward, Duke—*m.*—(ii) Victoria of—*m.*—(i) Emich Charles, of Kent / Saxe-Coburg-Saalfeld / Prince of Leiningen
VICTORIA
1. Charles—*m.*—Marie, Countess of Klebelsberg
Ernest
2. Feodore—*m.*—Ernest, Pr. of Hohenlohe-Langenburg
1. Charles
2. Eliza

Lady Augusta——*c.* (i) Murray
1. Sir Augustus d'Este
2. Augusta d'Este

Lady Cecilia, widow *c.* (ii) of Sir George Buggin (Created Duchess of Inverness)

9. Augustus, Duke of Sussex

7. Elizabeth—*m.*—Landgrave of Hesse Homburg
no children

6. Augusta

8. Ernest, Duke of—*m.*—Frederica of Cumberland and / Solms-Braunfels King of Hanover

Prince George of Hanover

PART ONE

1

The King stood before a tall cheval glass. He was simultaneously trying on a new coat and listening to his secretary, Sir William Knighton. The frogging of the coat held more of his attention because Knighton was being tedious and talking business. This the King disliked. Once, when he had been Prince Regent, affairs had interested him. Now they bored him. He simply wished to be comfortable.

Knighton was being particularly vexing, advocating that the Duchess of Kent and her two daughters be invited to Court. It would, he said, be prudent.

The King sighed by way of an answer. Then he sighed a second time. He disliked his sister-in-law. She was tiresome, a dumpy, managing, obstinate female. She had lived through a pair of elderly husbands – first old Prince Leiningen and then his own rather ridiculous brother Edward – and she was as vigorous and as objectionable as ever. If Edward had not died of a chill in unfashionable Sidmouth, probably she'd have bored or bossed the poor devil to death.

Knighton was droning on. He was insistent that the boy and the girl from the Duchess's first marriage mattered not in the least, but the Princess Victoria was becoming increasingly important.

'It won't do,' snapped the King, interrupting the secretary's flow of talk.

'Sir, she is exceedingly close to the throne.'

'Thomas,' said the King to his page. 'Tell me candidly how this sits to my shoulders.'

'A second skin. A caress. It is perfection, your majesty.'

The King frowned. 'So it should be for I can't abide slipshod tailoring. Nor,' he added, turning to face Knighton, 'can I stand my brother's widow.'

In no way abashed, Knighton continued: 'It would be tactful

and prudent to acknowledge the Princess's closeness to the throne.'

'Tactful!' repeated the King. He seemed to swell with anger. For a moment he almost resembled the First Gentleman of Europe he had been in his youth. But his rage quickly died, and he was fat and sixty-three again; upholstered, corseted and raddled. 'Very well,' he said resignedly. 'Arrange it . . . No; ask Lady Conyngham if she would kindly see to the matter.' The King smiled because he enjoyed a little malice. 'She is so much more capable at these refinements than you, Sir William.'

'As your majesty commands.' Knighton bowed himself from the room.

Thomas poured the King a huge glass of cherry gin and he drained it in three gulps. His rouged and painted face cracked into a grimace. 'My poor brother Edward,' he said.

2

'Ma'am, it would be the very best thing.'

It was Sir John Conroy talking.

'The very best thing,' he repeated.

There was a silence. It lasted so long that the child behind the tree thought they must have seen her. She breathed out through her nose and screwed her small face up into a determined frown of stubbornness.

They should not say she was listening intentionally.

She would tell them they were wrong.

But then the silence was broken by her mother's voice. 'Maybe,' she said. And that was all.

Now this was peculiar. In her native tongue the Duchess of Kent was a chatterbox. Victoria had overheard someone saying so. Even in English she generally spoke rapidly.

Evidently the matter was very important.

'It's my advice to accept, Ma'am,' Sir John insisted.

'Thank you. I am obliged for your opinion. But . . .' Again

3

there was a long pause. 'But would he take to 'Drina . . .?'

The child flushed pink with vexation. For a long time she had disliked her nursery name. 'Drina for Alexandrina was a curds-and-whey name. She wanted people to use her more peppery name, Victoria. Elizabeth had been her father's choice, but the Regent had altered everything at the Christening. In a great bad temper he had also refused the suggested alternative Georgiana Augusta and, after a great deal of bickering over the font, the nervous archbishop had named her Alexandrina Victoria. She hated the way her mother reduced the two to 'Drina . . .

So busy was she thinking of this, and pursing her lips into a little 'O' of disapproval, she failed to notice that Sir John and her mother had walked on. When she did, she peered round the tree trunk to see how far they had gone. A slight sound to her left made her spin round again.

'So! Your royal highness has become a Paul Pry? A spy? A deceitful, sly young lady?'

Her governess, Fräulein Lehzen, was wagging a scolding finger.

Victoria was highly indignant. 'I am no such thing.'

'I saw you as I walked over the lawn . . .' Lehzen paused. The Princess was a wilful child, but never had she been found telling a lie. She told the truth no matter what it cost her – or anyone else. If a plain girl had asked the Princess Victoria for a frank appraisal of her looks she would have got it. There was no subtlety or compromise in her nature.

'Very well,' said Lehzen. 'Explain.'

Victoria did so, saying that her eye had been caught by a glitter in the trees and she had turned off the path to see what it was. In fact it had been no more than an evergreen leaf reflecting the sun . . . and she had not known anyone was nearby. It was an elaborate explanation, and appeared far-fetched. But Lehzen knew it was the exact truth.

'Yet you listened?' she said.

Victoria looked at her defiantly. 'Yes,' she said. 'I was interested.'

Secretly, Lehzen was delighted by her candour. And she could not punish her because she herself was at fault in dis-

4

obeying the Duchess's explicit command that the Princess should never be left alone. It meant that, sleeping and waking, the child never knew the luxury of privacy, and so occasionally Lehzen was discreetly disobedient to the general rule. She would permit her charge to run ahead on a walk in the garden, and on one never-to-be-forgotten occasion she had even allowed her to wander alone in the saloon, keeping watch herself outside the double doors, so that the little girl could wander where she wished, looking in the cabinets and picking up the bits and pieces of bijouterie without anyone telling her not to touch. Lehzen was a Hanoverian pastor's daughter but she had a softer, gentler upbringing than most of her class and kind, and she wanted Victoria to enjoy some of the same sort of sweets and liberties of childhood. They could not be many. Against the Duchess's regimen for an heiress to the throne of England there were few opportunities for liberty.

She sat down on the moss below the tree saying: 'It will mark my gown – but, then, it can be cleaned.'

Victoria thought this was wonderful. To be able to defy moss stains. 'Lehzen, why don't you chew your seeds,' she suggested. 'And then I can tell you why I was interested.'

What a pert little seven-year-old, said Lehzen to herself. How knowing of her to sense that I share her interest, and am vastly curious.

She patted the ground indicating that Victoria should also risk moss stains and sit beside her, and she helped herself to half a dozen caraway seeds from a small silver box. It was a private indulgence which she much enjoyed. Many ladies took snuff – and in huge quantities. She chewed caraways.

'Now, child,' she said.

Victoria told her what she had heard: that Aunt Gloucester had invited them down to Windsor where they would see the King, but that Mamma was not certain if it was wise to go.

'And Sir John?' prompted Lehzen.

Victoria grinned. She showed her talent for mimicry by repeating Sir John's words in a squeaky version of his voice: 'It's my advice to accept, Ma'am.'

'Victoria!' exclaimed Lehzen ... yet she could not prevent herself from laughing. It was scandalous to mimic the

5

Comptroller or the Duchess of Kent's household – but how well the child did it.

Suddenly she found herself being hugged. Not often did the child show such spontaneous affection. 'Oh, Lehzen,' she cried. 'I do love you for calling me Victoria. I hate the name 'Drina. I hate it.'

Lehzen hugged her back. Poor little royal sparrow, she said to herself. 'Victoria it shall be for the present,' she promised aloud. 'But only, dear, when we are alone. I must address you as your royal highness in other people's company.'

'As Sir John does,' said Victoria pouting. 'And I do not really like Sir John.'

Lehzen rebuked her. 'Now that will do, Victoria. You are not to say such things. Get up and brush the leaves from your dress . . . and play. Yes, play near here.'

'What at?' asked the practical little girl.

'Pretend to be Daniel, dear; being put into the lions' den by wicked Nebuchadnezzar.'

Victoria considered. 'I'd prefer, I think, to be one of the lions.'

3

Victoria dearly loved her half-sister Feodore. Dutifully she also loved her half-brother Charles although he ruled in Amorbach and she had no recollection of ever having seen him. Feodore had been close to her all her life and was her dearest friend.

In that summer of 1826 when Victoria was seven, Feodore was eighteen and as lovely a girl as any in Kensington – or England for that matter, said Victoria.

'You will be the belle of Windsor,' she told Feodore when the invitation, and their acceptance were announced officially by Sir John.

Feodore was pleased but not flattered. Her life had been so secluded that she had small chance of comparing her charms with those of other girls. She hardly believed what her mother or her maid said of her looks. Lehzen, entirely wrapped up in Victoria, never gave an opinion.

To her astonishment, on their arrival at Cumberland Lodge she found that Victoria's view was the common one.

The Duchess of Gloucester kissed her on both cheeks, held her at arm's length exclaiming: 'My goodness! My goodness!' and then rounded on the Duchess of Kent to ask why such beauty had been kept in seclusion.

'Like rhubarb,' chattered the Duke of Gloucester. 'Like rhubarb under a pot.' Not for nothing was he called Silly Billy, but Feodore gave him a smile to show she appreciated his good opinion of her looks.

'Gloucester,' said his wife imperiously. 'We will have none of that now, if you please.'

At this the Duke gave a little giggle and bowed to the company.

Princess Mary, Duchess of Gloucester, was the next to youngest of all George III's daughters. On the Kents' first evening at Cumberland Lodge she quizzed Victoria on all manner of subjects, and, when she was taken away to bed by Lehzen, congratulated her sister-in-law on having an eminently sensible daughter.

'As indeed is dear Feodore,' she added with a smile. 'Though she, fortunate girl, has none of our Hanoverian blood which needs watching so closely.'

The Duchess of Kent did not at all care for this, rose to her feet and announced that she would take her dish of tea upstairs. It was a signal for Feodore to accompany her, but Princess Mary claimed her rights as hostess to sweep Feodore away for a quiet walk, she said, in the delicious night air of Windsor Park.

She walked Feodore up and down the terrace and then led her through a nut plantation, saying how delighted she was that Victoria seemed so steady and uncomplicated.

'Because most of us are not,' she confided. She looked towards Windsor Castle. 'I never go there now. Not if I can avoid it. I used to with the Queen my mother and it was shocking to hear the dear King run on so. Poor blind madman – with his white beard and flannel dressing-gown, playing on a flute or eating cold meat while standing to attention. We all loved him so. It is uncomfortable to go there now.'

Feodore turned to make an expression of sympathy but to her surprise the Duchess lightly brushed it off. 'It's past and done and finished with,' she said. 'And none of us has lunacy in such concentration.' She allowed herself to chuckle. 'Though we're a quaint lot, a very quaint lot.'

There was nothing, thought Feodore, that she could say, so she remained silent.

'Take my Gloucester for example. He's my cousin, too. And Silly Billy suits him well. Not that he's vicious like my brother Edward.'

Feodore was startled. Edward Duke of Kent had been her stepfather and Victoria's father.

'Vicious?' she stammered.

The Duchess nodded. 'Cruel as a stoat,' she said. 'Caused mutinies and was court martialled. And then,' she added reflectively, 'there is my brother Cumberland.' She cast an eye at Feodore. 'You know about him, of course?'

'No, Ma'am.'

The Duchess evidently decided it was wise to leave the girl in ignorance about these two members of the family for she turned to her brothers the Dukes of Clarence, Sussex and Cambridge and afterwards enumerated some of the peculiarities of the King himself.

'The King?'

'Yes, George my brother. George the Fourth of England. Prinny.' She chuckled. 'I love him dearly and especially for his oddities.' She looked once more towards the Castle and shook her head. 'No, none of us has it in such concentration. Now, dear, it's turning chilly. We will go indoors and take tea. Duke of Gloucester,' she cried at the top of her voice. 'Ring for tea.'

8

4

Victoria had very much looked forward to the Windsor visit. Kensington she knew too well, and the routes chosen for walks when they were staying in Tunbridge Wells or Folkestone were equally familiar. Windsor, like Claremont, the country house of her mother's brother, Uncle Leopold, had the attraction of being largely unknown. She discovered that though Windsor Castle had recently been redesigned and new terraces and gardens made at enormous expense, the King still preferred to be at the Royal Lodge. This was very much his own home, a small tied cottage converted and enlarged into an extravagant house which suited him well. But there was only room there for his household and the large family of Lord and Lady Conyngham. Other Windsor visitors were obliged to stay with the Gloucesters at Cumberland Lodge and drive over to pay their respects to the King.

Her first sight of Royal Lodge made Victoria catch her breath. The roofs were reed thatched and the windows mullioned and the inside and outside were decorated and furnished with his excellent taste.

She pressed Feodore's hand. 'It is just like the forest cottage in Lehzen's tales,' she said.

But there was no time to study the Royal Lodge in detail. Aunt Gloucester was leading them into a hall where the King awaited them.

With eyes cast down Victoria curtseyed, a deep deep curtsey.

She had seen her uncle three years before, when she had been taken to Carlton House to thank him for a birthday present. He had been fat then, and tall. Now out of the corner of her eye she could see he was immense. His clothes were huge so was his wig, and so were his jewels. His voice, though, was neither as gruff nor as deep as she expected from such a big man.

'Give me,' he said, and smiled, 'your little paw.'

She returned his smile and held his hand.

'Excellent,' he said. 'Excellent, my dear Mary.'

The Duchess of Kent was not permitting her sister-in-law of Gloucester to take undeserved credit. Sweeping a curtsey to the plump satyr before her she said: 'My daughter is always your majesty's most loving and faithful niece and subject.'

The King frowned.

Hastily the Duchess of Gloucester presented Feodore.

'The Princess Feodore of Leiningen, your majesty.'

The King's eyes lighted. He was a connoisseur of such beauty as Feodore's. He bowed stiffly in return to her curtsey.

'Sister-in-law,' he said to the Duchess of Kent. 'You are to be congratulated. Excellent. Excellent.'

Which pleased that pained lady to such an extent that for the remainder of their visit she was unusually agreeable to everyone.

The King bade Victoria kiss him and she stood on tiptoe to touch his painted, wrinkled face with her lips. He smelt beautiful. Quite beautiful. Yet she did not care for his rouge. It was too thickly put on and uneven. One cheek was more raddled than the other. Uncle Leopold's pages were more careful in painting their master's face.

'And here,' said the King, 'is a small gift for my niece Victoria.'

He showed her a picture of himself set in diamonds attached to a blue ribbon.

'Lady Conyngham will pin it on for you,' he said.

The Duchesses of Kent and Gloucester exchanged glances, questioning to each other the propriety of such an action while that lady calmly stepped forward and pinned it to Victoria's left shoulder. 'All the royal princesses wear his majesty's picture as an Order,' she said in the child's ear.

Victoria smiled at her. Lady Conyngham was a plump, grandmotherly sort of person. Without any difficulty she could become fond of her.

'Thank you, my Uncle King,' she said. 'I shall treasure it.'

The King beamed down at her with pleasure.

Lady Conyngham took charge of events. While the elder

members of the party were refreshed with a collation in the small dining-room, the younger Princesses would be taken for a drive in one of the Royal Lodge pony chaises.

'Not Princess Feodore,' said the King to everyone's surprise. 'She, I am certain, would relish raspberries in wine.'

Victoria and Lehzen were led outside by Lord Mount Charles, one of Lady Conyngham's children, and there stood a perfect little chaise with a pair of grey ponies at the shafts. There was barely room for the three of them.

Lehzen eyed the ponies nervously and asked the young Conyngham if he could drive.

Lord Mount Charles reassured her, took the reins and whip, and shouted an order to the outriders. Off they went, across the park, down rides and avenues, to Sandpit Gate Lodge where the King's menagerie and aviary were kept. There were chamois and gazelles and some American deer called wapitis. Victoria said she preferred them to the others, though Lehzen remarked that for her taste they held their heads too high. One, attracted perhaps by the smell of Lehzen's caraway seeds, seized a piece of her coal-scuttle bonnet and nibbled at it gently. Victoria earned herself a rebuke for laughing at an old woman's distress, but she didn't accept it. 'You're not old, dear Lehzen,' she said calmly. 'And he hasn't harmed your hat.'

The King was not about when they returned to Royal Lodge. He had left a command for Victoria that on the next day she was to accompany him fishing. The Duchess of Kent was not at all sure whether this was safe or desirable, but she said little. She was too perturbed about another matter and wanted to return to Cumberland Lodge. There, in the peace of her room, she could think about her new problem and consult with Sir John.

That evening Victoria spoke with her uncle the Duke of Gloucester about the mysteries of fishing. She had been invited to fish with the King, she told him, emphasizing the last word self-importantly; and, to be truthful, she knew nothing about the art of angling. Would he be very kind and instruct her in the first principles?

'Why, bless you,' chuckled Silly Billy. 'Fishing with the King involves no effort. You don't have to do anything. Nothing at all. Just sit there and listen to the band.'

Puzzled, Victoria frowned: 'The band?' she queried.

'Yes, my dear. The band. Te-he. Te-he.'

'Duke of Gloucester,' came an imperious voice from the other side of the room. 'We will have none of that now, if you please.'

5

The King, Lehzen told her, was late rising and there was no point in fretting herself because it was nine in the morning and she was still at Cumberland Lodge.

'Your aunt of Gloucester has driven to Royal Lodge, and we are to meet them later on the way to Virginia Water.'

Only half pacified, Victoria pouted.

'We are to walk over,' Lehzen said. 'Which will be good for all of us. From there we shall use the pony chaises.'

'Lehzen,' Victoria switched to another subject, 'why did the King not give Feodore one of his pictures?'

Lehzen looked at her, wondering how much she knew or guessed. 'The Order is only for English princesses, and Feodore though she is your half-sister is a princess of Leiningen.'

Victoria put her head on one side. 'Is that why the gentlemen raise their hats and bow to me, but not to Feodore?'

'Why, yes . . .' began Lehzen, surprised at the question.

But Victoria did not let her finish. 'Then I think it very unfair and very unkind. Feodore is the darlingest sister in the world.'

'Most darling,' corrected Lehzen – and then, rapidly, before Victoria could continue her questioning: 'Why don't you go and find her? Maybe she will tell you about fishing.'

Victoria shook her head doubtfully. 'Girls don't often know about such things. And even Uncle Gloucester did not know.'

* * *

It was much later in the morning that the party walking from Cumberland Lodge met the Royal Lodge pony chaises.

The King was in the front chaise – a highly sprung yellow-coloured phaeton drawn by four grey ponies. Next to him was the Duchess of Gloucester.

He smiled on the Cumberland Lodge party and raised his hat to the Duchess of Kent, Feodore and Victoria.

'Pop her in,' he said to his sister.

The Duchess lifted Victoria into the yellow phaeton. Her mother was alarmed. It looked such a dangerous chaise.

'Take care . . .' began the Duchess of Kent, but Feodore laid a hand on her arm.

' 'Drina will be all right,' she reassured her mother.

The King cracked his whip and off went the yellow phaeton, tittupping up and down and from side to side on its high springs. His wig and that of his sister were all that could be seen from behind. Victoria, seated between them, was too little.

The procession of courtiers' chaises went at a more restrained pace and by the time it reached Virginia Water the King was already preparing to embark on his Chinese junk, *The Mandarin*.

Victoria held her breath. It was a perfect place to spend a summer's day, a more colourful scene than any she had seen before. There was an island with a Chinese temple right in the middle of the lake, the lacquer and gilding of the pillars and roofs shining brightly against the greens and blues of the trees and the water. Around the lake there were other temples, and a classical ruin put together from pieces brought all the way from Greece. Then there were canvas and silk pavilions on the water's edge, where Victoria guessed, and correctly, they would all eat luncheon. She realized that her Uncle Gloucester had been right. This was no ordinary angling expedition. She would not need to show her ignorance of rods and lines and hooks and baits. She was there to keep her uncle company and listen to the band.

It was a surprise to see so many musicians sitting in a long open boat moored out in the lake. She wondered what would happen if it rained. Would they be able to scramble ashore before their uniforms and instruments were spoilt? Or did they have umbrellas lying at the bottom of the boat? Besides the bandsmen there were large numbers of royal servants: keepers, bargemen, watermen, fishermen, gardeners, estatemen, grooms, and the King's personal pages, one to help him change his blue coat for a more sporty subfusc, another to present him with a glass of cherry gin, another to bait his lines and hand him the rod.

'Now, Victoria,' he said to her. 'Are you ready?'

She took his free hand and together they stepped from the landing stage into *The Mandarin*. The royal band immediately struck up the National Anthem which the King acknowledged with a careful bow. Afterwards he settled to his fishing and the band settled to an hour or more of Handel, Gluck, Piccinni, Mozart and Rossini.

The pleasure of that day was to remain a memory with Victoria for many years. The King caught two fish. Neither was very large but, then, neither was very small. On each occasion, as the royal quarry was drawn over the side of the Chinese junk, the band played the last four lines of the National Anthem.

> *Send him victorious,*
> *Happy and glorious,*
> *Long to reign over us;*
> *God save the King.*

The King bowed in acknowledgement and while one page rebaited for him, another handed him a glass of cherry gin. Victoria was interested to see how the fish were killed, by being knocked on the head with a mallet called a priest.

That evening, the last of their stay at Windsor, the Duchess of Kent took her two children over to Royal Lodge by special invitation of the King.

She did not want to take them. Victoria was being too much of a cynosure for the good of her character. She ought, rightly, to be tucked in her bed with Lehzen watching over her. As for Feodore, the King's high opinion of her attractions was too

14

obvious. His way of leering was revolting. Feodore must be saved from this royal satyr.

She made her point by preceding her daughters into the room. The precedence which should have been given Victoria as a princess of England and Heiress apparent was subject to the dignity of a royal mother.

The King paid no attention. He was too full of cherry gin and had eyes only for the two half-sisters: Feodore because her demure beauty fascinated him, and Victoria because she was a good and kindly girl who unlike many of the children he met when driving in Great Park did not shrink away from him in terror.

'Child,' he said to her. 'Tell me what you would like my orchestra to play and they shall play it.'

The musicians who had played on Virginia Water were now decked out in fresh clothes and played in the conservatory lighted by coloured lanterns. Victoria considered. Then she said, 'I think, Uncle, that I should like to hear "God Save the King".'

The King chuckled. He had no idea if she was a flatterer or genuine in her choice. But he liked her, pinched her cheek, and sent word to the bandmaster. 'I like it, too,' he said.

6

George the Fourth's liking for the Princess Feodore of Leiningen did not pass unremarked.

Feodore herself merely smiled when she heard by indirect routes that the King was devoted to her and would make her his wife. She sensed that the rumour was wrong.

Lady Conyngham sensed the same. She knew that her royal lover had a curious preference for elderly women like herself. A beautiful and young princess was something he could appreciate just as he might a good piece of lapidary work or a new dish at dinner. Her husband, the Marquess of Conyngham, was less sanguine. Old men have strange whims and fancies and there was nothing to prevent the King marrying again in order to try and produce an heir for England. This would not suit the Conynghams at all. Not at all. His only consolation was the thought that the King was possibly too idle to alter his way of life in the smallest particular.

The Duchess of Kent said nothing to anyone except her Comptroller, Sir John Conroy. It was this which had made her uneasy from the first moment the King's eyes lighted on her eighteen-year-old daughter. In either case she stood to have a daughter on a throne, but there was a difference, Sir John suggested, and a large one, between a queen and a queen consort. Should Feodore marry the King and produce an heir, she and not her mother would be Regent of the kingdom; whereas if common expectations were fulfilled and both the King and his brother William of Clarence died in the not too distant future, the Duchess's position as mother to the Queen would entitle her to be Regent. The privileges of such a post were many and enjoyable; the responsibilities would be lessened by the willing and secret aid of her confidential friend Sir John Conroy. It was a telling argument, and was strengthened further by talks with her own mother, the Dowager Duchess of Saxe-Coburg-Saalfeld, who visited England with Prince Charles of Leiningen early in the autumn and stayed at Claremont.

Leopold invited his sister to be there with Feodore and Victoria, and as Victoria had never seen her half-brother she was very excited at the prospect.

It turned out to be a dull sort of holiday.

Charles was conscious of his own importance as a reigning Prince and at the age when young men can't abide being bothered by little girls. Moreover it was Victoria's daily duty to accompany her grandmother for long and uncomfortable carriage drives and listen to talk about Germany and her Coburg relations. Afterwards she could only remember two things which had stood out in all that enormous welter of talk: that at Rosenau, the Coburgs' country home, there was an abundance of storks, and that the neighbouring Duke of Saxe-Gotha-Altenburg, hoping to win Napoleon's friendship, had given him a carriage shaped like an egg and painted gold and apple green.

The Duchess of Kent was frank with her mother, and her mother was equally frank in return. Feodore was a dear child, but Sir John had been right to emphasize the difference between being mother to a queen consort and mother to a reigning queen. Besides – and here the bent old lady leant towards her daughter – there was her plan to consider, the Coburg plan. This was to enlarge the ever-growing influence of the house of Coburg. She was busy herself supervising the schooling of the royal brothers Ernest and Albert. They were cousins to Victoria, Albert was about the same age, and both in every way fit for a dynastic marriage. Yes, Feodore was a dear child, but she would not be allowed to stand in the way of the Coburgs.

So the Duchess was persuaded to a course which in her heart she had already decided upon. Feodore would return with Charles and make her home at Amorbach until a suitable German princeling had offered for her hand and had been accepted.

Feodore reacted curiously. Kensington had been her home for more than seven years. She had come to England with her mother for Victoria's birth. She had been with her in the Sidmouth cottage when Edward of Kent had caught his chill and died. She had understood their acute shortage of money and the embarrassment of being unable to pay the Duke's many debts. She had been on the best of terms with all the servants and members of the Kent household, and she had been a devoted companion to her half-sister and mother. She knew that Victoria's life was hard and tedious enough already and without her friendship it would be the more unbearable. Yet, because she had shared the prison-like seclusion of Kensington she was overjoyed to be going to Amorbach. With her beloved Charles she would be as free as a liberated cage bird. To her mother she showed the pleasure. To Victoria she showed the pain.

'Dearest sister,' she said, hugging Victoria. 'It was inevitable. We could not always be together.'

She had not told the child the real reason for her exile: simply that it was considered best that for the moment she should be at her brother Charles's Court.

Victoria stuck out her determined chin. 'You are not to go.

Don't go, Feodore.' Her lips trembled and tears began to trickle down her cheeks. 'I cannot be without you, Feodore.'

Feodore looked over her head at Lehzen with questioning eyes. What was she to do to alleviate the girl's distress?

Lehzen took Victoria's arm. 'Dear, dear,' she said. 'You must not be so unhappy.'

It was as though she had released a spring.

Victoria stood to her full height. It was not much but it looked more. She threw off Lehzen's arm and tossed her head.

'This,' she snapped, 'is a royal matter. It has nothing to do with you.' And then she added cruelly, 'What can *you* know of such things?'

Feodore was aghast. 'Victoria!' she cried. 'If my leaving makes you so unjust and spiteful, then it is time I left. You will apologize to Fräulein Lehzen.'

'I shall not.' The chin was pushed out farther; the lips trembled even more. 'I shall not.'

'Then I shall go, and I shall not trouble to say goodbye to you on Friday when I leave.'

The threat broke Victoria's spirit. She loved Feodore so much, she said, and to be parted from her was a terrible thing. She begged Lehzen's pardon, and had it freely. Lehzen hugged her and Feodore hugged her, and she hugged them both in turn.

When Friday came Victoria was calm. She dutifully kissed her grandmother and Charles. She was still calm when she kissed Feodore, though she could not keep down a sob when the carriage began to move. Lehzen noticed, too, that not once did the little girl look at her mother. She would not, could not bear to look at the person who had driven dear Feodore away. Lehzen thought that probably Victoria would never forget that day. She was right.

7

The Princess Victoria was barely civil to anyone in the household. The servants bore with her because they sympathized with her loneliness. Apart from her governess and Madame Späth, the Duchess's lady-in-waiting, she saw no one; and she was sadly missing her adored Feodore. Sir John on the other hand recommended to her mother that she be disciplined for her sulks and tantrums. The Duchess demurred. She knew why Victoria was behaving badly and it seemed not unreasonable. Until the pain of Feodore's absence smarted less, the child would remain the same. It was a question, she said, of time. There was no point in alienating Victoria any further.

Old Madame Späth was there and she agreed. 'I don't believe she'll alter, your grace; not until Christmas.'

'Christmas!' barked Sir John. 'Ma'am, I'll not put up with her pertness until Christmas.'

'That is,' went on Madame Späth, 'unless she is given some sort of companion.'

They looked at her.

'Surely you have a daughter, Sir John, who is about the Princess's age.'

'Yes,' he nodded. 'My second daughter, Victoire.' He thought for a moment, then turned eagerly to the Duchess. 'I believe Madame Späth has suggested the best remedy.'

The Duchess agreed. She was fond of her Comptroller and especially valued his services because he had been a loyal friend to her husband Edward, but she was by no means blind to his faults. He was quite as ambitious as she, and he had immediately sized up the advantages of having a daughter in the close confidence of an heir to the crown. His mind worked as hers did. Therefore she could understand and respect him. 'The two girls must study together,' she said.

Lehzen was required to arrange things. As general supervisor of

Princess Victoria's education she asked Mr Davys, the Welsh clergyman who taught Victoria, if Victoire Conroy might conveniently be admitted to his classes.

The experiment was a success. The two girls took to one another, though being with someone of her own age was such a new experience that Victoria found it a little bewildering at first. She was stiff with Victoire Conroy, anxious not to be too familiar, anxious as well not to be distant and offend. Victoire, on the other hand, was a naturally cheerful child. She was not especially intelligent, but she was spontaneously good and kind. It was what Victoria needed after being deprived of Feodore and though Victoire never received the same sort of confidence she became a daily intimate and helped to fill the dull hours which passed between getting out of bed and getting back into it again at night. Only occasionally was anyone of their age allowed to penetrate the seclusion in which they lived at Kensington.

8

Two close relations lived in apartments at Kensington Palace; an aunt and an uncle whom Victoria grew to love. Aunt Sophia was the youngest sister of the King and between forty and fifty years old. She lived a strange life largely alone, refusing to have a permanent lady-in-waiting and making do with ladies who came to read aloud to her at appointed times. She visited the Kent apartments more regularly than any other member of the family and very often she brought small gifts for Victoria which no one else would have thought of giving . . . an orange stuck all over with cloves, an autograph of Lord Nelson, a glass bottle containing tiny seashells, an agave plant growing in a pot, a pistol made entirely of confectionery, and a flint arrowhead. There was a mystery about her. Victoria sensed rather than knew it because whenever she had questioned Feodore her half-sister had never given a satisfactory answer.

Madame Späth almost did once, or looked as if she was going to when Lehzen, clucking exactly like a hen and beetling her eyebrows, stopped her from going on. Victoria intended to find out about this secret one day.

Then there was her Uncle Augustus, Duke of Sussex – a huge man who was never without a black skullcap and was always attended by at least a dozen yapping dogs and a small Negro page, named Mr Blackman, dressed in gold and scarlet. His apartments at Kensington were full of books and clocks. The former he knew and loved so well that he was accepted as the scholar of the family; the latter were his hobby, and at the hour made such a confusion of ringing and chiming and striking the music from musical boxes that the noise sounded through the walls. Uncle Sussex, as Victoria addressed him, had a way of appearing in her schoolroom to see how her education was proceeding, and he was held in high regard by Mr Davys and all her other teachers. He, too, though, was mysterious. He had had a wife and two children so they said, and yet Lehzen denied it. They weren't ordinary, but a special sort of wife and special sort of children. No, not like her cousins the Fitz-clarences whose father was her Uncle William; these were called natural children, and did not belong to her dear Aunt Adelaide who visited the Kents at irregular intervals and was always very kind. And apparently Uncle Sussex was thinking of getting another special sort of wife, a widow called Lady Cecilia Buggin.

Victoria found her relations fascinating, at least those on her father's side. On her mother's side they were duller. They did not have special or natural children and complicated households. Her mother's brother Uncle Leopold was typical of them; a thoughtful and wise adviser and generous in his hospitality. He had come to England to be the husband of the King's daughter Charlotte, but she had died a year later and he had found himself a stranger cut off from his own country, living grandly in a house given to him by the people of England. Victoria wished that they could pay more visits to Claremont. The food was more exciting there and usually something interesting happened.

Apart from the oddities of Aunt Sophia and Uncle Sussex

21

there was little of interest at Kensington. That was why birthdays were so important. On May 24th each year Victoria was assured of an interesting day. Her relations came to visit her and brought birthday gifts, and sometimes interesting strangers came as well.

A visitor on Victoria's ninth birthday was one of her special heroes. Lehzen had introduced the girls to carefully chosen works of the best English poets, and Sir Walter Scott, a Scotsman, had been included. They liked his verses more than anyone's, and when he came to be presented to the Princess she was enormously excited.

Lehzen had arranged for Victoire Conroy to be there as well. It was Victoria's birthday but as the two little girls had read all Scott's poetry together, it was only just that they should share the pleasure of talking to him. The Duchess of Kent put an end to this plan. Victoire had no sooner been shyly led into the drawing-room by Lehzen than the Duchess told her to leave.

It spoilt Victoria's pleasure in meeting the poet. She had planned to name her favourite poem – and, if he wished, to recite a few verses for him. As it was, she only thanked him for the pleasure his poetry had given her and after that was silent. The great man talked to her mother and eyed the Princess. That evening he confided to his diary the impression that she already knew her destiny, that though people said she could not be aware of her position, he believed she did. He was wrong. She did not know for another eighteen months.

During this time her mother was anxious to bring her before the world's notice and planned long and hard how most effectively it could be done. Eventually she decided that the child must be presented to society under the aegis of the Church. The country was then in an uproar about Catholic emancipation. The Tories were violently anti-papist; the Whigs inclined to be tolerant. Some of the Coburg family were Roman Catholics and the Duchess knew how important it was to re-assure the English people that Victoria was being brought up in the Church of England. So she invited the Bishops of London and Lincoln to visit and examine her daughter. Victoria proved she was an apt pupil. Her replies delighted the bishops. They wrote in their report that the Princess was knowledgeable and pious and this was discreetly released to the newspapers. The King was also reminded of her existence from time to time in reports sent by Sir John to Lady Conyngham, or in formal letters written by the Duchess of Kent. Victoria once sent him one of her pictures. It was a copy of a sketch done by Westall her drawing-master, and the King was delighted. 'Drawn by the Princess Victoria, and given to me by her,' he scrawled on the back, and kept it.

Lehzen eventually judged the time was ripe for Victoria to realize who she was and where her destiny might lie. It was a March day, only the eleventh, and still winter outside Victoria's schoolroom when Lehzen showed her a genealogical tree of the sovereigns of England. She was ten years old and well able to follow the descent from William the Conqueror through the different dynasties which had occupied the throne. Lehzen noticed her start, but she said nothing for some time. Clearly she was returning back up the tree to its source in William I. Then she followed the tree down again to her own grandfather, her uncle and her father.

'Uncle Clarence will be the next king?' she asked to make sure.

'He will,' nodded Lehzen. 'And he has no heir. No son or daughter to follow him. Your cousins the Fitzclarences are natural children. Their mother is not your Aunt Adelaide of Clarence.'

'She has no children?'

'No . . . She had a baby daughter but it died, poor little thing. And since, though several times it seemed as if she would, she has had no more.'

Victoria's stubby finger moved to the right and stopped at the name of Edward, Duke of Kent.

'Then I shall be Queen!'

'Yes,' said Lehzen. That was all. There was really no point in saying anything else. There would be plenty of time later to instruct her in her duties and make sure she was as good a queen as possible.

But the child seemed to have decided this already for herself. She closed the book. 'I will be good,' she said.

Afterwards Lehzen made some attempts to teach her history,

23

but her heart was not in it. Nor did she have very much of her pupil's attention.

9

Victoria was not greatly changed by the realization of her inheritance. Being a child, the present mattered more to her than the future or the past. And the present was dull, unbearably dull.

Lehzen tried her best to help. No one could have been kinder, and Victoria loved her dearly. With Lehzen she felt entirely safe. Just before falling asleep in the small bed in her mother's room she took comfort every evening from the sight of Lehzen guarding her, the governess's gaunt figure by the fire in winter time, with her chair close to the window balcony in summer. But even Lehzen could not break her feeling of being imprisoned. She wanted to get out, away, to see things as other girls did. Victoire Conroy was there only two or three mornings in the week and then she told Victoria of the world beyond the palace gates. It tantalized. Worse, it intensified the boredom of being shut inside the gates. She became apathetic, disinclined to make any effort at all.

Her listlessness was noticed by the Duchess of Kent. She and Sir John were mildly concerned. They would have taken her to Folkestone for a change of air but the Duchess decided she did not care to leave Kensington in the spring and the idea was abandoned. They told her that if the idea pleased her Victoire could share more of her lessons – but just at that very time the two girls had quarrelled. It was a small matter and neither was deeply offended or hurt, but it made Victoria say no, she saw enough of Victoire Conroy already.

Lehzen said her condition was simply the Princess's age. Madame Späth was of the opinion Victoria still fretted for Feodore. Her mother thought her idle and Sir John said she was sly.

A new set of rules for behaviour and conduct in the royal schoolroom was thought out by Uncle Leopold's adviser Baron Stockmar and tried out on Victoria. She accepted the new regimen as she accepted the liquorice powder and castor oil administered whenever necessary by Lehzen. Simultaneously she made the sensible decision to avoid trouble by keeping out of people's way. Instead of wondering how best she could please her mother and Sir John, she studied how to be inconspicuous and refrain from annoying them. Madame Späth she did not mind, nor, of course, Lehzen or Victoire. Hardly anyone else saw much of her.

Madame Späth became increasingly important to Victoria. This was not at the expense of her relationship with Lehzen, but the child sensed that the old lady was as unhappy and as lonely as herself. Even Feodore had called her 'poor old Späth' and Lehzen was often at pains to make a fuss of her, which the astute Victoria knew meant Späth was really undistinguished and did not amount to much in her mother's household. So, to her, it was one need for companionship and sympathy meeting another; but Späth also delighted her by making speeches on the English nation and the English throne with a fervour and a grasp of her material surprising in a German lady. Lehzen, Victoria's official history teacher, happily approved of Madame Späth's romantic approach to royalty. No Jacobite could have been more fervent in her belief in the Divine Right of Kings.

Then Lehzen was made a Baroness of Hanover. It was by command of George the Fourth and at the special request of the Princess Sophia. Sir John was also honoured with the Hanoverian Order, but it didn't spoil Victoria's pleasure that her Lehzen had been rewarded for her loyalty and affection.

Madame Späth of course said it was a sign of the highest confidence by the House of Brunswick and thereafter she made a greater fuss than ever of her old friend Lehzen.

'But you are a baroness yourself, dear Madame,' protested Lehzen, trying not to laugh at the old lady's absurdity.

'Ah, yes,' replied the other, adding cryptically, 'but not as deserving as you are.'

She had a happy hour telling Victoria about orders of chivalry and how her uncle as King of England was one fount of honour and as King of Hanover he was another. It was a good opportunity to explain again what seemed particularly mystifying to Victoria, how by the law of Hanover a female could not be sovereign and, as she could not succeed to the throne, one of her younger uncles would become King of Hanover when she became Queen of England. More than likely it would be Ernest, Duke of Cumberland.

Späth spoke his name with bated breath.

Victoria wondered why. True her uncle looked frightening because the left of his face was scarred and his eye was distorted. But this came from an honourable wound in battle and he kept it decently hidden behind long whiskers and a high neckcloth. Besides he was far more elegant than any of his brothers. They were all tall but whereas they were plump and looked seedy Cumberland was always very erect and very slim. Even Victoria, though, had sensed that in other ways he was different from the rest of the family. She plucked up her courage and asked why Madame Späth had spoken of him in such a way.

Späth turned pink. Her round, chubby face puckered into a frown. She was a silly woman but not lunatic enough to frighten the child with wild stories of her Uncle Cumberland. Yet she did not know how to answer her quite, and had to take refuge in the grown-up's last resort with a curious child. 'Späth,' she said, 'knows best.' And that was that.

A little later when Victoria ran off to find Lehzen, Madame Späth fanned her hot face relieved beyond measure that she had managed to evade such a dangerous subject. The current scandal about Cumberland was that, enraged at being deprived of the English throne through 'that squab of my brother Edward's', he would not hesitate to harm her if he could. He had strong support from Irish Protestants and the Tory party and those who preferred kings to queens and called themselves the Salic Set. This Salic Set was an ever-present menace to the romantic Späth, and was even taken seriously by the Duchess who hated Cumberland and believed all the hot talk about him – even that he had murdered his valet and given his own sister, Princess Sophia, a child. Possibly a real fear of his malice was at the back of the nursery rule which prohibited the Princess

Victoria from ever being alone. Sometimes her food was tasted before she was allowed to eat it; most often by the devoted Madame Späth who, teased Lehzen, would gladly have eaten cyanide to show her profound respect for royalty. Lehzen was a sensible, solid woman, with a better appreciation of the Duke of Cumberland than either the Duchess of Kent or Madame Späth. He was stiff, bigoted, reserved, stubborn and often ruthless; but by no means as atrociously wicked as they made him out.

'Madame Späth,' she teased one day when that romantic lady ran in from the Park to say she had seen the Duke of Cumberland ride by. 'Did you smell the brimstone? Did he emanate sparks?'

10

It was a hot June day and a small knot of the family was gathered on the lawn beneath a giant cedar.

Princess Sophia was there, talking about nothing in particular to the Duchess of Kent. Both had parasols to ward off any sunbeams able to penetrate the cedar branches. Surprisingly the Duke of Sussex was also there. He sat a little apart from the rest wearing the inevitable skullcap with his black boy standing beside him. He did not consider himself part of the group. Driven to the garden to enjoy the warm air, he had his reading with him: an open copy of John Horne Tooke's *The Diversions of Purley* which made him sniff and grunt and exclaim 'Such bosh! Such bosh!' a score of times; and on the table, in case he could not bear to read any further and required alternatives, there were copies of Carlyle's *Life of Schiller*, Henry Hart Milman's *History of the Jews*, and a novel called *Granby* which, because novel reading was hardly proper in the company of ladies, he was prepared to describe as a social history of the lower orders.

Lehzen was busy with her workbox and Späth was teaching

Victoria to cover cardboard boxes with tinsel. The conversation was desultory and, with an eye on Uncle Sussex, it was hushed.

Victoria was not paying close attention to what she was doing. It was too hot. On such days she felt exactly like her mother's dog which panted uncomfortably in one shady place and then moved on to pant uncomfortably in another. There seemed to be no way of keeping cool. Her underclothes stuck to her and were prickly, and her chin was sore from coming in contact with the edge of her collar. It was too hot for concentration; too hot for anything.

Then the little group was disturbed by the Duke of Sussex's equerry. The young man came over the grass, bowed to the ladies, and said something quietly to his master.

The Duke looked up from his book. 'Eh?'

Softly the equerry repeated himself.

'It is bad news, ladies,' said the Duke. As he climbed to his feet he removed his skullcap. 'The King is dead.'

There was a stunned silence. King George had been ill for weeks, for so long that the announcement of his death took them all by surprise.

Princess Sophia who had loved him dearly began to sob out her grief.

Victoria, too, was in tears. She had the kindest memories of her Uncle King, but she was quietly and expertly removed by Lehzen, marched over the lawn and taken to the schoolroom. There she threw herself into her governess's arms and cried for the dead King. Later in her life she learnt of his terrible suffering, how they had drawn pints of fluid from his dropsical legs, and how, distorted, overblown and revolting, the King who more than any other in his dynasty cared for beauty and elegance had felt the shame as well as the pain of his appearance. If she had known it then, she would have cried the more. As it was she mourned him because he had been unexpectedly kind and gentle with her.

Lehzen waited until Victoria had finished crying and dried her tears. Then she tried to make her realize what this death meant. She was now Heir Presumptive. Unless her Aunt Adelaide had a child, she was next in succession to the throne.

PART TWO

1

Madame Späth was shocked to hear that King William the Fourth had begun his reign with such zest. As the chief mourner at his brother's funeral he had gaily followed the coffin smiling and nodding and waving to acquaintances in the crowded congregation, even going so far as to leave the cortège to shake one of them warmly by the hand. But it was characteristic of the man not to pretend to a grief he did not feel, and in any case he was known to be mildly eccentric. For years he had been gargling daily to prepare his throat for the day when he would have to make royal speeches by the dozen. He had practised his writing ready for the time when he would have to scribble 'William R' again and again. He had taken extra exercise as a prince because he knew he would not have time for it as a king. To avoid the chance of a chill carrying him off as had happened to his brother, Edward of Kent, he was careful in wet weather to wear galoshes. He was a seaman, and a jolly friendly man, delighted to be King and clearly intending to enjoy it.

If Späth was shocked at first by his *joie de vivre*, she was able to reconcile his undoubted good nature and sense of duty to her ideas of kingship. He treated England like a man-of-war and expected obedience from all hands. That being so he saw no reason why captain, officer and crew should not enjoy themselves.

Sir John considered him a nautical clown, and said so, an old salt who knew rather less about kingship than anyone in the family. He underestimated the butt of his jokes, but he cemented the Duchess of Kent's opinion of her brother-in-law William. She despised him and was not tactful enough to hide it. Almost from the first day of his reign they were at cross purposes.

To begin with the Duchess insisted that Victoria's position

and her own be made official, applying to the Duke of Wellington as leader of the Tories for the rank of Dowager Princess of Wales and a substantial increase in income to match her new dignity. Wellington refused. The Whig leader, Lord Grey, agreed with Wellington, calling her 'a tiresome devil'.

The King when he heard about this was in a paroxysm of wrath. Queen Adelaide did her best to calm him and she persuaded him not to write directly to his sister-in-law. Instead, in a roundabout way, the King's views were made known to her: that his brother Edward could never have been created Prince of Wales under any circumstances and therefore it was ridiculous as well as insolent for his widow to claim she was a Dowager of Wales. In passage the message was somewhat softened, but it still made the Duchess of Kent gasp with anger.

Parliament solved her dilemma and the King's.

A Regency Bill was debated and Victoria was named, apart from any possible children of King William and Queen Adelaide, as heir to the crown. In the unlikely event of the King leaving an heir, Queen Adelaide was to be Regent. Should Victoria succeed to the throne before her eighteenth birthday, the Duchess of Kent would rule as Regent. An additional £10,000 a year was voted for the household and education of Princess Victoria.

Still smarting at his sister-in-law's impertinence, King William was determined to cut her when she announced her intention of bringing Victoria to join the royal party on a visit to the House of Lords. But, again, gentle Queen Adelaide took the sting out of his action by making a great deal of the Duchess, even more than she did of Victoria.

The little Princess was the cynosure of all eyes. They cheered her in Palace Yard. They cheered her inside the building. She walked slowly and gracefully, as Lehzen had taught her, turning from side to side. The mourning black she wore and the trailing black bands contrasted with her rosy complexion. She looked composed and content. It masked her real terror at this great public function. She felt sick. She felt resentful, too. She had just been told that the Duchess of Northumberland was to be her official governess. No one should supplant her beloved Lehzen, not even a duchess. No one.

King William bobbed along, beaming at the peers, looking behind him from time to time at the small Princess Victoria. Had he fathered her himself he could not have been more fond of her.

2

Victoria's fear was groundless. Lehzen carried on as before — and always would, she promised. The Duchess of Northumberland simply attended certain classes, and wrote a regular progress report for the King. But Uncle William did try to insist that Victoria should come regularly to Court.

He came himself to Kensington to speak on the matter, and Victoria, waiting with Lehzen to be summoned to the drawing-room, heard at least half of what he said — for he roared as though ordering topsail men on a man-of-war.

He emphasized his right to command his niece's presence. But the Duchess of Kent refused. Her child, she said, would not go to a Court where the King's natural children swarmed and thrived. The inference was plain. Victoria was too pure a lily to be contaminated by Mrs Jordan's children. Her waspishness drove the King into a frenzy. She was insolent, less courteous and kindly than his own wife. When, at the time of their marriage, he had ordered a portrait of Mrs Jordan to be removed from the house, Adelaide would not hear of it. 'She is the mother of your children,' she had said, 'and this is where her picture properly belongs.' Such affectionate sympathy made William her slave and the recollection of it intensified his fury now.

'How, Ma'am,' he roared angrily, 'is your child to be fouled by contact with mine? Did not her own father live with Madame St Laurent for nigh on twenty-seven years, and has she not a half-brother, Ma'am, called Wood? Robert Wood?'

The Duchess did her best to interrupt the flow, but he was too angry.

'What bosh is this? On my birthday all my royal brothers would keep me company and visit Mrs Jordan with our children. Your own husband, Ma'am, was invariably there. He brought his band to entertain us. And the Prince of Wales led Mrs Jordan into dinner and sat on her right. It is stuff, Ma'am, this talk of propriety. It was for an heir that I was obliged to leave Mrs Jordan and make Adelaide my wife, and at the same time it was for an heir that my brother Edward left Madame St Laurent to marry you.'

He won the battle of words. His sister-in-law was driven into a thunderous and frozen silence. Yet she won in the end, for she defied his commands and continued to keep Victoria from Court.

The half-understood revelations about her father were made clear by Lehzen. Victoria was Hanoverian and precocious for her age. It was wiser to leave her in no doubt as to the truth. Victoria appeared more interested than shocked, but found herself on the side of the King and resenting her mother's interference. Disliking her mother was a treachery she would not even admit to herself. Keeping it bottled in, hidden from everyone, added to her nervousness.

Mr Davys inadvertently gave her another burden. He was a good and pious clergyman and though he lived in the rarefied and unnatural air of palaces he was also aware of the social conditions in the world around him. He failed to understand the true nature of such things as poverty and hunger and slavery and injustice, yet they distressed him. Not being a man of action, he could do little in a practical way to remedy the bad social sins of his generation, but he tried his best by writing small pamphlets and booklets addressed to the poor, trying to teach them patience and how to hope for better things.

Madame Späth admired Mr Davys a great deal. He could easily make the tears start to her eyes by telling her of the callous way children and women and the very old were used as draught animals in mines and pits and on the canal towpaths of Great Britain. Späth passed on a watered-down version to Victoria, less to give her an all-round picture of the land she would rule than to make her grateful for the comfort and security she enjoyed herself. It did neither. Victoria was horror-struck. She did not think of her own position in contrast to theirs, and that one day she would be their Queen. She simply believed that nothing could be done except grieve for them. This she did, spilling over her misery on to Lehzen, who sought out Späth and thoroughly scolded her for frightening Victoria. She was bidden to hold her tongue, and Mr Davys was bidden to write for the poor and not for Princess Victoria. If they made her wretched again the Duchess of Northumberland should hear of it and she would tell the King.

Lehzen was naturally trying to protect her charge but this time she made a mistake. The more the future sovereign could learn about the condition of her poorer subjects the better. Instructed carefully by Mr Davys, Victoria could have developed a social conscience from her natural sympathy for the poor. She would have learnt to care for them. As it was, she was momentarily sorry for them; but then the events of that year made her fear them.

3

Victoria's uncle, Prince Leopold, had been offered the crown of Greece, and he was by no means indifferent to the idea.

Once a penniless Coburg princeling, now the widower of a Princess of Wales, he was ambitious to rise still further. Yet choosing between a comfortable life in England on £50,000 a year, and a second-rate throne on the Aegean Sea was not at all easy. Ultimately the death of his father-in-law made him decide against Greece. King William was an old man, and despite his health precautions he could not be expected to live for very long. Leopold saw himself sharing a Regency with his sister. Even when the details of the Regency Bill were published, he still saw himself as being the prime influence over her actions.

Then he became less certain.

He visited Kensington once a week – Uncle Leopold's Wednesdays as Victoria called them – and he noted with growing concern the increasing influence of Sir John Conroy. His sister appeared to depend on her Comptroller more and more. Even Princess Sophia seemed to treasure every word that dropped from Sir John's handsome lips.

What, Leopold asked himself, is happening here?

He observed, grew more anxious, and went to consult the Duke.

Only the Duke of Wellington was referred to as the Duke. He liked to advise members of the royal family and was constantly at it. Prince Leopold's confidential inquiry drew a quiet retort from him that presumably a good-looking Irishman let loose among a lot of women could create the devil.

Leopold said no more, but on his next Wednesday visit he was careful to counsel his sister to be reconciled to the new king. It so happened that Conroy was present, and he immediately gave the contrary advice.

Leopold flushed scarlet. He was unused to being interrupted, and it was particularly galling to be contradicted by his sister's Comptroller. He reminded her that it was his duty and privilege to advise her on such matters.

She would not listen to him. Sir John, she said, was in a better position to judge the matter than he was.

He stared at her in bewilderment. Her behaviour was quite out of character. She was, in fact, so unlike herself that, there and then, she took occasion to criticize him for the first time in many years. She asked if he would please do something about his strange appearance. He was getting himself laughed at by wearing a feather boa and shoes with three-inch-high heels. His wigs, too, were outrageous, and he was overpainting himself. In a plain man these eccentricities would not matter, but he happened to be good looking and his oddities were bringing the family into disrepute. Moreover – she went on rapidly before he could say anything – his affair with Caroline Bauer had gone on long enough. It ought to stop.

'Victoire, you wrong her,' he broke in to protest. 'She is Stockmar's niece and we have known her since we were children.'

'She is an actress,' said his sister warmly, 'living in one of your cottages, accompanied by her mother.'

Both statements happened to be correct and Leopold was too good-natured to allow his sister's asperity to anger him. 'Come,' he said. 'We must not quarrel . . .'

'It is as you wish, brother,' she said in a tone of cold indifference. 'I have merely expressed my point of view.'

For the first time Uncle Leopold's Wednesdays became irregular. He had decided to leave the field clear to Sir John who would undoubtedly ruin himself with his insolence. If his sister wished to be so foolish, then she was at liberty to do so. He would now concentrate his attention on Victoria, and help her to prepare for the day when she would be Queen. This was his intention and he would have carried it out in person, but sudden dramatic events in Europe made it impossible for him to be often at Kensington.

Victoria missed him more than anyone. She really needed his advice, and, in this household of hostility, she wanted to be able to confide in someone from outside.

Moreover the very events which were keeping him away were beginning to frighten her.

Lehzen gave her the bare facts.

The French had rebelled, she said, and had driven out their King.

Späth expanded this. She was in a great flutter; fascinated yet alarmed that the barricades had been thrown up in Paris, the Hotel de Ville seized, the tocsin rung, the tricolor hoisted, and Charles the Tenth driven from his kingdom by a mutinous Army.

Victoria caught a part of her alarm. She asked why the French had rebelled, why? But Späth did not know. She supposed it had been caused by mobs, a word which meant to her everything that was lawless and terrifying. All she could think of was the poor Bourbon King living uncomfortably in the damp and cheerless Holyrood House. 'Which is all the Tories dared give the poor King, all they dared. Revolution is in the air.'

Even allowing for Späth's romanticism and her excitability, there certainly seemed to be cause for some anxiety. If the mobs were out of control in France, they might be anywhere.

Leopold, with wide interests in Europe, was not there to calm her and give her a sense of proportion.

When four weeks afterwards the people of Brussels rose against the Dutch, it seemed to confirm Späth's prophecy that the mobs would take over. The rebellion was put down, but another rose in September and this was successful. The Dutch were driven from Brussels.

At the same time there were agitations and political troubles in England. The King was abused while driving through London. Law and order were threatened. The dissenters, manufacturers, merchants and the lower orders called out for Parliamentary reform. Large and rich towns like Birmingham and Manchester, Leeds and Sheffield had barely any members to represent them in the House of Commons whereas some town corporations and many private individuals virtually 'owned' seats and either gave them to favourites or for cash to the highest bidder. The gentleman who sat for the constituency of Old Sarum represented himself, a grassy mound, and a ruined wall. Radical rabble-rousers denounced the traditional rulers of the country, the landowning aristocracy, some Tory, some Whig. Inflammatory speeches were made by republicans against the monarchy and nobility. Trade unionists preached open revolution if Parliament was not reformed.

The Duke of Wellington's Tory ministry tottered and fell. Huskisson, leader of the Tory Canningites, might have taken power but, just at this vital time, he was killed, being run over by a slow-moving locomotive at the official opening of the Manchester and Liverpool Railway. Lord Grey, the Whig leader, formed a ministry which promised some measure of reform.

Simultaneously the poor of Great Britain began to react violently against their intolerable conditions. There were riots in the industrial areas and riots in small country villages. Looms and engines were wrecked because men feared that they would be replaced by machinery. In the countryside the price of corn and the labourers' inability to supplement their diet drove them to burn standing ricks and growing corn.

The penal laws were severe; Mr Davys said they were worse, they were savage. For burning a rick a man could be hanged. For taking a hare or a rabbit a man could be imprisoned or deported for seven years. The laws were in defence of privilege and property.

The aristocracy and middle classes were in a fright. Everyone believed revolution was close at hand. Jewels were buried, plans made to emigrate with the most valuable of portable possessions. Fantastic suggestions were sent in to Lord Melbourne, the Whig Home Secretary, amongst them that the French and the Jesuits were behind the disturbances and that the ricks were set alight by fireballs shot from guns disguised as umbrellas.

Lord Melbourne remained calm. It was not an affectation. During his few leisure moments while the worst of the rioting took place he was continuing his study of Druidism and reading *As You Like It*. His mood of confidence was infectious. He refused to consider more severe legislation against rioting, but forcefully applied the penal laws which already existed. Once brought to court, his order was that the guilty should be condemned with all the severity the law allowed – on the principle that afterwards, when the fuss was over, they would be quietly reprieved. But it was neither a quick nor an easy accomplishment, and for a long time Britain was open to the threat of widespread revolution.

A good deal of all this was kept from Princess Victoria, but Späth could not hold her tongue, nor could she resist embellishing a tale. By the early autumn Vitoria was in great dread of mobs. Mr Davys tried to reason with her and put the rioters' point of view. It only made her fractious. She became jumpy, given to starting at any unusual sound. Her cheeks paled. She slept badly and when she did sleep she had nightmares.

Then, one night, she saw a crimson sky to the south of Kensington village and knew that ricks were blazing there. She was convinced the palace would be attacked. It was a natural target for republicans who would wish to seize the heir to the throne.

Lehzen tried to calm her. First she was forceful. Then she coaxed her. But Victoria was in such a state of nerves that the governess decided it was her duty to send for Dr Clark the household physician. He had some claim to fame, having tended the poet Keats on his deathbed in Rome, as well as being a well-known fanatic about the qualities of fresh air, and Lehzen was nervous at having disturbed him. But he was quite undismayed. 'Not at all! Not at all!' he said, and after examining Victoria he prescribed laudanum and a hot posset.

'She must sleep,' he told Lehzen. 'Otherwise I should recommend her being sent by carriage to see the burning ricks. She would then know that these country labourers bear her no malice. It would be wholesome medicine.'

Lehzen was aghast at the suggestion. 'I'd not risk a hair on her head,' she said forcefully.

They were whispering, but Victoria in her small bed could hear what they said. She lay looking up at the ceiling. The red sky to the south was slightly reflected by the white plaster above her. It burnt rosily, and sometimes it flickered.

She closed her eyes when Lehzen tiptoed over to see if she was asleep. Then she heard the whispers again. Lehzen was saying that she would see the doctor out.

The door clicked behind them.

Victoria opened her eyes again. In the familiar ceiling she saw the mob, hundreds and hundreds of faces looking down at her. Some were smiling cruelly. Others were ferocious. There were women as well as men, even a few children. All were unkempt and dirty. One stretched out a hand. It grew larger as it came closer . . .

She sat bolt upright in bed holding her head in her hands, shaking it from side to side, wanting to empty it of the faces there, of the menace, of the mob.

She longed to be comforted. Where was Lehzen?

The red light brightened. The rick had fallen in on itself and sent up a blaze of sparks. Terrified, the child jumped out of bed and ran to the second door which led into her mother's private drawing-room. Without knocking she turned the handle and ran in to throw herself in her mother's arms.

But someone else was there, very close to her mother, and her mother spun round with a startled exclamation.

When she saw the little girl she frowned with vexation. ' 'Drina,' she asked, 'what are you doing here?'

Victoria saw that it was Sir John in the background.

'I was . . . I was dreaming, Mamma.'

'Then go to Lehzen,' said the Duchess angrily. 'Go to Lehzen, child.'

39

At that moment Lehzen appeared behind Victoria in the doorway. 'Lehzen,' snapped her mistress. 'Look after 'Drina. She has been dreaming.' She nodded, and added distinctly. 'Yes, she has been dreaming.'

It was some time before Lehzen could soothe Victoria's fears. When, at last, she had done it, and had tucked in the covers and kissed her, the girl suddenly said: 'Lehzen, why did Sir John have his arms about Mamma's waist?'

Lehzen caught her breath. She managed to force a laugh. 'I've not the least idea,' she said.

4

Fortunately for Victoria the local riots were quickly and quietly subdued. But she did not forget what she had seen in her mother's private drawing-room.

Instinctively she wanted to talk about it, and it was no use consulting Lehzen. She had a way of avoiding questions. Madame Späth, on the other hand, never failed to answer questions. Victoria went to her and told her the facts. She wanted to know if she was wrong to feel jealous of Sir John.

Späth was flabbergasted. Being a born courtier she could wear two faces and she had the cleverness to hide her dismay while she talked mildly with Victoria and said there did not seem to be any real cause for jealousy. But for herself, the more she thought about what she had heard, the more fluttered she became. She felt strongly her responsibility as the Duchess's lady-in-waiting.

It was some days before she decided on her plan and during this time she constantly observed her mistress. Small incidents which before would have had no significance began to mean something. She noticed, as well, how the servants reacted to a situation which, clearly, was not new. Without saying a word they showed that they knew precisely what was happening.

Late one afternoon Späth had her opportunity. Her mistress was preparing for dinner and the maid who usually brushed and dressed her hair was unwell and unable to be there. Späth took on the duty herself and as agreeably as she could broached the awkward subject.

She hinted, merely hinted, that the Duchess's indiscretion was fairly widely observed.

She bungled it.

The Duchess was quickly on the defensive and prickly to the faintest hint that her behaviour had been anything but circumspect. Späth, with barely anything said, found herself cut short and told to send a substitute lady's maid to attend to the hair.

5

Queen Adelaide was entertaining friends.

Besides her ladies there were a few well-chosen guests, and Princess Sophia, who had been asked not because she was a particular friend but because she lived at Kensington and probably knew precisely what was going on.

The Queen wished to know. At one time she had been a regular visitor at Kensington and would go when she wished. Yet now she was kept waiting in a small room until the Duchess chose to appear because this emphasized her own importance as mother to the heir of the throne. Adelaide, though a queen, felt it keenly. Near to the window where they were sitting at that very moment there was a marble effigy of a small baby, the Princess Elizabeth, the only one of all her children to live. For four short months a long time ago the baby had stood between Victoria and the throne.

Carefully the Queen introduced the topic of Kensington and then was frank, regretting the quarrel between the King and his sister-in-law of Kent.

'We long to see the Princess Victoria, and she ought to be

seen by the Court, but her mamma is obdurate . . .' She left the sentence in mid air.

'Her mamma is thoroughly German,' said Princess Sophia.

It was not the most tactful of remarks as Queen Adelaide was a Princess of Saxe-Meiningen, but to everyone's astonishment the Queen nodded.

'There are light and heavy Germans,' she agreed with a smile. 'And the Duchess of Kent is of the heavy variety. I told the Prime Minister not long ago that the Kensington squabbles do not surprise us in the least. The cause is that German *morgue* and little-mindedness which is so rampant there.'

It was a direct invitation to Princess Sophia to comment on the Kensington squabbles. She did not take it up.

'It is so mortifying,' went on the Queen, to tantalize her further. 'Victoria was not even permitted to come to Court for my birthday.' She sighed: 'Such behaviour is very heavy German.'

Princess Sophia at last responded. They were not all German at the Duchess's Court, she said. Many of the Princess's instructors were English, and the Comptroller Sir John Conroy was Irish.

'Ah, yes,' said the Queen softly. 'I had forgotten Sir John.'

She eyed the long face of her sister-in-law. The faintest possible heightening in the colour of her cheeks made it clear that Sophia was taken by Sir John.

'And dear Lehzen and Späth are light German,' she continued. 'As light as raised pastry.' She sighed. 'It is so sad that Späth is to be dismissed.'

The assembly buzzed. Most had already heard the news, but did not wish the Queen to know they knew.

Princess Sophia said nothing.

'You know, of course, about poor Späth's going?' said the Queen. 'It will make a great noise in the world.'

The buzzing grew again. Princess Sophia silenced it. 'Why?' she asked abruptly.

Evenly the Queen replied, 'Because undoubtedly it will kill her. Yes, kill her.'

'It will,' cried one of her gentlemen named Paget. 'It will. Oh, who can be responsible? I'll not believe the Duchess herself guilty of such cruelty.'

The Pagets were great favourites at Court and therefore very much against the Duchess of Kent and all her household, in particular the Comptroller, Conroy. The innuendo that he was responsible for Späth's dismissal did not remain unchallenged.

'Pray, Mr Paget,' said Princess Sophia tartly. 'Name whoever you believe to be responsible.'

'No names,' said the Queen. 'No names.' She went on to lament at the Princess's upbringing, that at one moment she was made too much of and at the next locked away from everyone's eyes. Her temper, too, was not sufficiently controlled.

'Is that not so, Princess?' asked the Queen suddenly and directly.

Taken by surprise, Princess Sophia nodded in agreement. 'She is, yes, wilful.'

'Ungovernable rages?' urged the Queen. 'Quite out of control?'

Princess Sophia would only admit that Victoria was a passionate child.

'Without Madame Späth she will be the more passionate?' suggested Paget.

'Indeed, no, Mr Paget; Baroness Lehzen has entire charge of the Princess. Baroness Späth is the Duchess's lady-in-waiting.'

'She was,' corrected the Queen.

6

'Ma'am, I have had the most strange letter from the Princess Sophia.' Sir John looked down on the small Duchess. 'She tells me the Queen and her ladies, even Mr Paget one of her gentlemen, spent last evening discussing the dismissal of Baroness Späth.'

The Duchess drew in a sharp breath. 'The insolence,' she hissed. Once she had been friendly with Queen Adelaide and had enjoyed her visits to Kensington. There would be no more now. It was an intolerable impertinence to talk of such matters about her Court. Then she was struck by a thought.

'Why should the Princess have written this to you, Sir John?' she asked.

He did not reply for a moment, but kept his eyes down. Then he looked at her and shrugged his right shoulder. It was so slight a movement as to be barely perceptible, but it told the Duchess all she wanted to know. Or rather, what she did not want to know. Sir John also had formal charge of Sophia's affairs and saw her in the course of business, but it was clear now that she had been setting her cap at him. The Duchess would brook no rival.

'Princess Sophia should not intrude,' she snapped. 'We do not interfere with her private life nor her weekly visitor.'

The visitor was the Princess's bastard son, a young Army officer named Garth. His father, an old general in the service of George the Third, had caught her eye nineteen years before at Windsor. This was the child which rumour said had been fathered by her brother, the infamous Duke of Cumberland.

Sir John smiled. He was well content. The Princess Sophia had served her purpose and could be now set aside. Knowing her to be a rival for his affections, the Duchess would be cold towards her sister-in-law. After what she had heard she would be cold to everyone else in the royal family, too. She was becoming more and more isolated as he had planned. After Späth, Lehzen.

'How has the Princess Victoria received the news?' he asked.

'Späth begged to be allowed to tell her herself. She is to say that health and family reasons make it necessary for her to leave us. It will come better from her because the child will not then guess she has been dismissed.'

Madame Späth's round face was crinkled with misery. Tears stole from under the rims of her spectacles and down her cheeks. She was trying with all her might not to sob out loud.

Victoria was less able to control herself. She threw herself into the Baroness's arms.

44

'Dear Späth,' she cried. 'Dear Madame Späth!'

The old lady found her tongue at last. 'I shall write: yes, I shall write to you. Often.'

'But why must you go?' Victoria sobbed.

'I'm an old woman, and not very well,' Späth pretended gallantly. 'It is time I saw Germany again. And it is decided that I shall go to our dear Princess Feodore.'

'Why? Oh, why?'

Späth held the girl at arm's length, and looked at her through tear-smeared spectacles. She told her the same lie again. She had to although it broke her heart. And it was a sign of her great distress that, though she invariably addressed the child as Princess or your royal highness, this time she called her Victoria.

'I am going now, Victoria . . . Yes, I am going directly. And you are not to follow me. No. I beg you. A royal princess must not be seen to cry in public. Baroness Lehzen will be with you directly.' The old lady took off her spectacles, with trembling hands, wiped them with a handkerchief and dabbed at the corner of her eyes. Afterwards, with great dignity, she swept a curtsey to the sobbing little girl before her.

'My love and my duty will always be with your royal highness,' she said quietly. Then she quickly kissed the girl's forehead. 'Yes, for ever, dear Victoria.'

Lehzen was waiting for Späth beyond the double doors.

'Go to her, Baroness, she is in tears.'

'Grief is difficult to share,' replied Lehzen. 'And she will not mind waiting for the short time it takes me to accompany you to your carriage.'

'Baroness, I forbid it. Your duty is to the Princess.'

'Madame Späth, we have been together in the Kent service for a very long time. I shall come with you to your carriage.'

Späth was moved to fresh tears, but these were of gratitude. The haste in which she had had to sort out her clothes and the hoarded souvenirs and little treasures of many years and supervise their packing into boxes and trunks had dulled the terrible fact of her dismissal. Now she was actually leaving her home she was acutely aware of it. She took Lehzen's arm and together they walked down to where the carriage was waiting. 'After so long,' she kept saying, half aloud. 'After so long.'

As they reached the foot of the staircase Lehzen's arms stiffened. She slipped away and curtseyed to the Duchess of Kent who was crossing the hall. Späth's hand caught at her dress and she would have curtseyed too, but just then all the hurt of her dismissal seared at her like a burn. She would not, could not be deferential or even courteous to the woman who had turned her off. With her head high she went straight to the door.

The Duchess started. A frown spread across her face. She was so outraged at the insult that she almost called Späth back, but wisely she refrained. Späth, she guessed, would have paid no attention. With a crimson spot on each of her cheekbones, she walked angrily from the hall.

The carriage which was to take Späth to Gravesend was piled high with her luggage. She was helped inside and the steps taken down.

Lehzen stood on tiptoe to kiss her old cheek. She asked to be remembered most affectionately to Princess Feodore. She wished Späth well, and a good journey. And then because Späth was crying so and she could think of nothing useful to add, she simply stood there, running her fingernail up and down the dusty window pane.

The grooms took off the horse wrappings and stood back. The footman leapt up behind. The coachman was ready and looked round for an order. Neither of the ladies said anything so he took it on his own head to whip up his team.

'Oh, Lehzen,' cried Madame Späth as the carriage jolted and began to roll away. 'Oh, Lehzen!'

The governess waved, and she waved. Then she sat back. She had wanted to say so much and had wasted her time in tears. But tears were a sign of a broken heart, and, truly, she felt her heart was broken.

She looked at the pattern made by Lehzen's fingernail up and down the dusty window pane. It made her burst into a final paroxysm of tears, and all she could mouth through her sobs was the same bitter regret: 'After so long. After so long!'

7

Victoria looked down from a high window to the carriage which was bringing her mother's new lady-in-waiting to the palace. All the reports of Lady Flora Hastings were excellent. She was young, between twenty and thirty, the eldest sister of Lord Hastings, and besides being pretty had a sharp wit and a great sense of humour. But neither Victoria nor Lehzen was pleased by her arrival. Victoria disliked her as a matter of course because she was replacing her beloved Madame Späth. Lehzen feared that a witty, pretty young lady might cause further havoc in a household already made restless by the Duchess's dependence on Sir John Conroy and her consistent rudeness to the King and Queen. She was right, the half subdued friction in the palace was aggravated by Lady Flora; but simply because she swiftly allied herself with the Duchess and the Comptroller and took to using her sharp wit on everyone else. Lehzen unhappily became her prime target. She never ceased to mock at her habit of eating caraway seeds and managed to make Sir John join in the ridicule. Up to that time he had hardly ever spoken to Baroness Lehzen; now she was vexed beyond measure by his condescending tone and his coarse laughter whenever she was detected eating caraways. And it did not at all endear Lady Flora to Victoria.

For the time being it appeared that Victoria's one aim and purpose in life was to re-establish Madame Späth in the Kensington household.

She had ferreted out the fact that she had been dismissed but no one appeared to know why.

Her Aunt Sophia told her most, which was rather strange because for some time Aunt Sophia had not been given to talking with her a great deal. But, then, Aunt Sophia was strange altogether these days. Once she had been often in the Kent apartments. Now she was seldom there. Once she had been in constant praise of Sir John's capable management of her affairs. Now it seemed he could do nothing right. Once she had loved to chuck Victoire Conroy under the chin. Now she openly bewailed that the child was permitted to share some of Victoria's lessons. It would not do, she said, and would simply give the girl ideas above her station. Moreover her influence over the Princess could not be considered wholesome.

Sir John accepted her criticism and insults without comment. He continued to be as bland and as suave as ever.

Not so the Duchess of Kent, who became shorter and shorter with her sister-in-law until they were barely on speaking terms at all.

If Aunt Sophia could have got back old Späth from Germany to please Victoria she certainly would have done so.

Victoria had hoped for help from her Uncle Leopold. But though he had listened sympathetically and had taken the trouble to talk for a long time in private with Lehzen about Madame Späth's dismissal, his sphere of influence at Kensington suddenly ceased altogether. The once regular Uncle Leopold's Wednesdays had already become very irregular and uncertain. Now they ceased altogether and the only way he could communicate with his sister and his niece was by letter. This was because he had at last become a king.

After the rebellion and Civil War in the Low Countries the Great Powers met to decide that Belgium should be separated from Holland and set up as an independent monarchy. Prince Leopold was invited to be Belgium's first constitutional king, and he had accepted.

He assured Victoria that he would return occasionally to Claremont, which he had no intention of giving up. And as Belgium was very near he would be in constant touch with her by letter. He would write to her privately and she was to reply in the same way.

It was some consolation for his departure although the vision of Madame Späth ever returning now disappeared for ever. Victoria was dejected. First Feodore, then Späth, and now Uncle Leopold. Fate seemed to deprive her of those she best loved one after the other. Only Lehzen was left, and she had nightmares that Lehzen would be taken from her.

For a time after Späth's dismissal Lehzen thought that the

Duchess might try to get rid of her. Her attitude altered and she was less than warm. But the Duchess of Northumberland and a number of other influential people made it clear that just as Lehzen had enjoyed King George's protection so she would continue to be protected by King William. She knew, then, that she was safe. If the Duchess attempted to get rid of her, the King would remove Victoria from her control. She puzzled how to reassure Victoria, for the girl was so very troubled and often cried bitterly at the thought of being left entirely friendless at Kensington. Not to tell her would leave her in a miserable state of uncertainty. In the end she decided it was better to be direct although, sadly, it drove another small wedge between the child and her mother.

8

There was more rick burning and smashing of machinery at the time Uncle Leopold left for Belgium. There were also political riots of a serious nature. The Whigs had prepared a reform bill, but it had been defeated and the King had been asked to dissolve Parliament. A newly-elected House of Commons had then passed the bill, only to see it thrown out by the House of Lords. The country exploded in political fury. There were riots in the larger cities and towns. Incendiary fires burnt all over the country. The castle at Nottingham was burnt to the ground. Bristol was in the hands of a looting mob for two days. The Birmingham Trade Union planned to march on London with two hundred thousand men.

This time Victoria was less terrified. Späth's going had brought one good and unlooked for fruit; the Princess looked at events through her governess's eyes rather than through those of the romantic and dramatic lady-in-waiting. Lehzen kept at bay the bloodstained, vengeful mob of her imagination by being factual; in no way embroidering and in no way underestimating them.

Reform she told her was inevitable. Those who were against it doubted the wisdom of upsetting the *status quo*. The landed aristocracy, Whig or Tory, had ruled for generations. They were born to it, experienced at it, and in the main they were prepared to make personal sacrifices to serve the crown. But the dissenters and the new mercantile and manufacturing classes wanted a say in things. They were inexperienced in governing but they wanted to try. This primarily was why they called for reform. Then there were the idealists with purer motives who saw reform as a way to alter the miserable lot of farm labourers and industrial workers. It was doubtful, though, if the lower orders would benefit one scrap from all their trouble to change the character of the House of Commons. Yet reform was bound to happen. The time had come for it, and, though the Duke and his followers might try to postpone the day, they knew they could not prevent it altogether.

She was proved right in this when Wellington left the House of Lords followed by about a hundred peers rather than vote against a newly-prepared Reform Bill. He could not vote for it but he realized that he could not vote against it.

The country was in such a state that the King doubted the wisdom of having an expensive coronation. He even wondered if it was possible to do without one altogether. His legal officers assured him it was not. Very well then, he would be crowned but to be extravagant at such a time would salt the wound. His brother's coronation eleven years before had cost almost £400,000, when he had worn an elaborate costume complete with jewelled orders, a vast collar and white kidskin knickerbockers lined with satin. King William would be content with a great deal less, and so he declared would the peers who were usually dined at the public expense after coronations. Some of them went so far as to object to this cheeseparing. If the King was going to be so parsimonious because of radical troublemakers, they would not take part and would keep away.

King William was unmoved. He merely observed: 'Then I may anticipate greater convenience of room and less heat.'

He insisted though that members of his family were present,

and especially commanded the presence of the Princess Victoria.

Sir John Conroy decided to show his hand.

9

Queen Adelaide was astonished at the change in her sister-in-law the Princess Sophia.

At just such an entertainment as when they had discussed the dismissal of Späth, and with equally well chosen guests, she confessed her surprise. 'Dear Sophia, you were once so stalwart. I declare you were his champion.'

The Princess muttered something which no one could catch.

'But, of late, Sir John has proved himself a scallywag?'

'He is coarse, sister-in-law,' said the Princess gruffly. 'Coarse in manner, coarse in thought.'

'He seems,' murmured the Queen, 'to be unduly skilful in fermenting trouble.'

Sir John's pride, or his delight in tormenting the King, had made him order royal salutes to be fired when Victoria was taken to Norris Castle on the Isle of Wight for a summer holiday. And whenever they crossed and recrossed the Solent there were more royal salutes. The King ordered it to be stopped. Sir John politely but firmly refused. It was his duty to see that proper honours and her Court precedence were always given to the Heiress Presumptive. For this reason he could not alter the order for royal salutes, nor could the Duchess allow the Princess Victoria to walk behind her royal uncles in the coronation procession. Her place was in front of them, directly behind the sovereign. As she had not been given this precedence, she could not attend the coronation.

Princess Sophia fanned herself. 'It passes belief that William should be subjected to such a parade of insults. I wonder he does not take Victoria from them.'

The Queen shook her head. 'The people would not stand for

51

it. Not at present. The crown is not overpopular and seizing the child from her mother would simply increase the dislike and make our position more uncomfortable.' She sighed. 'Sir John has the whip hand.'

'For the time being,' said Princess Sophia. 'Only for the time being.'

10

Three days after the coronation the Duke invited Charles Cavendish Fulke Greville to dine with him quietly at Apsley House. It was a *tête-à-tête* meal because the Duke wished to gossip and make inquiries.

Mr Greville had been Clerk to the Privy Council for the past ten years, had a wide circle of gossiping acquaintances and the sharpest nose for titbits in all London. He was, therefore, a capital source of information. Moreover, though he adored tittle-tattle, he would occasionally undertake to keep a matter confidential and had never been known to break his promise.

The Duke kept a good table although, by the standard of the times, he was a sobersides himself. He let Greville eat, plied him with wine, and listened to his views on the coronation. His own part in the ceremony had prevented him from seeing it in the round. Greville's contacts had given him the whole picture and he was of the opinion that, despite the King's parsimony and his point blank refusal to be kissed by any bishop alive let alone the whole Bench, the coronation ought to be counted as a social success.

'Except,' suggested his host, 'the absence of the heir to the throne?'

The Duchess of Kent's obduracy, admitted Greville, had been unfortunate. He had heard, on good authority, that the Princess had watched the coronation procession from an upper window of Marlborough House, and had cried because she could not be there.

The Duke enjoyed dessert. The cover was removed and he settled to enjoy an indigestible mixture of port and walnuts.

'King William,' he said suddenly, 'won't make old bones like you and me, Greville.' He considered: 'He's too pink; runs about a great deal; always fussing. And he's too portly.'

Greville was cautious. There might be something in what the Duke said.

'So I wish to talk to you about the Kent girl, the Princess Victoria.'

Greville cocked an eye at him. 'Politically?' he said. 'You know she has been brought up the most drab and snuff-coloured Whig there is?'

'I do,' said the Duke. 'And it's unfortunate. But I'd rather hear about her as a girl. When I've dined at Kensington she's been brought in to be admired, but otherwise we never see her. She's kept close, by God.'

'She is,' agreed Greville. Then, to prove his excellence as a source of information, he proceeded to tell the Duke exactly what he wanted to know.

The Princess, he said, was Hanoverian in most things, self-willed, energetic, inordinately bad-tempered, and often enchanting. But, unlike her uncle, she was always entirely truthful and was exceedingly decisive. Once her mind was made up neither reason nor persuasion could make her change it. It was said that she could be very kind to servants but hated to be threatened by her teachers and instructors. Her music mistress had once used the word 'must', at which the Princess had snapped down the lid of the piano, narrowly missing the teacher's fingers, and swept away.

'At present,' concluded Greville, 'she has a great hunger for freedom but it is being stifled. This can't be good for her.'

'No, by God!' cried the Duke. He thought for a moment. 'She's too young yet for marriage, but has there been talk of suitors?'

Greville nodded. 'Indeed, your grace. The King favours the Dutch royal family. The new King of the Belgians favours one of the Coburg princes.'

The Duke wrinkled his nose. 'Neither would be very agreeable.'

'There must be at least six others,' suggested Greville. 'Names are bandied about, but it is nothing more as yet.'

After a dozen or so walnuts and two glasses of port the Duke returned to the subject of Kensington.

'I'm concerned at what I hear,' he confided. 'I want to know about Conroy, Greville. Tell me about him, please.'

'The facts, your grace, or my opinion?'

'Facts first.' The Duke cracked a walnut. A piece of shell skidded over the polished table. 'Always facts first.'

Greville spread his fingers. 'You know he is of an Irish family, and not unconnected. I doubt, though, if his people could be considered grand. He was appointed equerry to his late royal highness, the Duke of Kent, and was an executor of his will. Since the Duke's death he has been Comptroller to the household but in no position of direct influence over the Princess Victoria. For a long time he has been on good terms with Lady Conyngham and the late King's Secretary, Sir William Knighton. Which accounted, maybe, for the fact that he was made a baronet in 1827.' Greville paused for a moment to take a pinch of rappee snuff. 'His wife is niece to Bishop Fisher of Winchester, once a royal tutor, and they have five children . . .'

'Greville,' broke in the Duke. 'I declare you're a marvel. You'll be telling me next their names. Go on man. Is it Tom, Dick, Harry, George and Charles?'

'No, your grace,' corrected Greville with a smile. 'Jane, Victoire, Edward, Stephen and Henry.'

The Duke put back his head and laughed. 'Take more port, Greville, and pass on to your opinion.'

This, said Mr Greville, would be not simply his own, but rather a distillation of the views of quite a number of informed people.

It was generally agreed that Conroy was handsome and well made, especially by the ladies for many of whom he had a sort of horrid fascination. Those who cared for him said he was loyal, honourable and courageous to stand up for his royal mistress against the bullying of the Court. The large majority who did not care for him at all described him as a trouble-maker, vulgar, over-familiar and unprincipled. Probably the truth lay between: that he was an ambitious, extravagant and selfish scamp.

'He sounds,' said the Duke thoughtfully, 'rather unprepossessing. I gather he is at the root of the Duchess's discourteous hostility to the King.'

'Without a doubt.' Greville looked into his wine glass. 'They are of the same age and he has great influence over her. In such a female household his male vanity is titillated and his male charms enhanced.'

'They are lovers?' asked the Duke sharply.

There was a long silence. At last Greville finished twisting the stem of his glass. 'I am forced to conclude so,' he said.

The Duke munched a walnut and cleared his mouth with port. 'I suppose,' he muttered, 'that you might be right.'

11

Victoria was trying to re-arrange her collection of minerals. Mr Davys had suggested she put them in some sort of scientific order: grouped as precious and semi-precious stones, ornamental stones, crystal, and so forth. She supposed he was right although it meant looking up each one to find out which group it ought to go in. Then she had to list them, her tongue protruding from her lips as she penned the words, and afterwards arrange them in the glass-topped drawers of her little cabinet. Perhaps it was better to be orderly and scientific but she hoped no one would expect her to remember names like axinite, apatite, chessylite, barytes and avanturine. That would be too much. Once the collection was rearranged, she examined each drawer in turn, and decided it didn't look as beautiful as before. When her Uncle Sussex had first given her the cabinet with a box labelled minerals she had instantly arranged them according to their colour. Now her four best reds, which she identified by her own pet names as the crinkly red, the candy red, the button red and the pyramid red, were in four different drawers and called scientifically wulfenite, crocoite, Indian carnelian, and fluor rose octahedron. More exasperating still was the way her five pieces of quartz were now in one drawer for the colours quarrelled with each other. There were two green pieces, one sea-green, the other darker, a sardonyx-coloured bulrush brown, an arabian mocha stone the colour of mutton fat and a multi-coloured jasper.

She asked for Lehzen's advice, and Lehzen laid down her sewing and went over to look at the minerals. 'They were prettier before,' she agreed. 'But your uncle is a scholar. He, I'm sure, would prefer to see them arranged as Mr Davys suggested.' She took out her jewelled pocket watch. 'We shall see, anyway. He will be here directly.'

She rang the bell for their outdoor clothes, so that Uncle Sussex would not be kept waiting when he arrived. To Victoria's delight he had proposed taking her to Oatlands, near Weybridge in Surrey, where her Uncle York had lived; a beautiful place with a huge garden grotto which had taken twenty years to build. She had affectionate memories of this uncle who had died four years before because he had once given her a donkey and had specially arranged a Punch and Judy for her in the garden at Kensington. She wanted to see where he had once lived, and she particularly wanted to go into the grotto which had several rooms all lined with shells, looking glasses, and pieces of mineral.

It would be a great adventure especially as Uncle Sussex was arranging it.

When he arrived that morning he was dressed in style, with a green coat, white embroidered waistcoat, feather choker fastened with a lion's head pin.

He examined the re-arranged collection of minerals with unfeigned interest, praising Mr Davys for suggesting the new classification, and Victoria for going to the trouble of following his advice.

'You can hardly do better,' he told her, 'than approach life and all its problems from a scientific angle.'

He did not inquire for the Duchess of Kent and refused an offer of refreshment from Lehzen.

'No, Baroness, we have a long drive.' He pulled a watch from his waistcoat pocket, studied it, shook his head, and pulled out another from his hip pocket. This appeared to give him more satisfaction. 'I thank you, but we must leave.'

He himself sat with his back to the horses, explaining that his eyesight was growing worse. He feared he was becoming blind as the result of cataract, and when the time was ripe would require the King's surgeon to remove it. Until then he kept dust out of his eyes if it was possible.

He put on smoked spectacles to protect them further, and a green silk shawl to protect his shoulders. Victoria and Lehzen sat facing him. Mr Blackman checked that the two large hampers were securely stuffed to the rear and then climbed up behind the footmen. The equerry, Major Keppel, rode alongside.

It was a beautiful morning and the warm September sun appeared to stimulate the Duke. He talked rapidly and very interestingly about a variety of subjects until the sun appeared to get the better of him and abruptly he fell asleep. After that Victoria and Lehzen talked quietly together, Lehzen pointing out this and that in the fields and cider orchards as they passed, Victoria, being twelve years old, wondering what was in the hampers to eat.

Then they passed through a village and the surface of the road changed from chips to cobbles. The noise woke up the Duke who went on talking as though he had never stopped. 'Sleep whenever you have the chance,' he told Victoria. 'A campaigning principle taught me by my brother Frederick. And he, whatever they say, knew a thing or two about military matters.'

'What do they say?' asked Victoria, but she was silenced by Lehzen who touched her arm and bade her not interrupt when her uncle was talking.

Sussex blinked. He had forgotten she was a child and could hardly be told that her Uncle York had been disgraced because his whore had made an excellent supplementary income from selling commissions and promotions.

'Very correct sort of man,' he said reassuringly. 'Interested in religion and good works. But only natural, I suppose. After all he was a bishop.'

'A bishop?' squeaked Victoria, and then, hurriedly: 'I'm sorry, Lehzen; and I'm truly sorry, Uncle, to interrupt you, but I was so surprised.'

'Quite all right, my dear,' said he genially. 'And when you come to think of it, it is surprising. Army Commander-in-Chief and a bishop. Yet true. My father made him Bishop of Osnaburg when he was a baby – and I recall he was always called Bishop until he was created Duke of York. At Oatlands you can see the set of china made for him by Mr Wedgwood. His bishop's mitre on every piece. Extraordinary.'

Privately Victoria was sorry to hear this. Her experience of bishops was limited but she didn't like them very much. Especially Bishop Fisher of Winchester. He had been tutor to her father and was Lady Conroy's uncle, and so he often called at Kensington. The 'Kingfisher' they called him in the royal family, though only behind his back, because he was such a toady and a snob. Victoria hated the way he made a fuss of her because she was a princess. Späth had done the same, but in a nice way. The Kingfisher was oily about it, slippery, eel-like . . .

'Victoria!' It was Lehzen, snapping her fingers irritably, and whispering her name to attract attention. Without words she was being told to mind her manners, sit up and pay attention to her uncle. He was still talking about his brother.

'. . . the most frightful funeral I've ever attended. No, the worst was Charlotte's. Your poor cousin, Victoria, who married your Uncle Leopold. Hers was worse, for the undertakers' men were cut.'

Even Lehzen could not forbear to interrupt at this. 'How very terrible,' she murmured.

He nodded. 'Drunk as fish,' he said gaily. 'At Frederick's they stayed sober, but there were dissenters selling pictures of him in the streets. Very peculiar, too. They'd drawn in angel's wings below his Field-Marshal's hat and made him look like an elderly Hermes. Prints went like hot cakes. But,' he added with feeling, 'it was the only hot thing that day. The chapel was arctic, no heating, no matting or carpeting, and all the draughts in Windsor were collected there. I caught a severe cold. So, I recollect, did Montrose, and so did Wellington. And Canning caught rheumatic fever. It's a wonder that half the congregation didn't die. The Bishop of Lincoln did.'

'He did?' asked Victoria.

Her uncle nodded. 'Yes, poor man. It's surprising he was the only casualty of any significance, though I understand the common people died by the dozen.' The carriage swung into a driveway. 'Why, here we are,' he cried.

The late Duke of York's house had been allowed to run down. It made his brother quite angry to see the changes.

'Frederica, his Duchess, would sit in the saloon with forty or more dogs while Frederick played whist throughout the night.'

'Imagine having forty dogs!' said Victoria.

'Mad on them. She doted on all sorts of animals; parrots, cage birds, monkeys, reptiles. We'll go and see her cemetery.'

The cemetery was outside the famous grotto; a long row of tombstones each inscribed with the pet's name and, in some few cases, a stanza or two of verse.

'All a lot of nonsense,' said the Duke cheerfully. 'Though I shouldn't like her to have heard me say so.'

The grotto came up to all Victoria's expectations. It was divided into four rooms with connecting corridors, and the spar and glasses on the walls reflected the candles held by Mr Blackman and two gardeners. One of the rooms was a boat house, the water clear as crystal and very cold. It was a beautiful and fascinating place.

In great detail they examined the minerals and the Duke was delighted because she remembered the name of one of them.

'Well done, well done,' he said and would have tested her further but at that moment a repeater began chiming in the Duke's pocket. He pulled it out, stopped the ringing, checked the time with three or four other watches he had about his person, and then said 'Luncheon!'

The contents of the baskets were better than anything Victoria could have imagined. The Hanoverians enjoyed the pleasures of the table, and the Duke of Sussex was as keen an eater as any of them. Mr Blackman and the footman laid out cutlery, plate, glasses and napery, and unpacked the hampers. There were a cold fowl, cold roast pigeons, a veal pie, a joint of pork, cold chops, a sirloin with the juices oozing from its centre, and a harvest rabbit pie. Then there were fish dishes, dressed crab, a lobster, some small fishes in aspic, besides salads, sauces, cheese, fruit, confectionery, wine and cordial.

Afterwards, Lehzen, quite unaccustomed to such sumptuous picnics, said she had eaten rather more than was good for her.

'Nonsense, Ma'am,' said the Duke cheerfully. 'Walk with me across the park and you'll be ready for more.'

When they were out of earshot the Duke made his purpose plain. 'Baroness, I should like you to give me an undertaking.'

Lehzen smiled, but her smile faded when the Duke said what it was.

'Promise me, Baroness, that you will not leave my niece under any circumstances.'

'I had no intention . . .' began Lehzen.

'That I know. Yet promise me, I pray.'

'Your royal highness, it is quite unnecessary,' said Lehzen warmly. 'I have not the least intention of leaving the Princess Victoria either now or later; that is, until she herself chooses.'

'Not if they push you, and pull you, try to bribe you and bully you?'

Lehzen saw no point in pretending she did not know what he meant. His apartments were in the same palace. He was an intelligent and observant man.

'There are limits, your royal highness,' she pointed out. 'If I should be dismissed as Madame Späth was . . .'

'If that should happen,' he interrupted, 'you are to come straight to me. Or tell Keppel should I be away. He will know what to do.' The Duke stopped. 'This I promise you, Ma'am; no one can dismiss you from your present post of responsibility. Unless it be the King himself, or, as his representative, me. Do I make myself clear?'

Lehzen curtseyed.

'This expedition,' explained the Duke, 'is by way of being a consolation to my niece for having missed the coronation. It has also given me an opportunity to speak my mind and understand your firmness. Very satisfactory, Ma'am. Very satisfactory.' He pulled out one, two, three, four watches one after the other. 'And now I think it time to think of returning home.'

12

The year 1832 must be accounted one of the most important in British History. Because of Wellington's refusal to vote against the Reform Bill, it passed through the House of Lords and received the Royal Assent. Parliamentary reform was a reality. And not long afterwards sections of the penal code were brought into line with the new thinking. Capital punishment was abolished for a number of crimes.

To the Princess Victoria it was a memorable year for other reasons. The first was sad. Sir Walter Scott died and to her it seemed to mark the end of an era. The second was joyful. Her uncle wrote from Belgium to suggest that she be taken on a series of private visits to meet the great families of England.

King Leopold was in the thick of troubles. The Dutch continued to oppose the independence of Belgium and defy the Great Powers. As a result, the French advanced and seized Antwerp, and the Royal Navy blockaded the coast of Holland. Despite all this Leopold found the time to consider what was best for his niece Victoria, and he consulted Baron Stockmar, his own personal adviser and physician. Stockmar said the Princess ought to accustom herself to going out in society and, now that she was thirteen, the people should be given a chance to see her.

Sir John Conroy considered King Leopold's suggestion and decided in its favour. He made one adaptation, however, which was to his own particular advantage. The Progress would be regal and as official as he could possibly make it. Complaints from the Court were largely based on the fact that the people saw nothing of the heir to the throne. They were best answered, he decided, not by taking Victoria to Court where she would have a certain independence, but by showing her and the Duchess as a model mother and daughter to carefully chosen Whig potentates. He and Victoire would accompany the progress and then the most important people would come to accept him as a natural and indispensable part of the household.

Victoria was excited by the thought of travelling because she pined to see something of the outside, ordinary world. They were to go by carriage and the royal yacht, *Emerald*, and her favourite possessions would travel with her. For instance, she would generally be able to sleep in her own bed from Kensington. It would precede her on each stage of the journey. And she would be able to exercise on her own pony, a dumpy but robust little mare called Rosy.

But there was one aspect of the journey which she did not care for. Her mother had decided it should not all be pleasure. She was to record her travels in a journal. In this way, said the Duchess, she would learn to be observant and critical, practise her powers of composition, and store up for future reference details about the places and people she would one day rule. She was given manuscript books with leather backs and marbled sides, and they had a solid, permanent look about them. They were records, more like ships' logs than a girl's diary, and their appearance told her that her mother would occasionally ask to see the journal. Doubtless Lehzen would be required to read it as well and so she could never write candid, secret things, which was half the attraction of keeping a diary. Every relation and friend would have to be described as 'dear' or there would be trouble, and this was a dishonest levelling between those who were truly dear and those whom she secretly detested.

To begin with she felt bogged down by the necessity to write facts. On the first day of their progress, when they made seven changes of horses, she felt obliged to include everything. Not a place name was omitted. And it looked as if she had her eyes on the clock.

We left K.P. at 6 minutes past 7 . . . 19 minutes to 1. We have just changed horses at Stony Stratford ... 1 minute past ½ past 3. We have just passed through Braunston where there is a curious spire ...

Apart from journal writing Victoria much enjoyed her first expedition into England and Wales. She was amazed to see the desolation and blackness caused by coal mining and industry. They stayed at Powis Castle where their host was the eldest son of the great Clive of India. She learnt to play billiards at Plas Newydd, and at Eaton Hall, fabulous home of the Marquess of Westminster, she saw an aloe plant which they told her only flowered once in every hundred years. At Chatsworth, the equally fabulous house of the Devonshires, she felt very important because they asked her to plant an oak tree, and afterwards she saw a Russian coachman in full dress, a fine collection of minerals which made her own seem paltry, and a mill where marble and Derbyshire spar were cut and polished. By October they were visiting the most fabulous place of all, the Earl of Shrewsbury's home at Alton Towers, where she and Lehzen enjoyed themselves trying to count all the curiosities in the gardens – streams, lagoons, canals, tanks, cascades and fountains, rockwork, shellwork, grottoes and caverns, turf stairways, mosshouses, ferneries, arbours, an imitation Stonehenge, a Grecian temple, an Indian temple and a Chinese pagoda decorated with bells and lanterns. A week later they were at Lord Liverpool's. As their host was a powerful Tory peer it looked as though Sir John had made a grand political concession. In fact, Lord Liverpool and the Duchess were old friends and his daughter Lady Catherine was one of her ladies-in-waiting. It was there that Victoria followed her first hunt in a carriage. She was delighted to be given the brush and teased Lehzen because the sight of blood made her feel faint. There was no squeamishness about her.

Then the huntsmen cut off for themselves the ears and 4 paws, and lastly they threw it to the dogs, who tore it from side to side till there was nothing left. We then went home.

And so it went on. It was all very exciting to Victoria except for the long speeches which people made as they passed through towns. Had the King seen the evidence of his subjects' affection for his heir he would have been gratified. As it was all he could think about was his sister-in-law's barefaced defiance of his order. He had commanded that the visits be private and unofficial. Far from obeying she and her Comptroller were taking every opportunity to bring themselves to the public's notice and did not care in the least that the King was annoyed and called them circus performers. The tour ended in triumph on November 8th at Oxford. The Duchess was given a formal address by the Vice-Chancellor and Sir John made an honorary Doctor of Civil Law. Then, directly afterwards, the corporation honoured them. The Duchess was given a second address, and Sir John was made a Freeman of the City. The Princess was less interested in these ceremonies than in Queen Elizabeth's Latin exercise book which was shown to her in the Bodleian Library. She turned over the pages written as a young girl by England's greatest queen, and was glad that Mr Davys could not see how much farther advanced the Tudor Princess had been. On the day following they returned home to Kensington Palace.

The royal progress was over.

13

Christmas at Kensington was kept in the German fashion with Christmas trees and present-giving on Christmas Eve.

The Duchess supervised, assembling everyone in the drawing-room after dinner, ringing a bell three times, and leading them into the cleared dining-room. There were three tables, two beneath Christmas trees and one without. They were heaped with presents.

Victoria clapped her hands with pleasure and ran forwards, but her smile quickly faded. Usually the two tables with trees were labelled for her mother and herself and the other had always been for Lehzen. This year her table and Lehzen's were still the same, but the other had been given to the Conroy family. Why? They were always there at present-giving but they received their gifts in their own home. Why had her mother changed the arrangements? And if they were to have a table why was it not like Lehzen's without a Christmas tree? Why had the Conroys been put on an equal footing with her?

'Where is your table, Mamma?' she asked directly.

The Duchess told them that it was upstairs. She had preferred to arrange it up in her own private drawing-room.

She gave no reason, nor could Victoria ask for one. The Conroys obviously knew of the plan for they showed no surprise and went straight to their table to sort out the presents.

Victoria quickly forgot her irritation in the excitement of undoing parcels. She had brooches, ear-rings, books, prints, a white bag, a silver brush, a satin dress, a fur-lined cloak, and from Lehzen a music book. She rushed over to her old friend and kissed her and thanked her. This did not altogether please the Duchess. Her own gifts ought to be recognized before anyone else's. And then there was Sir John's.

' 'Drina,' she said. 'You have not thanked Sir John for his silver brush.'

The girl curtseyed to him. 'Thank you, Sir John,' she said. 'I could not know for certain that it was intended for me.'

He laughed at this. Some gentlemen in Parliament had requested that Victoria's name be changed to Charlotte, and the matter was at present under serious consideration. The King had approved and so had the Duke. Lord Grey's cabinet had expressed no strong view either way. Victoria herself hated the idea, as Sir John well knew, and to tease her he had labelled the silver hairbrush, 'For the Princess Charlotte'.

'It occurred to me . . .' he began; then flushed red with embarrassment.

Victoria turned away from him to speak to her mother.

'Thank you, Mamma, for the very lovely dress and the jewels.'

' 'Drina,' said her mother, shocked, 'Sir John was speaking to you.'

65

Without turning to look at him Victoria said: 'Was he? Then I beg his pardon, Mamma. I did not notice.'

This was the last straw. ' 'Drina,' began her mother, panting with indignation. 'You will go to your room . . .'

'Ma'am.' It was Sir John's charming, Irish voice. 'Take no account of it. Take no account of it. 'Tis Christmas Eve. The Princess is out of humour.' He chuckled. 'No doubt the Baroness will give her a draught?'

It took all his soothing to calm the Duchess. Meanwhile Victoria seethed inside. How dare that coarse creature make a fool of her before everyone . . . and to suggest she needed one of Lehzen's purges . . .

Lehzen took her arm, and by the gentleness of her touch and her whole attitude rather than by any words, began to coax the Princess out of her ill mood.

Victoria lost it altogether when her mother suddenly said, 'Sir John is right, 'Drina. You are a wicked, wicked girl, but it is Christmas, and we must love one another.' She sounded so sincere and affectionate that Victoria responded by kissing her and asking Sir John's forgiveness.

Then, harmony restored, they all went upstairs to see the Duchess's presents, and a special gift for Victoria which had been put in her drawing-room and was entirely unexpected. It was an exact reproduction of a toilet table she had seen and coveted on their travels at Barton Hill near Anglesey, a table with pink and white muslin over it trimmed with lace.

She threw her arms about her mother's neck. 'Oh, Mamma!' she cried. 'How grateful I am.'

Before she fell asleep that night she felt genuinely ashamed for having almost spoilt the present-giving; and told herself she ought not to be so sensitive about Sir John's teasing. Obviously her mother had great faith in his judgement and he served them all to the best of his ability, so she ought not to dislike him.

'Lehzen,' she called through the darkness. 'Is it *very* wrong of me to dislike Sir John?'

Lehzen reflected. She wanted to reply: 'Not at all, hate him as you will,' because he did not even trouble to disguise his hostility to her. She had met a look or two of Conroy's which meant in as many words, 'Were you not so powerfully pro-tected, Baroness, you would join Madame Späth in Germany by the next packet boat.' Yet there was no advantage to be gained in disliking someone in so close a unit as the Kent household. Feuds and bitterness merely wore down the spirit. 'I think,' she said slowly, 'that you should try to control your dislike – for your mother's sake.'

She heard a sigh. Then Victoria said: 'Very well, dear Lehzen. I will try. For Mamma's sake. And yours.'

14

Victoria did try to keep her promise and to a large extent she succeeded. She grew closer to her mother than she had been for years, and she was politely deferential to Sir John. Virtue appeared to bring its rewards because everything started to go well for her. The King kindly made her tutor Dean of Chester, though Mr Davys was not to live away in the north. His duties were still at Kensington. Then to her relief the odious idea of changing Victoria's name was dropped and never brought up again. Next she went to Drury Lane to hear *The Barber of Seville* and lost her heart to Italian opera. She was enchanted, dizzy with the pleasure of listening to Almaviva, Rosina and Figaro, and though later in life she developed a fondness for German music she was never truly seduced away from her first love. And finally, Sir John gave her mother a small Cavalier King Charles puppy called Dash, and, seeing how much it delighted Victoria, her mother passed it on to her.

She was devoted to the puppy, and for a time was absorbed in him to the exclusion of all else. To begin with Victoire Conroy shared her delight. They took Dash for walks, fed him, decorated his basket, made him ribbons, brushed him, clipped his claws, and bathed him. But then Victoire, consciously or otherwise, began to feel jealous of the puppy. Victoria would talk and think of nothing else, and when her friend tried to distract her she paid no attention. This made Victoire sharp; sharper, anyway, than she generally was with the Princess Victoria. She called her stupid to dote so on a dog and to be forgetful of all the good times they had had together in their friendship.

Victoria was smaller than Victoire. She frowned, looked up in the other's face, and asked, 'What good times?'

'Why, everything we have done together,' said Victoire, who was flustered by that look. 'You've forgotten them all. You're ungrateful. You've forgotten me just because of Dash. Just because of an ordinary dog.'

'Dash,' snapped Victoria, 'is not an ordinary dog. He is my dog.' Her eyes hardened. She would have said more if Victoire had not been Sir John's daughter. As it was, she snatched the dog away and, hugging him to her breast, left the room.

Lehzen followed at a distance.

Five minutes later Victoria asked, 'Did I do wrong?'

Lehzen's face betrayed nothing. 'I am not your conscience, Victoria. You must decide some things for yourself.' She looked at her pendant watch. 'Now it is time to get dressed for Gloucester House. Your aunt is expecting you.'

Aunt Gloucester was in high spirits. She had persuaded her husband to go down to the country for a time and felt free of her responsibililty to control his eccentricities. Now she could indulge her own – and shout at the top of her voice, satisfy her huge appetite for high food, visit innumerable friends, for her circle was large, and see her equally numerous relations.

When Victoria and Lehzen were announced she seized the girl, kissed her, held her at arm's length to look at her properly, dragged her to the window where there was more light, and announced to Lehzen's keen satisfaction that she would do.

She asked after Victoria's health and progress in lessons.

She then admired Dash.

Nothing could have drawn her so quickly to Victoria's heart; and she listened patiently while her niece described Dash's beauty and many virtues.

'I hope,' said her aunt with pretended solemnity, 'that you give a little of your love and time to other things.'

This came so close to the subject of her quarrel with Victoire that Victoria was suddenly abashed and silent.

'What is it?' commanded her aunt. 'Speak plainly.'

Victoria told her. As she did so the Duchess was thinking rapidly. Conroy's daughter ... an undesirable influence? ... hard to tell ... the child needs young people about her ... we must find others. ... Ultimately she said: 'Be gentler with your friend. Animals are never, never as important as human beings – except, of course, radicals!'

The advice given she called for biscuits and wine.

Lehzen suggested gently that the Princess was unaccustomed to wine.

'How perfectly dreadful!' exclaimed the Duchess. 'Then she shall begin to accustom herself to it directly.'

Victoria found herself eating ratafee biscuits and sipping madeira. She liked both, but she thought it wise to refuse the pinch of snuff she was offered.

'Your mother takes it?' inquired the Duchess.

'Yes, Aunt, but very moderately.'

'I,' declared the Duchess, 'do not care for moderation.'

'No, Aunt.'

Lehzen and the Duchess chatted together, apparently about trivia, but with great subtlety they were giving each other information; the Duchess learning how matters stood at present between the King and Kensington, and how best they could be improved. If the King was to be persuaded to invite himself to Kensington would he be readily received? And if so would the little person act as cementing agent between them? Then would not a royal ball please everyone?

'Oh yes, Aunt,' said Victoria breathlessly.

'Child!' exploded her aunt. 'You are not supposed to have understood a word. Have you understood?'

'Yes, Aunt.'

The Duchess's face relaxed into a broad smile. She raised one hand. 'Then there shall be a ball,' she announced magnificently.

Lehzen indicated that they should be leaving. Victoria had yet to feed her ponies and Mr Westall the drawing master would arrive at half past two. And that was not the end of it.

After an early dinner they were going to the ballet of *Kenilworth*.

The Duchess rang for a servant to see them out. She repeated her promise and kissed Victoria goodbye.

In the carriage Victoria practised her art of mimicry. 'There *shall* be a ball,' she said in a near perfect imitation of Aunt Gloucester's deep voice; and even while Lehzen was getting the breath to rebuke her, she continued in the same voice: 'Duke of Gloucester, Duke of Gloucester. We will have none of that now, if you please!'

15

The Duchess of Northumberland, Victoria's official governess, was a great friend of the Duchess of Gloucester. Between them they made it possible for the King to invite himself to dine at Kensington.

The Duchess of Kent was agreeably surprised. Sir John sent to the Court for a list of guests, and was informed that beyond certain members of the royal household the King was happy to leave the list to his sister-in-law. Such a compliment was unusual, and further gratified the Duchess. She told Sir John the dinner ought to be out of the ordinary. He translated this to mean it should be magnificent, and magnificent he made it, both in guests and food.

The day before Victoria made clothes for Dash. She would not herself be dining but was to be present before and after the meal, and Dash she decided should be with her, and he should be suitably dressed for the occasion. As gently as possible Lehzen attempted to persuade her that a scarlet jacket and blue trousers do not become a Cavalier King Charles spaniel, but Victoria would not be moved. Lehzen left it at that. It was too small a matter to make a fuss about, yet on the next day when Victoria proudly produced her dog for the royal inspection, she wished she had.

At the last moment the Queen found herself unable to be present, and so did the Duchess of Gloucester. The King was supported by his two brothers of Cumberland and Gloucester. And the guests included the Archbishop of Canterbury, the Lord Chancellor, the Commander-in-Chief, and the Prime Minister besides the Dukes of Devonshire, Norfolk, Somerset, Gordon, Rutland, Northumberland, Sutherland and Cleveland.

As she and Lehzen went into the grand saloon after their own dinner Victoria's first thought was how much Madame Späth would have enjoyed such an illustrious gathering.

The King beamed at her and kissed her as did Silly Billy of Gloucester. The Duke of Cumberland was almost a stranger to her, and she thought him a huge, imposing man and very kind to keep the maimed side of his face away from her as he bowed and she curtseyed. But wasting no time on civilities he bawled out: 'Why is that dog absurdly dressed?'

Victoria flushed. 'It is the mode, Uncle.'

'Then the mode should be changed. It is silly. Excessively silly, by God!'

The Duchess of Northumberland took the child's arm and led her away. Cumberland's asperity was well known, and suffered by most people in silence, but for one dreadful moment it had looked as if Victoria would give him an angry reply. As official governess the Duchess of Northumberland was responsible for her actions.

'Dear Baroness,' she said to Lehzen. 'Do take the Princess away – and scold her.'

Victoria was trembling with rage. She said nothing until they reached her room. Then she burst out: 'Why does the Duchess say you are to scold me? Why should I be scolded? Why?' She stamped her foot. 'My Uncle Cumberland is a bad, wicked man as everyone knows; and he should not have been rude to my Dash.'

Lehzen concealed her surprise. She asked as lightly as possible: 'And when did you come to the conclusion that your uncle was a bad and wicked man?'

Victoria set her lips defiantly. 'Victoire says so . . .' Taking Lehzen's look as one of disbelief she went on fiercely. 'She *did*.

71

She said he was an ogre. She told me everyone says he is evil and a murd—'

'. . . Which is nonsense,' cut in Lehzen. 'Victoire is a naughty girl to say such things. As you are for repeating them. The Duke of Cumberland is your father's younger brother. You have a duty to him.'

Lehzen decided the Conroy girl was becoming a considerable nuisance. She would have to be checked and corrected.

'Now do you understand, Victoria, you are not to say such things.'

Victoria lowered her eyes.

'Tittle-tattle does not suit princesses,' said Lehzen sternly.

'But, Lehzen, I like tittle-tattle.'

Victoria's naïvety was irresistible. Lehzen smiled. She could not help it. Kissing the girl's forehead, she said: 'Well, dear, you must try not to gossip, however much you like it.' She kissed her a second time and suggested they removed Dash's uniform. 'Your uncle has a rough tongue, child; but truly I think he is in the right . . . There is no point in pouting. You could curdle milk with such looks . . .'

It took about an hour, but Victoria was at last coaxed into a good humour. Dash, lacking jacket and trousers and obviously much more comfortable, looked better. She had to admit it.

Lehzen's quiet but unspoken prayer was that when they went down again after dinner, Victoria would have the honesty and the courage to admit it to her Uncle Cumberland.

Victoria did. She went to her uncle and told him he had been right, and immediately she won his respect and admiration.

The band of the Grenadier Guards was playing and the Duke offered her his arm to walk the saloon. They walked up and down together, he in time with the martial air, she taking two paces to his one — he the hope of the Tories, tall, saturnine, with an atrocious reputation; she, hope of the Whigs, small, grave, with her hand on his arm; both very conscious of themselves and their own importance.

It was remarked that though the Duke of Cumberland never ceased to curse that he could not inherit the English throne as well as that of Hanover, from that evening he never harboured any personal grievances against Victoria.

The King, who from personal experience knew how difficult his brother Cumberland could be, was proud of his niece's conquest. He told her so. 'Dear child, if you charm your subjects so they will be your devoted slaves.'

'I have no subjects,' she reminded him. 'Nor would I have if the sad event that will bring them to me could be avoided.'

'Eh! Eh!' cried the delighted King William. He turned to the Lord Chancellor. 'Do you hear that, Brougham? They tell me you're the finest talker in my domain, but I'll wager you couldn't have mouthed that happy sentiment at such a tender age.'

Brougham had the highest sense of his own dignity and drew himself up to say he had not caught the Princess's observation; but the King had already left him, marching off with Victoria on his arm to congratulate her mother on possessing so fine a daughter.

'And you must not prevent us, Ma'am, from giving a ball on her birthday next month. Yes, indeed. The Queen insists that we do her honour, as does my sister, Mary.'

'It would be very gracious . . .' began Victoria's mother.

'An honour, Ma'am,' interrupted the King. 'Make no doubt there will be great larks and sparks. Yes, Ma'am, larks and sparks.'

16

The first part of the Duchess of Gloucester's plan had been a conspicuous success. The dinner at Kensington brought the two opposing parties closer together. The Duchess of Kent felt perhaps she had been over-hasty to despise her brother-in-law. He had gone out of his way to be attentive and respectful and kind. She began to regret some of the steps she had taken to emphasize her position as Victoria's mother. And the King, while not altering his dislike for Sir John Conroy, guessed that his sister-in-law had been unduly influenced against him. He was hopeful that in future she would be more complaisant.

Both, in this, underestimated Sir John. He was determined that the birthday ball should not cement the new cordiality between Kensington and the Court.

When the guest list was sent for the Duchess of Kent's approval he found fault with one or two omissions – the children of old friends of his master the Duke of Kent. Stifling his irritation the King ordered the list to be amended. Sir John then found it weighed too heavily in favour of Tory families. In the battle between his perverseness and the King's good nature, the King won. He cared too much for Victoria to refuse her the promised ball.

Subtly the Comptroller turned his attention to the Duchess of Kent. Had she, he asked, studied the ball list of guests? Had she noticed the absence of anyone at all whom her brother King Leopold might have considered a suitable suitor for the Princess? Victoria was about to be fourteen and it was not too early to be thinking of her marriage in a few years' time. Evidently the King had it in mind. The list was replete with his nominees – beginning with her cousins George of Cumberland and George of Cambridge.

It was a clever move. Leopold's ambitions for the Coburg family coincided with his sister's. Neither wanted Victoria to marry a Hanoverian cousin in which case their own spheres of influence would be greatly reduced. The Duchess did not actively dislike George of Cambridge who was a good-looking boy only two months older than Victoria, but he was a great favourite of the King and Queen and lived more with them at St James's than with his own parents. This was because his father, the deaf, bewigged Duke of Cambridge, lived in Hanover as viceroy and would do so until the Duke of Cumberland succeeded as king. No, George Cambridge could never be considered. He was of the King's party and very much prejudiced against his aunt of Kent. As for George of Cumberland, not only was there something wrong with his sight, but any question of an alliance with the hated Ernest of Cumberland was quite out of the question so far as the Duchess was concerned. She was actually afraid of him and admitted it on this occasion to Conroy.

He seized on it as a lucky chance to strike at Lehzen. The

more genuine grievances against her he could put to the Duchess, the more chance that one day, Court or no Court, she might be turned off as Spāth had been.

He told her he could understand her fear, which was shared by the majority of informed people – though not, he said, by Baroness Lehzen. It seemed barely credible but she had been angry with Victoire for telling the Princess that her uncle was unpopular in society; so angry that the child had gone to him in distress and he, in turn, had felt it his duty to remonstrate with the governess.

'At which,' he repeated, 'this much admired governess of your daughter turned into a virago. She was terrifying.'

'Not,' said the shocked Duchess, 'not before your Victoire?'

'Indeed yes, Ma'am.' He lied, and nodded after a pause. 'It makes one wonder how sane she can be.'

The Duchess shuddered at the thought of a madwoman being in charge of her daughter.

'Surely . . . Surely, she cannot be insane?'

'No,' he replied at once – in exactly the tone a man might use to reassure someone when the truth is too hurtful to hear.

Here was a gambit which had not occurred to him before. He stored it away for future use, and returned to the list of ball guests.

There was nothing, he supposed, that could be done. It would offend the King to carp at his list (the Duchess did not know of the previous amendments), but it might be worthwhile making sure the Princess did not become unduly friendly with any of her partners.

'You are right,' said the Duchess decisively. 'I will speak to her myself.'

The morning of Victoria's birthday arrived. She received many messages and many presents: diamond ear-rings from the King, a turquoise brooch from the Queen; pearls from Aunt Glouccester, Aunt Sophia and Uncle Sussex; turquoises from Uncle and Aunt Cumberland, and from Prince George of Cambridge a brooch in the shape of a lily of the valley . . . Her birthday table was loaded, but the surprise which gave her the greatest pleasure was the unexpected arrival of her half-brother Charles of Leiningen. He brought with him Feodore's love and a promise that she would visit Victoria next year. He brought, too, a tumbler and a plate of Bohemian glass from dear Madame Späth. Victoria was touched to tears.

Perhaps the best present of all was a magnificent painting of Dash, but she would never admit it because it had been given her by Sir John. She knew it was wrong. She knew she was behaving badly. She knew she ought to be as sincere in her thanks to him as anyone else, but she couldn't. There was an obstinately honest and unswerving streak in her which made it impossible. That was that. If Lehzen had given her the picture she would have thrown her arms about her and thanked her for being so kind and generous and thoughtful. As it was, she went to Sir John and gravely thanked him for the picture saying it was an excellent likeness. He was puzzled, then hurt, then vexed. He did not care for Victoria, regarding her as a high and mighty, hoity-toity girl far too much like her father to be likeable. But he did recognize her importance to his own comfort, and he was determined to break down her stiffness and bridge the gap which had been growing between them. Therefore he had gone to considerable trouble to get her picture and wanted her gratitude as his just reward. When she deprived him of it he was incensed and liked her less than before.

He made a point of reminding the Duchess to speak to her daughter before the ball, hoping maliciously that it would spoil it for her.

It did, almost. Victoria could not see why each of her partners had to be vetted in turn, and not simply by Lehzen but by the Duchess herself. If Uncle William considered the boys and young men were suitable partners for her at a ball then surely they were.

'Not at all,' said her mother shortly. 'It is I who shall judge.'

'It will be very embarrassing,' pleaded Victoria.

'I can't help that.'

'And it will anger the King,' persisted Victoria.

The Duchess caught her breath. 'Impudent girl!' she cried.

'For this defiance you shall not go to the ball at all. I shall send word you are indisposed.'

The sudden collapse of all she had been looking forward to was almost more than Victoria could bear. 'Oh, no,' she whispered. 'Please, Mamma, please. I wish to go of all things . . .'

'Victoria, you are a wilful, insolent, thoughtless child!'

'Oh, please, Mamma,' she begged.

For what seemed an hour the Duchess hesitated. At last she nodded. 'Very well. But you must do as I have said. And you must not be contradictory. It is undutiful and unladylike.'

17

Although she had had all her own way, the Duchess was somehow convinced that she had been slighted. Dining early at a quarter to six upset her digestion and she arrived at St James's suffering from acidity as well as an overblown sense of her own importance. When the orchestra struck up, the doors were opened and the King led Victoria into the ballroom, it was made clear to the Duchess that, whatever she might say or do, everyone was determined to enjoy the ball. She sat there smouldering with imagined grievances and was chagrined by the King, who took the simplest, though the most offensive way out of his dilemma, by behaving as though she was not there.

Lehzen sat with the Duchess of Northumberland, eating caraways in great excitement, and watching Victoria. She was very proud of her. So was Victoria's dancing mistress.

The Princess was dancing with her cousin Prince George of Cambridge. He was her age but a head taller, a solidly-built, yellow-haired boy who smiled and danced with great energy. He did not lack elegance, though; and Victoria herself had enormous poise.

Madame Bourdin was very proud of her, but she made the mistake of saying so to the Duchess.

'The Princess has such natural ease of deportment,' she said, sweeping a deep curtsey to the Duchess. 'And what a pretty couple their royal highnesses make!'

Had she gone to the trouble of thinking it out the dancing mistress could hardly have said anything worse.

'You are wrong, Madame,' snapped the Duchess. 'They are ill matched. Ill matched. And it does not please me to see the Princess stoop. However gracefully she manages the quadrille, however neat her footwork and balanced her poise, I do not care to see her rounded shoulders.' She thought for a moment. 'It shall be corrected,' she announced. 'Tomorrow she must have holly pinned below her chin. A sprig of holly. Kindly ask Baroness Lehzen to see to it.'

Madame Bourdin swept another curtsey and went away to tell Lehzen.

'So cruel,' she bewailed. 'Her poor dear chin will be pricked.'

Lehzen, her face dark with anger, could not trust herself to speak for a moment. When she did, she said sourly, 'I suppose we should be grateful that she did not send for a sprig of holly here and now.'

The Duchess of Northumberland said hastily, 'You are jesting, Baroness. No one would do such a thing.'

Lehzen agreed. 'No one of sensitivity could, your grace; though I fear her royal highness might.' It was indiscreet of her, she knew. The Duchess of Northumberland was the King's nominee as royal governess and her own attitude and what she had said would go back to the King. It would make matters worse between Kensington and St James's. But this time Lehzen did not mind.

Prince Charles's face clouded when he saw the vetting process taking place. It was mortifying to the young men and to their host the King. When he had an opportunity he went over to say so.

'Mamma,' he murmured in her ear. 'It's too bad of you really, to make poor Victoria bring up her partners.'

He had forgotten her temper. She put him down in an instant, and, as a sovereign prince unaccustomed to being scolded by anyone, he took it badly, bowed stiffly, turned on his heel and walked away.

Victoria was blissfully unaware of what was going on. She dutifully presented each partner in turn and then forgot everything in the pleasure of her first ball. It was an infectious pleasure which made the smile return to Madame Boudin's face, and Lehzen chew caraways once more. The Duchess of Northumberland forgot about sprigs of holly as she watched her charge dancing so ecstatically. Even her mother caught some of it. As to the King and Queen, never, they said, had they been so rewarded for their hospitality. Victoria was more alive than anyone had ever seen her before. The music, the candlelight, the ball dresses, the ornate decoration of the ballroom, the stately formality and the intricate interweavings of the quadrille in its five distinct sets, and the freedom at last to dance with boys of her own age made her so happy that she radiated it to everyone. She believed she was a little in love. Her cousin George was so handsome, and so much less grave than the other boys. As their hands met and they passed close to each other in the set he himself shocked her by whispering comments on the family. She pretended to disapprove when he gently mocked Uncle Sussex and Uncle Cumberland and Silly Billy, the uncle of Gloucester, but in fact she found it enthralling. No one since Feodore's departure had ever treated her as an equal. Because of this she thought she might be a little in love with handsome George Cambridge.

She would have been more certain if young Lord Brooke had not caused her to feel the most unusual sensations. He was older than George, at least fifteen, and a rapid question to Lehzen had told her that one day he would be Earl of Warwick. He had been allowed from school to attend the ball at St James's and was quiet and distant, hardly saying a word. This silence, with his undeniable good looks, had a powerful effect on Victoria. She believed she was rather more than a little in love with Guy Brooke. There were others as well: Charles, the Earl of March, a boy of fifteen at Westminster School; his thirteen-year-old brother Lord Fitzroy Lennox, and another thirteen-year-old George, Earl of Athlone. By Stockmar's schoolroom regimen she had never been allowed to receive or talk to any boy over the age of seven, and had very rarely seen any. The sudden and delicious experience at the St James's ball almost overwhelmed her.

Possibly it was a realization of this which decided the Duchess to leave before the end of the ball. Lehzen believed so, and so did Prince Charles. Unfortunately, though, hardly anyone else did. Clearly the King considered his sister-in-law was only being perverse and enjoyed exercising her prerogative as Victoria's mother. The Queen was of the same mind and was vexed at the slighting of her hospitality. Victoria, hot and excited and suddenly told they were to leave, was crestfallen to the point of tears. In her heart she could not help thinking that they were leaving because she and not her mother was the centre of attention. Unreasonably it made her impatient with everyone except her mother. Why had not Sir John and Charles and the King and everyone made a great fuss of Mamma? Did they not know she needed attention? If Mamma could have been courted and admired she would not have minded Victoria dancing until daybreak. As it was the Kensington party left at close on midnight.

George Cambridge claimed his right as a cousin to bid Victoria goodbye, and he tried to charm his aunt, promising himself the pleasure of calling on her. The Duchess did not spare him. She said neither yes nor no, but her severe look warned him to keep away from Kensington until he was invited there. Much embarrassed he bowed and went to the back of the party.

Victoria ached for him. She longed to tell him he would always be welcome. More than this she wanted publicly to dissociate herself from her mother's restlessness and cold lack of hospitality. But neither was possible.

The linkboys took their places beside the carriage. Then the steps were taken away, and they were off.

Victoria sat quietly in her place in the first carriage.

'Are you not well, child?' asked the Duchess.

'I am tired, Mamma,' she explained.

It seemed to satisfy everyone for no one bothered her again and she could close her eyes and live through her first ball once more. Instinctively she knew that no other ball would ever seem so wonderful. She dwelt on each incident in turn, but one kept returning, knocking the events out of order – the quadrille she had danced with Guy, Lord Brooke.

Agreeable as her cousin had been, she now felt certain that Guy Brooke had taken a part of her heart. She could not know how much. Not yet.

Nor could she know that a boy who had danced with her that evening and who was at that moment returning silently to his father's London house, was feeling the pain as well as the joy of having lost his heart to her. Young Lord Fitzroy Lennox was burning with the first love of a boy. It had all the sweetness and power of calf love but was more enduring and Victoria lay at the centre of his heart all through his life. Only his death by drowning in a steamer shipwreck at the age of twenty-one ended the undeclared and exquisite passion which began as he danced with the Princess Victoria on that May night at St James's in 1833.

18

A sprig of holly was pinned to Victoria's bodice the next morning. Lehzen took Victoria and the holly and a pin to the Duchess. The inference was clear ... if you wish this to be done, you ought to do it yourself.

Quite unconcerned the Duchess pinned on the holly, tested it to make sure that at the slightest tilting forward of her daughter's head it would come in contact with the prickles, and gave her a short lecture on deportment.

Victoria did not seem to mind. She bore it with composure. It almost amounted to indifference. Lehzen could not understand it, especially when Victoria was embroidering and, in order to see the work and avoid the prickles, she had to hold her embroidery at arm's length away from her face. She said she was like Moses holding up his arms for the battle, and she accepted the nuisance quite cheerfully. Lehzen did not know she was consoling herself by thinking about Lord Brooke.

Victoria could not be certain why, but she realized straight away that she could not confide her feelings for Guy Brooke. It was not that her old friend would have betrayed her, or mocked at her; and in anything else she would at once have tried to share her pleasure with the governess, but this time, no, she sensed it would be more prudent to say nothing at all.

Her only other confidante was Victoire Conroy, but they had not been such friends since their quarrel about Dash and Victoria thought there was just about the right distance between them. It was more comfortable for them both.

Victoire had also been at the birthday ball and had enjoyed it to the full. And, not long after Victoria had finished her stint of embroidery, Victoire sought her out, led her to a corner of the room where Lehzen could not hear, swore her to secrecy, and confessed her great liking for Lord March. It was more than a great liking, she admitted; it was a great love, an absolute devotion. She was passionately attached to Lord March.

Victoria's own feelings for Guy Brooke were somehow strengthened by Victoire's announcement, but she did not exchange confidences. Instead, and with great enjoyment, she listened to Victoire describe Lord March's charms . . . the way he held his shoulders, his beautifully cut coat, his cravat, his engaging habit of touching his cheek with a forefinger, his way of glancing sideways while passing in a set, the excitement of his nose which had been broken in a fall, the thin whiskers at his temples and the downy shadows on his upper lip and chin, the colour of his straight hair, above all, the colour of his eyes . . . Victoria and Victoire spent a great deal of effort in trying to find a blue similar to the colour of Lord March's eyes. Lehzen's embroidery silks were ransacked but without success. It was agony for Victoria because the holly sprig prevented her from looking down, and Victoire was in too great a state of excitement to hold up the silks for her to see. But afterwards in the long gallery when they went to examine all the paintings for a corresponding blue, Victoria, her head tilted back, was able to help. In the end Victoire herself found it, in her brothers' birds-egg collection when the colour of a blackbird's egg was an exact match.

Within a day or two Victoire had sworn so many people to eternal secrecy about her love that it was common knowledge. Victoria was thankful she had said nothing about Lord Brooke. She did not think she could bear to hear people talk about her private feelings, as for instance, Lady Flora did about Victoire and Lord March.

Lehzen watched both girls carefully, one at this stage in her life so withdrawn, the other so open and talkative. She advised Victoire to guard her love from other people's tongues, keeping it apart as something very special and very precious. It corresponded so exactly with what Victoria was doing herself that she began to wonder if Lehzen had guessed anything. In fact it was simply good advice, given gently and kindly to a volatile, rather spoilt girl who was already regretting she had confided in so many people. When Lehzen was out of earshot Victoire called her all manner of names, and concluded by asking nastily what a dried-up old dame like Madame Caraway knew about love anyway.

Victoria was shocked. In Victoire's voice she could hear all Sir John's vulgar scorn for her beloved governess. And there was a trace of Lady Flora Hastings, too, in that hurtful name 'Madame Caraway'.

She defended Lehzen, and so vigorously that Victoire was at first surprised and then indignant.

'She's only your governess,' she retorted.

It was the worst thing she could have said.

Victoria drew herself up to her full height. Almost any other girl would have looked ridiculous trying to assert herself with a sprig of holly below her chin. But Victoria managed it. She was smaller than Victoire, yet somehow she looked taller.

'You are incorrect,' she said. 'The Duchess of Northumberland is my official governess, Baroness Lehzen is my lady-in-waiting.'

'You know what I meant,' said Victoire sulkily.

'Indeed I do not,' Victoria continued to be regal. 'When you are disrespectful to my lady-in-waiting you are being disrespectful and unkind to me.'

Victoire would not allow herself to be put down. She said, and with some justification, that it was unfair for Victoria to be her friend at one moment and royal at the next.

In her heart Victoria wanted to finish the quarrel by saying, very well, she would be regal all the time, and that was that. But it would have finished their friendship altogether. Victoire wasn't a particularly good friend, and after today she would probably be worse, but when you only have one friend of your owne age in all the world you think twice before throwing her on one side. Victoria swallowed her pride. 'Perhaps you are right,' she said. 'But I wish you would not be horrid about Lehzen.'

Victoire was ungenerous in her victory. 'She is exactly what I said, and you know she is, Victoria.' She tossed her head, and added: 'Madame Caraway indeed.'

19

Though she had tried to keep Victoire Conroy's friendship even at the sacrifice of her own dignity, Victoria had failed. Victoire had joined the secret sneerers of the household, those who behind their hands smiled at her discomfort over the holly. She, though, didn't hide her sneers and her giggles. They were open and hurtful. The Duchess of Kent happened to notice it and she immediately told Victoria to remove the sprig of holly. She was having her own daughter laughed at before her eyes. By inference it was a slight to her as Victoria's mother.

Victoire's cheeks whitened as the Duchess rebuked her. 'We have a German word, Miss Conroy, which is used to describe taking pleasure in other people's discomfiture.'

'Yes, Ma'am,' stammered Victoire.

'Tell her what it is, Victoria.'

'*Schadenfreude*, Mamma.'

The Duchess nodded. 'And you, Miss Conroy,' she added icily, 'have a mean sense of *Schadenfreude*. It does not become you.'

'No, Ma'am.' Victoire hung her head.

This public rebuke finally removed any chance of the old

friendship being restored. Victoire continued to share Dean Davys's lessons, and to accompany Victoria and Lehzen to the theatre and opera, but their friendship was dead.

Victoria attempted to put the matter out of her mind by thinking of Lord Brooke and enumerating his charms as she and Victoire had done with the Earl of March. But it was difficult at this stage to remember the precious colour of his hair and eyes, and how his other features differed from everyone else's. She tried, but then she gave it up. How glad she was that she had not told anyone of her liking for the boy; and no one could accuse her of being fickle. She realized that the magic of the ball must have filled her with dreams.

Now that it was over she confided in Lehzen about Lord Brooke and told her as well that her friendship with Victoire had died.

She was better without that influence, Lehzen felt. She suspected that Sir John had intended to use his daughter to implant some of his ideas in Victoria's head. And Victoria had been lucky to escape so easily and unhurt from her first impressionable contact with boys of her own age. Yet she was lonely. She saw too little of her relations. Even those who lived at Kensington Palace barely ever saw her. Nowadays the Princess Sophia seldom went to the Kent apartments and never when Sir John was present at dinner. The Duke of Sussex was far too preoccupied with his latest interests; studying the early Church Fathers with Lord Melbourne the Home Secretary, and pressing his suit on the Lady Cecilia Buggin. Victoria's own mother hardly ever saw her. Feodore was a married woman with children and Charles Leiningen was seldom in the country. Lehzen's love, though deep and plentiful and protective, was not sufficient. What could be done? How could her lonely life be altered?

As though in answer to Lehzen's troubled question came a letter from Germany. The Duchess's sister, Antoinette, Duchess of Württemberg, proposed her sons Alexander and Ernest for a visit to Kensington. Lehzen calculated that they were considerably older than Victoria, but both were unattached. She hoped they would not be too grown-up to spare a little time with their lonely cousin Victoria of England.

20

Lehzen's secret hopes were realized.

Victoria's cousins arrived on a Sunday in June. That evening she wrote in her journal:

> They are both *extremely tall*. Alexander is very *handsome* and Ernest has a *very kind expression*. They are both EX-TREMELY *amiable*.

The Duchess also found her nephews amiable and hand-some. They reminded her of her own youth and suddenly the daily round at Kensington seemed humdrum. She wanted to get out herself and enjoy the London season. And so there were dinners and balls, family visits, picnics and boating trips, ex-peditions to the theatre and opera, drives and rides through the parks, a visit to see an exhibition of water-colours, and another where there were pictures by Reynolds, West and Lawrence.

Victoria was almost always allowed to accompany her cousins and fell head over heels in love with both. Lord Brooke flew from her mind and never returned. Her journal, by necess-ity a restrained document, was nevertheless splashed as never before by underlinings, the use of capitals and a quantity of exclamation marks. Her dilemma was in choosing which cousin she preferred, and if in her journal one was spontaneously de-scribed as 'dear and affectionate' the other was instantly de-scribed in the same way. It was a dilemma which she did not want to avoid or solve. If she loved one more than the other everything would alter. She was sure of it. Both of them would become stiff and withdrawn. So she resolved to love both and she had the most romantic season of her young life.

Later that summer the house party moved to the Isle of Wight in a string of carriages, Sir John in the van in a post-chaise, then a second chaise, a landau, a barouche, a berlin, a family coach and a household coach. The royal yacht *Emerald* carried them over the Solent, and a fly took the Kents and Württembergs from Cowes to Norris Castle and the Conroys to the cottage in the grounds.

Even her mother's unpredictable and embarrassing behaviour did not spoil that visit for Victoria.

The Isle of Wight had different attractions to offer from Kensington. There was sea bathing from bathing machines. There was shrimping. There were rides down the dusty lanes and picnics in carefully chosen places. There were walks with her cousins who helped her to collect wild flowers for pressing. When she had the idea to collect seaweed when the tide was out they even volunteered to help in that messy and tedious business, jumping from rock to rock, feeling for weed in the pools left by the ebbing tide. It took a great deal of patience, and time to make a collection fit for a queen, and that is precisely why Victoria wanted it. They were soon to be visited by Maria da Gloria, the young Queen of Portugal who was only a little older than Victoria, and the seaweed collection was for her. They experimented to find the best way of preserving and pressing seaweed. Neither was easy, but by brute strength the little pods were all popped and flattened, twisted stems were unkinked, and, when sun-dried, the leathery fronds were glued into an album. It was not an especially impressive gift and smelt strongly of gum arabic and the sea but Queen Maria da Gloria was young enough to appreciate it, and gave Victoria in return an herbarium of Brazilian plants.

The very thought of her cousins leaving cast Victoria into a depression. Lehzen told her she was stupid to spoil the last precious hours of their visit by being dejected. But, though she tried, Victoria could not even pretend to be cheerful. Already she had developed a tendency to anticipate the worst.

It was almost a relief when they actually left, and she went inside to sob over her journal and underline how much she would miss them.

Lehzen made no attempt to comfort her. She sat by the open window chewing caraways and rocking in her chair, wise enough to know that sometimes people do not want to have their grief reasoned away, that they do not want to be consoled. She estimated that Victoria would be out of her glooms by tea-time if not before. Then something happened to upset her calculation.

At a little after a quarter to ten they both heard a galloping horse outside. Victoria ran to the window. She was too late to see anything.

'It was a courier,' said Lehzen.

'A courier?'

'Yes, in a great hurry.'

'Could we go down?'

Lehzen considered, deciding that Kensington protocol need not be strictly enforced when they were on holiday. She led the way down to the Castle Norris drawing-room.

A royal estafette, his uniform dusty from the roads, stood before the Duchess of Kent. She was reading a dispatch.

Without warning her hand flew to her mouth and she paled. Simultaneously Lady Flora and Lehzen moved to support her, but it was not necessary. She turned the page and finished reading.

'Are you able to ride without delay?' she asked the young estafette.

'If there is a fresh horse, your royal highness.'

'There is,' said Sir John. He bowed and left the room to arrange everything.

'What is it, Mamma?' asked Victoria.

Her mother was already on her way to the writing-table. 'Your Uncle Alexander,' she said over her shoulder. 'He has died.'

For a moment Victoria did not know whom she meant. Then suddenly she realized; Duke Alexander of Württemberg, father of her beloved cousins who had left only two hours before. Lehzen's arm was already about her and guiding her skilfully from the room. Then Victoria stopped. 'Will you please add my condolences to your own, Mamma.'

The Duchess did not look up but she nodded. 'Very well,' she said.

It was a long time before Victoria was herself again. In her imagination she had followed the estafette to Dover and seen him hand over his terrible dispatch to the unsuspecting Alexander, now reigning Duke of Württemberg. She felt so sad for her cousins. Sad that they had gone, sad that they had lost their father.

She was sufficiently miserable and silent for Lehzen to say that she needed a purge – a suggestion which brought on one of Victoria's famous rages. She stood in the centre of her room trembling with anger, clenching and unclenching her fists, her crimson face set in an obstinately defiant look. She would not take any purge, she swore. All she wished was to be left alone. It was insulting to offer her liquorice water when she was simply mourning for her uncle. She would not take it. Never . . .

Lehzen had looked after her for nine long years. She knew to a minute when the eruption would subside and simply stood there with the draught in her hand until Victoria took it from her.

'Lehzen, you are hateful, so unkind,' she said, and drank it down, grimacing because the undissolved powder cloyed the roof of her mouth. 'Hurry, please hurry,' she cried.

Lehzen quietly poured out a small glass of grenadine and handed it to the girl. 'Better?' she inquired.

'No,' moaned Victoria.

'Be just, child,' said Lehzen, smiling.

'Well . . . yes, the taste is better,' Victoria admitted. Then she discovered she felt less disgruntled than before. Being angry always cleared her head. She felt fresher, as though it had rained at the end of a hot, dusty day.

'Lehzen,' she suggested. 'Let's ask them to saddle my Rosy and your Isabel.'

Lehzen clapped her hands. 'What a very good idea.'

21

The Corporation of Plymouth had sent an invitation for the Kents to visit the city. Moreover the admiralty and dockyard officials and the military attached to Western Command associated themselves with the invitation. It was hoped that the Princess would present new colours to the 89th Regiment of Foot.

Sir John had his temporary Comptroller's office in the butler's pantry, the butler having been exiled elsewhere, and it was in an atmosphere of wine, biscuits and silver polish that he considered the complications of such a visit and its advantages to him.

No matter what the King had commanded, such a visit could never be kept private and unofficial. Plymouth would not hear of it. The people themselves would not allow it. Therefore the King should be told nothing and the invitation accepted. It would establish his own place and power in the eyes of the public.

He instructed Lehzen to prepare the Princess for an unofficial visit to the West Country while he busied himself in making sure it had the authentic Conroy touch. They would travel by the royal yacht *Emerald* and there would be formal addresses, street decorations and illuminations, banquets, naval and military reviews, receptions and bands.

Steam was the thing. The Duchess had it firmly in her head that she need not suffer from seasickness if they travelled to Devon under steam. The *Emerald* being engineless, Sir John arranged for her to be towed along the coast all the way to Plymouth. No one else cared for the idea. It was inelegant, something of an insult to the Royal Yacht Squadron, but the Duchess wished for it. Therefore it was done.

Within half an hour of casting off she wished it had not been.

There was a heavy swell that day and the towing steamer rolled like a sea-cow. Every time one paddle was out of the water she slewed a fraction, and every time she rose out of a trough she plucked at the *Emerald*. The swell and the rolling and the bucketing aboard the *Emerald* had a disastrous effect on the Duchess, and almost everyone else. The Duchess and Lehzen felt so ill that they lay below for the whole voyage moaning and gasping and praying with all the fervency of bad sailors to arrive in Plymouth.

Victoria was ill herself for about thirty minutes, but then it passed off, and by one o'clock she was hungry.

She went down below to ask Lehzen about luncheon. Lehzen moaned. She half sat up and then leant back again. She glanced at the Princess and quickly closed her eyes. From a flickering sign made with trembling fingers Victoria guessed that her governess wished to be left entirely alone. And so she went off by herself to see the steward, and order a hot mutton chop to be served on deck.

She ate her meal alone, feeling rather grand in her isolation and enjoying the way the cutlery and glasses tinkled and jumped up and down. Because she was alone she did something she had never been allowed to do and she gave the chop bone to Dash. He tried to bury it first in the deck, then in the scuppers, then in a coil of rope, and finally he ate it.

Afterwards Victoria marched up and down talking grandly to the seamen. Saunders the helmsman was even favoured by being allowed to hold Dash in his arms, despite which extra responsibility he carefully followed the steamer until Plymouth hove in sight. It was four o'clock by then and suddenly the swell became less noticeable.

Sir John came up on deck with an unhappy expression on his face. Despite the opportunities it offered to him personally, he wished with all his heart that he had never accepted the invitation. He was followed by other members of the household, finally by the Duchess herself. Mostly they were in the same dazed state and in no condition to receive the Commanding Admiral who came aboard to pay his respects.

Sir John did his best. The Duchess did not even do that. She could not make the effort to be courtly. Lehzen stood there swaying. Lady Flora had the best control. Except the Princess. Victoria was entirely herself.

Guns boomed and she heard a tinkle of music from the distance as the old admiral bowed low and kissed her hand. He spoke with her for a moment, and prepared to stand with her for the rest of the tow. She was proud to be at his side. He had commanded a ship at Trafalgar under Lord Nelson.

Orders rang out through speaking trumpets. Bells rang. The towing steamer surged up on her paddles and plucked at her tow. The *Emerald* was under way again.

Then it happened.

91

She ground suddenly into a hulk. As she fouled the shock snapped her mainmast. The admiral put a protective arm round Victoria. Hearing the timber go he reacted instinctively: ' 'Ware deck!' he barked. ' 'Ware deck.' A section of the mast thudded down not far away. 'There, Ma'am,' he said. ' 'Tis over and done.' But the noise continued. The *Emerald* shuddered as she heaved against the hulk, while seamen shouted and cursed and women screamed.

As suddenly as it had begun, the noise stopped. Saunders the helmsman had heaved on the tow rope and jerked them clear of the hulk.

He was the hero of the hour. The *Emerald*'s mainmast had snapped in two places, but miraculously only a fraction had crashed to the deck. Her side was deeply scored and holed and her steering apparatus knocked out of true. But she was still afloat and no one at all had been hurt. If Saunders had not acted so quickly they might have been in the greatest danger.

Lehzen, her face yellower than ever, pushed her way through the crowd of seamen and threw her arms about Victoria. She cried and swayed from side to side with relief.

'Saunders saved us, Lehzen,' said Victoria. 'Truly he did. And,' she added proudly, 'not once did he drop my darling Dash.'

22

The Duke of Wellington and Lord Grey, the Whig Prime Minister, were talking together at a levée in St James's. Though political opponents they were friends, and both were concerned with a non-party problem.

'Whom,' asked the Duke, 'will she marry?'

Grey shook his head. 'I've an impression; but, mind you, it's only an impression, that the King favours the Prince of Orange.' He lowered his voice. 'But very probably that is merely because the Duchess of Kent approves of her brother's suggestion — one of the Coburg princes. His majesty still finds it impossible to forgive her for taking the Princess to Plymouth without his permission.'

The Duke sighed and snapped his fingers, deprecating the open hostility between Kensington and St James's since the sea collision. 'A compromise third party would be best,' he said. 'It's a thousand pities that Cumberland's son is blind. A thousand pities.'

The advantages of the future heir to Hanover marrying the future heiress to England were obvious. But now, clearly, it was out of the question.

Lord Grey pointed out that there was always Prince George of Cambridge.

Wellington considered. 'At a pinch. Maybe. Yes, he might do.'

'For what?' asked a voice at his elbow.

It was Lord Melbourne, Grey's Home Secretary.

The Duke made him welcome. 'We were discussing Kent's daughter, Melbourne. Would she make a wife for George of Cambridge?'

'No,' exclaimed Melbourne immediately. 'It'd never do at all. They're too close by blood.'

Involuntarily they all looked towards the King on the other side of the saloon. He had left the throne and was plucking at the grey hair on his crimson pineapple-shaped head. Added to this he was roaring with laughter.

'You're right,' said the Duke thoughtfully. 'Damned eccentric lot. Wouldn't do to mix cousins. They'd breed something odd. Ten to one on it.'

'That argument,' Grey pointed out, 'excludes the Coburg cousins, too.'

'Exclude them by all means,' said Melbourne cheerfully. 'Our royal family has only come to life since it came to England, and it may have been mad, depraved, even downright evil, but it has never been dull or ungenerous. I'd not find it difficult to choose between civilized, sparkling wickedness and uncouth German virtue.'

Lord Grey urged him to lower his tone. 'In view of the King's age and health,' he murmured, 'I should say the decision will probably be made by the Princess herself. Or by her mother as Regent.'

'God forbid!' exclaimed the Duke fervently.

'In which case,' continued Grey, 'her choice will be limited. I'm informed that only German visitors stay at Kensington. Last year, there were the Württemberg princes; this year the Duchess's brother Ferdinand who has three sons, and now there is Princess Feodore with her husband.'

Lord Melbourne frowned. 'Therefore the prevailing influences upon the Princess are teutonic, which is not a very happy prospect for the future of England.'

The Duke nodded gloomily. 'He's right, Grey. Germans don't suit the English. Too thorough and humourless. And, by God, they can be very odd. D'you recall old Blücher after Waterloo – thinking himself pregnant of an elephant, and fathered by a French soldier at that?'

Melbourne smiled: 'Such an original German would be very welcome, but I'm afraid most of them are damnably dull.' He reflected. 'I wonder, though, if any prince in the world would suit the Princess at the moment. She is difficult to please. Sussex tells me that apparently she is not at all contented with her lot. She is short and wishes to be moderately tall. She is plump, inclining in fact to stoutness, and wants to be sylph-like. Her chin and nose are pointed and she would cheerfully blunt both. Then, by nature, she presents an alarming prospect as our future ruler, having the force and obstinacy of a tyrant but not the intelligence which can make tyranny tolerable and even beneficial. Her mind is vapid, and her taste non-existent because she is crammed with information rather than taught how to get the finest savour from life. For instance, she will spend a morning absorbing complicated details from a visiting lecturer on hydrostatics and dynamics and afterwards will entertain herself at a pantomime of Old Mother Hubbard.'

'Come, come,' objected Lord Grey. 'That is natural at her age.'

'Just so,' agreed the Duke.

'On the contrary,' said Melbourne. 'It is natural for a girl to enjoy Old Mother Hubbard, but not to have a mind stuffed with hydrostatics and dynamics.' He sighed. 'There it is then. I suppose we should be grateful that she speaks English and French as well as German, and that she has the best possible teacher in every subject from crochet-work to ballroom dancing.' Sighing once more, he added: 'I only hope England can stand it.'

'Melbourne,' said the Prime Minister uneasily. 'If I didn't know you better, I'd say you were a determined republican.'

'My dear Grey, you don't know me in the least,' came the laughing reply, and Melbourne slipped away to talk to the Duke of Sussex about the early Fathers.

'An enigma, by God,' chuckled the Duke.

'Precisely!' said the Prime Minister.

23

Victoria was just fifteen years old when Feodore arrived at Kensington with her husband Ernest, Prince of Hohenlohe-Langenburg, and their two small children.

Both had been looking forward to the visit with extreme excitement, but they kept it bottled up. Six years had passed since last they had seen each other. It was too long a time for Victoria. Shyly she could not believe that her busy, grown-up half-sister wanted to waste any time talking to her. Feodore, realizing that these six formative years had made Victoria into a very different child, did not want to thrust herself forward. Patiently she waited.

Victoria made a great fuss of her children. No doubt through the children they would renew their old intimacy. Meanwhile Feodore observed her half-sister from a distance.

What she saw she did not altogether like. Victoria was certainly moody and appeared to be secretive, too quick to find fault, and surprisingly she showed signs of being indifferent to Lehzen. Once she had adored her; now she resented being told what to do and did not trouble to hide her resentment. This worried Feodore so much that she plucked up her courage and spoke to Lehzen about it. They went for a walk in the park together while Victoria played with the children.

After an amount of skirting the subject Feodore found the courage to say what she thought.

To her surprise, but also to her relief, Lehzen chuckled.

'Dear Feodore, how thoughtful of you. And how observant to notice my little rebel in the middle of her rebellion.' She took Feodore's hand and kissed her cheek. 'Believe me, it is nothing. She lacks companions and therefore I have to be the butt of her displeasure as well as everything else. When we have visitors I am relegated to the post of unpopular governess. When the visitors have gone, I am restored to favour.'

Princess Feodore frowned. 'No one but you would tolerate such ingratitude,' she said. 'And I'm not sure that you should.'

Lehzen led her to a garden seat and explained that Victoria now seemed to be incapable of giving her full love or putting her full trust in more than one person at a time. Those who loved her – and, sadly, they were very few – could understand this trait. Others called her sly and ungrateful.

'But I am confident,' said Lehzen, and she sounded quite sincere, 'that she will develop beyond this, that she will mature sufficiently to be capable of loving several at once and trusting many simultaneously.'

Feodore went out of her way to be friendly to this new, enigmatic, adolescent sister. But she had no success. Far from helping to bind them together as she had hoped, the children were being used by Victoria as a barrier between them.

Whenever Feodore tried to re-establish their old relationship and talk confidentially, Victoria would quickly play with the children, or talk about them, or remember something that needed doing for them. She still had a convinced belief that Feodore could not possibly be interested in anyone who was so much younger. Fortunately they were bidden to Windsor for the races. It was impossible for her to be timid and elated at the same time, and she was in a fever of excitement and chattered of this and that to her sister as they prepared for Windsor. Feodore decided to leave her children behind at Kensington so that they could no longer act as a barrier.

Furthermore Sir John decided to stay behind. The King had told everyone that if his niece had been drowned off Plymouth it would have been entirely Conroy's responsibility, and very probably Sir John did not wish to risk a royal explosion of temper. His absence relaxed Victoria and made the occasion more of a family affair, though it was not until after dinner on their first evening at Windsor that the sisters regained their old intimacy.

Dinner at the Castle on the night before the races was exceedingly formal.

Feodore's husband led in the Queen. They were followed by the King, who led Victoria on one hand and her mother on the other. He held them, everyone noticed, at a distance, like a pair of swaddled spinning tops, nodding his pineapple head and being excessively polite to the Duchess. Mutual dislike made their smiles fixed and brilliant. They were followed by Princess Feodore, led in by the Duke of Richmond.

Victoria sat between the King and the Duke of Dorset. Secretly she had hoped George Cambridge would be closer to her. He had smiled when she had given him her hand in the anteroom. She hadn't smiled back, but she had wanted to. Now he was far away down the table. Only by hunching herself forward over the soup could she just see the tip of his chin in the distance. Perhaps it was as well. Her mother, Lehzen, everyone had made it quite clear that she wasn't to be too friendly with her cousin George.

Victoria was very fond of the King but the noise he made was tremendous, and it was something of a relief when he turned away from her to shout at her mother, and she was free to talk to the Duke of Dorset. Privately she thought he was extraordinary. He was tiny, but unlike most small men, he was vain of his littleness and had used it to good effect as a jockey. He told of his successes at Newmarket. He and his brother, he said proudly, had won many races in their time. And her good, sweet uncle had won a lot of money on them. Which uncle, she asked politely, would that have been? Why the Regent, he told her, afterwards King George, his own special crony, though he'd been friendly, too, with her uncle of York. What times they'd had together, he began – but he broke off and fetched a sigh. Victoria's rank, sex and youth forbade any sort of account of their adventures. Instead he asked her if she had seen the statue to her Uncle York being raised in Waterloo Place. And when she said she had and she thought it a good likeness, he winked confidentially and said it was common talk the lightning conductor sprouting from his head would be a useful spike for his unpaid bills. Victoria was abashed. Because of her own father's debt she was sensitive to any mention of bills, but this little duke, screwing up his face and laughing merrily, made fun of it all. After a moment she smiled. The thought of Uncle York, Field Marshal and Bishop, with bills spiked on his lightning conductor was irresistible. They laughed and chuckled together, and he felt encouraged to amuse her with other discreet stories of the past. By the end of the dinner, everyone at the head of the board had been included and they were all laughing at his wit. Victoria was as merry as any of them.

In the drawing-room excitement made her rush naturally to Feodore to tell her how charming the Duke of Dorset had been. 'He has such a way with him, Feodore,' she said.

'Indeed he has,' laughed Feodore. 'Like all rich single men over the age of forty.'

She was overjoyed that Victoria had run to her spontaneously. Gingerly, she invited more confidences. 'But Dorset is by no means as handsome as your cousin George,' she said.

Victoria smiled. 'So you saw him smile at me before dinner?' she asked.

'I did. And I liked his boldness.'

Victoria told her about the birthday ball, at first hesitantly but then, when she was certain that Feodore was really interested, she spoke rapidly in her old way. She confessed her strong but only temporary feelings for Lord Brooke. 'A dark, silent person, the very opposite of cousin George.' Then she spoke of Victoire's grand passion for Lord March, and this led her to admit that she and Victoire had quarrelled.

'We still see each other every day, but we're no longer friends.'

'Do you really mind?' asked Feodore.

Victoria considered. 'No, I don't think so,' she said slowly.

'Probably you are better without her,' said Feodore. 'Though it's such a great pity you have no one of your own age to keep you company. Lehzen told me you are lonely.'

Victoria shrugged. All the gaiety had suddenly drained away. 'But isn't that what I shall be all my life?' she asked flatly.

'Oh, no!' Genuinely shocked Feodore tried to make her see that being royal need not cut her off from all society. She would find a husband, as she had done, and learn to love him and her children. And she would have friends . . .

'Not in the sense that you can have friends,' said Victoria. 'Already I am different from everyone else because I am heiress to the crown. As a ruling sovereign I shall be truly isolated. Ask Späth,' she added with a smile. 'Späth will tell you about the loneliness of being exalted. So perhaps it is as well that I have hardly anyone to talk to at present. I am rehearsing for the great day, just as Uncle William rehearsed by keeping his writing-hand supple and his throat well gargled.'

She turned to look out on to the tree-tops below the window. Feodore wondered if she was being caustic or simply morose, but not by any sign did she show her feelings. 'Do you so much regret the prospect of being Queen?' she asked.

'It is inevitable,' replied the other. She picked up a fold of the red velvet curtain as though to examine the material and let it drop at once. 'Therefore, I am indifferent. Or rather I must try to be indifferent.'

'Let Lehzen help you. She is anxious for you.'

A tiny frown appeared on Victoria's face. 'Lehzen worries too much,' she said.

Feodore caught her hand. 'Now don't disappear again, I beg.'

'Disappear?'

'Yes. It has taken all this time for us to return to where we were six years ago and your face shows warning signs that you're going to be shy and stiff again.'

Victoria smiled. 'Not with you,' she said. 'I promise, not with you.'

'Nor with Lehzen, either,' insisted her sister. 'She is the very best friend you have, Victoria. Don't hurt her.'

Victoria wanted this explained. Like most other children of fifteen she could see very little farther than her own immediate needs and concerns. It astonished her to hear Feodore say that by being thoughtless she could bring great unhappiness to Lehzen. 'Oh, no,' she exclaimed. 'I would not hurt Lehzen for the world.'

'Not willingly, I know,' soothed Feodore. 'But don't take her too much for granted. And remember that, though she is merely a part of your life, you are more than that to her. She has given up home and family and friends for you. You are everything to her and she deserves well from you.'

'But, Feodore, I don't think she really understands me.'

'How?'

'Well ... It's difficult to explain, but can't you remember how she holds you in? She's like a bit on a pony. Occasionally I want to be entirely alone. I want to run away. I want to be free. She doesn't seem to realize that, because I can't have these things, I feel like exploding.'

'I think she does realize,' said Feodore quietly. 'She knows you better than you think. And, remember, she's the only one who ever allows you to be alone – that is, when she can.'

Victoria nodded. 'Yes, you're right. She does.' She sighed. 'It's not Lehzen's fault. It's the rules.' She grinned and said in a fair imitation of her mother's voice. 'The regulations governing the upbringing of young princesses.'

She would have said more but the Queen called them to the large oval table where the royal party sat with their closest guests.

She caught Feodore's hand. 'Stay close to me, dearest sister, and I shan't disappear again.'

Feodore returned the pressure of her hand. 'I know,' she said. 'It is a long way to Hohenlohe, but if ever you need us, if ever you need me, Victoria . . .' It was unnecessary to finish the sentence.

As they approached the table Victoria whispered gently in her ear. 'I hope you go down to the races with the Duke of Dorset.'

Feodore chuckled. 'It ought to be your pleasure.'

As it turned out neither of them was so fortunate. In the procession of carriages to the racecourse, Victoria travelled with the King and Queen and her mother, and Feodore was in the second carriage with the Queen's lady of the bedchamber in waiting and a pair of duchesses. It was Baroness Lehzen who enjoyed the company of sweet Uncle George's midget crony, Charles, fifth Duke of Dorset. He at once asked her what she took from the little silver box and insisted on trying a caraway seed. He was so droll he made her laugh, and once or twice so outspoken that she turned to a delicate flamingo pink. He gave her unasked for and very mysterious hints on judging horseflesh and advice on laying wagers. He then prophesied rain. Her pretty bonnet would be ruined, he said. It wouldn't be ordinary rain but terrible, cats and dogs, Ascot week rain.

Unfortunately he was absolutely right, and Lehzen's bonnet was completely spoiled.

24

Lord Melbourne's butler coughed to attract attention.

'Your lordship!' he murmured. 'Your lordship!'

But the figure beside the shaded library lamp was asleep; a volume of the *Noctes Atticae* of Aulus Gellius open upon his knees.

The butler cleared his throat with a very lound and unpleasant sound.

Lord Melbourne opened an eye. 'Yes?'

'A messenger has come from Westminster, your lordship.'

'Then bid him wait,' came the cross reply.

He had been Prime Minister since Grey's ministry had fallen at the end of July, muddling along as a caretaker minister (he called himself the political undertaker) and not enjoying the muddling. For it was wearing, enervating. Very wearying. Public affairs prevented him from enjoying the company of cultivated people as much as he wished. His reading time was limited, so was his theatre-going and his exercise. Policies came before being sociable and charming in the great houses of

London. Even his quiet evenings with Mrs Norton had often to be sacrificed to cabinets. Public affairs stopped him from going down to his country house at Brocket, though public affairs should not make him move from his London house and he resolutely refused to occupy 10 Downing Street. For four months he had been King William's First Minister. A short time, but already he was very weary. And they would not even let him rest.

Once more aware that his butler was still standing by the chair he said: 'They will not leave me alone. They will not. So they must learn. Bid the messenger wait.'

'With respect, your lordship,' said the butler. 'He bade me tell you it was very urgent.'

Unless he was drunk – a not infrequent occurrence – his butler was not usually so persistent, and clearly he was not drunk on this occasion.

Melbourne sighed. 'You are sure?' he asked. 'Absolutely sure?'

'Very urgent,' repeated the butler solemnly.

So he was bidden to bring the man in with a glass of something hot – a toddy would do – and as he went to fetch the messenger he heard his lordship cursing and blinding with the skill if not the energy of a costermonger.

'His lordship is expecting you,' he told the man. 'And he's in the devil of a bate at being woken up.'

As soon as he saw the man wore the livery of a House of Lords servant, Melbourne guessed it was a message from one of his ministers. They were so easily teased by Tory questions and dreaded committing themselves. He held out his hand, but the messenger had nothing written.

'Verbal, your lordship,' he said.

'Then it can wait until I've drunk my toddy.'

The butler made an elaborate performance of mixing toddies. Melbourne watched the ritual appreciatively. Then he took the glass, sat down, sipped, nodded, drank a little, smoothed his trousers, sighed, and said, 'Well, man. What is it?'

'Your lordship I was bidden to say the Houses of Parliament are afire.'

Melbourne put down his glass. 'Both Houses?'

'Yes, your lordship.'

'Seriously?'

'Past stopping, they say, your lordship.'

The Prime Minister stood alone beside the River Thames. He had gone immediately to Westminster to see if anything could be done. Only parts of the palace might be saved. The remainder was doomed, most of it already a blazing holocaust. Ministers and Members of both Houses came to ask what should or could be done. Nothing, he told them, nothing. Then he went away by himself to stand close to the river and watch the reflection of the fire in the water. He showed to the world a cynical, sceptical side, but secretly he was grieving. It was not so much that he was seeing the destruction of a building but the end of what to him it stood for. In the Commons he had sat at the feet of Charles James Fox and then at the feet of Canning. In those days, before reform had let in members of another type, Parliament had sheltered a ruling, lettered, aristocratic class who governed England from one point of view or from the other but almost always for the benefit of England and not for any section of society. Now everything was altered and altering. As the King's First Minister and belonging to the traditional governing class of England he was in a position to control the speed of change, but he could not prevent it happening. His lot he felt was like that of Lepidus, an Aemilian patrician bargaining for the world with Antonius and Octavius, neither of them principled or likeable, neither of them gentlemen, neither with a real feeling for Rome and its traditions, both aggressive plebeians, and yet both with talents and a new tremendous power. Change was unavoidable but regrettable. Melbourne was absolutely certain that the world was no longer such a good place to live in.

A few peers came to join him. He was cool and appeared resigned to the loss of Parliament, cooler than any of them, they judged, and a perfect example of how one should behave in the face of calamity. They envied him his poise and his detachment, not knowing that inside he was mourning for so much which he loved and respected, and which, like the buildings before him, was being reduced to ashes.

25

Two nights later the Prime Minister was to dine with the Duchess of Kent at Kensington. He knew quite well why he had been invited but he accepted as an inevitable part of his duties the tiresome business of having to hear complaints and appeals from the royal family. And he took the opportunity of arriving early at Kensington in order to visit his friend the Duke of Sussex. Only after an interesting hour's discussion on patristic writings could he face the pleas and food of the Duchess of Kent.

The Duke of Sussex was in an ebullient mood and delighted to see him.

'I had hoped you would call, Melbourne, for I am to dine with the Kents as well.'

'That, your royal highness, is something of a relief.'

The Duke smiled. Melbourne was famous for his frankness. Often it appeared he said the very first thing that came into his head. But he was also famed for his ingenuity. You never quite knew whether he was being naturally frank or deliberately frank in order to invite your confidence. It appeared on this occasion he was simply being candid. 'Her royal highness is bound to say a number of disagreeable things and ask for the impossible. With your help, sir, I shall survive the ordeal.'

'And how may I help?'

'By emphasizing, if you will be so kind, that I have no real power, that I am caretaking and therefore any undertaking I might give could, in fact would, be revoked as soon as I fell from power.'

'Now, Melbourne,' laughed the Duke. 'That simply isn't true.'

'For me, sir, you should be prepared to tell a lie, but, as it happens, it is quite true. Will you wager with me? I have no real following in the Commons. In the Lords I am cliff-hanging. The King will tire of it very soon and he will send for

Wellington and Wellington will advise him to send for Peel. A wager? That this happens before the year is out?'

'Fifty guineas!' said the Duke, who cared little about the intricacies of politics but loved a bet.

'Done!'

Each made an entry in his pocket book, and Mr Blackman was ordered to bring brandy. 'And now, my dear Melbourne, you must see what Patrel has sent from Paris.'

They sat at a writing-desk examining three volumes of the Greek text of Lactanius, and before long were gently disagreeing; the Duke having a special regard for this Anti-Nicene father, the Prime Minister favouring Gregory Thaumaturgus.

The company was small. The Duchess preferred it so because, as Melbourne had suspected, he would have to earn his dinner. Beyond the Duke of Sussex and his equerry, the Princess Sophia and her reading lady, the Duke and Duchess of Gloucester, and Sir John and Lady Flora from the Kent household, the only other guests were the Duke of Northumberland and the Earl of Durham.

Melbourne frowned when he saw Durham. They had served together in Lord Grey's ministry until Durham had been given an earldom a year before. What, said Melbourne to himself, was he doing here?

The Duke of Sussex pulled his arm and begged him not to be so outspoken.

'Did I say something aloud?' whispered Melbourne in amazement.

The Duke nodded. 'But no one heard,' he whispered back.

It was little wonder, thought Melbourne with his lips firmly pressed together, that he spoke out aloud when confronted with Radical Jack Durham. Of all his colleagues he found him the most difficult to get along with. Durham was everything he disliked: vain, a bit of a bully, and an idealist. And his honesty was suspect. How could a man go on and on and on and on about the poor, as Durham often did to the agonized boredom of his colleagues, and expect to be regarded as their spokesman when he was noted for his extravagance? It was inconsistent, and therefore irritating to Melbourne, for Durham spoke of starving Midlanders while spending no less than £90,000 on redecorating his country house. Further he was a Pandora's box of emotionalism. At meetings of ministers he had sulked, shouted, pleaded, wept, stormed, shaken his fist, beaten his breast, pulled his own hair, threatened to harm himself, threatened to harm others, and altogether been impossible. He would not make a comfortable dinner partner. Melbourne decided to avoid him as far as possible, and was icy, as only Melbourne could be icy, when Sir John effected the usual presentations.

As the meal proceeded Melbourne saw exactly why he had been asked. He was to be reassured of the Kents' support of the Whig cause. There wasn't a Tory in the room. He was being offered a continuance in office should anything happen to the present king, and the full support of the heiress to the throne. But clearly on conditions. There would be conditions.

At first everyone wanted to talk of the fire and how Parliament was to be rebuilt. Durham, as Melbourne knew he would, said the conflagration had been fortuitous – a splendid way of wiping out the inglorious past. As *The Times* leader had remarked, when such things happened one had to be practical and utilitarian and not sentimental. Did not Lord Melbourne agree? But Melbourne refused to be drawn. He would not speak publicly on things which mattered to him. Certainly not between the entrée and the roast. The Duke of Sussex came to his assistance to some extent and answered for him. But Durham would not let it alone.

'And how,' he asked, 'would the King's First Minister review this happy episode?'

Had Melbourne not been a guest he would have suggested economizing by using the Bloody Tower for the Commons and Drury Lane for the Lords. Instead he simply said he had no views to offer at present, and accepted a sorbet.

The Duchess of Kent hastily moved on to another topic. It was one she had close to her heart. She spoke down the table to the Duchess of Northumberland who was sitting next to Melbourne. 'Tell the Prime Minister, your grace, how well the Princess does at present.'

The royal governess did so, not particularizing but clearly approving of Victoria's upbringing. In fact it appeared she was a little too warm in her approval to suit the Duchess of Kent.

'Come, your grace,' she called down the table. 'We don't wish to give anyone the idea that my daughter is a prodigy. Indeed . . .' She paused deliberately to make sure she had everyone's attention. 'Indeed, as we are family or close friends here tonight, I may say that in some matters Victoria is not as forward as she might be.'

'We can't all have brains,' said the Duke of Gloucester, suddenly without his usual cheerfulness. Such a remark from him at that moment was rather pathetic.

His wife was moved to shout at him across the table: 'You're right, Duke of Gloucester, you're right. But when a man's good-natured and considerate he don't need brains.'

It was a sincere compliment in which the Duke of Sussex joined by nodding vigorously. Silly Billy sat back, looking very pleased with himself.

'Is that not regrettable, Lord Durham?' asked the Duchess of Kent – determined not to allow the conversation to wander and ignoring her royal relations-in-law as though they had not spoken.

Durham was a skilful diplomatist and was not going to commit himself just yet. 'You may indeed be right, Ma'am,' he replied.

Lehzen championed her darling though she would have been wiser to let the topic rest. 'The Princess, Ma'am, has good reports from all her teachers. Monsieur Grandineau has the highest opinion of her French. Mr Westall has said that were she born for lower things than a throne she could have done well as a professional painter. Madame Bourdin, Mrs Steward, the Dean – all are delighted with her progress. Her frequent visits to the opera have deepened her love for music and she has spent a great deal of time in the past few months studying that subject, singing and practising upon the harp.'

'The harp?' It was Lord Melbourne who interrupted. He could not help himself. In his imagination he saw a small portly young lady attack the harp with German determination and ferocity.

'The harp,' repeated Lehzen. 'At St Leonards and in Tunbridge Wells.' She was pink with the exertion of listing

Victoria's virtues. 'All in all she has done very well.' She turned for confirmation from Victoria's official governess. 'As you have already said, your grace.'

'Just so,' agreed the Duchess. 'And as she matures she will improve still further . . .'

'Matures,' said the Duchess of Kent, interrupting her. 'Now that is just the word that worries me.' She looked round at her guests. 'May I be frank?' she asked.

Melbourne longed to say no, on no account could she be frank, for he knew it would involve some sort of trouble. Generally a robust eater he pushed away his pudding untasted and listened, with a sinking feeling, while the Duchess confessed her anxiety that the Princess was maturing too slowly.

'In the sad and calamitous event of the King's death,' she said with blithe hypocrisy. 'I shall be there to help and guide my daughter as Regent of England until she is eighteen.'

'The official coming of age of an heir to the Crown,' added Sir John, quite unnecessarily for everyone knew it. It simply showed Melbourne the Comptroller's personal interest in the matter.

'But I am wondering, we are all wondering, if even at eighteen she will be sufficiently mature to take the responsibility as well as the Crown.'

'How can we tell?' asked her brother-in-law of Sussex with a sarcastic edge to his voice. 'Must she sit an examination of royal competency?'

'Duke of Sussex, I beg you not to treat this lightly,' returned the Duchess. 'It is a matter of greatest concern.' Then, abruptly, it came: 'Do you not agree as Prime Minister, Lord Melbourne?'

He was her guest and had to reply. 'Until her royal highness is eighteen the question is hypothetical, Ma'am.'

'In three short years,' she said. 'Come, I insist on your giving us your advice. Would a Whig ministry consider lengthening the Regency under such special circumstances?' Having asked this bold and direct question which had Melbourne gaping for a moment, she slightly turned to Lord Durham and asked his opinion were he a Whig minister of the Crown.

'Without a doubt, Ma'am, I should vote for an extension,'

said Durham cheerfully for he found it difficult to resist the flatteries of handsome women.

So, thought Melbourne, that was why Durham had been asked: to set the pace, and force some sort of answer from him.

'It would be a mistake,' he said slowly, 'to anticipate hypothetical events.'

'But we must,' said the Duchess with a shake of her head.

'If you will permit me to disagree, Ma'am, I think it would be a mistake to anticipate hypothetical events.'

And that was all she could get out of him.

Afterwards he did something which was unusual for a man accustomed to let things be. He sought out Lehzen and said how much he regretted the Princess was ill and had not been able to dine that evening.

'But, my lord, she is not ill,' said Lehzen swiftly.

Melbourne cocked an eye at her. 'No?'

'No, my lord. She had dinner in her room with her maid. Her mother intimated that matters would be discussed at dinner which the Princess ought not to hear.'

'A pity,' said Melbourne. He was thoughtful for a moment. 'Give her, please, my humble duty, Baroness.'

Five minutes later he and the Duke of Sussex were seated in a corner of the saloon continuing their gentle disagreement about Lactanius and Gregory Thaumaturgus. The Duke of Gloucester sat with them, nodding his head occasionally, as though to agree with one or other of the points of view, and beaming all the time.

26

Taught by Lehzen, Victoria had already become acquisitive. She was a hoarder, a magpie who could throw little away, and she was already a compulsive collector. In the next few months she added to her minerals and dressed dolls two more collections.

The lesser in importance was her collection of autographs. It was a hobby encouraged by her Uncle Leopold, who saw in it an interesting and painless way of studying history, a subject which he considered to be of extreme moment to a modern constitutional ruler. He enclosed autographs with the many letters he wrote to her, and she began with an interesting batch, autographs of Louis XVI, Marie Antoinette, Henri IV, the Duke of Marlborough, the Empress Maria Therese, and Lafayette.

The second collection was very different.

Twice in a short time Victoria found herself in the plain black bombazine dress kept for family mourning.

The Duke of Gloucester died. She had not known her uncle well but she remembered his kindness to her years before when they had visited Cumberland Lodge at Windsor. And she had seen the devotion of Aunt Gloucester for her Silly Billy. Now he was gone, with his kind smile, and way of wrinkling his nose in perplexity exactly like a hungry rabbit, and his habit of repeating the many long words which he didn't understand. In his last illness Victoria and her mother sent messages asking after his progress, and on the very day he died he said to Aunt Gloucester: 'Tell them that I say, God bless them, and that I love them.'

Victoria was deeply moved when she heard this and tried, though without much success, to convey her feelings in her journal.

The next family death was of her mother's sister who had married Count Mensdorff Pouilly. She died far away in Bohemia, and though Victoria had seen her only once she was shocked at the circumstances of her death which had been unexpected and had taken place, on a journey, in a rough Bohemian cottage. She did her best to comfort her mother and devoted several pages of her journal to describing how they had received the news, how her uncle and four cousins grieved and how splendid the funeral had been.

Thereafter she began to collect funeral mementoes.

Lehzen was cautious. She consulted the Duchess of Northumberland, but neither could see any real harm in Victoria's interest in weeds, black crêpes, mourning rings, hair lockets, plaster doves and lilies and hands clasping, and all the other paraphernalia and trappings of death. And her mourning when members of the family died was at least genuine and a real expression of her love.

But her mother was shocked. Wallowing in death was a grisly business more suited to Latin peasants than to princesses of the blood. The morbid collection of funeral mementoes was condemned, and would have been thrown out but just at that time the Duchess had other things to disturb her peace of mind. Victoria was soon to be confirmed and her mother was balancing the advantages and disadvantages of being awkward with the King.

The truce made between them at Windsor had long since fallen to pieces. He was too excitable. She was too indiscreet. It had been ruptured when he heard, through his sister Sophia, of the Kensington dinner party, and the blatant probing of Lord Melbourne. This had made him so angry that he let it be known it was his sole wish to live long enough to deprive her of any regency at all. He caused the insult by repeating publicly what the Duke of Wellington had said about her: that she was a damned, mischievous, meddling woman.

Mortified beyond belief, the Duchess then spent months endeavouring to inflame the King's irascibility. She succeeded. The war between Kensington and St James's blazed as brightly as ever. Nevertheless when Victoria's confirmation came under discussion the King gave an explicit command. It was a royal occasion. The rite was to take place in the Chapel Royal in the presence of the royal family.

For a time the Duchess considered the pleasurable self-indulgence of disobeying. She could insist on her right as a mother and have Victoria confirmed where and when she chose – at St Leonards, Tunbridge Wells, or even Kensington. But she hesitated, and it was this which occupied her mind and saved Victoria's funeral collection from being jettisoned. Ultimately she decided to be cautious. It would not be to her advantage to stay permanently away from things. Therefore Victoria would have to be confirmed in the King's presence in the Chapel Royal as he had commanded.

And so, on an intensely hot July day, they drove up to St

James's, the Duchess having given her daughter a little talk on filial obedience and three puzzling handbooks about confirmation.

Dressed in white lace with a white crêpe bonnet decorated with roses, Victoria dipped into the books and despite Lehzen's comforting presence she felt very apprehensive. The solemnity of the occasion deeply impressed her. She was enrolling, the Dean had told her, as a loyal soldier in the Army of God, but it was not easy to think of this when they reached the King's Closet and she was greeted by the royal family. The King kissed her and chuckled and chattered as though they were about to witness a naval review or a cricket match. And the Queen beamed fixedly and took great quantities of snuff. Already emotional, Victoria recollected it was the first time the family had gathered together since Uncle Gloucester's funeral. The tears stole from her eyes as she kissed her Aunt Gloucester, black in her widow's weeds, and still very genuinely mourning her Silly Billy. She squeezed her aunt's arm and would have spoken but she was pulled away by her mother to take her place in the procession into the Royal Chapel.

At this point there was an hiatus. Because of the smallness of the chapel the King had given strict instructions about the size of the royal party, and he now somewhat reduced the solemnity of the occasion by personally counting the Duchess of Kent's retinue. And at the top of his voice. To his undisguised delight he found it one too many and promptly asked Sir John Conroy to leave.

The Duchess wept. The King was adamant and implacable. He would not have the place overcrowded, and he would have his instructions obeyed.

This inauspicious beginning was followed by a full-scale session of Morning Prayer with the Litany and then a sermon of immense length and profundity. Victoria was the only candidate and the Archbishop preached at her as though he were addressing a congregation of hardened Newgate felons. She was moved to tears and felt ill because of the heat.

She was moved to tears once more after the service when the King kissed her warmly and gave her a set of emeralds. The Queen gave her a tiara of the same stones. They kindly invited her to spend the summer with them at Windsor. She was growing up now, and would enjoy herself. They particularly hoped she would be their guest as it would give them both so much pleasure.

Through the tears Victoria told them she loved them truly, and would always honour them as kind sovereigns and her very affectionate uncle and aunt.

Half an hour later she was forced to realize how difficult it was going to be to keep to the good intentions she had only just made. She was sitting opposite to her mother in the carriage back to Kensington, and was obliged to listen to a catalogue of all the insults and damages imagined and real which had been heaped on their heads by the King and Queen. By not speaking out Victoria felt she was betraying her uncle and aunt and had already revoked the solemn promises given at her confirmation, yet she had been taught all her life that obedience to her mother was the sovereign Kent virtue. Nothing matched up to it. Lehzen was beside her but, in front of her mother, she could not ask for advice on this bewildering matter. It appeared that if she was loyal to one she must be treacherous to the other. For the third time that morning she relieved her feelings by crying.

Her mother thought she was crying out of sympathy for her and was gratified. 'There, my dear,' she said offering a handkerchief. 'How wicked it was of your uncle to upset us so on your confirmation day.'

'Oh, no, Mamma,' sobbed Victoria. 'On the contrary to me he was very kind.'

The Duchess pursed her lips. 'Oh, was he?' she snapped. At once she tried to spoil all Victoria's appreciation of her uncle's kindness by suggesting he had been kind simply to vex her.

'That cannot be,' said Victoria, a finger to her mouth. 'Truly not, Mamma.' The tears streamed down her cheeks.

'Child,' said the Duchess sententiously. 'You have no notion how wicked some people can be.'

'Ma'am,' said Lehzen suddenly, unable to restrain herself any longer. 'I rather believe she is learning.'

27

'She must go, Sir John. I will not have her teaching my own daughter rebellion. Nor will I stand her insults.'

The Duchess raged up and down the carpet of her private drawing-room. She was beside herself and the Comptroller was doing all he could to calm her.

For the twelfth or thirteenth time she repeated what Lehzen had had the effrontery to say to her in the carriage and how she had followed her offensive, suggestive and insolent remark by sitting in stony silence for the rest of the journey.

'On the child's confirmation day, as well,' screamed the Duchess. 'Her confirmation day.' She rounded on the Comptroller. 'Sir John, I say she must go. She MUST!'

He was able to calm her at last, but he could not make her see the practical difficulties of dismissing the Baroness Lehzen for no apparent reason.

'No reason!' cried the Duchess, her bosom beginning to heave once more. 'She was insolent, man, insolent.'

'What she said, Ma'am, was capable of three interpretations; as a deliberate insult to you, as a cynical observation, or as a statement of fact. You choose the first interpretation, but the King would choose one of the alternatives.'

'I choose . . .!' The Duchess gasped. 'Sir John, I was there. It was to me that she addressed her insulting remark. The King would have no choice but to believe me.'

Sir John gave up trying to reason with her. It merely added to her over-excitement. Instead he undertook to look into the matter and see how – for a dangerous moment he had almost said 'if' – the Baroness might be dismissed.

His promise cooled the Duchess's wild anger. She cast herself on a chaise-longue and asked him to summon her maid. He rang the bell, told the woman to look after her mistress, and went himself out into the Park. After such a scene he needed fresh air.

It was merely a figure of speech for there was nothing fresh about the air that afternoon. It was heavy and moist and hot and thick with small black insects which foretold a storm. He ran a finger between his neck and stock reflecting that probably the weather as much as anything had contributed to the Duchess's vapours. He hoped so, or that it was simply caused by her age, because he was seriously concerned about her lack of self-control. If she continued to have such passionate outbursts she would present a formidable problem. For the time being she would have to be placated, if not with Lehzen's head on a charger then at least with a token.

He puzzled over this as he followed a path through a tunnel of clipped evergreens, and on the lawn beyond was confronted by Lehzen and the Princess Victoria. He was visibly startled by the sudden appearance of the subject of his thoughts, but quickly pulled himself together. He bowed.

'Good afternoon, Sir John.' The Princess sounded excited. 'We have had such good news from Germany. Princess Feodore has a third child, a little girl.'

'And we are off this very minute to inform the Duchess,' added Lehzen.

'My felicitations,' said Conroy. 'You will be happy to have another half-niece, your royal highness.' He bowed again. 'How is it, though, that her royal highness your mother has not yet heard the news?'

'The message came by estafette and was addressed to me,' said Victoria proudly.

'I make no doubt,' said Lehzen hastily, 'that the Princess Feodore ordered this knowing how it would please her half-sister.'

'But, to be candid,' said Sir John, 'it will not please their royal mother.'

'That is as it maybe,' said Lehzen with a toss of her head.

'Baroness . . .' Sir John paused. He chose his words carefully. 'Baroness, her royal highness the Duchess is overwrought at present. This close heat, you know, and the small fracas at St James's this morning . . . Contrive, please, if you can to make her believe she is the first recipient of the news from Hohenlohe.'

'You would have me reseal the dispatch?' asked Lehzen.

'And present it as though addressed to my mother?' asked Victoria.

Sir John bowed. 'I would,' he said. 'She will not look at the direction, and in any case she will probably ask you to read it to her.' He paused again and spread his hands expressively. 'A little adjustment of the wording ... A small alteration to suit the case and save her royal highness from an excess of excitement ...'

'No!' said Victoria bluntly.

'That is, of course, as I guessed,' said Conroy blandly. 'And so, if you will permit me, I shall carry the dispatch to her royal highness and make the painless adjustments myself.'

'No,' said Victoria again; but Lehzen laid a hand on her arm.

'Sir John knows best, dear. There is no purpose served in needlessly upsetting your mother.'

'Just so,' said Sir John. He held out his hand for the dispatch.

Reluctantly Victoria gave it to him. 'She is to be christened Adelaide Victoria Mary Louisa Amelia Constance ...' she said; then broke off for the Comptroller was looking over her shoulder with an extraordinary expression on his face. 'Sir John! What is the matter, Sir John?'

'Ladies,' cried Conroy. 'Stand behind me.' He stretched out both arms protectively.

Victoria turned. 'Why it is Mr Tunbridge Wells,' she said, and she laughed.

Lehzen also laughed in great relief. 'I thought you had seen a monster, Sir John.'

Conroy looked from one to the other. Mr Tunbridge Wells or whoever he was had popped out from behind a large bush and was bowing and kissing his hands in rapid succession towards the ladies.

'Is he a lunatic?' he asked quietly.

'Eccentric,' explained Lehzen. She confessed they were not really on speaking terms though both she and Victoria had seen the man on odd occasions for some time past. Apparently he had fallen madly in love with the Princess and was in the habit

116

of leaving *billets doux* attached to trees and the Park railings. He lived in Tunbridge Wells and drove up regularly in his own barouche to woo the Duke of Kent's daughter.

'But, great heavens! He might be dangerous, Baroness. He should be restrained, looked after.'

'He is,' said Lehzen reassuringly. 'Look carefully in the shrubbery behind him.'

Sir John did so, and could just make out a glazed top hat.

'A peeler,' he exclaimed. 'One of Peel's new policemen.'

'Yes,' said Lehzen. 'In fact there are two: Contable Osborne and Constable Mount. But they are kind to Mr Tunbridge Wells and always keep in the background so as not to embarrass him. Now, as you are to take the dispatch to her royal highness, with your permission we will continue on our walk, Sir John.'

He bowed. They curtseyed and walked away across the grass. Sir John saw Mr Tunbridge Wells sidling along parallel with them, keeping about the same distance away. Two glazed top hats were now in evidence and the swallowtail coats of the new police force. They were also moving in the same direction, keeping themselves as hidden as possible and always at a discreet distance.

He was dumbfounded. As much by the coolness of the Princess and Lehzen as by the fact that a lunatic was loose in the Park. If it hadn't been for the peelers no one could have guaranteed Victoria's safety. Was Lehzen being negligent, over-careless?

The combination of circumstances made him recall the idea which had first occurred to him some time before. The suggestion that Lehzen was impossible, eccentric to the point of craziness, and not at all fit to look after the Princess Victoria, was the only one that could reasonably bring about her dismissal. The King would be obliged to accept such a telling reason for getting rid of her. Yet it could only be implied. It could not be proved.

Sir John continued walking. He walked up and down the dry and springy turf to stimulate and exercise his mind.

Eventually he went inside the palace. In his hand he had the dispatch from Hohenlohe which, as he would read it out, ought

117

to please the Duchess and wean her a little from her hysterical desire for revenge on Lehzen. But if she was obdurate, if she still demanded the governess's head, they would have to concoct a plot between them to show Lehzen's incapability.

28

The storm broke that evening.

First the thick moist air was stirred by a breeze which blew in from the east. It was barely perceptible to begin with, hardly ruffling the beech leaves. It was followed by a darkening of the skies. Deep violet clouds, flecked here and there with silver, rolled in from the sea. They were chased hard by grey and black clouds which seemed to swallow up all the evening light. Then, across this sky, huge streaks of lightning flashed. It was ghostly. There was no sound of thunder yet. Only the lightning, jagged and brilliant. The breeze freshened and turned to a wind. It blew dust and bits of insects through the open windows of the palace, and there were menacing growls in the distance. Only just in time did the servants close the last windows. Simultaneously a great clap of thunder shook the building and it began to rain. It wasn't merely rain whispering down to earth. It lashed and sheeted down. And all the time the thunder pealed and rolled and the lightning flashed.

Dinner was over. Lady Flora and the other ladies had gone to their rooms. Lehzen and Victoria had decided to spend the rest of the evening in Victoria's little room. Sir John and the Duchess sat in her private drawing-room, and both were more relaxed than they had been all day.

They had made their plans.

They had tested them this way and that, and if all went well Lehzen would be gone within twenty-four hours. They were to bypass the Duchess of Northumberland and see the King and Queen to ask their advice. They would say they were at their wits' end because Victoria's lady-in-waiting had recently proved incapable and irresponsible and possibly a danger to her royal charge. Victoire Conroy would be asked to accompany them to say her piece about Lehzen's violent tempers. Lady Flora could probably be persuaded to add something telling in addition. And one or two others in the household, who had less cause to be loyal to the Baroness than to their royal mistress, would add their corroboration.

Sir John rubbed his hands together. He did it slowly, almost with sensuous pleasure. He was well content. The Duchess had been soothed and she had put herself further in his debt by her eager acceptance of the plan. Furthermore, without Lehzen, and with perhaps a candidate of his own in her place, he would be in a far stronger position to control the Princess.

He went to the window to look out on the storm which raged beyond and did not hear the knock on the door. The first thing he heard was the majordomo's voice announcing that the Duke of Sussex was in the great saloon. He exchanged glances with the Duchess. Both had the same thought. The Duke could easily get from his apartments to theirs even in a tremendous storm like this, but he was not given to calling at any time, certainly not after dinner and certainly not unannounced.

Sir John felt less confident as he followed the Duchess down the stairway, and when he saw the Duke he was distinctly uneasy.

The Duke had come in some state. He was dressed in Court breeches and a cut-away, and wore the ribbon and star of the Garter. This was in strong contrast to the crimson satin dressing-robe, silk cravat and pair of Persian slippers which he usually wore about the palace. He was also wigged and powdered, carried a snuff-box in one hand, and a cane in the other. Mr Blackman was behind him; Major Keppel was beside him. Another equerry stood to the rear.

He bowed deeply to his sister-in-law; then rapidly took snuff, transferred the box to his embroidered waistcoat pocket, and picked up his quizzing glass. Clearly he wanted to be impressive. And he was.

The Duchess offered refreshment.

'I thank you, no, Ma'am,' he said. 'We have already dined.'

He had come, he explained, to apologize for not being at Victoria's confirmation that morning. It had been unavoidable but he felt the negligence keenly and he would not wish her to regard it as a sign of lack of interest or respect on his part.

His sister-in-law curtseyed. She understood, she said; and the family had been well represented at the ceremony. Perhaps he would like to see Victoria? In which case she would at once send for her.

The Duke held up his hand. 'No need, Ma'am, no need. For I saw her this afternoon. I have come this evening, Ma'am, to make my apologies to you as her mother.'

Sir John stirred. 'You have seen the Princess, your royal highness?' he asked politely.

The Duke put up his glass again and peered at Sir John.

'Yes,' he said brightly, and, turning to the Duchess, he continued: 'She visited me with the dear Baroness late this afternoon. And I was able to give her my regrets for not being present this morning.' He breathed on the glass, polished it, and looked deliberately at Sir John again. 'I understood there were, shall we say, one or two unfortunate little contretemps.'

The Duchess flushed with anger at the thought of Lehzen and her daughter discussing these matters with the Duke of Sussex. 'They were of no real significance,' she said shortly.

'I am so glad,' purred the Duke. 'Then it was just as the good Baroness said. Small mishaps of small significance.'

Sir John saw the way it was going. He could not help showing his anger. 'It seems inappropriate for the Princess's lady to tittle-tattle about such affairs.' Instantly he wished he had not done so. The Duke quizzed him through the glass as though he was an unidentifiable insect. After a long silence he said: 'Really?' and turned back to his sister-in-law.

'I was glad to hear that all, in the end, went well; and I could see from my talk with Victoria how excellently she is coming on. What a lot we all owe to Baroness Lehzen for her continuous and affectionate care for the heiress to the throne. How wise you were to choose her, sister-in-law; and how wise I have been, if I may say so myself, to give her my special protection and the assurance of the protection of the King.' He took snuff. 'As I wrote to his majesty this evening when conveying my congratulations on the confirmation of his heir, we are all so indebted to the Baroness and grateful to her loyalty, her common sense, and her excellent example to the Princess. I hope to persuade him to make her a marchioness. She deserves it, I am sure. And so is the Duchess of Northumberland.'

Once more he quizzed Sir John, refused further offers of refreshment, kissed his sister-in-law's hand, bowed, and turned to go. He stopped.

'If, Ma'am, you would convey my humble duty and love to your daughter, I should esteem it as a favour.' He turned to Sir John. 'And perhaps you would have the goodness to give the Baroness Lehzen my sincere compliments.'

Sir John could not trust himself to make any reply at all. When the Duke's party had left he stood staring after them at the closed doors.

'How could he have known?' the Duchess whispered in his ear.

He sighed. 'He didn't. All that happened is that the Baroness is far more intelligent than we supposed. Knowing how angry you were this morning she anticipated trouble and sought their confidence before anything could happen. And now,' he added bitterly, 'nothing can happen. They would never now listen to any complaint against her. Madame Caraway will be with us for a long time yet.'

29

Almost immediately after Victoria's confirmation the Kent household moved to Tunbridge Wells. Victoria knew perfectly well why. She wished very much to go to Windsor and the King wanted her there as well. Therefore, automatically, her mother chose to move to Tunbridge Wells. It would have been better, she thought bitterly, if her uncle and aunt had pretended the opposite, that a visit from Victoria would cause them inconvenience and anxiety, for assuredly it would have made her mother send her to Court. As it was they left for Tunbridge Wells and spent August sweltering on Mount Ephraim.

Outbluffed by the governess he had hoped to ruin, Sir John's anger was black for a week or more. Then his mood altered. He became haughty and was insufferably overbearing towards Lehzen. She tolerated his insolent bullying for Victoria's sake and she said nothing.

To Victoria herself Sir John began to show a familiarity which she did not care for at all and she was quite unaware that, for the first time in their relationship, he was genuinely trying to be agreeable. There was a reason for it. He had realized at last that she alone was the gateway to his future security and position. Therefore she was worth troubling over and he set himself out to be congenial. But he failed. She appeared cool to the charm which so many other women found fascinating. In fact she was frightened of him. For too long he had been a bogey to her. The new Sir John was simply unrecognizable. He tried in every way he knew to please her. She merely withdrew farther into her shell and would have nothing to do with him. She made it plain she resented being called his little woman. She resented being patted in an affectionate way on her forearm. She was affronted by his odious familiarity, and, in the face of her icy, regal distaste, he suddenly gave up the game and became snappy and short-tempered.

To revenge himself he watched like a cat for ways to hurt and tease her and he was far more clever at his probing than she was at concealing. Very soon he discovered her weaknesses. One made her exceedingly vulnerable. She could not bear it when he scorned her love of the Italian opera. If he had known nothing about it she could have relieved her feelings by classing him as an uncultivated boor, but, on the contrary, he knew what he was talking about. Or he appeared to, which was just as bad. What with the heat and hearing her beloved opera challenged, Victoria became quite flustered. Before long he had wormed out a special secret which she had confided in no one, not even Lehzen: that she had a particular admiration for Luigi Lablache.

Probably at no time in his life was Conroy a really wicked

man, but he was always a vain rascal and he took a boy's pleasure in tearing the legs and wings off his victim. Finding out about Lablache must have made him rub his hands. It was a classic passion: the sixteen-year-old, plain-looking girl still in the schoolroom for the forty-one-year-old, highly successful maestro.

Lablache had made his début in England five years before and enjoyed a high reputation both in society and in musical circles. He was a first-rate comedian and portly, both of which attributes, in Conroy's experience, would make him especially attractive to lonely adolescent girls. Victoria had heard him sing several times at the opera; but this spring and summer more than most. Then had come her special concert at Kensington. Knowing of her enthusiasm for Italian opera the Duchess had given her this concert as a birthday present. The singers had been Malibran, Grisis, Rubini, Ivanoff, Tamburini, Costa and Lablache, and they had enchanted everyone. Especially Victoria. Sir John recalled how she had gone quite pale as Lablache sang *Dove vai?* from *Guglielmo Tell*.

Now, down in Tunbridge Wells, he twigged Victoria mercilessly; nodding and winking when no one was by as though to remind her that they alone shared the secret of her infatuation. She could have screamed aloud. It was not an infatuation. Her feelings for Lablache were like those of a daughter for a father. She was devoted to him and admired and respected him. She longed to shout it out for everyone so that there was no secret to share with the hateful Conroy, but somehow she could not. He had had revenge for her previous attitude. She was no longer ice-cold and regal; rather a red-faced, angry girl, wincing whenever he chose to throw a little salt into the wound.

Wisely he did not drive her too far. His instincts of caution told him not to lose this valuable hold. He wanted to keep something in reserve.

Victoria, hating the heat and hating Sir John, could not understand why the persecution dribbled away to nothing. But she was greatly relieved. Having the focal point of her dreams held up to ridicule had been a searing experience. Lehzen, seeing her distress, wanted to help; but Victoria found it embarrassing to say anything at all about Lablache even to

Lehzen. It was the same as when she dreamed of young Lord Brooke. These things were apart from ordinary life as they lived it in the Kent household. Only Sir John's treachery had got it out of her and threatened to reduce her great devotion for Lablache into something false and puerile.

Mr Tunbridge Wells, now on his home ground, provided a diversion at this point by evading his vigilant constables and climbing a tree to get a better view of the Princess. Not being sure where in this hired house she had her rooms, he had fixed in his mind that a certain window encircled with ivy must belong to the object of his devotion. The cedar close by gave him a perfect vantage point from which to blow kisses, and Lady Flora, whose window it was, fainted right away when she saw the enterprising Mr Tunbridge Wells wooing her as she thought from the branches of a cedar tree. This disconcerted him so much that he fell from the branch and was found unconscious on the ground by Constables Osborne and Mount. He was not dead, but he had to be removed to hospital, and Victoria heard through Lehzen that he would be prevented from any further eccentric displays of his love for another month.

Victoria settled into a quiet routine of seeking shade from the heat, playing the harp, reading Madame de Sévigné's letters, and thinking about Luigi Lablache. If she could not be at Court, Tunbridge Wells was, perhaps, the next best thing. Then to her dismay she discovered that Sir John was arranging another progress, this time into the north country.

Victoria begged that the progress should be cancelled or at least postponed, because she suffered so much in hot weather. Her mother would not hear of it, and, having a great deal of stamina and being indifferent to heat and cold herself, she was dry of pity for anyone less fortunate. Girls of sixteen, Victoria was told, never suffer from such things. It was all in her imagination. Furthermore the Archbishop of York had been kind enough to invite the whole household to Bishopthorpe, and this would be a saving.

Whenever she talked of making economies it was a sure sign that the Duchess was upset. Having been married to one of the most extravagant of English princes, and coming from careful

German stock herself, the Duchess was terrified of debts. The late Duke of Kent's obligations had been allowed to rest, both by considerate creditors and by the Duchess herself who considered the most effective way to deal with debts was to believe they did not exist. Her adequate if not handsome income from the government was used to meet current expenses and put a little by. But the fear of debts always lay underneath and came to the surface when she was angry or feeling low and dispirited. Then she became exceedingly mean and practised economies which were as embarrassing as they were ineffective. Living on the Archbishop of York was an example. Fractionally it might cost less for them all to go to Yorkshire, but that was a good enough reason for the Duchess.

The only possible way to make her change her mind was to find the cause of her anxiety and try to put it right. Old Späth had once done it. For all her fluttering, bumbly ways she had been the perfect anodyne for the Duchess's moods. Sir John, too, could manage it because he was close in her confidence; and so, on occasions, could Lady Flora. But neither had any reason to want to stay in Tunbridge Wells. Progresses, with the opportunities they brought for self-advertisement, were very agreeable to Sir John, and Lady Flora had been told she could go home to her family while the household was in the north. The two who wanted to stay were in no position to do anything about it; Lehzen because of her recent rebellion, and Victoria because at this stage there was hardly any confidence between mother and daughter at all.

It was with ill grace that Victoria settled to accept the fact that another progress was unavoidable. She sulked for days, until Lehzen begged her not to, claiming that no one but she really suffered from her moods, and it was not her fault that they were off to the north country. Victoria saw the justice of this. Her sulks soon vanished, and instead she enjoyed a game at which she was expert, that of finding fault. Nothing escaped her keen eyes. Her own maid, the housemaids, the gardeners, Rosy's groom, the kennelboy, even the Dean who travelled down from London to teach her Latin, were all pained by her critical attitude. Sir John escaped it. So did his arrangements for the progress. She dared not find fault with someone who had tormented her as he had done. But she was outspokenly scornful of her mother's meanness in timing their departure from Tunbridge Wells to correspond with a visit of the Duc de Nemours. It meant the Duchess could claim that their late arrival at Kensington and the need to go on their way early the next day made it impossible for her to receive him in her own apartments. The carpets were rolled up, half the servants were away, and so forth. The Princess Sophia was persuaded to offer her apartments instead.

'Mamma, it is not the same,' Victoria pleaded. 'He will be offended.'

'Nonsense,' snapped her mother. 'He is barely twenty-one and won't notice such things. Depend on it he's coming to look you over and won't think of anything else. Not,' she added warmly, 'that you are to give him the least encouragement. His father may be King of the French, but his throne is wobbly, and Nemours is only a second son. He is not for you.'

Victoria flushed. She disliked talk of the European marriage market. It reduced her to a beast in the farmyard. How far distant were such affairs from her tender feelings for Lablache.

'It seems so unkind to trouble Aunt Sophia,' she said.

'She will not be troubled,' replied the Duchess. 'I have made it clear that we shall not expect her to be present.'

Victoria opened her mouth to protest. She wanted to say it was outrageous to keep Aunt Sophia out of her own rooms. Instead she said something mild to the effect that it must involve her in some cost.

Not at all discomposed her mother said: 'She can afford it, 'Drina. And, of course, it will be a saving to us.'

Victoria had a special reason for wanting to receive the Duc de Nemours as correctly as possible. His sister, Louisa, had recently married her beloved Uncle Leopold of Belgium, and though Victoria had heard much of her in letters from Uncle Leopold, she had not yet met her or any of her relations.

At the reception in poor Aunt Sophia's rooms, she found the young duke attractive. He was tall, slender and fair, his only obvious drawback being that he was very timid. This was understandable in view of her mother's fierceness. She made it obvious that she thought he had come over to look at her daughter as though she were a piece of meat, and she treated him as an undesirable suitor. When he produced a letter for her from his mother, the Queen of the French, and a set of mathematical instruments as a present for Victoria, she barked her thanks at him so fiercely that he was reduced to a hopeless state of shyness. Only with the greatest difficulty could he manage to give her a message from her brother Leopold of Belgium; that at the end of September he planned to bring his Queen to England and he hoped it would be convenient for them all to meet at Ramsgate or some other convenient post.

The Duchess mellowed. She was genuinely fond of her brother and wanted to meet his wife.

Yes, she told the frightened Nemours; she would write directly to the King of Belgium, and her Comptroller would take lodgings and hotel rooms for the Kent household and their royal guests.

She then reverted to her role of suspicious mamma, and offered her guest refreshment in a tone which made it impossible for him to accept or refuse. He simply stood there with his mouth open.

Sir John and Princess Victoria between them came to the young man's rescue. He was persuaded to drink a little wine, though he would eat nothing. And out of nervousness, not because he wanted any, he helped himself out of a large snuff-box on the table. Looking up and finding the Duchess's eye on him, he took too large a pinch and began to sneeze uncontrollably.

He left that evening with a vivid picture in his mind of the formidable Duchess. For the rest of his life he recalled her as a terrifying gorgon of a female, and all he could remember of the young Victoria was that she was kind and that, in the mode of the moment, she looked exceedingly pear-shaped.

Triumphant at having kept the designing young man at bay, the Duchess of Kent swept to her own apartments where, despite the rolled-up carpets, she enjoyed an excellent dinner.

127

30

'Are we not fortunate, your royal highness?' she said to Victoria. Victoria's attitude to the progress was entirely altered by a chance remark made by Lady Catherine, the lady-in-waiting who was to attend her mother in the north country.

'The concerts at York are always so good.'

'Concerts?'

'Yes, at York. We shall be there for the Musical Festival.'

Victoria's instant reaction was to demand why no one had told her before. Apparently Lehzen had not known about it. Nor had Sir John realized that their visit would coincide with a music festival. Her mother warned her that, even if he had, he would not have troubled to mention it. 'Provincial entertainments, dear, are not particularly exciting.'

Victoria appreciated the warning, but the thought of finding any sort of concert at the end of the long, hot journey made the prospect of their tour much more bearable.

Yet another credit was Sir John's absence. He had been obliged to go to Ramsgate to make arrangements for the visit of the Belgian royal family and could not join them for some time. By the second day of their journey Victoria was quite reconciled to the progress, and had begun to enjoy herself.

On that evening they reached Barnby Moor, a little village in flat, wooded countryside on the Great North Road, and to the Princess's delight they stayed in an old inn. There was a garden behind to explore, and Lady Catherine, a beefy, no-nonsense sort of girl, found a piano in a parlour which promised well for after dinner. The meal itself was a change from the plain and unimaginative food served up as a rule at Kensington. There were grouse brought down from the Yorkshire moors, plover pie, a roast leveret, a ham baked in short pastry and then sauced with burnt brown sugar, and a good firm Trent salmon served with a rose in its mouth. The Duchess dined in her room so without her there to say it would be a saving if they left the ham and the pie untouched and tell Victoria not to gobble, and without Sir John to spoil everything with his pessimism and say though this meal was good the last had been terrible and the next was sure to be as bad, the small company enjoyed their dinner.

Later they set out for Lady Catherine's piano and listened to her playing variations of Herz and Hünten. After that the Princess was persuaded to stand up and sing *Il rival*. Her voice was true and clear. Lehzen could seldom hear her without being moved to tears. Tonight was no exception. They were obliged to comfort the Baroness until her sobs subsided, but she was not herself until Lady Catherine made her bold suggestion. Why not ring for the waiter, she proposed, and order in a bottle of wine, a dish of plums, and the remains of the plover pie? A little something would not harm their music. Such a daring idea dried Lehzen's tears in an instant. Her eyebrows shot up in disapproval. But then they descended again. Except for her they were all young and had healthy appetites. Lady Catherine was right. It was an excellent plan. The Baroness rang the bell herself and gave the order . . . a bottle of wine, a dish of plums, and the remains of the plover pie.

The next evening they reached the Archbishop's palace almost three miles from York, and there Victoria found her new contentment continuing.

She was fascinated by their host the Archbishop. He was so courtly and kind and seemed so immensely old. In fact he was seventy-eight but already he wore many of the frailties of old age. He was gaunt, his skin slimy and crinkled and loose, his eyes watery and opaque, and he stooped over his cane. His bagwig appeared to be too heavy for comfort because he kept lifting up his head and shaking it from side to side, and this made him look like an ancient and amiable tortoise. Only his voice was still strong and robust, though hearing it coming from such an antique setting was rather unnerving.

There was a large house-party to greet the royal guests. To Victoria's delight it included the Duchess of Northumberland, who in all their relationship had never been anything but just and kind to her.

'Dear Duchess!' she said kissing her and raising her from her curtsey. 'We shall have to promise to behave.'

'Not at all, your royal highness. I am here unofficially, as wife to a Percy of the Border, and not as your governess. You may be as wicked as you wish.'

'Don't give her permission, Duchess,' came a voice from behind them. 'It will halve the pleasure.'

Victoria was amazed to see it was her mother. Clearly she must have heard the last sentence but, instead of being angry as Victoria would have expected, she was as lighthearted and cheerful as everyone else. She took her mother's arm. It was a rare sign of affection to which the Duchess quickly responded.

Victoria had noticed that on the rare occasions when she and Sir John were apart her mother became quite a different person. It was so now. Within an hour or two she had completely forgotten that being there was a saving. It was a great relief to Victoria. Her mother's fractiousness and parsimony could so easily have spoilt what promised to be a very enjoyable stay in the country.

The promise was fulfilled.

To begin with she took enormous pleasure in spoiling the Archbishop. She was full of sympathy for him, thinking of him as a poor old man, and was very attentive, running for cushions to put behind his back and offering to read to him. The Archbishop was amused. He was not exactly in want, being so very, very rich in this world's goods that his contemporaries called him the sumptuous prelate, and besides ten settled sons and a married daughter, he had two unmarried daughters at home to look after his needs. Moreover he was still hale and hearty and felt well able to look after his province and see. In fact he was to do so for another twelve years until he died at ninety. Yet being cosseted by the heiress to the throne as though he was a poor, decrepit old man was rather enjoyable. He did not disillusion her and gracefully submitted to her spoiling.

Then on the very first evening Victoria discovered that one of the Archbishop's granddaughters, Lady Norreys, who was also staying at Bishopthorpe, was a pupil of Tamburini. Tamburini, the great Tamburini whom she had first heard at the age of

130

thirteen, and who was an associate of her dear Lablache. As if this was not enough, one of Lady Norreys's cousins called Miss Vernon was also staying, and she too was a pupil of Tamburini. After dinner Victoria asked them to sing and the applause was loud and genuine when they had finished singing a duet from *La Gazza Ladra*.

Victoria was in raptures. Could they not sing again, she asked. But she had forgotten they were in an archiepiscopal palace. It was time to go to chapel for evening prayers.

Very late that night – at half past eleven – Victoria was finishing writing her journal. It had been a happy, eventful day, but no more than on any other day could everything be included. It was too public a document, as open to inspection and criticism as a schoolroom composition. She sucked the end of her penholder wondering if *'We then went to prayers'* made a suitably rounded finish. It did, but there was one little fact to add. With her head on one side she laboriously penned into the journal:

After that I sang the *Barcarola* from *Faliero*, frightened to death.

31

'I can't believe it.' Victoria jumped up and down. 'It's not possible. I shan't, won't, can't believe it.'

She was holding in her hand a copy of the York Festival programme, which had just been given her by the butler. Grisi was to sing in Handel's *Messiah* and, two days afterwards she would sing again at a day concert. But this, deeply as she admired Grisi, was not the cause of Victoria's excitement. Listed to sing with Grisi were Signor Rubini and Signor Lablache.

'I shan't, won't, can't believe it,' she cried again, to the astonishment of the butler, and then ran off to tell Lehzen.

Lehzen had the greatest difficulty in calming her.

'Very well, don't believe it,' she said in a matter of fact voice. 'But if you continue so excited you'll throw yourself into a fever and miss all the concerts.'

Victoria paled. 'Oh, no, Lehzen!'

'Then compose yourself. Really, the fuss and scrimmergy you make about a few singers . . .'

'A few singers!' expostulated Victoria.

'Yes,' said Lehzen firmly. 'For that's what they are. Isn't Grisi a woman? Aren't Rubini and Lablache ordinary men . . .?'

'*No!*' Victoria jumped up and down again, and then she spun round in her agitation. In a torrent of words she tried to describe the music they made, their artistry, their power, their beauty of soul. But all she got out of Lehzen was another warning. 'Too much excitement – fever – bed – no concerts.'

Sir John was put out. He had made all the preliminary arrangements for the Belgian visit and travelled to Yorkshire without delay. For all his pains he considered he had barely received a civil thank you. The Duchess was too intent on enjoying herself as the Archbishop's guest. Moreover, as he had noticed before, it was never easy re-establishing their old relationship after a few days' separation. This showed at bottom how frail the relationship really was, which, in view of his hopes for power and influence at the Court of Queen Victoria or her Regent, was a serious matter.

Once more he was obliged to realize that only through Victoria could he achieve the influence he longed for. How imprudent it had been to torment her in Tunbridge Wells. And how imprudent, as well, to show such hostility to the Baroness. Lehzen led to Victoria. Victoria led to power. Coldly, methodically, he set out to cultivate them afresh.

Lehzen was the first to notice his changed attitude. Normally she did not eat caraways in his company. It opened her to his scorn which she did not enjoy. When she did, she was particularly careful to do it unostentatiously, almost secretly, in the hope that he would not notice what she was doing. On the day of the big concert when they were waiting for the carriages to return to Bishopthorpe she absent-mindedly took the caraway box from her reticule, and, even as she popped a seed in her mouth, she noticed that Sir John was looking at her. Instantly she snapped the lid to and replaced the box in her reticule. She drew herself up in a bold attempt to defy his scorn. But there was no need. He was smiling. Surely it could not be at her? She looked over her shoulder. No one behind was looking in Sir John's direction. He was actually smiling at her and not in contempt, but with genuine warmth. It was past belief. She scowled at him and turned away.

As they jogged out of York she asked herself why Sir John should suddenly alter. She had not known him to look so genial in a matter of eleven years.

She could not give the matter much thought because Victoria was rhapsodizing about the concert. She lauded Rubini to the skies. She raved about Grisi. She was almost violent about Lablache.

Here, thought Lehzen, was another mystery. Grisi had taken luncheon with them at the deanery; a bobbety little woman with dreadful clothes and bad breath – but with a voice that was electrifying. Rubini too had sung his heart out in the cathedral, making superb, long notes soar to the roof. But Lablache had not been up to his usual standard. There was no denying it. Yet Victoria, a better judge of singing than she would ever be, gave Lablache first place. Had it been a sentimental occasion for her? They would not hear such singing until next April at the opera. Without thinking she took another caraway or two, and remembered Sir John again. His look. It had surprised her, but not pleasantly. Like expecting tea and finding the drink is coffee. What, she wondered, was he up to?

She discovered very soon because she was with the Princess when Sir John came with his proposal.

Because Lehzen was there Sir John was careful to address her as Princess Victoria and he explained that he and the Duchess had arranged a great treat for her. Mrs Anderson, chosen because she was a pupil of Felix Mendelssohn, would continue to give the Princess music lessons, but for the training of her singing voice Signor Lablache would be engaged in the following year.

Victoria's face lit up. 'Oh, Sir John, do you really mean it?'

'Of course,' he smiled down at her. 'I should have arranged it sooner, but then, I was busy on your affairs down in Kent.'

'Signor Lablache will teach me next year?'

'As soon after the beginning of the opera season as he can manage it!'

For one horror-struck moment Lehzen believed the Princess would have kissed Conroy out of gratitude.

'Victoria!' she said when, heavy with the girl's thanks, Sir John left the room. 'You almost disgraced yourself.'

'Oh, Lehzen, is it not marvellous? Am I not the luckiest girl in the world?'

'You almost disgraced yourself,' repeated Lehzen quietly. She explained.

Instantly Victoria was indignant. 'I should never do such a thing,' she cried. 'Lehzen, you know I should not.'

'I saw it with my own eyes. You came as near as may be to kissing the Comptroller to your mother's household.' Her eyes narrowed. 'Simply because he has gone out of his way to do something which is not his concern at all and has found you a new singing teacher.'

The girl's confusion told her what she wanted to know. 'So,' she said gently. 'It is the singing teacher you would rather kiss. Is that not so?'

Victoria tossed her head. 'Now you are being unkind as well as unjust,' she said. 'I admire Lablache a great deal and Sir John has put me in his debt by making such a welcome arrangement. That is all there is to it.'

Lehzen folded her in her arms. 'If I did not love you, child, I should not care; but I do not want you to be a victim of Sir John's clever wiles. You know what he is, and I do hope that you will not allow yourself to become so indebted to him that you feel you have to make a return which would be neither good nor wise.

Victoria made no reply.

'You see, dear, he is a very unscrupulous person. He clearly wants something from you.'

'What?' asked Victoria.

'I haven't the least idea. But isn't it true? Have you not

always disliked each other? When he gave you that picture of Dash were you not made uncomfortable by his generosity? And suspicious?'

Victoria admitted it.

'He has been generous again,' warned Lehzen. 'Why has he been so generous? What does he want? Neither of us knows the answer yet, but you would be prudent to keep on your guard.'

32

The time arrived for the Kents to leave Bishopthorpe. Victoria had enjoyed herself and she regretted leaving. The Archbishop looked so exceedingly antique and fragile that she decided mistakenly she would never see him again. This cast her down. So did the thought of travelling so far, from the seat of one nobleman to the other, all the way to Kensington. For some unknown reason she had begun to feel very tired, and she had bad headaches. Being polite to strangers and dressing up at all hours had become a strain.

She tried to take pleasure in the journey, but she had so little energy. Even looking at a view, or appreciating a house, or enjoying someone's company, required energy and she felt her supplies were running very low. At Belvoir Castle, for example, when they were the guests of the Duke of Rutland, she could raise little enthusiasm for the Gobelin tapestries and the collection of Dutch and Italian paintings, though her morbid interest in death revived her sufficiently to enjoy the mausoleum. There a carved figure of the late Duchess appeared to soar up towards her four dead infants who were marble-winged and lit by blue and yellow glass. This impressed Victoria but the rest of the progress was full of vexations.

They passed through King's Lynn on the way to the Earl of Leicester's and the townspeople showed their loyalty, but vastly irritated the tired Victoria, by insisting on dragging her carriage round unfamiliar parts of the town with such force that they ran over and injured an innocent bystander, and made them an hour and a half late in arriving at Holkham Hall. It was the same on the visit to Euston. Victoria could barely keep awake; and she was increasingly captious.

At last they reached Kensington. But it was only for a few days' visit. On September 28th they had to leave for Kent.

Lehzen was worried and she took Victoria in hand. Lessons were stopped for the time being. She was forbidden to ride and made to rest for a large part of each day. In addition she was dosed and fed on red meat and burgundy. As a result, she had much more energy when they travelled to Ramsgate to receive the Belgian royal family.

Sir John's arrangements for the visit bore his authentic touch. King Leopold had particularly asked for no fuss at all. He would travel privately with his Queen and her brother, the Duc de Nemours, and the royal suite would be minute. Sir John permitted himself to adapt this simple request. He had arranged unpretentious lodgings for the Kents in a private house, and for the Belgians in the Albion Hotel. He had also impressed upon the Mayor and Corporation the necessity of regarding the visit as a quiet and private one. All communications from the muncipality with regard to the visit were to be addressed to him, solely to him. This established his importance locally. Then, when the Belgian royal yacht anchored off Ramsgate there was cannon fire to greet the King and Queen. Conroy's taste for salutes was gratified by a battery of cannon temporarily lashed to Ramsgate pier. They almost shook the structure to pieces, and put off the bandsmen who had been hired to play martial music at the landing stage, but Sir John was quite indifferent. He stood there alone, as the Duchess of Kent's Comptroller, ready to welcome the King and Queen of Belgium – apart from the crowd, a fine figure, stiff and straight-backed, with greying hair and whiskers, and he wore full military uniform with the stars of five orders blazing on his breast. He greeted them with precisely the right formality, had himself presented to the royal suite, and afterwards led them the short distance to the Albion Hotel where the Duchess and the Princess were waiting.

Victoria threw herself into her uncle's arms. She had not

seen him for four years but he seemed hardly a day older. And privately she considered him handsomer than ever. Evidently he was very much in love with his new wife, and Victoria could understand why. She at once adored her new aunt, particularly as she was bidden to regard her as a sister and confide in her as she had in Feodore. It was an irresistible invitation to a lonely girl.

33

King Leopold was struck by the change in his niece. If four years appeared to have made no difference to him, they had made all the difference to her. He had been writing to her regularly but in his mind's eye he had thought of her as a child, not as the young woman he saw in Ramsgate. He took an early opportunity to talk privately with Lehzen.

It was not his way to be outspoken. He edged and he hinted. But from what he said she guessed he wanted to be reassured that the relationship between his sister and his niece was as cordial and trusting as it ought to be. She was sorry, she said, but she could not give him this reassurance. On rare occasions the Duchess showed a loving concern for Victoria, but they were becoming rarer. King Leopold hedged and hinted again. He was really asking if there was a special reason for this breakdown in their affection. Yes, said Lehzen bluntly, there was, but she would not elaborate and she left it to him to guess the reason.

He was silent for a moment. He was remembering the prickly situation at Kensington before he left for Brussels. He remembered Wellington saying he supposed a good-looking Irishman let loose among a lot of women could create the devil. He distinctly recalled his sister breaking with long-established custom and taking Conroy's advice in preference to his.

To Lehzen's relief he did not pursue the matter. Instead he changed the subject altogether. He regarded her, he said, as the lynchpin of the household and he would be grateful for her help in his plans for a Coburg marriage for Victoria.

'You have the greatest influence on my niece,' he said. 'And it would please me if you could persuade her to think kindly of one of my brother's sons.'

'Sir,' replied Lehzen. 'You may be sure I shall do all I can to make the Princess happy. I could not undertake anything more.'

He laughed. 'You mean that she is not easily persuaded? That I know. It is a Coburg streak. We share precisely the same obstinacy.' He reflected. 'Let me put the matter in another way. If, Baroness, you could present the young Princes in a favourable light, I should appreciate it. I shall suggest that their father brings them to England – early next summer. It will be their first adventure to a great Court and young Germans, fresh from the nest, are inclined to be gauche. Rather than underline anything you personally might find unpleasing in their manner, you could underline all those things which are attractive.'

Lehzen smiled. 'It would be wiser, Sir, to depend on your niece's good sense and feeling; but as you have asked me, why, yes, I shall remark on the Princes' qualities rather than on anything else.'

'Baroness, you place us all in your debt,' said Leopold. 'Being without a father it is so important that she be happily and suitably married within the next two or three years.'

Much relieved he left her, not noticing that, quite suddenly, her expression had altered. Realizing the truth of what he said, that in the near future her darling would be married and given absolutely into a stranger's power, made her face whiten and her fingers tremble. It was the sort of thing which, in the contentment of the moment, she had never much thought of, let alone put into words. *Within the next two or three years*. It was a painful realization. Deliberately she put it at the back of her mind.

Queen Louise had been making some dispassionate estimates on her own account. Hints of the Conroy – Duchess of Kent scandal had travelled through Europe though at the Belgian Court there was a natural reticence to discuss the scandal as it

138

concerned the King's sister. The Queen wished to judge for herself, but she saw no sign, heard no word which was in any way indiscreet or compromising. Yet instinctively she knew that her sister-in-law was bound in some way to her Comptroller, if not by ties of passion, then by something equally strong.

Her second estimate was of Victoria. Her name had been so often on Leopold's tongue, and he so often wrote her long letters that Louise had come to think she must be a very special person indeed. Her own experience of royalty was limited. She recognized that her husband, though he had come far from homely Coburg and had a quicksilver mind, still belonged to the bourgeois royalty. Her own father, though distinguished by birth and brought up by his father's mistress – the bluestocking authoress of ninety books – had made it his policy to be bourgeois, and was proud of being a citizen-king who had supported himself as a teacher in Switzerland, and had lived in the United States of America and an English village. Therefore, convinced that Victoria must be representative of a more august and sublime sort of royalty, Queen Louise had arrived at Ramsgate with a preconceived picture of what her new niece would look like and how she would behave.

The reality astounded her. Victoria was entirely, completely, unromantically ordinary. She had some talents, played the piano and harp, sang very well and drew beautifully. Moreover she could manage languages. But she gave no sign of having any extraordinary accomplishments and intellectually she was as dry as a biscuit. When she did express a point of view it was unlikely to be original and it had to be squeezed out of her. As to her looks, these did not matter for doubtless they would improve as she grew up but there was no denying her unprepossessing appearance at present. The most debased place-hunter could not have called her beautiful. By most standards she was not even pretty. Her chief advantage in looks was her poise, but she only carried herself well when reminded to do so by Baroness Lehzen and then she pushed herself along more like a small duck breasting water than a swan gliding with grace and power. Generally, as she trotted about Ramsgate, she simply looked plump and undistinguished. Anything less like the picture she had imagined Queen Louise could not conceive.

She was affectionate and eager to please, and the way she admired her aunt's Paris dresses and bonnets was quite flattering. Nor was there any doubting her fierce family loyalty. Nevertheless the Queen was disappointed. She said so to her husband and he smiled.

'Unprepossessing at the present, yes,' he agreed. 'But occasionally, only very occasionally she shows her true blood. I saw it in her cousin Princess Charlotte; not often, but it was enough to put me in my place.'

'You?' said Queen Louise. 'Surely not?'

Leopold's smile broadened. 'Indeed, yes.'

The Queen waited hopefully, but while she enjoyed her company, Victoria continued to be as mousey as ever. Then, two days before the Belgian party was due to leave, she saw what perhaps her husband had meant.

It happened for the strangest reason – because Victoria was ill.

King Leopold had given a dinner at the Albion and, while the cover was being removed for dessert, Lehzen leant forward and quietly asked the Princess if she was unwell. Victoria's face was ashen grey. She replied, equally quietly, that she felt not quite herself, apologized to her uncle and aunt and left the room. It was done without fuss or display, and yet it commanded everyone's sympathetic attention. Something had come to her rescue to save her the embarrassment of being simply a girl feeling sick at dinner. She left the room in such a way that everyone instinctively recognized as truly regal. It was astonishing.

34

King William and his First Minister strode up and down the ramparts at Windsor. The early October sunshine was surprisingly warm and heated the royal head. The King sent for a hat.

'That water-drinker, Melbourne, has been disporting himself on the Ramsgate sands.'

The King disliked Leopold of Belgium because he was brother to the Duchess of Kent, had objectionable marriage plans for Victoria, and because he took his brand new crown too seriously; most of all he despised him because he had once refused to drink wine at his table.

'Do you know why he is at Ramsgate, Melbourne?'

The Prime Minister confessed he did not. He would have liked to add that he was completely uninterested and if this was the reason why the King had asked him to travel all the way from London, he thought it a very poor one. But he held his peace. His precarious ministry was opposed by the Church, the bar, the agricultural and monied interest, and a large minority in the House of Commons, and the King himself was a notorious Whig hater. There was no point in exciting the old gentleman and exacerbating the situation still further.

'Then you ought to,' said the King crossly.

He rejected four of the five hats offered by his page, and accepted the one with the widest brim. This he put on his head and continued bobbing up and down along the ramparts.

Melbourne patiently followed.

Abruptly the King stopped. 'Lord Melbourne, I require you and your colleagues to discuss my niece Victoria's marriage prospects. I shall expect you to propose a union with the House of Orange.'

'Very well, Sir.'

The King looked at the Prime Minister suspiciously. Generally he took a great deal of persuading to any course of action.

'You are sure?' he asked.

'Indeed, Sir,' said Melbourne blandly. He knew how important it was to give way occasionally especially on minor matters which the King thought were major.

The King was so pleased that he asked him to stay and dine, an unusual tribute to a Whig at William's Court. Then he reverted to Leopold's visit.

'I can't think why we weren't told,' he complained. 'Doesn't protocol demand it, Melbourne?'

Lord Melbourne reflected. 'His Majesty is still a citizen in

receipt of a large government pension and the owner of Claremont and other property in the country.'

'All a great mistake,' interrupted the King.

Melbourne politely reminded him that Leopold had once
been married to the Princess Charlotte.

'Are we to keep him in a lifetime's ermine and gold because
of a twelve-month marriage?'

Melbourne admitted it was, perhaps, regrettable.

'Regrettable!' shouted the King. 'It's damnable, utterly
damnable. A week's stay in my kingdom, with cannons popping
and a great deal of fa-la, and no one troubles to tell me. I
suspect he was plotting, my lord, plotting with that sister of
his. Plotting about my niece. He might, you know! Great God!
He is a water-drinker.'

The King spat expertly over the ramparts as though to clear
his mouth of the offensive word.

The Prime Minister had some sympathy for King Leopold.
When he and his ministers had last dined with the King, they
had been invited on the strict understanding that each drank
two bottles of wine in the course of dinner. It had been a trying
occasion.

'A plotting water-drinker, by God!' roared the King. 'And in
my kingdom, Melbourne, I beg you to see it don't occur again.'

35

Dr James Clark was not in the least frightened of responsibility nor of making decisions. Once physician to Princess Charlotte and Prince Leopold, he had delivered their
stillborn son and watched his illustrious patient die before his
eyes. And five years afterwards, in the moist air of a Roman
winter, he had attended the dying Keats, working ceaselessly
but unavailingly to save the poet from the blood cough which
wrung his lungs. Nevertheless, when Lehzen sent for him to
examine Princess Victoria two days after the departure of the

King and Queen of Belgium, he admitted he was anxious. She was wrong, he told her, to think the trouble was unimportant, a mere indisposition.

The Princess moped and sat about doing nothing. She had a mild fever and a constant headache. Occasionally she felt sick. Once her nose bled. The doctor was worried. He insisted she be put to bed. Then for two days he observed that her fever was variable, low early in the day, higher towards the evening.

Lehzen became alarmed when he said he felt the need of a second opinion and sent for a local practitioner. She was present while they made their examination, and she heard their cheerful questions to Victoria and their muttered remarks to one another with a fast beating heart. Afterwards they talked quietly together on the landing and Dr Clark saw his colleague out.

He returned to Lehzen and beckoned her out of Victoria's room.

Before he spoke she had guessed. She tried to fight down the rising fear inside her. 'Is it typhoid?' she asked.

He nodded. Then he said, 'I wonder if you would go with me to see Sir John?'

'At once, Doctor.'

They found Conroy walking alone in the garden.

Dr Clark was short and businesslike. The Princess he said had typhoid. For the time being she would have to be isolated. To avoid the possibility of infecting another room he suggested that she be left where she was and that the Duchess and Lehzen should exchange rooms. The fever had been growing for some time and there was no question at all of moving her back to London. Would Sir John kindly inform the Duchess? He himself would undertake to engage local nurses for day and night.

'Ought the King to be informed?'

Sir John's question surprised the doctor, until he appreciated that any illness of the heir to the throne was of interest to the country at large. 'You yourself are the best judge of such things, Sir John.'

Conroy insisted. 'If she is very ill it is my duty to send a courier to Court.'

The doctor spread his hand. 'If you are asking whether or

not she will die,' he said bluntly, 'I can only reply that I cannot tell. People frequently do die of typhoid, and the Princess might be unfortunate, but she is young and we shall take great care of her.'

'Then I judge it right to tell the King.'

Lehzen sat by the bed in the darkened room. Most of the time the Princess lay still, gazing at the moulded ceiling. Sometimes she turned on her side and, with a pointed finger, traced the outline of the pattern on the wallpaper. Occasionally she would stretch out a hand to touch Lehzen. She cried, too; very often; at first silently and then in deep, strangled sobs. She called again and again for her uncle and her aunt. She called for Feodore. Once she even called for Späth. Always to reassure her that she was not alone, Lehzen would take her hot hand and stroke it.

As the fever heightened pale rose-coloured blotches appeared on Victoria's skin. She lost her plumpness and became emaciated. This confirmed Dr Clark's diagnosis. He told Lehzen that the nursing must be constant. She must make sure the Princess was never left alone. And because she was a capable woman he warned her that the symptoms would all get worse. Her tongue would dry and turn brown like leather and her frail body would shake in nervous spasms. It would be a distressing sight, but the Baroness was not to lose hope. As he had remarked before, the Princess was young and she was being well looked after.

Tight-lipped Lehzen continued her vigil, praying continuously that her darling would not die.

A thin arm, the wrist and fingers trembling from the elbow, stretched out towards the grate where there was a fire. In the flames Victoria could see the rick burners and she wanted to catch one; to hold him between her forefinger and thumb and study him closely. Then she would have liked to squeeze him for frightening her. But then the light by the fireplace altered. It was like sunshine on a book-page, the butter colour dimmed to whey when a fast-scudding cloud passes overhead. Her hand fell on to the counterpane and she closed her eyes, listening to the crackle from the grate and the sound of rain sheeting on to the window pane outside. There was another recognizable noise; a nipping sound as Lehzen bit through a caraway. She opened her eyes to find Lehzen, but a strange person was there – gaunt and ancient, as old as the Archbishop of York, old, old, old. She blinked and he was gone. She blinked again and saw the dead Duchess of Rutland soaring up towards her marble-winged babies. Her kaleidoscope changed in the same way; every shake made a fresh pattern. Now every time she shut and opened her eyes someone else swam into view. For a moment it was the man they had run over at Lynn. He lay on the ground, his face screwed up with pain. Then he opened his mouth. He was going to accuse her.

'Dearest, will you not take a little?' Lehzen's voice was far far away. But what did she mean? And where was she?

She tried to sit up in bed. 'I'll not have holly beneath my chin. I won't, Lehzen.'

But there was only Saunders there, at the wheel, with Dash in his arms.

36

The Duke of Wellington never knelt except to royalty and only then, as he made it clear on several occasions, to British royalty. In church he crouched to pray, his bottom propped up by the edge of the pew, his head on his hands, his eyes covered. Nor generally did he listen very carefully to what was being said in church. At Stratfield Saye his chaplain's voice was muffled, in London his parson had a new-fangled sort of pronunciation which the Duke didn't hold with at all. Besides which he whistled. But though on that November Sunday the prayer was full of sibilance and the parson was whistling and hissing like a kettle, he held the Duke's attention and approval.

'Amen,' said the Duke firmly at the end of it.

He felt truly grateful to the Almighty that the Princess Victoria had been saved from her 'late dreadful visitation'. It was not, though, so much because he was glad for the girl's sake. He hardly knew her, and found her dismayingly ordinary. But, if she'd died at Ramsgate, Cumberland would have been heir – and the thought of so bigoted a Tory on the throne was not to be borne, even by the leader of the Tory party. Cumberland was too reactionary – voting against the Great Western Railway because he said the noise would disturb the Eton boys and because railways facilitated the transport of radicals from one place to another. He would have made politics impossible and set himself up as a non-constitutional tyrant.

'From Ernest of Cumberland good Lord deliver us,' he said.

From a sudden pause in the whistled praying and from the surprised glances of his neighbours he supposed he might have said it out loud. Well, there it was. The truth would out.

37

Four and a half weeks of watching and nursing had worn out Lehzen. She was obliged to retire to bed herself for a time, but now that Victoria was on the mend and there were good nurses to prevent a relapse, she obeyed Dr Clark and did keep to her bed. She tried to sleep, but she was nervously exhausted and sleep would not come until he gave her a draught. Then she slept at first deeply and then fitfully for the larger part of three days.

It was during this period that Sir John Conroy took his opportunity.

He had had some bad moments in the past weeks when the source of all potential power had been so close to death. Now that the threat was gone he became once more a dedicated careerist. He felt he owed it to himself to improve his position. It was essential that he should be guaranteed a place closer to the throne. The most influential post would be that of confidential Private Secretary and, with the Duchess of Kent's enthusiastic agreement, he went to the Princess while she was convalescing to ask her for the appointment.

She looked a pathetic little thing; her eyes deep set, her cheeks hollow, her limbs still emaciated and trembling as she lay on her daybed. Worst of all was her lack of hair. In a desperate effort to keep down the fever, Lehzen had cut off most of her long thick tresses. What remained lay in thin lifeless strands. The new hair was growing through them.

Sir John remained standing and congratulated her on her recovery.

'I fear you will be a long time getting your strength, but we will all do what we can to help.'

She thanked him. Her voice, too, had altered. It had no timbre.

It sounded as though she were speaking into an empty tumbler.

'I do not need your thanks,' he said jovially. 'We are like one family, and we are anxious to help. I, in particular, want you to be well and strong in time for Signor Lablache's lessons in May.'

It was a neat reminder of what he had done for her. Being under a debt of obligation would make it that much more difficult to refuse his request.

But, to his chagrin, she did refuse.

'It is not in my power to make you confidential Private Secretary, Sir John.'

'I accept that, of course, your royal highness.' The emphasis on the title was implicit with the understanding that never again would he call her his little woman, or pat her arm in an affectionate way, or be in any way familiar.

She was unmoved. 'I can't do anything at this stage.'

'You could make a promise,' he insisted. 'Give an undertaking.'

Still she refused. 'I am sorry, Sir John,' was all she said.

For a second time he spoke to her mother.

'Obstinate girl,' said the Duchess with feeling. 'Does she not realize all you have done for her?' She did not herself know of Sir John's private relationship with her daughter. 'She must give you the post, or the promise of it.'

'I tell you,' said Conroy warmly. 'She will not.'

'Then she must be constrained,' declared the Duchess. 'I shall speak with her.'

The Duchess had visited her daughter very little during her sickness. This had been by command of Dr Clark because typhoid was contagious, and by her own inclination because she could not bear to be with ill people. They offended and frightened her.

When, then, she swept into the sickroom to coerce Victoria into giving Sir John the appointment, she was appalled by her daughter's appearance.

'I was told you were well again,' she said. 'Why did Lehzen tell me you were well?' She looked about her. 'Where is Lehzen? I wish to speak with her.'

Victoria's altered, hollow voice came from the bed. 'She is resting, Mamma; watching over me has made her ill. And I am better, Mamma,' she added hurriedly because it looked as though, ill or not, Lehzen was to be sent for. 'Lehzen told you the truth.'

The Duchess obviously decided to leave the matter at that. Peremptorily she ordered the day nurse to leave the room as she had something private to say to the Princess. Then, still standing at the foot of the bed, for she had no intention of going any closer, she asked why Victoria had not agreed to Sir John's request.

Victoria stared at her mother with her deep-set eyes. 'Surely, Mamma, he did not tell you about it?'

'Of course,' snapped the Duchess. 'He, like me ...' She stopped for Victoria had given a loud, low sigh.

'Forgive me for interrupting you, Mamma; but I find it hard to believe he would have been so shameless as to confess his ambitions in such an open fashion.'

The Duchess blinked. There was a pause. Then she exploded, saying she doubted the evidence of her own ears that Victoria could say such terrible things ... to speak of ambitions in connexion with their good Sir John ...

Again Victoria interrupted her. 'You will pardon me, Mamma, but he was never *my* good Sir John. I have obeyed him and honoured him for your sake as he is the Comptroller of the household. But he has asked for an appointment which I am in no position to give. And if I was, I should refuse it.'

The Duchess was finding difficulty in getting her breath. 'Chit of a girl!' she cried. 'How dare you speak so disrespectfully of one who has always had your interests at heart?'

Victoria was frightened. She had never been quite so outspoken to her mother before. And in her physical weakness she would have consented to anything rather than submit to such bullying. Had the Duchess stopped haranguing her at that moment and demanded as a matter of filial duty the appointment of Sir John, Victoria would have consented. But the Duchess did not know this and in her arrogant vituperation she went too far and suddenly pricked Victoria's pride into action again.

She held up a thin trembling hand. It was a strange, unfamiliar gesture which so surprised the Duchess that she stopped abruptly.

'I do not think you are justified in blaming me so,' said her daughter in that strange, hollow voice. 'Nor ought you to speak so highly of a gentleman who is no more than a member of your household.'

' 'Drina!' White to the lips the Duchess drew herself up in furious indignation. 'You will apologize and beg my pardon this instant.'

But she could not quell the stubborn pride she had herself aroused. Victoria said she saw no need to apologize. She had but spoken the truth as she had always been taught to do.

The Duchess made a last attempt. 'I cannot believe you will disobey me. It is inconceivable that you can think you know better than your mother. 'Drina, I must insist that you promise Sir John the appointment, and that you keep to it.'

By that time Victoria's pale cheeks had flushed. She felt ready to faint but anger drove her to say: 'Madam, I will not. Sir John Conroy is not fit for it. You should realize the great difference between a Comptroller to a private household and confidential Private Secretary to the Queen of England.'

Without another word the Duchess left the room.

* * *

Sir John panicked. He tried once more on his own account, going into the Princess's room with a paper and a pencil. He had written out her promise of the post and her mother commanded that she sign it. He thrust the paper under her nose.

'I cannot read it,' she said.

'There is no need to. I have told you what it says. Merely sign.' His tone was peremptory.

'I must read it,' she insisted.

'Sign it,' he said between his teeth.

Victoria longed to tear up the paper and thrust the pieces in his face. She knew that she would hate him for the rest of her life. She would never forgive him, nor would she ever forget that terrible day. But she was too weak to argue any more; too feeble even to give him the edge of her tongue.

Her eyes told the nurse what to do. She went to the door and opened it. 'Sir John, the Princess is very tired and ought not to be disturbed any longer.'

He did not trouble to look round. Instead he waved the paper in Victoria's face. 'Will you or will you not sign this undertaking?' he demanded.

'Sir John.' The nurse's voice had hardened. 'I must insist. The Princess is overtired. She must not be disturbed any longer.'

He looked down once more at the unhealthy-looking girl who had resisted every persuasion, and he sighed.

'Sir John. Please leave the room.' The nurse had her hand on his arm.

'Very well, very well,' he said, shaking himself free. He left.

An entry from the Princess's journal, dated Thursday, November 5th, 1835:

Dear good Lehzen takes such care of me, and is so unceasing in her attentions to me, that I shall never be able to repay her sufficiently for it but by my love and gratitude. I never can sufficiently repay her for all she has *borne* and done for me. She is the *most affectionate, devoted, attached,* and *disinterested* friend I have, and I love her most dearly . . .

38

As she recuperated from her illness Victoria decided that, if it could be managed, she would lead her own quiet life. She preferred in future to see less of her mother, and as little as possible of Conroy. When Dr Clark announced she was fit enough to travel she was thankful beyond belief. The Ramsgate house had been too small. At Kensington it was easier to avoid people, especially as the Duchess had taken over some extra rooms in the Palace. Victoria settled into new apartments, gave up visiting the Conroy house, and tried to forget what had happened at Ramsgate.

For her part, the Duchess regretted having tried to coerce Victoria, not because it had caused the girl distress when she had been in an enfeebled state, but simply because it had closed an important door to her own future security. Moreover Sir John, denied his own way in anything, was apt to whine. And after whining he snarled. It was imperative to placate and reassure him. She suggested that when the time came Victoria would no doubt be very content to make Victoire Conroy one of her ladies-in-waiting. Meanwhile they would have to return to the first phase and persuade the politicians to extend the Regency beyond the official coming of age at eighteen. Lord Melbourne as leader of the Whigs, had proved particularly unsatisfactory; making no undertakings and treating the whole matter with an unfitting levity. The Duchess now turned her attention to the Tories.

On the last Saturday in February 1836, there was a large dinner party at Kensington Palace. It included Aunt Gloucester who eyed the new apartments and asked caustically how her dear sister-in-law had managed to persuade the King to let her have seventeen extra rooms. The Duchess of Kent replied by laying a finger against her lips and closing one eye, a device which told the Duchess of Gloucester what she knew already — that the rooms had been seized without the King's permission or even knowledge. Archbishop Harcourt and Miss Harcourt were also there; the former looking so frail that everyone considered it a marvel he had withstood the journey up from York. The hostess's prime targets, the *raison d'être* for the party, were the Duke of Wellington, who had led many Tory administrations, and Sir Robert Peel, a shy, tall man who had been Prime Minister for a short time and promised to be the next.

Victoria, being sixteen and a half, was naturally there, sitting silently between the Duke and the son of the Russian Ambassador. Her presence would have been a disadvantage to anyone more sensitive to other people's feelings than the Duchess of Kent. With sublime disregard of what her daughter might think she hinted that in the lamentable event of the King's death a longer Regency than the one already provided for by law might be desirable. What, she asked, did Sir Robert think? Sir Robert Peel was one of the canniest statesmen of the day; yet in the face of such blatancy he was entirely at a loss. He looked down the table to his wife for help. She was expert at answering difficult questions, but on this occasion she refused to catch his eye.

'Well, Sir Robert?' said the inexorable Duchess.

'Not being in the present ministry . . .' he began wretchedly, and stopped.

The old Archbishop sitting at the Duchess's right came to his rescue. 'I believe Sir Robert's courtliness prevents him from forming an opinion of so delicate a matter.'

Wisely the Duchess let the subject rest. Afterwards she would speak to the Duke. He really was the source of all power in the Tory party. For the present, and to Sir Robert's great relief, she talked of other matters.

Victoria had at once realized what her mother was trying to do. The Duke who was hard of hearing had not caught the conversation, but she knew he would be approached afterwards to give his view on the possibility of an extended Regency. She set out to prove herself in no need of regents.

To begin with she talked of family matters – telling him how pleased they all were that her cousin Ferdinand had married the Queen of Portugal. Wellington's deafness, or pretended deafness, was rather wearing. She was obliged to repeat what

152

she said, and he merely nodded making no comment. She persevered, saying that her cousins Ernest and Albert of Saxe-Coburg were coming over for her birthday. Their father would accompany them ... the reigning Duke of Saxe-Coburg and her Mamma's brother. Did the Duke know him?

'Eh?'

The question was repeated.

'No,' he replied shortly.

Bravely she went on, praising her Uncle Leopold's benign rule of his new kingdom, and his excellent advice on political affairs. To her surprise the Duke came to life.

'Advice' he snapped. 'To whom?'

Victoria tried to explain how her uncle had been advising her on the duties and privileges of a constitutional monarch, directing her historical studies, and her other reading.

But the Duke's interest disappeared almost as quickly as it had occurred. He simply shook his head when she asked if he did not think Uncle Leopold a fine, sagacious man; so she presumed he did not want to talk about affairs. Instead she tried him on minerals, but to this he made no contribution at all. She talked of tetragonal crystals and lapis-lazuli while he silently ate sauced turbot and sipped a German wine. Frightened that she was being tedious she began to speak faster and faster. He paid little attention.

After that she gave up. Miserably she decided that far from proving she didn't need regents, she might have done the exact opposite.

She need not have worried. Privately the Duke accounted her a fearful bore, and he sincerely hoped that when she was their reigning monarch she would not dement her Court with such awful small talk; but not for one moment did he underrate her capacity to rule. And he made this very clear when the Duchess of Kent approached him after dinner with her proposal that the Regency be extended.

'I want to know, Ma'am, why you think your daughter's in need of a Regency?'

'She is so young, your grace; so undeveloped and immature.'

'Then, Ma'am, the very best thing we can all do is let her

grow older, let her develop and mature a little before we come to any definite conclusion. Am I right, Ma'am? Am I right?'

39

Sir John had a mind to prevent Victoria from being taught singing by Lablache. But the Duchess herself said the arrangement could not be cancelled. At great inconvenience to himself the maestro had agreed to come regularly to Kensington throughout the opera season, and it would never do to put him off at this stage. Reluctantly, for if he could have hurt Victoria he would, he was obliged to agree with her.

In May there began for Victoria an enchanting time when she saw the figure of her dreams almost daily. Lablache was not unaware of her devotion, nor was he unaware of the potentially dangerous position in which he found himself. He was over twice her age and in a position of trust. It was for him to choose whether to rebuff or accept her love. The little figure who stood beside him at the piano, and put such passionate effort in attaining and holding top C, was afire with her feelings. He was Italian and a realist and therefore would not dismiss it as a passing calf love. He knew that it gave her as much joy and as much hurt as any that would follow later in life, perhaps more so, and, if he could, he was determined not to damage anything so precious. He did this and managed to maintain his difficult position by the judicious use of laughter. He was as great a clown as a singer, mixed hilarity with wistful sadness, and by self-ridicule, pretended pouting, light teasing, and practical jokes, he taught her a great deal about human values. With great skill he held them both in that difficult but not unpleasant state when love can never be fulfilled. And all the time he was waiting anxiously for his replacement. This was his plan, to cherish her feelings but guide them painlessly in another direction.

Lehzen realized how fortunate Victoria was in her kindly

understanding singing master. Hiding such strong feelings from the household's curiosity and laughter was very exhausting, and the girl could not keep up the pretence with her governess. Again Lehzen experienced smarts of jealousy, but she generously offered herself as a safety valve for Victoria's pent-up feelings. She heard about Lablache and nothing but Lablache until she almost felt in love with him herself. They used code words to eliminate the danger of the affair becoming known, and made sentimental pilgrimages to the music room where the maestro taught her.

Lehzen, like Lablache, was waiting for his replacement. It might, perhaps, have been young Lord Elphinstone. He fell deeply in love with the Princess and was as assiduous in his wooing as Mr Tunbridge Wells; but after a day or two's uncertainty Victoria decided that he was making himself ridiculous. Certainly he carried his love to extravagant lengths and one Sunday morning in church he was actually seen by the Duchess sketching her daughter's profile. That was the end of young Lord Elphinstone. The Duchess brought pressure to bear on his family and his regiment. He was shipped off to Madras without delay. Then there was the possibility of young Prince Augustus of Saxe-Coburg-Kohary, who came with his father and brother, both called Ferdinand, on their way to Prince Ferdinand's new house in Lisbon. Augustus was young and blond and handsome and vigorous, and he had a charming manner, but though Victoria was fond of him he never stole her heart away from the maestro. It took another cousin to do that . . .

Duke Ernest of Saxe-Coburg-Gotha, eldest brother to the Duchess of Kent, brought his two sons on a visit to England for Victoria's seventeenth birthday. King William was enraged. The Whig ministry had done its duty and declared in favour of the Prince of Orange, but the Duchess had refused point blank to entertain the idea. Nor would she tolerate the Duke of Wellington's plan to marry Victoria to blind George of Cumberland. But the King was equally strong against the Coburg plan. If he could have prevented the Duke and his sons from arriving in England he would have done so. He summoned Lord Melbourne and sought his advice. Could the ducal party be stopped from landing? Could they be forcibly returned to the continent? Lord Melbourne was not often alarmed, but the King's proposition made him literally clutch at his hair. By no means, he told his royal master, by no means in law or anything else could they be turned back and refused hospitality. He stayed at Windsor until he was sure the King had accepted his advice and had agreed to be civil to the Coburgs at the State Ball on Victoria's seventeenth birthday.

Lablache had reigned in the Princess's heart for a long time, but now a boy of sixteen, her cousin Albert, reigned in his place. Victoria confided to him. It was a sign of the high trust and regard she would always have for her singing master. Her cousin, she told him, was the one they all hoped she would one day marry. He was three months younger than she, highly intelligent, and absolutely beautiful. This was precisely how she described him, and from it Lablache knew that he was a free man again. She admitted there were drawbacks. The English way of life, staying up until one or two in the morning and lying in bed until a late and heavy breakfast on the following day, did not suit Albert at all. He grew paler as the evening wore on, and twice was caught sleeping on his feet. On the day of the State Ball for her birthday he felt unwell, danced a few steps, almost fainted and had to be taken home.

'He is so delicate, maestro, so very delicate that I am anxious for him. And yet he is so absolutely beautiful.'

He kissed her hand and wished her every happiness. Then they sang a duet together – *O amato zio* from her favourite *Puritani*. Both sang strongly and joyously.

40

Despite a number of hints from the English Court, some so vague as to be not understood and others so broad as to be offensive, King Leopold of the Belgians was determined to keep up and use his English house at Claremont. Occasionally he wished to entertain family friends informally without the protocol of a royal Court and his gift from the English nation was eminently suitable for this.

In the high summer of 1835 he invited the Kents to join him there, and, barely giving them time to settle in the rooms, he sought out Lehzen to thank her for keeping her promise.

'But, Sir, I did nothing.'

'Come,' he said. 'I believe you are over-modest. My niece has written feverish letters about her cousin Albert; one might say ecstatic.'

'I assure you, Sir, it was none of my doing. The Princess was instantly attracted to him and nothing that I might have said either in favour or disfavour of the Prince would have made the slightest difference.'

'How astonishing!'

She smiled. 'Perhaps, Sir, you are surprised because your plan achieved success so easily; or perhaps, as his uncle and a man, you cannot see the Prince's very obvious attractions.'

'Baroness, nothing you say will convince me that my nephew is a paragon . . .'

'You will forgive me for interrupting, but I have no intention of doing any such thing. Between us, I may say he smiled very little and complained rather a lot. He was always ready to sit down or rest or go to bed, and he was invariably taking care of what he ate; neither of which attributes generally commends itself to young people.'

King Leopold laughed. 'In fact he was ponderous?' he suggested.

'Quite . . . Yet, none of these things made any difference . . .'

She broke off for Victoria was approaching down the corridor.

'Dear Uncle,' she cried. 'I have hurried so that I may talk to you. Writing is not the same. I wish to talk.'

Lehzen curtseyed to them both and turned to go. But Victoria stopped her. 'Nothing I may say is private from you, dearest Lehzen.'

'His majesty, your uncle, may have private things to say to you,' said Lehzen; and she insisted on leaving.

'What I would do without Lehzen . . .' began Victoria looking after her. 'Uncle, you could never understand, no one could, how much I owe to Lehzen.'

He led her to an ottoman. They sat side by side and he took one of her hands in his. 'I guessed from your letters and I heard from other sources that you have had some difficulties since I last saw you.'

She nodded.

'And therefore,' he continued, 'I am inexpressively relieved that you have the Baroness with you. She, I know, will always be loyal and affectionate.'

'Indeed, yes, dear Uncle.' She knew he could not say more without condemning her mother who was his own sister.

'I wish,' he went on, 'that I were closer, but it would not do for us to be too often at Claremont, and besides, I do have a great deal of work in my own kingdom. And so I have planned to send you my *alter ego*, Baron Stockmar.'

Victoria would have preferred her uncle in person. Baron Stockmar had made the severe rules under which she had been trained for the throne. She hardly knew how but she guessed he would be just as severe as his rules.

Her reluctance showed itself.

'He is a good man, Victoria,' urged her uncle. 'And has been my own tutor in sovereignty. A large amount of the advice I write to you has its foundation in Stockmar's teaching, and I can give you no better present for the future than that he should come and reside here in England as your confidential adviser and helper. No one, no one at all will be able to exert pressure on you either when you come of age or when you come to the throne if Stockmar is beside you.'

Victoria was convinced. If Stockmar was so knowledgeable and so indifferent to power he would be a valuable asset.

'Thank you, Uncle, I should appreciate his help. When will he come to England?'

King Leopold considered. 'Not yet, I think. It would be prudent to wait for a few months until you are eighteen and of full age. He will be of most value to you then and thereafter.' He smiled. 'And now,' he said, 'let us walk outside and talk about Albert.'

She sprang to her feet. 'Oh, yes,' she cried. 'For I love him so much, and I worry constantly because he is so delicate.'

On their walk King Leopold was able to reassure her that after a short time Albert would easily adapt his system to English hours and English food, and then he would be like other young men. There was no weakness in his physique, and certainly none in his mind. He had already gone off on a grand tour through Bavaria and Switzerland and on to Italy to equip himself against his possible destiny as consort to the Queen of England.

Victoria asked shyly if he had said anything of her after the visit to England.

But, of course, he said; the boy was full of admiration for his cousin. It pleased Victoria who blushed prettily. Leopold wondered if she really was so naïve, or if she pretended to save herself from hurt. She must, surely, realize Albert's position, and that his family and German vanity made him rebel at being a mere chattel in the marriage market. He had been agreeably surprised to find their cousin Victoria was neither a horror nor a wanton, but was cynical enough to know that it would have made no difference if she had been either.

41

William the Fourth, as was quite often the case, was in a state of fury.

It had been sparked off by his ungrateful natural children. This summer they had been clamorous in their demands for more and more money. He had settled them well, given them rank, and married off the daughters to respectable members of the nobility. And he dearly loved them. But they caused him an unnecessary amount of anxiety and anger, and, one after the other, they seemed to take pleasure in hurting his feelings. Then his fury had been stirred into a blaze by the most constant source of all his troubles, the Duchess of Kent. He was not a well man. Heart disease, asthma and bronchitis were grasping him tighter and tighter. Bronchitis, although uncomfortable, he did not mind: it was a truly English disease. The remainder he despised but he recognized they were killing him. Essentially good-natured he had offered an olive branch to his sister-in-law. His own birthday and his Queen's fell in August; so did the Duchess of Kent's. She was invited to bring Victoria to Windsor for all those birthdays so that the family could be jolly together. The Duchess accepted, but only on her terms. With malice or stupidity – it was difficult to decide which – she said they would only come for the King's birthday, which fell last of the three. This deprived the King of a chance to be generous to her on her own birthday. Worse, it was a slight to Queen Adelaide whom he adored.

Therefore the King was already in a temper when he woke up on the day his sister-in-law and niece were due to arrive from Claremont. It was worsened by an early dispatch from the Admiralty reporting their lordships' decision to reprieve an insubordinate royal marine whom the King had wished to hang from the highest yardarm in the Navy. As bad came the realization that he had to go all the way up to London to prorogue Parliament, and it was a beautiful day far more suited to cricket or angling.

He became more equable on the long drive from Windsor.

More than any of his brothers he was like his father and though he knew far less about farming than the management of ships of the line he liked to appear as the Squire of Windsor. Seeing fields of fine standing corn, he leant out of the chaise window to shout congratulations to the farmers and their labourers, and he stopped the carriage on a village green so that he could get out and inspect a flock of geese, pronounce them 'sturdy', and give the gooseboy a sixpence.

But then, on the outskirts of London the dust began to aggravate his asthma. He was forced to have the windows closed and he sat wheezing heavily, his mouth protected by a handkerchief.

The King was tired but in a calmer and more reflective mood when he set off for Windsor that evening. Proroguing Parliament had taken the shortest possible time. He had stormed

160

into the House of Lords and out again so quickly that Lord Melbourne, his eyes twinkling, congratulated him on a royal record. He had eaten sauced codfish, chops, beefsteak pudding and brawn with his brothers Sussex and Cumberland and in sufficient quantities for such a hot day to give any but those Hanoverian princes a fatal stroke of apoplexy. Wine, which all three dearly loved, had been served liberally, and under its soothing influence the King had grown sentimental about their niece Victoria. 'It will touch every sailor's heart to have a Queen to fight for,' he exclaimed, not altogether to his brother Cumberland's liking. 'They'll be tattooing her face on their arms and chests, and thinking she was named after Nelson's flagship.'

The same tender feelings made him decide to call at Kensington Palace to see the shell which had contained his dear niece for the greater part of her life. He had not dined there for a very long time and had never seen the Kents' apartments.

There were no public demonstrations of loyalty as the royal chaise bowled along the road. But, at least, thought the King, they didn't throw stones and worse as they had in the vexatious time of reform. One or two individuals did raise their hats politely and bow to the chaise, and this pleased him a great deal. Once more he visualized Victoria sitting in his place. They'd cheer right enough then, for she was a dear and pretty girl, and he, well – if the truth was to be admitted – he now found the crown less comfortable than an admiral's hat and the common people knew it.

They were at the Kensington Lodge gates. Immediately they were thrown open and the chaise rolled on up the drive to the Clock Court and the palace door. The footmen jumped down and ran to ring the bell. The King's eldest daughter, Lady de Lisle, had been housekeeper at Kensington for the past six months, and she was at once summoned to meet her father. He kissed her and said he had come on a sentimental journey – to visit the rooms of his niece and heir.

The coachman threw his reins to an ostler boy. The King's habit of inspecting places as though he was doing the rounds of a ship always took a good deal of time. He'd stretch his legs, beg some stout at the kitchen, perhaps even manage to suck a pipe. As it turned out, he was able to enjoy none of these simple pleasures. Indeed hardly had he climbed down to the ground when he saw the King walking rapidly out of the palace again, followed by an anxious-looking equerry. In the rear was Lady de Lisle. She was wringing her hands and weeping.

'Windsor: Windsor!' ordered the King, his face pink with exertion as he leapt into the chaise.

The King reached Windsor at ten o'clock.

He had been smouldering all the way. The Duchess's effrontery in seizing seventeen extra rooms was almost unbelievable. He remembered that she had asked for them. He also remembered that she had not troubled to ask personally but through her factotum Conroy, and he had been so pert in manner that the request had been refused.

'I must remember she is female, I must remember she is female,' he kept saying over and over again, the implication being that had she been male he could have physically attacked her; and no sooner had the chaise come to a halt than he was running, literally running this time, to the drawing-room where he knew the house party would be assembled. The double doors were opened in front of him one after the other. He was fairly out of breath when he arrived; even so, his entrance was sufficiently precipitous to take the company by surprise.

The band stopped playing Mozart and began the National Anthem as the King bounded over to his Queen and kissed her. Then he looked round the company. Victoria was standing close to her mother. He went straight to her, kissed her, and clearly through the strains of *God Save the King* he welcomed her to the Castle, said how pleased he was to see her there and how much he regretted that she was not with them more often. The National Anthem ended. He turned to the Duchess of Kent and bowed low. In a voice of suppressed fury, yet quite loud enough to be heard by some of the company, he said:

'Ma'am, I have this evening been to Kensington. To my palace there, Ma'am: and I have found that the most unwarrantable liberties have been taken with it. Without my consent, in fact contrary to my express command, you have taken possession of certain apartments there.' He turned away, but clearly considered this rebuke was insufficient. 'You ought to know, Ma'am,' he continued, 'that your sovereign is seriously displeased.'

'It was so humiliating, Lehzen,' sobbed Victoria. 'He reproved her in front of everyone.'

Lehzen took her in her arms. 'No one who heard would have been shocked. The King is always outspoken and his quarrel with your mother is well known.'

But it was not so much the publicity of the reproof which upset Victoria as the fact that her mother deserved it. 'How could she take those rooms when he had forbidden it? It was so stupid. He was bound to discover it one day.'

'Your mother does not respect the King, my dear.'

'But she should, she must,' said Victoria, outraged. 'He is her King.' She seized Lehzen's hand. 'If, when I am Queen, anyone should treat me with such scant respect, I believe I could not bear it. No, I could not bear it.'

Lehzen reasoned with her. She ought not to be too hard on her mother. She was not always advised very well, as they both knew. Moreover, respect had to be earned as well as inherited. Perhaps the King had been over-familiar with his subjects and that was why the public treated him as a figure of fun, and some people in high positions took liberties with him.

'It is too cruel,' said Victoria. She was genuinely devoted to her uncle and aunt. Seeing them pilloried was hurtful. 'But it determines me not to make the same mistake. To everyone but my beloved Albert, and to you, dear Lehzen, I shall be an iceberg.'

Lehzen seized on the mention of Prince Albert as a means to lead the conversation elsewhere. Victoria was over-sensitive to family scenes at Court; and much, much happier rhapsodizing like any ordinary girl about the boy who had her heart.

One of the King's sons, Lord Adolphus FitzClarence, saw his father the next morning and, though it was his seventy-first birthday and there was plenty to occupy his mind, he was still in a passion about the seventeen stolen rooms at Kensington. Lord Adolphus prophesied, and not without relish because he disliked the Kents, that they had not heard the last of that business. Not by any means.

He was right.

That night, at the royal birthday banquet, the King responded to a toast in a strangely feverish way. He rambled for some minutes, running bird-like from point to point, not having, apparently, any theme. The Duchess of Kent sat on his right. She looked exceedingly bored. The Princess Victoria sat across the board in front of her. She looked dutifully interested, but she was as perplexed as any of the hundred guests. Everyone wondered what the King was driving at. Then, unfortunately, it became all too plain.

Suddenly he lowered his voice, so that everyone had to strain to hear him. 'I trust in God that my life be spared for nine months longer,' he declared, and looked slowly round the tables.

No one knew quite what to do. They all wanted him to go on living for a long, long time; but to cheer at this point would be open to misinterpretation. They did not want him to think they limited their hopes, like him, to only nine months. The reason for this peculiar restriction he made clear.

'For nine months longer,' he repeated. 'After which, in the event of my death, no Regency would take place.'

The Duchess of Kent stiffened in her seat.

'I should then have the satisfaction,' he continued, pointing suddenly across the table at Victoria, 'of leaving the royal authority to the personal exercise of that young lady, the heiress presumptive to the crown.'

The guests chose this as a suitable moment to applaud. But the King had not finished. He quietened them by raising a hand.

'And not in the hands of a person now near to me,' he said, in an electric silence, 'who is surrounded by evil advisers, and who is herself . . .' He raised his voice just in case it could not be heard '. . . incompetent to act with propriety in the station in which she would be placed.'

There was a light buzzing from the tables. The Duchess of Kent sat like a stone. Queen Adelaide made bread pellets. Victoria felt her neck redden and the colour rise higher and higher. She wanted to think about Albert and so escape from this terrible scene, but it wasn't possible.

Having started so dramatically, the King continued at the

top of his voice and at a great rate, thundering out that he had been insulted, grossly and continually insulted, by *that* person, and he was determined to endure it no longer. 'Amongst many other things, I have particularly to complain of the manner in which that young lady has been kept from my Court.' Once more his forefinger pointed to the crimson Princess. 'She has been repeatedly kept from my drawing-rooms, at which she ought always to have been present.' The arm fell. He half turned towards his rigid sister-in-law. There was no doubt as to whom he was referring to now. 'I would have her know that I am King, and I am determined to make my authority respected, and for the future I shall insist and command that the Princess does upon all occasions appear at my Court, as it is her duty to do.'

The hundred guests were made up from the household, special friends, and a number of local gentlemen with the ladies who had been invited to join the birthday celebrations. They were unaccustomed to royal quarrels and to such outspokenness, and they were agog. Already they were longing to get home to pass on this remarkable story. Their only fear was that though they had the dining-out story of the century, possibly no one would believe them.

Victoria could not control her tears. They coursed silently down each cheek. Her mother made no sign of her feelings except that she sat in profound silence until the end of the meal. Afterwards, when the ladies retired, she became very voluble. She ordered her carriage, required postboys to be sent on ahead to warn Claremont of their immediate arrival, and declared neither she nor Victoria would stay another hour at Windsor Castle.

Somehow Queen Adelaide and Victoria prevailed upon her to change her mind. They never knew how they did it. Very probably the fact was that at last the King had partially subdued his cantankerous sister-in-law. She knew now it would be unwise to throw such a thoroughly angry, bitter man into another rage by outward defiance. Instead, she would revenge herself in quieter ways, by ignoring him, by laughing at him behind her hand, by keeping him waiting for his meals, and by refusing to allow Victoria to be at Court.

42

The Prime Minister's relationship with Mrs Norton was proved in the courts to be platonic. Her husband's malicious action against her for committing adultery with Lord Melbourne had been dismissed. Justice cleared them both. Only they knew how far justified the verdict was, and they continued to enjoy their friendship as before.

Mrs Norton was not quite respectable and yet she was confidante to the highest *ton* in London. A Sheridan by birth she skirted the periphery of the demi-monde and received statesmen, men of letters, painters, the Army and the Navy. They were seldom accompanied by their wives though this might just have been possible. The truth was that Caroline Norton liked to be a candle-flame to moths and therefore preferred men without their wives. For her dear William, Lord Melbourne, she gave intimate little supper parties, and they were for him alone.

Caroline's intellect hardly matched Melbourne's but it was still considerable. Her mordant wit was stimulating. So too was her *brio*, her adventurousness. In so many ways she was a cast of Melbourne's disastrous Caroline; the wife who had fascinated with her liveliness and sparkle and charm, the wife who had driven him into himself, rent with self-reproaches, while she gave him an idiot child, enjoyed a hectic, wild affair with the poet Bryon, and then went mad. Now, after many years, a widower and his backward son dead, Melbourne was quite alone and he found the best of the old Caroline in his new Caroline.

She made few demands on him. She did not even require him to be a constant visitor. If private or state affairs kept him away for a week or a month or more, it was all one to her. Friendship she believed transcended regular contact. All she wanted was that he should appreciate the quality of their friendship. He did. She was one of the most exciting women he had ever known and yet in her presence he could relax and unwind as he could with no one else. He was not in the least in love with her, but he needed the company of a pretty and accomplished woman.

When he was tired he went to her for solace. When the situation in which he found himself became too ludicrous: that is, as head of a progressive ministry when by inclination he was quite as reactionary as Wellington; he could tell Caroline about it and somehow she understood. And only she could be relied upon to hold her tongue when he unburdened himself of any large secret. She knew how tired he was of witnessing royal squabbles and as month followed month towards the Princess Victoria's eighteenth birthday she alone shared the Prime Minister's knowledge of what was happening.

He often came to her direct from Windsor, where, he said, the King's health grew worse and worse. He told her that on some days the old man wheezed and choked so much that conversation was impossible. On others, bouts of coughing caused him acute pains in the chest and prostrated him. Generally he was quiet, sitting with his feet up on a day bed, his face no longer rosy but a livid grey. In this state it was natural that he should fret about little things. Seeing a uniform incorrectly worn made him irascible for hours. So did the sight of sloppy livery, or people standing about doing nothing when he considered they ought to be working. And his prejudices deepened. Protocol required that King Leopold should be invited to Windsor but he was warned that his host would expect him to drink wine. Leopold compromised by having a full glass of wine with a small glass of water hidden behind it, but the King, well aware that Leopold was that hated thing, a determined water-drinker, examined his cover and detected the little glass. The following scene was painful. 'God damn it!' the King had shouted. 'I won't allow *anyone* to drink water at my table.' Leopold promptly found a good reason to leave the Castle, and the King had an attack of asthma which was so bad that he was an object of pity to all who saw him.

It upset Melbourne more than he would have admitted to anyone but Caroline Norton. The Queen's devotion was touching, he told her. When the King was beside himself with pain from his heart or gasping for breath she drove away his attendants and nursed him herself. She was prepared to be the butt when weakness and fright made him bad-tempered. She adored her William, but she was also a realist. She asked Melbourne what she would have to do when the King died. What were her responsibilities?

'It was pathetic, heartbreaking,' murmured Melbourne.

Caroline saw how moved he was. She would not let him say another word until he had eaten. The food she had prepared with her own hands. She served him at a round table in her dining-room, telling him to think only of his supper. Afterwards, when he had eaten, they could talk again.

He ate a dish of wild duck, a salad of forced radishes, and cheese sent up from the West Country. Finally he ate a pear. There was nothing, he said, quite like a pear for rounding off a meal – unless it was a handful of cherries.

They drank wine together and were very content. Eventually, he returned to the subject which was troubling him.

The bad news from Windsor was aggravating a crisis at Kensington. Though both he and Wellington had refused to consider it, the Duchess and Conroy were doing everything in their power to have the Regency extended. Surprisingly Princess Sophia and the Duke of Sussex had agreed in principle. But they were entirely uninterested in the self-aggrandizement of their sister-in-law. They were concerned, they said, for Victoria. The crown might well be too great a burden for her until she was older. Therefore a Regent, congenial to her if not of her choosing, should be empowered to rule on her behalf. This was not at all to the Duchess's liking. Her influence over her daughter had dwindled to nothing. If Victoria had to choose a Regent it would probably be the Duke of Sussex. But then she and Conroy had gathered support from an unexpected quarter.

Victoria's half-brother, Charles, Prince of Leiningen, had recently arrived in the country and he had come to the conclusion that his mother was right. Victoria *was* too immature to hold the reins of authority at the age of eighteen. He had said so openly to various members of the royal family and to the Prime Minister.

'Maybe he has seen things which we know nothing of,' said

Melbourne wearily. 'But it all amounts to a conspiracy and is a damned, bad nuisance.'

Caroline soothed his forehead with her fingers.

'And is the Princess worth our trouble?' Melbourne asked. 'From the little I have heard I judge her to be a forceful if not pigheaded young lady.'

'Come, William,' chided Mrs Norton. 'You are unjust. She has a powerful personality, yes. I have heard the same. But I have also heard that she is gentle and kindly disposed . . .'

'To lapdogs and ponies,' interrupted Melbourne. 'And, of course, to Albert of Saxe-Coburg.'

'Now, William, I'll not have you so ungallant. I think it romantic beyond measure that she has fallen in love with a supplied suitor.'

'Supplied, though, by her Uncle Leopold.' He put his feet on a faldstool. 'Are they not the oddest lot in the world, my dear? I heard only today that young Leiningen has tried to enrol Uncle Leopold on his side in the conspiracy. He of course has the influence to persuade Victoria to ask voluntarily for a Regency. And what is Leopold's answer? Neither a flat yes or no; simply that he is sending Baron Stockmar, the uncle of his own discarded mistress, to look into the affair. Agree with me, my dear; are they not a very curious lot?'

43

Lord Melbourne had barely done justice to the King of Belgium. Leopold had no intention of furthering his sister's scheme and he was determined to scotch the Regency conspiracy. He made his views clear to Baron Stockmar before he left for England. His nephew's appeal was to be refused as politely and as diplomatically as possible and, should that young man persist, he was to be told plainly that no reasonable person could support the Duchess of Kent's candidature as Regent of England. As she had proved herself incapable of managing her own daughter, it was unlikely that she could successfully rule a kingdom. Beyond this Stockmar was given no particular instructions. He was free to make his own judgements and decisions, and he was to advise Victoria and her mother, and – if necessary – consult with King William or the Prime Minister.

To begin with the Baron was regarded by both sides at Kensington as a type of celestial arbitrator. Charles of Leiningen felt obliged to accept his uncle's point of view though he continued to work for an extension of the Regency. Conroy confessed his ambitions to the Baron. He simply wanted, he said, to be Victoria's Private Secretary, and he also wanted to curb the insidious influence of Lehzen. Victoria told Stockmar how much she disliked her mother's Comptroller and in every detail she told him why. Stockmar decided that a compromise between them would be the only effective anodyne. He told Sir John that so far as he could see the Baroness had never attempted to turn Victoria against him, and he recommended a grand apology for all shortcomings. It ought, he said, to work wonders. Sir John went so far as to write one, but a second reading and Irish vanity made him tear it up. Stockmar also tried to persuade Victoria not to be so determined. She must relax and give some ground away in order to make progress in more important directions. He found she was an enemy of compromise, and after her harrowing experience at Ramsgate, she would not give an inch.

Shortly after Stockmar's arrival the King played a card of his own which heightened the crisis. He sent his Chamberlain, Lord Conyngham, with a message written especially for the Princess Victoria. It was to be given to no one else under any circumstances.

Sir John held out his hand for the package and his eyes blazed when Lord Conyngham refused to do as he asked. 'I was bidden, Sir John, to place it in the Princess's own hands.'

Conroy went off to fetch the Duchess.

Eventually she faced Lord Conyngham and she held out her hand. 'Sir John understands, my lord, that as the King's messenger you are not permitted to give him the letter for the Princess. And so I, as her mother, have come for it myself.'

'Your royal highness will appreciate ...' began Lord Conyngham but he was cut short.

'I appreciate,' snapped the Duchess, 'that my daughter is a minor and I am her legal guardian. Kindly give me the letter.'

Conyngham decided it was wiser to say nothing. He bowed with great politeness, but he did not hand over the letter.

Pink with mortification the Duchess gasped: 'I shall remember this, Lord Conyngham.'

He bowed again and lower this time. The Duchess swept from the room, followed closely by Sir John.

In pettiness they kept him waiting for forty minutes. Then, to insult the King, instead of Sir John escorting him to the Princess an underservant was sent to do it.

Conyngham found her in a small drawing-room attended not, as he had expected, by Baroness Lehzen but by Lady Catherine Jenkinson.

The Princess was nervous and ill at ease.

He told her why he had come and handed her the letter. 'I was bidden to remain, your royal highness, and answer any questions which might occur to you. Pray regard me as entirely at your service.'

Lady Catherine told him it would not be necessary. She rang for a servant to show Lord Conyngham out, but he did not move.

'My instructions were explicit,' he murmured politely. 'I was to see her royal highness read the letter with her own eyes, and afterwards reply to any questions which she might like to ask.'

Victoria suddenly broke the seal and opened the paper. She read it carefully and slowly. Not by a flicker of movement or any other sign could Lord Conyngham measure her reaction to what was written there. She read it through a second time, carefully folded it, and slipped it into her reticule.

'Will you please thank his majesty, Lord Conyngham? I shall reply as soon as possible.'

'You have no queries?' he asked.

'None, I thank you. It is very clear. Convey, please, my love and my duty to their majesties.'

Conyngham kissed her hand, bowed, and left the room.

The door had hardly shut before a door opened on the opposite side of the drawing-room.

'And what,' demanded her mother, moving swiftly to Victoria, 'did your uncle write?'

Sir John was with the Duchess.

'I should prefer, Mamma, to read it again before deciding anything.'

'You!' said Sir John contemptuously. 'You decide?'

The Duchess laughed, and so did Lady Catherine. 'Do not be offended, dear; it is not for pretty young heads like yours to make decisions.'

Victoria was enraged. She was tired of being humiliated. She gave the letter to her mother as though it was of no account at all, and said with an edge to her voice. 'You forget, Mamma, that I alone of all of us here was born to make decisions.' She left it at that, and went to find Lehzen.

'Hoity-toity,' said the Duchess. 'What a waspish, vain girl I have.'

'Brought up so, Ma'am, by Madame Caraway.'

'That, I agree, is likely. Now . . .' Quickly the Duchess opened the letter. 'Let us see what our nautical sovereign has to say . . .' She read for a moment; then gasped. She read on. By the time she had finished the letter her hand was trembling. She gave it to Sir John. What he read made him very angry.

The King had offered Victoria £10,000 a year for her own exclusive use, to be used as she wished and without her mother's supervision. A friend of his sons called Stephenson would act as an independent Privy Purse to manage her private affairs. And she was now given the right to appoint her own ladies.

In no way could the King have better contrived to infuriate his sister-in-law and Conroy.

A reply was drafted without delay. In it the Princess accepted the additional income, but in view of her youth and immaturity she begged that her own mother should have the care of it.

Sir John took it to Victoria's private sitting-room.

She read through the draft and then handed it to Lehzen.

Conroy frowned. 'That is a confidential document, your

royal highness. The Baroness ought not to see a communication between yourself and the King before it has been sent.'

'Why not, Sir John? You have seen it as chief and most intimate adviser to my mother. It is right that the Baroness should see it as my chief and most intimate adviser. But in any case,' she added, 'the question of privilege does not arise. This is not a letter from me to the King. I shall not sign it.'

Sir John's face darkened. 'I think you will, Victoria,' he replied.

'I will trouble you to address me correctly, Sir John,' she said shrilly.

She wanted to hold out. Why should she sign the letter and give her uncle a false impression? Why should she make herself out to be a nitwit not able to spend an income without the help of her mother? But Lehzen advised her to give way.

'In only a few days, my love, you will be eighteen. The poor King is so unwell that he might die at any time. It is not worth the struggle, the endless bickering to defy them in this. It takes too much out of you.' She repeated it several times. 'It is not worth it.'

Surprisingly Baron Stockmar counselled the same.

He examined the problem as soon as he arrived and came to the conclusion it was a small matter. The King was intelligent enough to see that such a letter, though signed by his niece, had certainly not been written by her. In this he was right.

As soon as the King read it, he said immediately: 'Victoria has not written that letter.' He sent for the Prime Minister and showed him the letter. 'My brother's widow is determined to vex me,' he complained. 'So I charge you, Melbourne, to deal with her.'

Lord Melbourne accepted the letter with the greatest reluctance. Of all things he wished to avoid being involved in royal squabbles. But he was the King's principal servant. He understood and recognized his obligations, and he undertook to look into the affair and be as discreet as the circumstances allowed.

'Discretion don't matter in the least,' gasped the King. 'But hurry, my lord, hurry. I haven't much time.'

173

44

On May 24th the King smiled as soon as he woke up. He smiled all through the doctors' morning examination. He smiled when his valet shaved him, so broadly that twice he was nicked and blood trickled down over his double chins. And he smiled throughout the day. His sister-in-law had been beaten by the calendar. The Princess Victoria was eighteen and of age. Unless the Regency Act was altered, the Duchess of Kent could never rule in England.

At Kensington a long white banner flew at the palace flagstaff. Across it, embroidered in letters of gold, was the one word VICTORIA. By the King's command her birthday was a public holiday. The Kensington lanes were strung with bunting and decorated with flowers, and all through the morning deputations waited on the Princess bringing their congratulations and good wishes. Victoria, dressed as for a ball, received them in the Great Saloon and kept silent while her mother made speech after speech. Members of the deputations were bewildered. Victoria herself was extremely embarrassed. How could her mother be so insensible to other people's feelings? Why had no one advised her to keep silent or, at best, say only a few words? It would have been more suitable. As it was, the Duchess reminded her listeners of the great personal sacrifices she had made in remaining in England to bring up her daughter for the English throne. She emphasized the cost of doing this effectively. She presented herself in the rosiest of colours and she hardly mentioned Victoria at all. At the end of this paean of self-praise from the Duchess, Victoria quietly thanked the visitors for their good wishes and waited for the next deputation to be ushered in and a further display from her mother.

After a humiliating morning, Victoria drove out with Lehzen and a maid of honour. She disliked the idea of showing herself off, but the people expected it on this important day and she knew it was her duty to oblige them. She half-expected her mother to go with them to draw the crowd's attention to herself but fortunately she refrained from proposing it.

That evening, though, the Duchess was determined to be right at the centre of interest at Victoria's birthday ball at St James's. Neither the King nor the Queen could be there, and so the honours were done by the oldest unmarried daughter of George III, the Princess Augusta. The Duchess of Kent, however, soon took over the management of things. She attracted attention from all sides by making Princess Augusta look thoroughly foolish, and then by openly sneering at the King's hospitality which she said was shocking and parsimonious. Amongst the guests she found targets for her malice and displeasure, pointing them out to Sir John and a small circle of toadies, and whispering things about them behind her hand.

Victoria saw it all; the looks, the whispering, and the mockery and found herself in tears. In law she was now free, a mature woman ready to receive the full powers as Queen Regnant of England. In fact, she was still a girl made wretched by her mother's louche behaviour.

45

Despite the King's indifference to discretion, Lord Melbourne thought the matter needed tactful handling and especially when he heard from Wellington that Conroy was trying to make it a party matter. Tories in and out of Parliament were being pestered to use all their influence to further his schemes.

'The rascal's desperate,' said the Duke. 'Must be to bring the girl up a Whig and suddenly change sides at this stage.'

Melbourne agreed. 'They'd change anything to get their way. Conroy wants the Private Secretaryship; she wants a new Regency Act; both are out to be rich, and both are implacably hostile to the King.'

'Then something must be done,' said Wellington.

They put their heads together, and tried a compromise.

They suggested to the Duchess that only £4,000 out of the King's offer of £10,000 should be for Victoria's private expenditure. The remainder could be used as she wished by the Duchess herself.

A curt refusal arrived from Kensington. The Duchess refused to entertain the idea of Victoria controlling any part of the £10,000. Ironically the letter was signed by Victoria.

'Tiresome woman!' snapped the Duke.

Lord Melbourne was equally acid, but he was coarser.

Cheerfully they would have left the matter at that, but both had a strong sense of duty to the King. They discussed further possibilities. Then Melbourne had an idea.

'If they really are leaning Torywards,' he said, 'why not send an old family friend who is a Tory to settle the quarrel?'

'Liverpool?' said the Duke quickly.

'Exactly. They have stayed at his home and his daughter Lady Catherine is one of the Duchess's ladies.'

'Excellent,' exclaimed the Duke. 'I will arrange it.'

Lord Liverpool's instructions were explicit. He was to find out exactly how matters stood at Kensington and do all he could as a mediator.

He was astounded to find that only the barest civilities were being maintained in the Kent apartments. The Duchess and her daughter had not spoken to one another for days.

His first interview was with the Duchess and not particularly successful. She greeted him as an old friend and repeated *ad nauseam* her claims to be Regent and continue looking after Victoria. Nothing he said could make her change her mind. She insisted on her rights as a mother.

Liverpool's talk with Conroy was equally unsatisfactory. He began by squashing the Comptroller's chief ambition. He was empowered, he said, to say the Prime Minister had already decided to advise the Princess not to have an official Private Secretary. Instead he would act as her confidential adviser, and a Privy Purse, with no political power, would be appointed to attend to minor matters.

Conroy's face fell. Then abruptly, and to Liverpool's dismay and disgust, he suggested the Princess would require a Private Secretary because there were serious reasons to doubt her sanity. He elaborated. The family history of lunacy was well known. To those who knew the Princess well and were in a position to judge, her actions and manner had been noticeably quaint of late. 'She could not possibly manage without a Private Secretary,' he insisted. 'Her tastes are frivolous, and she thinks of little but dresses and fashion. Believe me, my lord, she is in almost every way immature and undependable.'

Liverpool said he would prefer to judge that for himself. For the moment he could do no more than repeat Lord Melbourne's decision. There would be no Private Secretary.

Conroy immediately asked for the Privy Purse.

'Maybe, Sir John; maybe.' Liverpool would make no promise. He could not, he said. But he would bear the request in mind. And now, if the Comptroller would be so good as to take him to the Princess Victoria's apartments, he would like to have a talk with her royal highness.

That evening Lord Liverpool wrote an account of his visit and went to see the Duke and the Prime Minister. Lord Melbourne had just returned from Windsor with grave news of the King.

'He is close to the end,' he told them. 'But he is struggling to keep alive until the 18th. Of all things he wants to see another Waterloo Day; but, whatever happens, the banquet is to go forward. He made me tell you this, your grace.'

Wellington was noticeably affected. 'The sons of George the Third,' he declared, 'have been villains, buffoons, exquisites and macaronis, and the damnedest nuisances to any sovereign state, but by God they've all a sense of occasion. They know about glory, by God. By God they do.' He blew his nose. 'Now, Liverpool, tell us about your arbitration.'

'It is hardly that, your grace, but I did make some discoveries.'

He told of Conroy's conversation.

Melbourne stirred restlessly. 'He must have few wits and be at the end of those to insinuate the Princess is a lunatic.'

Liverpool grimaced. 'I share your distaste, my lord.' He went on to tell them about his talk with Victoria. 'I saw her alone, a procedure which I believe is unusual, and she struck me at once as extremely tense. She has, maybe, an extravagant force of temperament, but fortunately for me she also has a remarkable simplicity of vision and was very lucid. Without demur she accepted your advice that she do without a Private Secretary, but . . .' The Earl spread his hands. 'My goodness, when I hinted that it might be as well to make Conroy her Privy Purse she went white with pent-up rage. I hardly had time to point out the office would be unimportant and she need see little of him, before she was listing his iniquities, as she called them, the many slights and incivilities she has had to bear through the years.'

'The years?' broke in Wellington. 'Is she a vengeful young woman?'

'I judge that, yes; very probably she is. Certainly she has not forgotten a single harm done her by Conroy. And she insisted that I ask my daughter for confirmation.'

'Did you?' asked Melbourne.

'I thought it quite unnecessary,' replied Liverpool, 'but I did. And Catherine vouched for the truth of what the Princess had said. There was one ambiguity, though, which I did not mention to my daughter.' He looked through his notes on the conversation. 'Yes, here it is.' He adjusted his spectacles and quoted: ' "The Princess said she knew things of Sir John which rendered it totally impossible for her to place him in any confidential situation near her." ' He laid down the memorandum and his spectacles.

Melbourne and the Duke exchanged glances.

'How does she know?' asked the Duke.

Liverpool offered him the memorandum. 'It is written here,' he said. 'If my memory serves me correctly her actual words were: "I know this of myself without any other person informing me." '

'Poor child,' said the Duke.

'Wellington,' said Melbourne sharply. 'We mustn't be sentimental. She is a Hanoverian who are a damned passionate lot, and we have all gone through these sort of shocks ourselves. They stun us for a time, but we come round.'

The Duke recognized how many shocks of this kind Lord Melbourne had had to sustain. He had borne a great many himself. After a moment he said: 'Yes, I see your point of view.'

'And I agree,' said Liverpool. 'From her behaviour today I should say the Princess was robust. In no way did she give me the impression of being a frail innocent. Yet her experience accounts for her implacable hostility to Conroy.'

Wellington nodded. 'But if she won't take him as Privy Purse how are we to settle it?'

'What would you recommend, Liverpool?' asked the Prime Minister. 'After your visit today.'

Lord Liverpool shrugged. Then, to Melbourne's great relief he said: 'I don't believe I can recommend anything, for nothing useful can be done at present. It is simply a question of waiting ...'

All three were silent then, as they thought of the old King; gasping and wheezing on his bed at Windsor.

46

Everyone was waiting.

Victoria was composed. 'Keep your mind *cool* and *easy*,' wrote King Leopold in some agitation from Belgium. 'Be *not alarmed* at the prospect of becoming perhaps sooner than we expected Queen.' He underestimated his niece. She was not in the least alarmed by that particular responsibility. Living, though, at Kensington while she waited was intensely difficult. After Lord Liverpool's visit she declared she would eat with Lehzen in her room. The Duchess at once forbade it, then abruptly changed her mind. 'What is the point?' she asked Sir John, and he, agreeing, said the table would be far more pleasant without Victoria pouting and looking sullen in her place.

He made one last attempt and called on the Speaker of the House of Commons, hoping for his help in persuading Victoria to promise him the Privy Purse. But that gentleman said he could do nothing under the present circumstances. His thoughts were at Windsor. He too was waiting.

Baron Stockmar only called occasionally at Kensington. He was not welcomed by the Duchess, who now considered him a spy, and he was unable to be of much service to the Princess. When she was Queen Regnant he would be there, his experience and philosophy at her disposal. For the moment he could only wait.

Ernest, Duke of Cumberland sat at a desk writing. He was listing the particular household pieces he wished to take to Hanover. The majority of the furniture could be left behind in his apartments at St James's Palace. He had no intention of taking his family into permanent exile, but for a time it would be a relief to get away from England. It was uncomfortable to be so liked and so disliked; made much of by right-wing Tories and hissed at by the mob every time he rode or drove through the streets. Once outside the House of Lords they had dragged him from his horse, but he had given a very good account of himself and thrashed them with his crop. It would be peaceful to reign in Hanover. Soon he would be king. It was only a question of waiting.

Caroline Norton prepared the Prime Minister's supper dishes with her own hands. He enjoyed his food and she went out of her way to please him, choosing Severn salmon, sea trout, lobsters, small rosy flounders, well-hung lamb, baked ham, veal pies, asparagus and cherries. By a happy chance the gulls had laid two clutches that year. Of all things he loved gulls' eggs, cold with watercress or hot and sauced with pepper cream. He had them as often as he wished. It could not be for much longer. Soon she knew she would see so much less of him for he was to act as Private Secretary to the young Queen as well as be Prime Minister. Their friendship would not alter in the slightest but their ways would separate for the time being. It was inevitable. Making the most of those last days, she waited for them to end.

* * *

The Duchess of Kent's patience snapped on the eve of Waterloo Day. She sent for her daughter and demanded that she give Sir John Conroy the post he deserved. 'This is my command as your mother.'

Victoria said not a word. She curtseyed and turned to leave the room.

'Undutiful wretch,' cried her mother. 'Stay where you are until you have my permission to retire.' Eventually Victoria was allowed to leave, but the Duchess's bad temper was not worked out. Later in the day she gave the abrupt command that her daughter was to be locked up. If Victoria would not be obedient she should suffer for it. Happily Charles Leiningen prevented it. He said they had gone far enough. They could do nothing more.

It was a lovely June. Queen Adelaide had the windows opened so that the King could see the tops of the trees in the Great Park. But he did not look at them. In the rare moments of peace from the turmoil of fighting for breath, he gaped at the ceiling, too tired even to close his mouth.

His wish was granted and he lived to see another Waterloo Day. Wellington sent down the tricolour flag to Windsor with his humble duty and loyalty. The King was deeply moved when he saw the flag and he moved his mouth. It was dry. Too dry to speak. The Queen hastily moistened his lips and in a little while he found his voice. 'Unfurl it,' he said to his eldest son, Lord Munster. 'And let me feel it.' His fingers touched the cloth. He was too feeble to clutch it. 'Glorious day,' he said, two tears stealing from his eyes. 'A glorious, glorious day.' Then he closed his eyes and in a short time was racked with gasping and wheezing. All he wanted now was to die; to escape from the strangulation in his chest and throat and the terrible pain at the bottom of his right lung. All he wanted was to die. But he, too, had to wait.

On the 19th, Victoria went to her mother and asked if they could drive down to see the King at Windsor. 'It would be a kindness to Aunt Adelaide, Mamma; and I should like to see my uncle before he dies.'

The Duchess was aghast. 'Certainly not,' she cried. 'Whatever will you think of next? How indelicate, how indiscreet it would be! Why, child, they will all think you have gone to see if the crown fits. Why, no, it would never do at all.'

Victoria flushed. 'Does it matter what they think, Mamma? My uncle and aunt have been very kind to me. I should like to see them today.'

'Would never do at all,' replied her mother firmly. 'You must be patient, child, and wait.'

Outside the King's room the Duke of Sussex mopped at his eyes with a handkerchief. He had seen his brother given the Last Sacrament and had heard the Archbishop praying. Then he had said goodbye. Of all his family, William had been the dearest. Life without him would not be quite the same.

'Augustus, for shame, to let the people see you weep.' It was his sister Mary, Duchess of Gloucester.

'And why not? I care not a fig if they think me a booby. I grieve for William.' Then he saw that she was crying, too. He blew his nose and took her arm. 'Come, we will go outside. It is a most beautiful June evening. There we can weep together.'

Four hours later the exhausted King took his eldest son by the hand. 'The Church,' he said softly, and then again in a louder voice. 'The Church.'

Then he died.

PART THREE

1

The porter at the lodge gates of Kensington Palace was woken out of a deep sleep. His bell was clanging and jumping. He dragged on his breeches and went outside to see who was making the uproar.

A postilion was tugging on the bell. He jumped with fright when the porter shouted at him through the grille.

'Give a bit of warning next time,' he said. 'Took me right by surprise, you did.'

'And what was you a-doing? Ding-donging on my bell at this hour of the morning.'

'Nibs,' said the postilion, nodding over his shoulder.

The porter focused his sleepy eyes on a carriage. The horses were sweating profusely.

'Who?'

'The Lord Chamberlain and the Archbishop of Canterbury and a doctor.'

'And I'm the King of the French.'

'Fact,' urged the other. 'Honour bright.'

The porter thought about this for a moment. 'What do they want?' he asked.

'Look, are you paid?' asked the postilion. 'Do you work here? Do you open gates?'

'All right, all right,' grumbled the porter. He went into his lodge to get a key. With one hand keeping his breeches up he unlocked the gates and swung them open. Being one-handed it took a long time and at the last moment he had to jump hard in order to avoid being run over. The carriage whirled through the gates and up the straight drive to the Clock Court. Again there was difficulty in waking the courtyard porter. The postilion rang and thumped and kicked at the doors. Then the porter refused point blank to believe what he was told.

Scarlet with indignation the postilion shouted: 'Open, you

zany! Have you nothing but cloth between your ears? We're not come from Windsor to be held up now. OPEN UP!'

The porter was at last persuaded when through his grille he caught sight of a gentleman in a clerical wig alighting from the coach. It might be any clerical gentleman, but just in case it was the Archbishop, he creaked open the doors. At the same time he sent a message into the palace.

Lord Conyngham, Archbishop Howley and Sir Henry Halford had galloped the whole way from Windsor to greet Victoria as their Queen. To be delayed by the slowness of sleep-befuddled servants was almost too much for Conyngham. He fretted and fumed and was especially angry when a servant came to say they could not see the Princess.

'Who sent this message?' he demanded.

'Her royal highness the Duchess,' replied the servant. 'She says the Princess is asleep and cannot be disturbed.'

'Young woman,' said Conyngham. 'Return to your royal mistress and say that we are here to see her majesty the Queen upon Affairs of State.'

The pattering of feet, then a swish as curtains were drawn back, half woke Victoria. With her eyes still closed she turned in the bed wondering why her mother should be by her bed. She knew it was her mother because she was being called 'Drina.

Victoria fought down her longing to drift away into sleep. She made an effort and opened her eyes. Bright sunlight pouring through the windows made her close them involuntarily.

' 'Drina! I insist, you must get up.'

'What is it, Mamma?'

'There are some gentlemen to see you.'

Victoria opened her eyes and sat up. She looked at her father's watch which hung at her bedhead.

'The Archbishop of Canterbury, Lord Conyngham and Sir Henry Halford.'

So it had come.

'Very well, Mamma,' she said. 'I will be with you directly.'

The Duchess left the room. Victoria slipped her feet out of bed and into a pair of slippers, took off her nightcap, adjusted her hair and put on a peignoir. She could hear someone in the next room waking Lehzen. She went to the window and looked out into the Park. Already there were heat shimmers over the lawns.

So it had come.

Her lip trembled, not because she was Queen of England but because her uncle was dead. In his odd way he had tried to look after her. She had much to thank him for.

There was a rustle. Lehzen was beside her. There in the morning light she curtseyed low to Victoria and kissed her hand. Victoria raised her to her feet and kissed her cheek.

'Dearest Lehzen.'

'Your mother is waiting,' said Lehzen quietly. 'Come.'

She led the young girl from the room. Outside they were joined by the Duchess of Kent. The corridor was still in close-curtained darkness. Lehzen slipped back into the room for a small candlestick, and while she was there seized a bottle of sal volatile. She gave the candlestick to Victoria and the three of them walked down the staircase and on to the room where the gentlemen from Windsor were waiting.

Victoria went in alone.

2

'What the devil were they about?' said the Prime Minister wearily.

The Melbourne carriage bowled along the road from London.

His secretary shook his head. 'Perhaps, my lord, they were carried away by the hour and the circumstances?' he suggested.

'An archbishop, a lord chamberlain, and an elderly respected doctor should have known better. Waking the girl unnecessarily. Melodrama. Fuss and bother. If they've thrown her into a tizzy, what are we to do?'

Lord Melbourne found he had no cause to be anxious. His carriage reached Kensington at nine o'clock and he was at once shown into the Queen's presence. He bowed low and was moving to kiss her hand when he found it was already under his nose. Such aplomb in so young a girl was rather extraordinary. He kissed the hand. It was very small and very soft. She then sat down and evidently felt no uneasiness at seeing him stand. Steadily and without a tremor she said it was her intention to retain him and the rest of the ministry at the head of affairs.

Melbourne was astonished. He realized he was listening, of course, to Stockmar, but even the good baron – for whom Melbourne had the highest admiration – could not have taught the girl her poise, her charm, her regality. These were natural.

'Ma'am,' he said. 'The ministry will serve you loyally and to the very best of its ability.' And it did not seem in the slightest bit odd that he, a tall and well made man of fifty-eight, should so address a small girl young enough to be his granddaughter.

He told her that he had already sent out the summonses to Privy Councillors. 'With his late majesty in so unhappy a state I had them drawn up and prepared,' he explained. 'The crown lawyers insist there be a Council as swiftly as possible. Has Baron Stockmar acquainted your majesty with the procedure?'

Yes, she told him, Stockmar had explained that a deputation would tell her officially that King William the Fourth was dead, and then she would have to make a declaration.

'I have it here, Ma'am.' Melbourne took a sheaf of papers from his tail-coat.

Victoria thought it an odd place in which to keep such an important document and was amused to see it kept company with letters, banknotes, memoranda of one kind or another, and – if she was not mistaken – a bill or two. Solemnly she took the declaration from him and read it out.

'Well done, very well done, Ma'am. Perhaps a little more force towards the end, eh? We've a number of deaf Councillors.'

He sorted through some more papers until he found a

memorandum from Greville, Clerk to the Council. 'With your permission, Ma'am?'

She bowed.

'Council to be held in the Red Saloon . . .' he murmured, and read silently for a moment. 'Yes, here we are. Now, would you like to be accompanied by the great Officers of State or will you enter the saloon alone?'

Instantly came the reply. 'Alone, if that is in order.'

'Quite in order, Ma'am. Quite in order.'

They talked of one or two more matters, and then Melbourne bowed his way out, promising to be at hand to answer any questions she might have.

Very few at that first Council of the reign knew what to expect from their new Queen. She was an enigma to the large majority and even those who did know her in varying degrees of intimacy were not in the least prepared for the magnificent way in which she entered the Red Saloon at eleven o'clock that morning.

The great doors were opened. Quite alone, a small neat figure dressed in black walked gracefully into the room and curtseyed to her assembled Councillors. There was an impressive silence. The Queen's uncles, the new King of Hanover and the Duke of Sussex, moved from their places to greet her; both of them massive and towering over their tiny niece. They led her to her seat at the head of a long table. Then the silence broke and there was a subdued hubbub all round the room.

The impression Victoria had made upon the company was extraordinary. It was also lasting. The Duke of Wellington wiped a tear from his eyes. Had she been his own dearest daughter he could not have desired her to play the part of Queen so well. Simply by picking up the declaration laid on the table before her, she immediately silenced the murmurers and the whispers. In a calm, clear voice she read her declaration: keeping it strong, as Melbourne noted with satisfaction, especially towards the end.

When her uncles knelt before her to kiss hands and give their allegiance, her pose was momentarily shaken. Seeing the whiskered grim face of her Uncle Cumberland and the dear familiar face of Uncle Sussex in positions of abasement, she flushed to the roots of her hair. It was only temporary. With the same calm gravity as before she sat there while Wellington and Peel and Melbourne and Palmerston were sworn in and kissed her hand. There seemed, she said afterwards, a very large number of gentlemen.

Then she retired. The double doors closed behind her and instantly the Red Saloon buzzed with excited chatter.

Viscount Melbourne saw the Queen several times that day. On each occasion he tried his best to help her in what, he considered, was an exceedingly difficult situation. He counselled moderation. It echoed King Leopold's advice. But Victoria frankly enjoyed her power. She found out from Stockmar and from Melbourne how far within discretion she could go, and to that limit she went. She gave audiences to the great Officers of State and to her ministers. She wanted to reward Lehzen for her loyal and constant service and have her always near at hand to be her closest confidante and friend. Lehzen wisely refused a grand title saying it would make other people jealous. She also very wisely suggested that, as the ladies-in-waiting and women of the bedchamber held political appointments, her tenure would be more secure if she was given an unofficial post. Lord Melbourne agreed, warmly commending the Baroness's prudence. Between them they concocted a new post and Lehzen became Lady Attendant on the Queen. Victoria also appointed Dr Clark to the Queen's household. And without any qualms she dismissed Sir John Conroy.

Conroy's sun was setting, but he picked up what he could while there was still a little light. He buttonholed Stockmar with a message to pass on to the Prime Minister: 'Make it clear, Baron, that though our brand-new Queen has dispensed with my services, she cannot easily dispense with my company. She cannot dismiss me from her mother's household; and there I'll stay – unless my terms are met.' He pressed a paper into the Baron's hand and begged that the matter be decided at once.

Stockmar had a weakness for rascals and he was forced to smile at Conroy's temerity. Melbourne, though, was not amused. He read the list with increasing incredulity and irritation. In return for his voluntary retirement from the Duchess of Kent's household Conroy demanded a pension of £3,000 a year, the Grand Cross of the Bath, a peerage and a seat on the Privy Council. 'If we were to divide these impudent proposals by half, and agree in order to rid ourselves of a villain, they would still be too much.'

'He can work any amount of mischief in the Duchess's household,' warned Stockmar.

'Why, then, if he must, he must,' said Melbourne wearily.

Later he came to regret this decision.

The Duchess of Kent lay in her large white bed. She could not sleep. The night was too hot, and she herself was too unhappy. The events of the day had given her dyspepsia and heartache, and had thrown her into a depression.

On each occasion when she considered it her duty to support her daughter her offer had been not so much refused as disregarded. She had offered advice as well. This had been firmly spurned. Conroy had been formally dismissed. She had been obliged to leave her daughter alone on several occasions. And now, for the first time in their lives, unless they had been separated by sickness, they were sleeping apart. Without consulting anyone, without a word to her, Victoria had ordered her small bed to be removed from her mother's room. Most hurtful of all, she was sleeping in a room on the other side of Lehzen's, and depending entirely on the governess, who had flouted the Duchess again and again.

At this stage of her life the Duchess's piety was of a strictly practical nature. She prayed in emergencies. Her unhappiness and her mortification made her pray that night. She knelt up in her bed, wondering for a moment if she looked silly kneeling there wearing a frilly nightcap, but her prayer was very sincere: that her daughter's hard attitude would soften, that she would not disdain her mother and keep her at arm's length for ever.

3

'My dear,' said the Duke of Sussex to his morganatic wife Lady
Cecilia, 'depend upon it this is going to be accounted a very
special year.' He began telling off the reasons, one after the
other on his fingers. 'Fox Talbot's photography has improved
beyond belief ... We have a new patent registered for the
electric telegraph ... Plans are prepared to cross the Atlantic
with a regular steamship service ... Pitman has invented his
admirable short way of writing ... Carlyle's *French Revolution*
is a masterpiece ... There's the young man Boz keeping us in
tucks and chuckles with his Pickwick ...'

'Your grace,' interrupted the Lady Cecilia.

'My love?' said the Duke, at once all ears to her command.

'You were originally telling me of the Queen's proclamation.'

'Indeed, yes, my heart. I merely remarked that her reign
begins in an *annus mirabilis.*'

'What did she wear?'

'Eh?' The Duke gaped a little. His powers of scientific observation were never practised on such things as women's clothes.
'Why, black, of course. And very pretty she looked. Inclined to
stoutness, but, then, few in our house are thin. I was impressed
most by her demeanour: grave, as befitted so solemn an occasion and when we are all mourning poor William, but she
was also serene. One would have expected her to be uneasy,
even a little alarmed. Not a bit of it. She had as much aplomb,
if not more, than yesterday at her first Council.'

'Poor child,' said Lady Cecilia and very sincerely.

The Duke held up a hand. 'Waste no pity on Victoria, my
love. She is young enough to enjoy the eminence of sovereignty
without yet feeling the loneliness of it. Her childhood was
cracklingly dull. Moreover, considering all things, for the heir to
so great a crown it was curiously mean. For years she has
dreamt of the day when the dullness would be over. And

yesterday as the trumpets sounded and we all raised our hats she was the shabby little girl transported into a glittering queen. I could see it in her eyes. They betray her sometimes. They were full of glory and wonder and triumph. For the time being anyway she will enjoy being Queen.'

'Bless her,' said Lady Cecilia.

To which the Duke replied with feeling: 'Amen.'

4

Three days after her proclamation Victoria drove down to Windsor. She had already given an audience to the Earl Marshal and Garter King at Arms about her uncle's funeral. It remained to visit the Castle, where his remains lay in state, and give her condolences to the Queen Dowager.

Despite her morbid interest in *mementoes mori* she did not enjoy this visit. The royal standard hung limply at half mast.

Queen Adelaide received her with a kiss and a few tears and led her to her own apartments. She was obviously determined to be brave.

Knowing how strong the affection had been between them, Victoria suffered for her aunt. Not only had she lost the man she loved best, but her homes, too, and her high station were all forfeit at his death. Victoria shrank from the thought that by inheriting the crown she was taking so much from her aunt.

In a businesslike way she discussed the arrangements that had been made for the King's funeral: she also discussed her aunt's future. Being businesslike was an excellent cure for low spirits.

Amongst the dispatches waiting for her on her return from Windsor was a letter which made her feel a little thrill of excitement. She read it before the others.

My dearest cousin, I must write you a few lines to present you my sincerest felicitations on that great change which has taken place in your life.

She clasped the letter to her breast for a moment. Prince Albert had been too often driven from her thoughts by the great events which had recently taken place. And he belonged there. She was sure of it. How agreeable he was to write so quickly.

She read on, skimming over the inevitable theological parts, hoping there would be something more personal. There was.

May I pray you to think sometimes of your cousins in Bonn, and to continue to them that kindness you favoured them with till now.

Albert no doubt considered he had been very daring, but what he said made Victoria frown. Had she not made her preference clear? Had not her uncle done the same? Why was he shyly writing of 'your cousins' as though Ernest was on an equal footing?

At that moment Baron Stockmar came in to help with her official work. She showed him the letter. This surprised him for he had guessed at the tender feelings she had for Prince Albert. He read the letter and tried to reassure her. The Prince was not blowing cold; neither was he being politely slow in his approach. It was the mode. Victoria tossed her head. If that was the German way of doing things, it was a very bad one. She preferred people to be outspoken, and to keep a situation moving. Taking backward steps and dodging the point had no place in her idea of friendship.

She put the letter on one side and proposed they get on with the official work. It was all so new and so interesting. Stockmar left the matter at that. He saw how fascinated she was by the paperwork of power and how quickly she forgot the pique which Albert's letter had caused her. He wondered privately if it would be very long before she forgot Albert himself.

5

Victoria enjoyed almost every aspect of being Queen. She liked the ceremonial. She liked being at the centre of things. She liked the formal courts at St James's and the day-to-day state affairs which were her constant concern. As much as anything she enjoyed exerting her power in independent ways. One of her first commands was to remove the hated Alexandrina from her official title. Henceforth she was to be known simply as Victoria.

As soon as she could she paid off her father's debts and gave personal presents to those creditors who had waited so patiently for their money. She was also considerate to her late uncle's bastard children, providing them with a substantial income from her privy purse. Lord Munster, the eldest, came to thank her on their behalf. They were all touched, he said, with so kindly a gesture, which was quite unasked for.

'My lord,' she said. 'Had circumstances been otherwise and had fortune played you better, our situations might have been reversed. I have your father's crown. It is only just that you and your brothers and sisters should have something of his private fortune.'

She felt very daring to spend so much money all at once and would hardly believe Lord Melbourne when he told her she could well afford it. 'You are not only rich, Ma'am,' he told her, 'but very, very, very rich indeed.' He directed the late King's Privy Purse and Confidential Secretary to make the position clear to her.

Such sudden riches after a lifetime of dancing grotesquely between luxury and parsimony were quite bewildering. So was her power to make decisions when up to that time almost every decision had been made by her mother, Lehzen, and the Duchess of Northumberland. She took an inordinate pleasure in commanding fresh supplies of Madeira and biscuits when the Prime Minister called, particularly as the previous supplies were fresh enough and, anyway, he never touched either. Feeling power was delicious. She confessed as much to Lord Melbourne.

'So it is, Ma'am; but it has to be kept within bounds.'

Already he was able to say this sort of thing without causing the least offence.

Victoria regarded her First Minister very much as a father. King Leopold had been her second. Melbourne was undoubtedly her third. But as there was no blood relationship between them she could not be so demonstrative as she had been with Uncle Leopold. She had to keep the Prime Minister at a certain distance and interview him with what Lehzen termed 'becoming gravity', which was not at all her inclination. With his soft voice and curling hair and beautiful eyes he had much the same effect on her as Luigi Lablache. But his eyebrows and whiskers were more luxuriant and he had a soft baby-face which made him look innocent and sad and gentle all at once. In full Court rig and with his commanding height he was an impressive looking man. That his character matched his appearance, and that he was invariably courteous and patient with her stupidities was a miracle to Victoria. She might so easily have inherited a very different kind of First Minister – perhaps a cantankerous intellectual who would have frightened her with his anger, or a condescending, jolly sort of man who would have teased her ineptitude and kept her in ignorance to secure his own position. Lord Melbourne was different; a patient intellectual who liked to share her pleasures and was always ready with information, advice, and if he felt she needed it, a warning.

Not long after her accession she discovered he had once been offered the Garter and an earldom by King William and had refused the honour. She repeated the offer, begging him to accept to please her. But still he refused. Viscounts, he said, were rarer birds than belted earls and he was quite content as he was.

Nevertheless he was touched and said so. 'Serving you, Ma'am, is all the honour I could require.'

Victoria thought him the most gallant and thoughtful First Minister any sovereign could hope to possess.

'How lucky we are, dear Lehzen, to have Lord Melbourne as our friend.'

This was said more than once. On the first two or three occasions Lehzen pursed her lips. In her opinion young oil of eighteen and old water of fifty-eight did not make a satisfactory mixture, and it became noticeable that Victoria spoke less and less of Albert. Then Lehzen examined the situation honestly and critically. She was not really concerned with Prince Albert. She had kept her promise to King Leopold by saying nothing against the Prince, but privately she considered him ponderous and too inclined to give way and demand sympathy. Ultimately she admitted to herself that Victoria's continual praise of the Prime Minister was pricking her disposition to be jealous. It hurt her to see the girl depending more and more on someone else, even someone so charming and gay and urbane as Lord Melbourne. But time and custom helped. She grew used to seeing him every day at Kensington and his private messenger arriving at any hour with confidential letters for the Queen. Melbourne was indeed assiduous. No one could have done more to assist a young sovereign at the beginning of her reign and Lehzen found herself increasingly grateful to him for all he did for her beloved Victoria. He was Prime Minister, Private Secretary, mentor and guide. Lehzen's smarting jealousy was finally liquidated by her growing concern for Melbourne himself. He was too overworked and too elderly to be riding backwards and forwards, backwards and forwards between London and Kensington Palace. It would be much easier for him when they moved to Buckingham House.

At no stage in her life did Victoria ever do anything by half. It was a characteristic which made her some enemies but endeared her to many more friends. Her move from Kensington Palace was typical of this. She was frank with Lord Melbourne. She simply wanted to get away from her mother. But the Prime Minister was equally frank. He told her it would give an undesirable impression at an early stage in the reign. If the Queen moved to Buckingham House, the Duchess would have to be given a suite of apartments under the same roof. Two households in close proximity would tend to quarrel, said the Queen.

Could her mother not live at St James's Palace? The King of Hanover had apartments there which he would soon be vacating. On the contrary, replied Melbourne, his majesty King Ernest had made it plain he was holding on to his English possessions. And it was vital for the Queen, as a young unmarried lady, to live in the same palace as her mother.

Victoria was bound to accept his advice, though she did so with bad grace.

She inspected Buckingham House – a Nash house ordered by George IV and never lived in either by him or by his brother King William. Few people seemed to like the building. Everything had been sacrificed to the stone façade including the convenience of getting from one state room to another. It was necessary sometimes to disappear through small doors into unseemly back passages in order to reach a saloon or a banqueting hall. King William had considered it a most ill-contrived house, and gleefully tried to give it to the nation when the Houses of Parliament were burnt down. Because they had refused his offer, Victoria now found herself mistress of this huge conglomeration of rooms and corridors with rows and rows of raspberry-coloured pillars. It still had an unfinished look. There were housemaids scrubbing the floors, and men laying carpets, but the Queen found a suite of apartments for her mother which could effectively cut her off from the rooms she had chosen herself, and, moreover, Dash liked the place. Some of her courtiers might call the place 'Brunswick Hotel' and express their disgust at the flaws in its design and decoration. Having so little taste herself she was less pretentious. The place would give her a new freedom and her dog liked it. That was that. Henceforth it was to be known as Buckingham Palace.

From the Queen's journal dated Thursday, July 15th:

Got up at 8. At ½ p 9 we breakfasted. It was the *last time* that I slept in the poor old Palace, as I go into Buckingham Palace today. Though I rejoice to *go* into B.P. for many reasons, it is not without feelings of regret that I shall bid adieu *for ever* (that is to say *for ever* as a DWELLING), to this

197

my birthplace, where I have been born and bred, and to which I am really attached! ... I have gone through painful and disagreeable scenes here, 'tis true, but still I am fond of the poor old Palace.

6

Lehzen took a great delight in her new post. She made copies of Victoria's most private correspondence, was always available to advise and explain, and without in any way offending the Mistress of the Robes and the First Lady of the Bedchamber, she became *grand-mère* to the household ladies. She was admired and looked up to by them all, loved by not a few. Whenever a girl was appointed to the household her mother would be sure to urge her to confide in and depend on the highly respected Lady Attendant. Even caraway eating, though the seeds were not to everyone's taste, had a passing mode. Lehzen's good sense and good humour assured an armistice between the Duchess of Kent's household and that of the Queen. Only one member of the former was never under any circumstances admitted to Court or the Queen's table, and in petty revenge Conroy stirred up as much mischief as he could.

It was Lehzen who advised Victoria to give way to at least a part of his demands. He was given his pension and a baronetcy, and the promise of an Irish Peerage when there should be a vacancy. It mollified him. He continued to enjoy spiteful gossip in the Duchess of Kent's drawing-room and she gave it out publicly that his daughter Victoire had been promised a place and the promise had not been honoured; but for a time his sting had been drawn.

Victoria was entirely free to enjoy herself, and that is exactly what she did.

Two months after her accession, and for the first time in two years, she began riding again; and she soon instituted the habit of taking a daily ride or drive wherever she happened to be. Sometimes she was accompanied by her mother or by the Lady Attendant in a pony phaeton, but she relished most mad gallops across the countryside with Melbourne and the gentlemen of her household. The Prime Minister was vexed with her because of the risks she ran. Her neck, he told her, was too important to England to chance at daily hazards. She promised to be careful and took less risks for a week or so, but then she forgot and took the gentlemen at such a tremendous rate across the parks that one of her favourite courtiers, Lord Alfred Pages, spoke of her as Boadicea. Being with Melbourne out on a gallop was one of her greatest delights.

She had many other pleasures.

She enjoyed the company of her ladies. Lord Melbourne had nominated the majority who were from great Whig families, but she had homely, ordinary girls as well, such as the Dean's daughter, Mary Davys. Men being all important under law and in society, she had a unique female experience of being free and at liberty. She saw a great deal of her aunts Mary of Gloucester, Sophia, and Augusta – the Cordelias of their poor mad father. 'No Regans,' he would say. 'No Gonerils. All, all Cordelias.' At last she became properly acquainted with the Duke of Cambridge. He returned from being Viceroy at Hanover and he and his family were, for a time, high in her affections. Meanwhile she continued to see a great deal of the Duke of Sussex who undertook to instruct her in English pronunciation. She was anxious not to make mistakes. Mispronunciations made her seem a foreigner, and the English were sensitive to the fact that since the Middle Ages they had not had an English sovereign. She discovered that her tutelage in this respect had not been particularly sound. Her mother, for example, always spoke of the London fogs as though they rhymed with 'rogues'. She insisted on being as correct as possible. Uncle Sussex was charmed to be her teacher. She also worked hard at statecraft with Stockmar and Lord Melbourne, and this with such men was a pleasure too. Finally she delighted in the royal round. Already she had become attached to sameness. Routine meant stability and, though she pined sometimes to go to the continent – against which Lord Melbourne set his face – she preferred regularity to adventurousness. She enjoyed the elaborate banquets followed by chess and whist at Buckingham Palace. She enjoyed the summer at Windsor and inviting her Uncle Leopold to come over with his Queen and their tiny child, another Leopold. She enjoyed two autumn months at Brighton, though not because of the exotic Chinoiserie which had so intrigued her uncle. Then came the return to Buckingham Palace and the completion of the year.

Almost always Melbourne was there. In her journal the Queen began to write of him as 'Lord M.'. Not even Lehzen knew how she thought of him in her heart.

7

'Caroline, you do not think it gauche of me to tell you this?'

'No.' Mrs Norton looked solemnly up into his face. 'Truly, William, I do not. Were I made ill with jeaousy it would be apparent to you. But I have small belief that affairs are heaven-made, nor do I have a belief in total relationships. The Queen has a precious part of you which I can never have. Yet the reverse is also true. Were you to give a scruple of my own special share of your love to anyone I should fight her and you with all my strength. But it would be childish, worse, it would be spiteful, to throw an attack of the vapours because you love a different person in an entirely different fashion from the way you care for me.'

'You are generous, noble,' he said, and he meant it.

'Nonsense. I am being severely practical. I repeat, I should be a hellcat in defence of what is mine, but she has not laid a finger on your affection for me. Indeed, perhaps I should thank her. The depth of your feelings for her has enhanced what you feel for me. Is that not so?'

He smiled down at her. 'You have a woman's way of seeing things, and I confess it is beyond my understanding. But I thank you, dear Caroline, with all my heart for hearing my prattle. I can confide in so few.'

'Prattle of love,' said Caroline, 'with the sound of desert fountains, makes the sweetest music in the world.'

When he had gone, leaving discreetly from the tradesmen's gate and accompanied by a footman, she rang for her maid to prepare her for bed. While her hair was being done she relaxed with closed eyes thinking of her dear William. He had become so pliable and down-like, and was so sweetly affectionate about his pretty young Queen. Again and again he had called himself the most fortunate man under the sky, because he, a man of fifty-eight with all the drawbacks of his age and temperament, and despite the sovereign and subject relationship between them, should have attracted the love of so admirable and so young a girl. Caroline – and quite dispassionately – held the contrary view, that the Queen was the most fortunate of young women to attract so estimable and cultivated a man as her William. She smiled. He had been so indignant when telling her of the Duchess of Kent's birthday present to the Queen: a cheap edition of *King Lear* with a passage underscored – 'How sharper than a serpent's tooth it is to have a thankless child!' Then his manner had softened when he told her of the Queen's absorbing interest in modern novelties; wanting to know for example how a balloonist raised himself from the earth, and, having gone up, how he got down again. And no father could have been prouder of his child when he spoke of her stern refusal to follow the modern mode and make her face pallidly ethereal by having the blood drawn from behind her ears by barbers' leeches.

Dear, good William. He was so deeply happy being in love with Victoria's youth and innocence. Caroline had the unexpressed opinion that probably their Queen was something of a goose. Very probably she also made unnecessary demands upon her Prime Minister because the love of young people is always as irresponsible as it is total and breathtaking. One day she would discard him. She would have to. How she did it depended on her character. For William's sake Caroline prayed it would not be too painful a piece of surgery.

8

After twelve months, when Court mourning for King William had finished, arrangements were made for Victoria's coronation. The festivities were to include a gigantic fair, balloon ascents, the distribution of largesse, the roasting of whole oxen, three state balls, two levées, a drawing-room, and a state concert.

By custom ruling sovereigns did not attend coronations. There were exceptions. The King of Hanover was there as Duke of Cumberland, immediate heir to the crown, and the Queen's uncle. Lesser royalties in the family also attended as a matter of right. Prince Albert's father, the Duke of Saxe-Coburg, came over with Victoria's half-brother and sister, Charles and Feodore. King Leopold thought of attending but, choosing to class himself as a major royalty, he preferred to stay away and send a representative as other sovereigns did. A galaxy of princes, counts and military commanders and ministers began to arrive in London. Their suites were composed of young noblemen famed in their homeland for their grace as courtiers, their prowess as dancers, and the size of their private fortunes. These attributes, it was considered, would ensure the young Queen's enjoyment of the state balls and banquets.

Victoria moved through these hectic events apparently composed and with a supreme confidence. Inwardly she was less so. Mistakes were made as was inevitable in so gigantic a piece of administration.

It enraged Louis-Philippe's envoy Marshal Soult, an old campaigner against the Duke of Wellington, that the first state ball of the coronation also celebrated Waterloo. *Le bal de Waterloo* as the French called it, was an error of tact. Other mistakes included the maiming of three artillery men in a badly-managed salute of guns; the issuing of tickets for some seats in the Abbey which did not in fact exist; the thoughtlessness of the Mistress of the Robes who had given the trainbearers long trains themselves so that having both hands on the long, heavy train of state, they kept tripping over their own and progressed inelegantly, like a troupe of Russian dancers, up the length of the Abbey nave; the overturning of a peer so ancient that, when he climbed the steps to pay homage to the Queen, he could not keep his balance and rolled backwards again; the heavy-handedness of the Archbishop, who, not remembering and not noticing that the ruby ring had been made to fit the Queen's fifth finger, squashed it with all his force on to her fourth, and afterwards thrust the crown so heavily upon her head that he scratched and hurt her; the clumsiness of the peer who, when touching the crown before kissing her hand, prevented himself from slipping by clutching on to it and jamming it still farther on to her head; and the ineptness of the Bishop of Durham, who, placed beside the Queen to guide her through the complicated ceremonies, was, in her own words, 'remarkably maladroit, and never could tell me what was to take place'.

Yet despite all these and other calamities, the crowning was a deeply impressive and moving ceremony. The Abbey was decked out in crimson and gold, with seating made in raised tiers and galleries for the huge congregation. The brilliance of the uniforms and dresses set a colourful stage, two in particular, belonging to foreign visitors, being the most dazzling of all. A Prince Eugène Zichy was there whose uniform was encrusted all over with turquoises; and a Prince Esterházy was so covered with jewels, right down to his boots, that an observer said he looked as though he had been 'caught out in a rain of diamonds and come in dripping'. Against this splendid background the Queen, tiny and looking hardly more than twelve years old and dressed in her Parliament robes of crimson velvet furred with ermine, moved with a truly regal dignity.

The coronation proceeded through its ancient course until the moment arrived for the crowning. The trumpeters sounded a fanfare, the peers and peeresses put on their coronets, and the Archbishop presented her to her people. Again and again the congregation was moved to spontaneous bursts of cheering but as the ceremony was somewhat loosely arranged, no one appeared to mind. They cheered the Duke of Wellington when he paid homage. They cheered Melbourne as well when with tears in his eyes he kissed the Queen's hand. She was almost moved to tears herself and looked up to exchange smiles with Lehzen in a box nearby; Lehzen the faithful who had suffered so many upheavals at Kensington on her behalf, now present at her darling's coronation and with another faithful at her side – old Madame Späth brought all the way from Germany for this special day.

Victoria did not catch her mother's eye. The Duchess of Kent, feeling diminished and utterly low on this great day, was so shaken with sobs that Lady Flora had to try and balance her coronet on the top of her head. Sir John Conroy was not present.

There was a collation and wine to refresh the chief participants. The Queen was surprised, and slightly shocked by the quantity of food laid out.

'This, Ma'am,' said Lord Melbourne, drinking champagne, 'is nothing to the breakfast they gave me in the Jerusalem Chamber before your arrival. Depend upon it, Ma'am, whenever the clergy has anything to do with anything, there's sure to be plenty to eat.'

Afterwards the Queen was dressed once more with crown, sceptre and orb, and led to the Abbey porch. There she entered George III's state coach; a heavy but elegant gilt carriage of panels and glass drawn by eight cream-coloured long-tailed horses from Hanover. The procession wound through the streets by a long route so that the people could see their Queen. The huzzas and hurrahs were tremendous. They loved her instinctively. At six o'clock after an absence of eight hours, she reached the palace. The newly-crowned Queen promptly went to her private rooms and there gave Dash a bath.

9

Having spent a year at the Queen's side Baron Stockmar advised her that it was time for him to return to Belgium.

She protested that she could hardly do without him.

'You have the Prime Minister, Ma'am,' said Stockmar. 'And it is better that I should go.'

Stories were circulating about the Court which generated strong feelings that the Queen was too much under the influence of foreigners. They began in the Duchess of Kent's apartments where Conroy waged his bitter war against the Queen. Baroness Lehzen was loved too well and her position was too secure for her to be greatly harmed, but the caricaturing of Stockmar and King Leopold as a pair of sly enemies of England was more serious. Stockmar tried to hint at this, but he was not sufficiently candid and Victoria's immediate reaction was to claim belligerently that she alone was Queen and she alone would choose her advisers. It would be craven, she said, for him to leave her for such a reason.

Smiling he agreed, and subtly he suggested another reason altogether. 'We have talked of Prince Albert's education,' he reminded her. 'I should like to have the opportunity of accompanying him on a tour through Switzerland and Italy.'

She looked at him sharply. 'Quite,' she said. 'And at the same time you could persuade my uncle that as yet there is no fixed engagement between us.'

'I could do that, certainly,' said Stockmar slowly. 'But if I may be frank, Ma'am; it seems to me that you and the Prince are destined for one another.'

'Destined? No such thing. Not at all,' replied the Queen in agitation.

Discussing Albert now excited her because he seemed a threat to her present happiness. At the coronation the Duke of Saxe-Coburg had told her the sovereigns of Europe were persuaded there was an understanding between Albert and herself.

To his surprise she had snapped that the sovereigns of Europe had better be unpersuaded, and very quickly. Albert was too young for her as yet. He needed to learn English as well as many other things before she could come to any decision. In reality, as everyone knew, she was refusing to give up Lord Melbourne for a callow boy.

Stockmar calmed her down. No one, he said, either would or could force her into a distasteful marriage. It merely appeared that at the present Albert of Saxe-Coburg was the most suitable match, but the choice was entirely hers.

Eventually she said: 'Very well, yes. Perhaps it would be a good thing for you to go to Belgium. You could make my views plain to King Leopold, and you can help to improve Prince Albert.' She sighed, remembering the handsome youth who had captivated her two years before at Kensington and who fell asleep, and complained of ill health, and would not eat, and talked of little but theology. 'He needs smartening up, that's my opinion,' she added firmly to Stockmar. 'Polishing.'

The autumn and winter of 1838 was a difficult time for both Melbourne and Victoria. After her first carefree year as Queen, Victoria began to wonder if she was becoming over-frivolous. She grew low-spirited, idle and fat. At bottom she had all the puritan's suspicion of pleasure, and the dismal certainty that grief follows joy and pain pleasure just as summer follows spring. Melbourne on the other hand had been brought up in the easygoing eighteenth century. When she accused him of not going to church regularly, he cheerfully made light of it. When she said she was rather ashamed of her uncles because of their hard drinking and scandalous behaviour, he defended them and called them scallywags but jolly fellows. There was this slight discord between them, but to Melbourne she was still the girl he loved and he lacked the heart to quarrel with her.

He was a voluptuary by nature, a lover of good food and wine, a loller-about on sofas and chairs, a man who valued wit and scholarship and good taste more than most things. Yet he tolerated her grumpiness and her limitations. When she was wilful and fretful and though she weather-cocked continuously between sombre pietism and her Hanoverian blood, he was seldom vexed with her. He tried hard to direct her, instructing her in history and affairs, guiding and encouraging her in her reading, telling her anecdotes, and entertaining her with his opinions on all sorts of matters – on vaccination, on thieving boys at Eton, on the old protocol which forbade people to wear spectacles at Court, on lion taming, and on marriage. She carefully recorded his rather daring views on the last:

Lord M. said that the happiest marriages are those when the woman's taken by force.

But, though he was bewitched by the Queen's youth and found it incomprehensible and unbelievable that she should care for him at all, he was not entirely blind to the reality of her situation. Being fastidious himself he was shocked because she could not be bothered to get up in the morning, and she hated bathing and washing her teeth. Clothes ceased to please her. Her hair lacked lustre because she could not bear to let her maid brush it regularly. She rode a little but not with the same delightful panache. She refused to walk if she could possibly avoid it, claiming that stones slipped into her shoes.

'Ma'am,' said Melbourne. 'You are the richest person in these islands and can afford a pair of tighter shoes.'

'Then they will only pinch me,' she said woefully.

Lehzen was blunter. 'This sort of listlessness, dear Victoria, is perilously catching. Seeing their mistress idle and despondent your household and the servants will be the same.'

'Lehzen, you are not to say such things to me.'

'And if I can't, who can?' Victoria turned to avoid her eyes so Lehzen placed herself squarely in front of her. 'Tell me, how do you think the boy Jones managed to live here without being found?' Jones was a waif who had penetrated into Buckingham Palace and slept there, under chairs, sofas, and tables, eating and drinking and seeing what he wanted, for the best part of a week. 'The servants are already too slack to detect and catch an intruder. And those who want to make mischief in the two households find it easier to do so when you are less watchful than you ought to be.'

Victoria's eyes filled with tears. She hung her head. 'What ought I to do?' she asked.

'Not a great deal,' encouraged Lehzen. 'Your people love you. All we wish is for you to be happy. Simply pull yourself together and make just that extra effort, and everything will adjust itself.'

Sooner than either Lehzen or Melbourne realized a shock came which forced Victoria to pull herself together. It was, in fact, so cataclysmic that it threatened her throne.

10

On January 16th, 1839, the Queen's journal referred to a long conversation with Lord Melbourne on her Uncle William's mistress Mrs Jordan. He told her that a statue had been made of her, so large that it would not fit conveniently into any house and no one quite knew what to do with it. It appeared her real name was Dorah Bland, and there never had been a Mr Jordan; that she had had beautiful legs and feet, was of Irish stock, and was fond of acting in men's clothes – as Hippolyta in *She Would and She Would Not* and as Rosalind in *As You Like It* – which, said Lord Melbourne, was 'the prettiest play in the world'.

Neither, apparently, mentioned an important conversation which had taken place earlier in the day.

Lady Tavistock had sent a message to the Prime Minister asking him to call on her. He had obliged. Not only was she one of the Queen's senior Ladies of the Bedchamber, but she was also married to one of his most powerful Whig supporters, the Marquess of Tavistock. He expected her to ask his help in some small matter relating to the Court or to use his influence in her favour on the Queen. What she had actually said made him at first incredulous and then thunderstruck.

Lady Tavistock had a forceful personality and no niminy-piminy reluctance to call a spade a spade. She reported that Lady Flora Hastings had returned on January 10th, from a holiday in Scotland and, from the look of her waistline, she appeared to be *enceinte*.

This was the Queen's view. Her observant eyes had noticed the differences in her mother's lady-in-waiting. She had consulted Lehzen and then sent for Lady Tavistock and Lady Portman to ask for their corroboration. They had covertly regarded Lady Flora and had come to the same conclusion. The obvious course would have been for the Queen to mention the matter in confidence to her mother, but, owing to the deadlock of hostility between them, this was out of the question. Lady Tavistock had, therefore, conceived it her duty to acquaint the Prime Minister with the facts. What was he going to do about them?

Melbourne hardly paused before telling her that true or false the facts were dangerously explosive. In the close atmosphere of the households at Buckingham Palace the courtiers were cut off from outside opinion. Any breath of such a scandal would harm the Queen's own reputation.

Lady Tavistock begged leave to disagree. If such a criminal relationship as that which existed between Lady Flora and Sir John Conroy was not exposed and punished, the Court was finished.

At this first mention of Conroy's name, Melbourne started. How did Lady Tavistock, how could anyone know that Sir John was the putative parent?

The two were inseparable, said Lady Tavistock calmly. They were devoted to one another. She had it from the Duchess of Kent herself that quite recently the pair had travelled long distances alone together . . .

Melbourne cut her short. He was sorry to be so abrupt, he said, but neither she nor Lady Portman was to say another word about the matter. He did not express it as his opinion. Rather was it a command. He could not have the Queen's reputation damaged by household tittle-tattle. With that he went off, presumably to talk to the Queen about Mrs Jordan, and describe *As You Like It* as the prettiest play in the world.

Lady Tavistock was furious. In as many words she had been

called a common gossip and told to hold her tongue. She was determined to prove herself right.

For a month she and Lady Portman cast critical eyes at Lady Flora's waistline.

So did the Queen and Lehzen.

One of Lehzen's deepest faults was her inability to forget wrongs done to her, and in her heart she wanted to be revenged for all the caustic remarks levelled at her in the past by Lady Flora. Because she enjoyed finding her enemies confounded she was particularly careful to make sure of the facts. Her observation was acute and penetrating, and it was with secret triumph that she found herself able to agree with Lady Tavistock and Lady Portman.

As for the Queen: her attitude was overwhelmingly prejudiced by her hatred of Conroy.

On February 2nd she wrote in her journal:

We have no doubt that she is – to use the plain words – *with child*! ! . . . The horrid cause of all this is the Monster & demon Incarnate, whose name I forbear to mention, but which is the 1st word of the 2nd line of this page.

The first word on the second line was 'J.C.'.

Lehzen advised caution. The Queen said little. But by now Lady Tavistock and Lady Portman were certain. They went jointly to see Sir James Clark, physician to both royal households and in the best possible position to settle the scandal. Evidently he had small respect for medical confidence, or perhaps he had been swollen by his knighthood to care more for the Queen's service than the Hippocratic oath, because he at once told the ladies that he was already treating Lady Flora. She had complained to him of pain and other discomforts some little time before, and he had prescribed ipecacuanha, rhubarb, and a liniment of camphor, soap and opium. But being a lady, and unmarried, it had never occurred to him that she could possibly be *enceinte*. Lady Portman pressed him. Had Lady Flora any symptoms which indicated that she could *not* be in that condition? No, said the doctor. He was appalled by what they said. Naïvely he promised to do as they asked, that was, to acquaint Lady Flora with the facts and demand that she accept a proper medical examination.

He handled the interview clumsily. Lady Flora turned scarlet with embarrassment. Then she was outraged. He pleaded with her to be calm. She would surely acknowledge the fact that her figure had altered? She set her mouth. He persisted. Had her figure not altered? Ultimately she acknowledged that it had. Why then, he asked, did she refuse to accept a medical examination which would expel all doubts? Tearfully she agreed; but only on condition that another physician was present.

Rubbing his hands together the doctor reported to Lady Tavistock. She and Lady Portman took the news to the Queen.

Unfortunately, Victoria was in one of her puritan phases. Though on occasions she could talk uninhibitedly about royal mistresses and paramours, bastards, morganatic wives and other aspects of concupiscence, there were times when she was exactly the opposite, falsely modest and almost ludicrously prim. Had she discussed this matter with Lord Melbourne, his breezy good sense would have made her see the folly of the course her ladies recommended. But at that moment she felt she could not. Sir James Clark was sent to tell the Duchess of Kent that it appeared her lady-in-waiting was pregnant and a medical examination, to which she had agreed, would resolve all doubts. Lady Portman followed the doctor with a verbal message from the Queen to her mother. Lady Flora was forbidden the Queen's table until her innocence had been proved.

The Duchess of Kent was scandalized. Her instinctive reactions were spirited and loyal to her own household. She promptly dismissed Sir James Clark from her service. She required Lady Portman to say that as long as Lady Flora was barred from the Queen's table she herself would refuse to appear. She also informed Lady Portman that in future she would not be welcome in the Kent apartments.

Melbourne did not catch up until after the examination had taken place. When he did, he was angry in that icy menacing way which is common to men who are usually calm and easygoing. He sent for Sir James Clark and his medical colleague,

Sir Charles Mansfield Clark, a noted London gynaecologist. He asked why they had been so unutterably foolish as to allow the palace ladies to lead them by the nose. Forcing Lady Flora to submit to such an examination was as unethical as it would prove dangerous.

'I understand,' he snapped, 'that you have provided the young lady with some sort of certificate.'

Sir James, a good deal frightened by Melbourne's bellicose attitude, admitted it.

'To prove her virginity?'

'Indeed, yes, Prime Minister. We felt obliged to advert that, after a thorough examination carried out in the presence of Lady Portman and Lady Flora's own maid, there appeared to be no grounds for believing she was pregnant or ever has been.'

'I could understand such a certificate being given to a New-market blood filly,' said Melbourne cuttingly. 'But not to a lady-in-waiting of her royal highness the Duchess of Kent.'

Sir James said nothing. Sir Charles was less inclined to take the rebuke.

'We were acting professionally on behalf of her majesty,' he began in a portentous tone.

Melbourne slapped the desk in front of him. 'No, by God,' he cried. 'You were doing no such thing. I'll not have it.'

Both doctors regarded him with amazement.

'The Queen's name is never to be mentioned in connection with this affair. Do you understand me, gentlemen?'

'That is as you please,' said Sir Charles stiffly. 'But it seemed just to provide the young lady with some sort of authenticating document.'

'Particularly as Lady Flora requested it,' added Sir James.

Sir Charles nodded. 'Exactly so!' Then he wagged his finger. 'But I personally hasten to inform you, my lord, that there might be some reason to believe that she is, after all, pregnant.'

Melbourne started. 'Yet she is a virgin?'

Sir Charles wagged his finger a second time. 'There are many reasons for believing pregnancy does not exist, but it is pos-sible.'

'Then why, for the love of God,' burst out Lord Melbourne, 'did you issue that damnable certificate?'

'It is Sir Charles's private opinion,' said the other. 'Not mine.'

As soon as she heard the doctors' verdict Victoria sent Lady Portman to apologize on her behalf for what had happened. She deeply regretted the incident and would be happy to see Lady Flora at Court that evening.

Lady Flora did not come. Nor did she appear at Court for seven days, during which time the Duchess of Kent declaimed her wrongs as publicly as she dared, and the Queen suffered agonies of suspense. When, pale and drawn after her experience, Lady Flora did at last appear at the Queen's Court, Victoria was so relieved that she threw her arms about the injured lady. Her apologies were, perhaps, too profuse. Her eyes swam with tears for a long time.

Lehzen watched the reconciliation with equal relief. Panic had worked magically upon Victoria, exciting her out of her lethargy and her indifference to daily affairs. But it had been acutely painful. Waiting for Lady Flora's gesture of forgiveness had so tormented her that she had been close to a breakdown. Now that it had come, she would need Lehzen's extra care to avoid being prostrated by nervous exhaustion.

Everyone in the palace except perhaps Conroy and the Duchess of Kent, was supremely glad that the whole disagreeable episode was over.

11

Lord Winchilsea was being shaved at ten in the morning when his friend Lord Hastings was announced.

'I thought you were down at Donington ...' he was beginning to say when he broke off. His visitor looked flushed and feverish. He climbed, still half-shaved, from his chair and held out a hand. 'Are you ill?' he asked.

'I have had influenza,' replied Hastings. 'But I had to come up.'

He gratefully accepted a chair, and Winchilsea sent his man for wine.

'By the look of your face, you still have a fever. May I offer you a bed?'

'No, no.' In agitation Hastings leapt to his feet. 'There is no time to be ill. I've come for your help.'

'Anything,' offered the other immediately. 'How may I serve you?'

'In an affair of honour.'

Winchilsea knew his friend was hot-tempered and not over-blessed with intelligence. If he had landed himself in some awkward scrape he would have to be eased out. He asked for details.

'I wish you to be my second,' said Hastings pacing up and down the little dressing-room.

'Who is the other principal?'

'Lord Melbourne.'

Winchilsea whistled. 'Undoubtedly feverish!' he exclaimed. 'Now do be good and stop tramping about. Sit down.'

Hastings was persuaded to do so and then he started on a long and rambling explanation. He was over-excited and not particularly explicit but Winchilsea managed to gather the bones of the trouble: that Lady Flora, whom he remembered as the eldest of Hastings's three sisters, and a long-necked, wide-eyed girl who wrote poetry and attended the Queen's mother, had had her honour impugned; that she had written to her brother a bare outline of what had happened; that Hastings had left his sick bed to see and hear from her own lips the sordid story; and that from what he had heard he had decided there was some sort of Whig plot against the Tory house of Hastings. Therefore the villain of the piece was the Prime Minister.

Winchilsea was an ultra-Tory, even to the right of the Duke of Wellington who would have taken any opportunity to harm the Whigs, but he would not accept the task of carrying a challenge to the Prime Minister.

'You're still feverish, Hastings. It wouldn't do. While you've been down in the country I've been here close to the centre of things and if there'd been any hint of a Whig plot I should have heard of it – or,' he added with a smile, 'I should have started it myself.'

He recommended that his young friend wait a day or two while his fever subsided and then ask for an appointment with the Prime Minister. 'Tell him you insist on your right as a peer to an audience with the Queen.'

Hastings seized on the idea, but he would not wait. He went off, there and then, to peal at the Prime Minister's door bell and insist on an immediate interview.

Winchilsea shrugged his shoulders, settled down to have the other half of his face shaved and sent out a knowing servant to find out if, of late, there had been any rumours of a scandal at Court, any rumours at all.

Melbourne was short with his early caller.

'You will appreciate, my lord, that a great deal of this is blown up and its importance exaggerated by the ladies themselves. Your sister's painful experience is lamented by all, but you will agree that in the end no harm has been done.'

Hastings disagreed entirely. His rejoinder that it was a pity that Whig ladies should be so criminally vexatious about a Tory innocent carried a hint which Melbourne found offensive. He rang for a servant to show his visitor out.

'Be good enough, my lord, to call at once upon your party leader. The Duke will reassure you. Good morning.'

'You will acknowledge my right to be heated in this affair?' demanded Hastings.

'Good morning, my lord,' was Melbourne's sole answer.

The Duke of Wellington had a fondness for being third party at the core of quarrels in high places. An intimate friend said he liked 'being mixed up in *messes*'. No denser, more squalid, potentially ruinous mess had ever presented itself for his attention than the Hastings affair. He already knew the salient facts before the angry Marquess burst in on Apsley House and was able to assure that young man that there was no Whig plot afoot. His own view corresponded with Melbourne's. The whole unhappy affair was the fruit of tittle-tattle. It was better left to subside. In that way it might be forgotten . . .

'Better!' cried Hastings. 'Better for whom?'

'For her majesty,' replied the Duke calmly.

Hastings appeared to struggle for breath. What, he demanded, of his sister's honour? It had been impugned. Salacious stories were still circulated about her. And she was from a family renowned for its respectability. If reparations were not made she was ruined in society. In justice, was this not of more consequence than the well-being of a young Queen who belonged herself to a notoriously libidinous family and whose present attachment to her Prime Minister made her the laughing-stock of European drawing-rooms? He snapped his fingers. He cared not that for the Queen, he shouted. And if she had a bad conscience about the matter so much the better . . .

Wellington was no longer young. Nor was he very tall. In his blue-tailed coat he looked more like an elderly finch than the victor of Waterloo. But with one look he quelled the furious young man who towered over him. Quietly he said: 'You forget yourself, my lord.'

Wellington worked hard to pacify the Hastings family.

He saw the Duchess of Kent and begged her to unbend a little. Her stern disapproval was widening the gap between those who defended Lady Flora and those who supported the Queen. His attempt failed. Anything which could inflame the situation had an instant appeal to the Duchess. She gave an audience to Lord Hastings, advised him to demand reparations in the shape of Sir James Clark's dismissal, and she sent her own personal sympathy to old Lady Hastings, his mother.

The Duke then saw the Queen. He warned her, more forcefully than Melbourne had brought himself to do, of the political consequences of this scandal getting out. She was still popular with her people, but republicanism was the mode. Should she become unpopular he would not answer for the consequences. She must make much of her mother, drive out with her in public, and not let anyone see or suspect there were any differences between them. He also advised her to see Hastings because it was his right as a peer to demand an audience.

When Lord Hastings saw Victoria she was exceedingly

nervous. She saw him alone in a formal throne room but she had been told what to say by the Duke, by Lord Melbourne and by Lehzen. In her anxiety she forgot it all, babbled her apologies and regrets, and point-blank refused to dismiss Sir James Clark.

Hastings was mollified by her apologies. They were sincere. He could see that. Why then would she not make reparations? He pressed her to dismiss Sir James. He would not ask, he said, for the dismissal of anyone else, though it was said that the Queen's Lady Attendant must bear a large part of the responsibility for what had taken place.

'My lord!' The Queen's eyes blazed. 'I have expressed my regrets that Lady Flora suffered so harsh an experience, but the disposition of my household is entirely my affair.' She held out her hand for him to kiss. The audience was over.

Afterwards she felt sick with fright. She was positive that soon the whole world would know the story, and that she could not bear. People would point fingers. They would demand to know the answer to one question; where lay the original source of the slander? Then they would know whom to blame and who ought to be punished. The thought was unbearable. Involuntarily she crushed her cambric handkerchief into a tight ball. She could not stand the waiting. It was like being haunted with the fear that some indecent act would be made public, that a hidden shame would be exposed. And the haunting had already gone on so long. It was the dripping of water on stone – waiting for minutes, days at a time, weeks, months until the whole world would know that she, the Queen of England, was the first author of the calumny.

She swayed a little, a small figure on the great throne. Then she covered her face with her hands and burst into tears.

12

Lord Hastings retired for a time to the country. Melbourne and Wellington breathed sighs of relief. Only the Queen refused to be persuaded that the affair was over. Lady Flora's brother had struck her as a very determined man.

She was right in this. He began a deliberate attack upon Lehzen, writing to Lord Tavistock and Lord Portman asking them to defend their ladies and Baroness Lehzen against the charge of being the source of the scandal. Both gentlemen were aware of what he wanted; a written reply which he could publish. Neither obliged. They defended their panic-stricken wives and exculpated Lehzen entirely. It looked as though Lord Hastings had lost his fight. He met with brick walls everywhere and could not even persuade his sister to leave the Court. By this time she was seriously unwell and in pain but she believed that going home would be an admission of guilt. Bravely she struggled on.

The inevitable happened.

The sort of poison which had spread so rapidly through the palace seeped into the streets outside. It spread into the countryside and abroad. The common people were at first loyal to the shy young Queen who had so caught their imagination at her coronation, but then they altered their affections. It was said that she was being cruel and obstinate. She had refused point blank to permit any further investigation into the affair of her mother's lady-in-waiting. Callousness of this order did not appeal to the Londoners who were notoriously sentimental. They began to ignore the Queen's carriage when she drove out, turning their backs on it in silence.

This outward show of hostility was balm to the Duchess of Kent and the party who by now were implacably opposed to the Queen. They whipped up strong feelings against the Court and though Melbourne and Lord John Russell, Wellington and Peel, publicly deplored the fact, they managed to make it into a political issue. The Tories began to castigate the Queen's Court as a seat of royal voluptuousness. She herself, they insinuated, was no better than her father or her uncles. And they had been bad enough. The Paget family with few good looks but enormous charm had high places at Court, and Lord Alfred Paget, a handsome youngster of twenty-two, was a great favourite of the Queen's. The Court was therefore called Paget Club House, and Victoria herself occasionally named 'Lady Alfred'. Generally, though, she was known as 'Mrs Melbourne'.

When it was too late Conroy saw it had been unwise to associate Lady Flora's cause with the Tories because automatically it aligned the Whigs with the Queen. They were not slow to couple the Duchess of Kent's name with that of her Comptroller, and they resorted to any means to blacken Lady Flora's character.

Finally the newspapers seized on what Mr Greville had called 'the grand scampiglio', and though some were responsible, others printed scurrilous reports which made the scandal flame burn brighter.

The Duke of Sussex hit upon the happy notion of inviting the principal political protagonists in the Hastings affair to a party. Lady Cecilia tried to dissuade him. She was not sanguine. But the Duke, with what he called his rational, scientific approach, was certain they would find it salutary to be confronted by each other's folly. Unfortunately he was wrong. As an experiment, it was a conspicuous failure.

Lord John Russell was uncle to the Marquess of Tavistock, and highly indignant when a Tory backbencher told him confidentially that Lady Tavistock was at the root of it all. Sir Robert Peel was equally indignant when a Whig spokesman suggested that Lady Flora would soon be slipping away from the palace to bear her child in the secrecy of Donington. Wellington was incensed when a Whig peer told him candidly that there never would have been an uproar if the Duke's party had not whipped up popular feeling against the Queen. As for Melbourne, he came close to losing his temper in public when the Speaker asked why he had not pressed for the dismissal of Baroness Lehzen. Melbourne recalled that the Speaker was a particular friend of Conroy's. Controlling himself, but only just, he said that the Baroness had behaved impeccably throughout.

'My dear Prime Minister,' said the Speaker, shaking his head. 'Lehzen is a snake in the grass. And the Queen? – why, she is a cruel, heartless child.'

Melbourne turned on his heel and walked away.

From the fastness of Loudon Castle, in Ayrshire, the Dowager Lady Hastings wrote an eight-page letter to the Queen. It was a woman to woman demand for justice for her wronged child. But it won no response from the Queen. She was blazingly angry. To begin with the letter had been sent care of her mother. To go on with, it contained indirect reminders that Victoria was young and inexperienced and therefore, by implication, rash, heartless, and even incapable of discovering the perpetrator of 'the atrocious calumnies and unblushing falsehoods' against Lady Flora. Finally the old lady demanded reparations – and Victoria was obstinately determined not to make any at all.

Melbourne answered the letter repeating the Queen's deep concern and saying that she was desirous to do everything in her power to soothe the family's feelings.

A second, shorter but no less stinging letter arrived from Loudon Castle. Lady Hastings addressed herself now to Lord Melbourne as the *maire du palais*. A third letter followed:

> I claim at your hands, my lord, as a mark of public justice, the removal of Sir James Clark.

Thoroughly incensed the Prime Minister dictated a reply:

> The demand which your ladyship's letter makes upon me is so unprecedented and objectionable, that even the respect due to your ladyship's sex, rank, family, and character would not justify me in more, if indeed, it authorizes so much, than acknowledging the letter for the sole purpose of acquainting your ladyship that I have received it.

As a matter of form the clerk subscribed:

I have the honour to remain, madam, with the highest respect, your ladyship's obedient and humble servant.

Which, thought Melbourne, as he scrawled his signature, is as nice a piece of humbug as I ever penned.

Thwarted by the Queen, battered by Lord Melbourne, the enraged Lady Hastings took her revenge in the public prints. She sent copies of her letters and the Prime Minister's to the *Morning Post*. They were published on March 7th.

Up to this time newspaper articles on the affair had been more speculation than anything else. Here now was something for the public to read and chew on. It did not like what it read. Nor did it like another letter published on March 17th, in *The Examiner*. This was a copy of one sent by Lady Flora herself, outlining all the facts of the case, to her uncle who was a resident in Brussels. In order to vindicate her he sent in the letter for publication, and went himself to London to join the rest of the family in their demand for reparations. He found he could do nothing.

13

The palace walls were unbreachable but the Court was vilified from one end of the country to the other.

The Duchess of Kent kept her household rigidly apart from what she publicly described as the contaminating influence of her daughter's ladies. Lady Flora, still stout and by now deathly pale, and often in great pain, was seen less and less.

The Queen remained silent.

To her ladies she looked careworn and her eyes had the pink and amber colour caused by sleeplessness. Her serenity was gone. This was all on the outside. Inside remorse was eating at her like a cancer.

Then, on March 22nd, when she firmly believed she had reached the nadir, she found there were still unseen depths of misery to be experienced.

Very late on the night of the 21st the Whig ministry was defeated in the Lords by five votes. For hours the Queen had to face the likelihood that Lord Melbourne would feel it incumbent upon him to resign.

She could not bear the thought. She retired to her inmost private room and there she sat, her back rigid, plucking with agitated fingers at the edge of her dress.

Lehzen was worried. Under ordinary circumstances she would have sent for Sir James Clark, but in the Queen's eyes he had become a symbol of all the trouble they had suffered in the past weeks. He would agitate her more than bring her relief.

Eventually Melbourne brought the best medicine of all. Lehzen saw from his face that the Commons had given him his vote of confidence and that he would continue in office. She left them, ostensibly to make ready for a deputation which very shortly was to wait on the Queen, in reality so that the Prime Minister could give Victoria the news in private.

He took her hand and kissed it. 'It's all right, Ma'am,' he said. 'The ministry's secure.'

Her eyes lighted for a moment. But she had gone through a great deal. She handed to him her journal, already half written for that day. He read a part of it:

I am but a poor helpless girl, who clings to him for support and protection – & the thought of ALL, ALL my happiness being possibly at stake, so completely overwhelmed me that I burst into tears and remained crying for some time.

'I'm sorry, Ma'am,' he said, shutting the journal, 'to be the cause of such distress.'

She took his hand. 'My good, kind Lord Melbourne.' She bade him sit down and they were silent together for a long time. He judged it was a good occasion to be entirely candid. Her delight that he was to continue in office would bolster her a little against the other serious news he had to tell her. So far, because he loved her, he had hedged round the exact truth, but it was essential that she should know how hostile her people were and how unpopular they had both become so that she could do her best to remedy the situation. Quietly but very seriously he told her the situation; that her most estimable advantage, the public's high regard for her innocence, and ingenuousness, was for ever gone; that her Court was decried and the sad affair had cast odium on the whole monarchical system; and that it was now too late to make any sort of reparations. The Hastings family might still demand vengeance on Lehzen and Sir James Clark, but their dismissal would benefit no one, least of all the Queen. He advised her that she had to shine again, to win her people by brave smiles and as cheerful an attitude as she could manage.

'No,' she muttered. 'No, Lord Melbourne, I cannot pretend to like them. Not after what they have done. Not after what has been said and written in the newspapers. The mob is a beast. I will not smile on it.'

He urged her. 'You may wring your hands in private, but you have to be calm and benign in public. It is your duty, Ma'am. And your sense of justice will teach you that your people cannot be blamed for the unhappiness you have suffered in the past weeks.'

She nodded. 'Yes,' she whispered. 'You are right. It has been our fault, here in the Court. And mine has been as great as any. Perhaps the greatest.'

Dumbly he accepted what she said. He loved her protectively and would have given anything to save her from pain, especially that which was self-inflicted, but wisely he did not contradict her. Instead he kept silent until, her face pale with anxiety, she asked if nothing could be done to make life more bearable.

'No, Ma'am. Nothing. We have to live with it.'

Said so simply it seemed less grave, but Victoria's hand flew nervously to her throat. The tears coursed down past the bridge of her nose and then over her chubby, pallid cheeks.

He took her hand. 'Nothing can be done.'

Her crying was silent. Unbearably silent to him.

'Everything has been attempted to silence their waspishness.'

The tears streamed down.

'Ma'am . . . we have tried.'

'Yes, my lord, yes.'

She could say no more. She wished to thank him, to say she appreciated his obvious concern, to say she knew or could guess what he had done and had tried to do for her. But speech was impossible.

There came a knock at the doors. Lord Melbourne stood up. One half of the doors opened. Only Lehzen would have interrupted their talk, and she had come to curtsey and say that the delegation had been admitted and was waiting.

'Very well,' sighed the Queen. She dried her eyes on a handkerchief.

Lehzen took a hare's scut from her bag and sealed the tear channels with an ivory powder. Then she handed the Queen a shawl.

Victoria inclined her head to Lord Melbourne and curtseyed. Without a word he returned the curtsey and bowed low. With her head erect she went to the doors. At a word from Lehzen both were opened from the other side. The Queen walked on, her grief subdued, in hate with the world and her own people, but no one now could see or guess it. She was England's Queen by blood and right, and blood and right kept her regal.

Melbourne, his own eyes brimful with tears, watched her go. 'By God!' he muttered in admiration beneath his breath. 'By God! By God!'

14

King Leopold was seldom subject to depression, but his niece's continued indifference to the Coburg marriage proposal made him exceedingly dejected in the spring of 1839. Victoria was hostile to Albert, and gave her opinion that he still needed improvement.

'She's playing for time,' consoled Queen Louise. 'The old viscount has taken her fancy, and she wants to enjoy him for a while.'

'But it is so exasperating,' declared Leopold. 'And it is humiliating for Albert. For two years she has governed his education. It is at her particular request that he and his brother are now enlarging their minds in Italy. What more can she want?'

'Has she been told of the Haustein scandal?' asked Queen Louise.

Leopold regarded her in astonishment. 'Why, yes, I imagine so'. He thought for a moment. During Albert's boyhood his mother had been divorced from his father for committing adultery with a Jewish Army officer named Alexander von Haustein. Afterwards they married, he was created Count Pölzig, and they lived in exile in Paris. A recurring scandal in European high society said that Prince Albert was not his father's son, that he was illegitimate, and half Jewish.

'Of *course* she knows,' exclaimed King Leopold. 'My sister would have told her. And if not, Melbourne would have done. But the scandal's of no account. No one, I think, believes it.'

'Albert does,' said the Queen shortly.

He blinked and opened his mouth to protest.

'I am certain of it,' she insisted. 'And I am inclined to believe it myself.'

'Louise!'

'Be calm, Leopold. There are a number of pointers.'

Briefly she listed them. Prince Ernest was exactly like his father the Duke. Neither was particularly good-looking, and both had the same sallowness, inflamed eyes and ill-fitting teeth. Both were selfish, and extravagant, and made instinctive, hasty judgements. Both drank a great deal and were notorious womanizers. Albert shared their Germanic thoroughness. He was methodical and plodded to the root of every matter. Otherwise he was entirely different from them. The strictly masculine university life at Bonn had suited him exactly. He had enjoyed the lectures, the company, the swimming, fencing, shooting and sketching. An English officer, Lieutenant Francis Seymour, had been sent off with the party to Italy with the specific duty of keeping the Princes unharmed and pure. Privately the family had hoped that Albert, at any rate, would elude his vigilance because to the present he had shown no particular liking for female society. Finally, like many young

Jews, he had the virtue of being confiding and he was outstandingly handsome.

As he listened to this catalogue of good reasons for believing Count Pölzig might have fathered his nephew, King Leopold wondered if even now it was too late to change boats in midstream. If Victoria was not eager to marry, but simply accepted it as a duty, she might prefer Albert's brother, Ernest – about whose paternity there could be no possible doubt. But he dismissed the idea as quickly as it occurred to him. Apart from Albert there was only one fine-looking bachelor prince in Europe – and he, the Hereditary Grand Duke Alexander of Russia, was as good as betrothed to a German princess. The horse-faced Bourbons would never appeal to Victoria, the Orleans princes were feckless, the Dutch prince ponderous, and the remaining bachelors in imperial Germany conspicuously third-rate compared with Albert of Saxe-Coburg. He could depend, he knew, on Albert's physical attractions to win Victoria. She was Hanoverian as his first wife had been. They found it difficult to resist a handsome man or a beautiful woman. But for powder to flash it had to be put with fire.

Begging his wife to keep her wild fancies caged in her pretty head, he settled down to write to Stockmar. It was time for the Princes to return from Italy. Somehow the Queen of England had to be persuaded to invite them to England.

15

The news flashed round London and thence to the country: the ministry had fallen and the Queen was obliged to send for the Duke.

A few received the news with undisguised pleasure. Chief amongst them was the Duchess of Kent.

Being excluded from her daughter's Court had bitten deeply into her soul. She now actively and consistently hated Victoria, and if she had a chance to be spiteful and hurt or damage her she took it without hesitation. The news from Westminster was a salve to her wounded pride. The unforgiving Conroy was equally delighted. He detested the Queen and spoke of her so viciously that Lady Flora, his old accomplice in so many adventures, was quite shocked and said so. He sneered at her. Lady Flora had played her role in the battle between the households. She was of no more use. If she had changed the colour of her favour she had better leave the Duchess's drawing-room. The poor young woman climbed painfully to her feet. She begged leave to retire; then, without waiting for formal permission, and with her head held proudly erect, she went from the room. Neither the Duchess nor Conroy paid any attention to her. With their heads close together, they imagined the fright and loneliness and despair of the girl they both hated.

Adolphus, Duke of Cambridge, had apartments at St James's and was trying to make music with his Duchess when the news was brought. His deafness was an increasing disability and he could barely hear notes from his own violin let alone the servant's voice. The news was shouted out. He nodded, laid down his bow and violin and drank water silently while he considered the implications of Melbourne's fall. He was not displeased. His own experience of sovereignty as Hanoverian Viceroy had been generously offered to his niece. She had declined it and not with much grace, saying she preferred to rely upon her excellent Lord Melbourne.

'I wish her well with Wellington,' shouted the Duchess.

She was thinking upon precisely the same lines as her husband. They were a close and affectionate couple who shared all their pleasures and had no secrets from one another.

'Indeed, yes,' said the Duke.

He picked up his violin and bow. She turned back to the harpsichord and nodded when he was to begin.

At Donington and Loudon Castle the news was very welcome. Neither Lord Hastings nor his mother had been able to persuade Flora to leave the Duchess of Kent's household. She would stay, she said, until she had proved by time, if nothing else, that the charges against her were scandalous and false.

No adequate reparations had been made. It was some solace to know that the *maire du palais* had been outmanoeuvred in the games of statesmanship and was at the centre of things no longer.

The Princess Sophia, now lonely in her Kensington apartments and without the mordant stimulant of afternoons in Adelaide's drawing-room, was turned in upon herself. Her son was being troublesome, making demands which could not easily be met. Sir John Conroy had managed her affairs in addition to the Duchess of Kent's and she had supposed him to be capable and careful. But something had gone awry. She had difficulty in meeting all her bills, and hoped the inconveniences were merely temporary. Meanwhile she economized on her already modest spending. Struggling, anxious and lonely, her good nature had corroded. More and more she took pleasure in other people's misfortunes. She had loved each stage of the grand scampiglio. Now, when she heard the news of Melbourne's fall, she rubbed her thin old hands and chuckled to think of Victoria's discomfiture.

Mrs Norton heard the news and, having asked her servant to repeat it carefully, she said she wished to be alone to rest. She lay back on the sofa and repeated the message slowly, word by word under her breath: *Lord Melbourne's ministry has fallen over the Jamaican Bill.* It gave her a sweeping feeling of elation. She made no attempt to fight it down as unworthy. It was natural. Though rationally she held fast to her conviction that her affair with William Lamb was entirely distinct from Viscount Melbourne's adoration of his Queen, she had ir-rational, animal moments of possessiveness. Her man and his other woman were being separated by fate. But the feeling of elation sank and died. She realized the situation had barely altered. It would merely make William unhappy to be sep-arated from his Victoria. She did not like to think of him as being unhappy.

The Duke of Sussex shared Mrs Norton's double view. Instinc-tively he was relieved to hear Victoria's grand vizier had fallen. It might allow him and his brother Cambridge a larger share in her counsels, which was their right as well as their duty. Yet he was fond of his niece and knew how deeply attached she was to her Prime Minister. It was a wretched business for them both; poor Victoria with her head right up in the air, and poor Melbourne, such an excellent scholar but with less time or taste now for patristic studies than for gallantry.

Then there were those who were dismayed to hear the news.

Queen Adelaide grieved for Victoria. She had seen little of her niece since the coronation but enough to know of her utter dependence, emotional and in every other way, on her Prime Minister. Princess Mary, Duchess of Gloucester, was also aware of her niece's feelings for Melbourne. From her heart she pitied her, hating the curious machinery of government which made possible so undesirable a change.

Privately Wellington did not wish his party to accept responsibility for the country in its rundown condition. Later, when things were better, and the Court scandal a thing of the past, the Tories would have been glad to guide the state. He foresaw, as well, endless trouble arising from the Queen's personal devotion to Melbourne. A Tory Prime Minister could hardly hope to rule satisfactorily if the sovereign was in constant touch with the leader of the opposition. Nevertheless it was his duty to answer the Queen's summons. He found her in tears, comforted her, told her that he himself although leader of the party, could not form an administration, and he advised her to send for Sir Robert Peel. He was shocked when she pouted and said she did not want to because she did not like Peel. Personal considerations were to be put on one side, he told her in a fatherly fashion but sternly enough for her to know that he meant it.

King Leopold was made distinctly uneasy by the change at Westminster. His special courier service brought him the news within a day. Of all the English statesmen, Melbourne had his warmest regard. Though he was leader of the more progressive party, Melbourne was a happy-go-lucky statesman, and a devotee of *laissez-faire* who was not likely to cause much ferment

in the councils of Europe. Peel, on the other hand, though he
had been Prime Minister for a four-month period in King William's reign, was still an unknown quantity. On the face of it
Leopold decided that a doctrinaire Tory was less likely to look
happily on the Queen's contact with the Belgian Court and on
the plan to marry her to Albert, than easy-going Melbourne. It
was a melancholy prospect.

Lord Palmerston was married to Melbourne's sister and had
been his Foreign Secretary. He was often in his company in
their first days out of office, trying to interest him in affairs,
and making a careful autopsy of what had happened.

Being a realist who understood the inevitable seesaw action
between government and opposition, he himself was not particularly concerned that the ministry had fallen, but the reason
for it vexed him exceedingly. Settlers in Jamaica had defied the
Whigs' proposal to legislate on behalf of their sugar workers,
and they had found enough support in Parliament to bring the
government down. This, to Palmerston, was intolerable. He
was the authoritarian of the Whigs, trained to wear a mailed
fist by his experience as Secretary at War under five Tory Prime
Ministers. Defiance of any kind to the might of the English
nation was offensive to him, and it was doubly so from insolent
expatriates, many of whom would have been of little consequence to say the least in their mother country.

He was chagrined to find that it left Melbourne quite unmoved. His brother-in-law was not in the least interested in
Jamaica. His thoughts were solely at Court, now brilliant for a
visit of Alexander, Hereditary Grand Duke of Russia, and
Prince Henry of Orange. Palmerston had no great opinion of
Melbourne as a Prime Minister except that, being aware of his
limitations, he had the good sense to delegate and gave his
ministers unprecedented powers. Nevertheless he highly respected him as a man. No one in his acquaintance was so
unaffectedly indifferent to the trappings of power, and few
could have borne so quietly his private burden of an unfaithful,
lunatic wife and a mentally deficient son. But there was no
stoicism about him now. He was utterly crushed because his
administration had been brought down. Under ordinary cir-

cumstances he would have accepted it with cynical amusement and gone off to his country home at Brocket to keep abreast with the latest German theology or make new plantations with his gardeners. Under the present circumstances his next to Roman fortitude in the face of adversity had entirely gone. It dismayed Palmerston to see him cast down in such a fashion. He would seize on news from the palace, otherwise he was lifeless. He ate little, drank rather more than usual, and, from the look of him, he was not sleeping properly.

On the Friday after Melbourne's resignation he was mostly silent throughout the day. Palmerston had a wretched time. It was a beautiful day and he wanted to get out. Had his wife been there he could have left Melbourne in her charge, but she was down in the country. He felt it his duty to stay in with his melancholy brother-in-law, and the enforced inactivity made him liverish. He snapped when Melbourne sighed and said he had no heart to go to the state ball that evening for the Grand Duke and the Prince of Orange. Then he apologized for his short temper. He tried to read, walked up and down the library, studied the globes, and went on fretting, until, after constant reference to his pocket watch, he decided the only thing that would properly calm his nerves was dinner.

'William,' he said suddenly, tugging at his orange whiskers. 'Can't we hurry along your people? A little meat would do me a great deal of good.'

Melbourne made no reply, but he rang for the butler and put forward the hour of dinner. When it was announced Palmerston gave a gusty sigh of relief. He took Melbourne's arm. 'What you need, William, is a plateful of meat; good honest meat.'

They dined silently together.

Whenever Lord Palmerston was there the housekeeper respected his well-known penchant for meat and hot sauces, and had given the cook the most particular instructions. That evening there was little fish and few vegetables. Palmerston, sometimes brooding on the Jamaicans, sometimes on Melbourne's unhappiness, attacked each course with gusto. He ate smoked ormers, eels, Westphalia gammon, roast beef, saddle of Cotswold mutton, ox heart, duck, and a dish of kidneys.

231

Melbourne ate nothing.

After a time Palmerston gave up pressing him, and munched in silence.

They were taking their wine when the butler came in. 'There is a letter from the palace, my lord,' he said.

Melbourne seized it from the salver and broke the wafer. As he read it his face paled.

Palmerston stood up. 'What is it, William?'

There was no answer until Melbourne had finished reading. Then he handed the letter to his brother-in-law.

Palmerston read the Queen's letter with growing incredulity.

Forming an administration was a lengthy process and although he had been First Minister for three days Peel still had not completed his arrangements. Now the Queen was holding him up. She wrote to say they were quarrelling about her ladies. Because they were Whig nominees he wished them to be replaced by ladies of his own party. She had agreed at first to some changes. But then Peel had irritated her and she had changed her mind. She had expressed the opinion that a king and his political lords-in-waiting was one thing, a queen and her ladies was another. Her ladies must stay. He had begged her to make this small public demonstration of her confidence in her new government. She remained adamant. No changes would be made except amongst the few gentlemen of her household who were also in Parliament. Peel had consulted with Wellington and they had decided that unless the Queen surrendered her most prominent ladies, the Tory ministry could not go on. Gleefully she wrote that Lord Melbourne must hold himself in readiness.

I was calm but very decided and I think you would have been pleased to see my composure and great firmness. The Queen of England will not submit to such trickery. Keep yourself in readiness for you may soon be wanted.

Palmerston laid down the letter in amazement. 'But she cannot do this,' he said.

Melbourne smiled. It was the first time that day. He took a

glass of wine. 'I confess I had not thought it possible,' he said. 'But she can be stubborn when she wishes, and she is clever enough to use a technical point to get her own way.' He stood up. ' "Keep yourself in readiness", she says. Pam, I believe we have forgotten her schooling by Stockmar. He is an expert on sovereign rights and privileges.'

Palmerston tugged at his orange whiskers. 'She has also been schooled by you,' he said. For a moment he hesitated, then he went on. 'William, will you permit me to intrude upon your private affairs?'

Melbourne's smile died. He sat down and twisted the stem of his glass. Abruptly, he nodded.

His brother-in-law was careful. 'I have seldom seen such unhappiness as yours since Tuesday,' he said. 'And I would not wish it again upon my worst enemy, let alone on you.' He put his hand on Melbourne's shoulder. 'Yet it will come again. You and she are bound one day to be separated by a handful of votes in Commons or Lords.'

'I accept that,' said Melbourne after a pause. 'But it can make no difference. The Queen's regard for me, her affection, if you will, is transitory. It is deep and it is true, but it is not eternal as is my love for her. No, Pam,' he said, as the other made a movement as if he would speak. 'Allow me my say, and then you may have yours. You and all my friends have been patiently considerate of my devotion to the Queen. No doubt you have kept things from me which might have caused pain, and you kindly show your concern that one day, by political circumstances, I shall be separated from my sovereign – who also has my heart. But neither you, nor even she, can understand my devotion. I do not fully understand it myself; yet I am certain I would not deny myself a day or hour or minute of her company if it were avoidable. Soon she will grow beyond me. If I am fortunate her affections will be watered down by time and distance to a high regard. She will marry – for love I hope, because I love her. She will bear children. As an old lady, when the personality I now admire has developed and altered out of recognition, when the skin I long to touch has shrunk and crinkled, when she has quite forgotten William Lamb, and he lies under a stone at Brocket, then my love will still continue circling the world – like light and warmth. It is immortal, my dear friend, and unalterable. It generously gives the most intense joy, and therefore I must also expect the sharpest pain.' He stopped and there was silence for a moment. Then he said, 'Now, Pam, it is your turn to speak. You will tell me my duty is to persuade the Queen to marry for England's sake?'

Lord Palmerston simply nodded.

'Very well, then. I shall.'

16

So there was summer again at the Queen's Court.

It was dramatically obvious to Lehzen. Quite suddenly the podgy, greedy girl who had come to dislike washing and who grumbled continuously, changed back to her dear Victoria, and once more was eager to please and was easily pleased. There was no difficulty now in persuading her to change her clothes, and *cercle* as she was obliged to about her guests each evening. She was good-tempered, full of energy and overjoyed to have recaptured her capacity for pleasure.

Everyone noticed the change. The common people took the Queen to their hearts again and called after her carriage, but the drawing-rooms, far less ready to change their opinions, were still censorious. Even the Grand Duke Alexander and Prince Henry of Orange noticed the difference after the Whigs had returned to power.

There was more zest in life, no more talk from the Queen of feeling exhausted and being obliged to retire early. She danced, she banqueted, she commanded concerts, she played and sang, she enjoyed mild flirtations with a glance or a touch, she was a romantic, exchanging romantic tales with her ladies, and alive to the quality of life as she had never been before. The sad and sombre pietism which had suited her winter moods was gone now that summer had come.

By some magical process, known only to himself, the Duke

had produced a miracle. He went to immense trouble and – believing Conroy to be at the root of all their troubles – he contrived to make him resign and go abroad. He was aware that threats would not have been effective. Nor, very likely, would promises of place and fortune. And therefore he used flattery which is the deadliest of weapons against Irishmen. He made Conroy feel important, and persuaded him he was making a noble sacrifice in resigning from the Duchess's household to live out of the country. Conroy relished the flattery and went. The *'certain wicked person'* who appeared so often in Victoria's journal was no longer there to torment her or the Baroness. It was time for a reconciliation with her mother. The Duke urged it. So did Melbourne. The Duchess, without Conroy to sustain her malice and feeling lonely, was prepared to be less hostile to her daughter. But Victoria was vengeful and inflexible. Not yet, she said, not yet.

This was the only rain cloud in that summer sky. Such perfection of existence could not last. It could not. Melbourne, with his eighteenth-century cynicism, knew it was an Indian summer. Victoria with her innate puritanism which expected pain after pleasure was equally sure. Yet they were determined to enjoy it, each in his own way. There was talk of the strangest things, all faithfully recorded in the Queen's journal:

. . . of the Horticultural Society, and Lord M. said, 'I took my name off about 12 years ago, when a man ran off with £120,000 . . .'

. . . of Bishop Heber's being drowned in a bath. 'He was a blundering, awkward fellow,' said Lord M. . . .

. . . of the Russians wearing no whiskers, which Lord M. said was because they thought it was French, and they hated the French . . .

. . . of the Nurse and Tutor calling children by their Christian names, which my brother said was done abroad, and which Lord M. said no one would think of doing here, that they always called them Lord, and Mr . . .

There was other talk which, for Melbourne, heralded the coming of autumn.

It seared him to talk of marriage yet he kept his promise to Palmerston. But it was not for England's sake. It was for her. He was sufficiently wise and candid to recognize that marriage was necessary for her ultimate happiness, and he loved her dearly enough to help in this as in everything.

He was careful and gentle in the way he went about it.

He reminded her of the Haustein scandal about Prince Albert's birth and found that, like him, she was still disinclined to believe it. As for the rest, he had to overcome his aristocratic disdain for bourgeois German royalty like the Coburgs. He merely told her the truth, that they were not popular abroad, especially with the Russians. Nor, he admitted, did he think it a good idea for first cousins to marry. Would it really be prudent, he asked, to tie herself in that direction?

He was surprised at the speed with which she said no. Prince Albert had written recently from Italy and had sent her an autograph of Voltaire's with a pressed Alpine rose. They were all reminders of the claims he supposed he had on her, none specifically expressed, but all understood – and therefore the more irritating to a girl like Victoria who objected to being reminded of her duty and found importunity detestable. She told Melbourne that Albert was being presumptuous. And she thought him dull and stodgy. Nevertheless, she said, she wanted to marry someone.

Seeing his surprised look she confessed she had changed her mind about marriage. Only a few weeks before she had told him she dreaded the thought of it. Now she realized it was the only way of getting free from her mother – and that she wanted more than anything . . .

More than anything? The first frosts of autumn. Poor Melbourne turned away for a moment. He did not want her to see the pain in his eyes.

Then she also admitted she was more than a little in love with the nineteen-year-old Grand Duke Alexander.

He made light of it, teasing her with spreading her regard equally over the gentlemen of the Grand Duke's suite; especially two of them, M. Pathul and M. d'Adlerberg.

She admitted it, smiled coyly, and said of course, they were good-looking young men, and danced most beautifully, and how enjoyable it was to be with princes and noblemen of her own age.

Of her own age. Another touch of autumn frost, to make Melbourne wince and feel each one of the forty years which separated him from the Grand Duke and his companions.

17

For the moment the matter of marriage was left. It was better so, said the Queen, though she would do as Lord Melbourne asked and write a list of possible suitors whom she might be prepared to consider.

It was never compiled.

Events now crowded together. The Queen's uncle, Prince Ferdinand of Saxe-Coburg, came on a visit to Windsor accompanied by his children Augustus, Victoria and Leopold, and another cousin, Count Alexander Mensdorff.

Victoria was reminded of earlier visits – when her cousins had been lights in the dreary nightscape of her childhood. Sentimentally she lived through those happy days again. She re-developed her sense of family. With a pricked conscience she sent letter after letter to 'dearest Feodore' in Germany, deeply regretting that temporarily they had been out of touch. She made much of her half-brother, Charles, to his surprised amusement. She wrote to her Uncle Leopold and begged him to visit England. He replied, suggesting that Albert and Ernest of Saxe-Coburg should visit her in the late summer. With a smile on her face she handed the letter to Melbourne.

'You wish them to come, Ma'am?' he asked.

'I do,' she said evenly. 'There is no objection at all.'

Pulled about by her emotions, the Queen was inclined to be

fretful. She was often rude to Melbourne. But he would not quarrel with her and, at length, it was brought home to her how much she depended on him. When things went wrong she needed his wisdom.

At Ascot there was a sudden manifestion of her continued unpopularity amongst the aristocracy. Two ladies hissed as her carriage passed the grandstand. A little later she was greeted by cries of 'Mrs Melbourne! Mrs Melbourne!' from all parts of the stand. Then word spread through the country that Lady Flora Hastings was dangerously ill. She had taken to her bed, and lay there, a thin pallid ghost made horrible by her distended stomach. There were those who still believed she was carrying a child. To the vast majority it was clear that she was in the grip of some mortal disease.

In her distress the Queen turned to Melbourne. He hid nothing from her. Though she wanted them flogged, the ladies who had hissed her could not be barred from Court. He warned her that fresh movements were being made by the Hastings family to demand reparations. Sir James Clark's inefficiency had been shown up by his own profession and all he did was busy himself with inventing a method to pump good air into Buckingham Palace while thinking of his hour of glory attending on the dying Keats in Rome. Melbourne strongly advised the Queen to visit Lady Flora on her sickbed. She refused. So Melbourne and Lehzen combined to make her change her mind.

Perhaps it was inevitable that the two who best loved Victoria should have made common cause when she became more and more independent. They never really liked each other. Infinitesimal grains of jealousy prevented it. But they had a high respect for one another, and for Victoria's sake they were prepared to work together. Lehzen was more forthright than Melbourne, telling Victoria that she could never lift her head again if Lady Flora should die before they were reconciled. Melbourne, pretending to be dispassionate, said it would be more prudent to visit Lady Flora. 'It's expected, Ma'am. Not to would offend. It wouldn't do at all.' Victoria was rude to both of them, and then went to see Lady Flora. She was piqued to be told Lady Flora was not well enough to see her that day, and she had to be re-persuaded by her devoted Lehzen and Lord Melbourne. When she did go, she went with the air of a martyr, and rather condescendingly. But afterwards she told them she was glad she had gone, and confided to her journal with a plethora of semi-colons.

I found poor Ly Flora stretched on a couch looking as thin as anybody can be who is still alive; literally a skeleton, but the body *very* much swollen like a person who is with child; a searching look in her eyes, rather like a person who is dying; her voice like usual, a good deal of strength in her hands; she was friendly, said she was very comfortable, & was very grateful for all I had done for her . . .

Ten days later Lady Flora died.

An upsurge of dislike for the Queen made her tremble. The corpse was to be taken by ship to Scotland and buried at Loudon. The Queen sent a carriage to join the cortège to the wharf. It was stoned and plastered with refuse and chunks of filth. Victoria turned to Melbourne as she had done in the past, and he, grateful for what he knew might be his last chance, was her support and strength for many anxious days.

18

Stockmar took to Brussels an excellent report of Albert's stay in Italy. He had studied French, English, practised on organ and piano, walked, played dominoes, talked politics, and had been received by the Pope.

The visit to the Vatican had been a political courtesy because, though interested in theology as an academic study, Albert's religion was informal and incapable of attachment to any known brand of Christianity. He was however by nature and inclination sufficiently protestant to giggle at the old gentleman who sat on St Peter's throne, and sneer at the Holy Week observances as totally absurd. He had not found it necessary or desirable to elude his mentor in virtue. Lieutenant Francis Seymour reported that nothing untoward had occurred.

King Leopold was highly gratified. He was soon to go to Windsor and would then cement the arrangement for the Princes Ernest and Albert to visit Victoria. Meanwhile Stockmar was to instruct Albert in English social life and manners. If he could work in the Lady Flora Hastings affair as a cautionary tale so much the better – though he must not permit the boy to be censorious. He had learnt himself that the one thing the English people cannot abide is a condescending prig.

Albert, unfortunately, did not have time to learn this lesson. His father, the larrikin Duke Ernest, was concerned to hear of his Italian adventures. Virtue had been a rarity in the family since the days of Praying Ernest. Now the Coburgs were a more swashbuckling and passionate lot in the grand tradition of Frederick the Bitten, a duke whose cheek was scarred for life in an explosion of strong affection.

Albert was sent for and closely questioned. His devotion to study was praised, his staidness was not.

He wrote a sober letter to Baron Stockmar to say his father had urged him to be more light-hearted and 'take more trouble about women'. For that reason he was to accompany the old rip to Carlsbad, a seedy watering place where Coburg wild oats had been sown for generations.

19

As the time drew nearer for her cousins to come to England, Victoria's heart sank lower and lower.

On his visit to Windsor at the beginning of September, King Leopold had tried to cope with her fears, assuring her that no one better understood her difficulties. As a Queen Regnant her choice was restricted, and it was natural to fear marriage with a largely unknown person. Nevertheless he could guarantee

Albert's steady application to his studies, and his willingness to take second place, which was always a difficult position for a man. Victoria was grateful for his concern, but she did not find his advice encouraging. He did not seem to realize that she did not want a studious bore. She would happily marry an idiot if she loved him. And she did not want her husband to take second place. In her home he must dominate, though outside her duties as a queen made her his superior.

Lehzen spoke up for the Prince. It was simply because she believed, like Melbourne, that for her own happiness the Queen must marry, and, privately for her own sake, she wanted it done as quickly as possible. The protracted courtship from a distance was a daily torment to her. She longed to get it over. So she helped to forward the suit of the man whose influence would one day replace hers. She reminded Victoria of her high regard, if not love, for Albert over a long period, and reminded her that it had only died down because of the preoccupations of queenship. Hearsay had told against him, too; as had his tedious, prosy letters which were more like philosophical treatises than sparkling declarations of constant affection. The Queen could rely upon her uncle. He would not propose a match which was unsuitable or uncongenial.

Victoria, well aware how much Lehzen dreaded the disruption of their even life together, was impressed by her old friend's generous attitude. It moved her more than any argument. For a time she was encouraged to be more cheerful. She took to consulting her relations about the possibility of marriage. She saw the Duke of Sussex who thoroughly approved of Albert because someone had told him the boy had a scientific bent. She saw the Cambridges. Her uncle was not averse from the match though her aunt, without giving a reason, was less than enthusiastic. Victoria guessed, and rightly that the Duchess had had hopes for her son George. Aunt Gloucester was severely practical. 'Marry him or marry anyone,' she said. 'But don't let it disturb you. Most marriages work well if you take a little trouble.' Aunt Sophia was romantic, as was Aunt Augusta. Neither gave good advice. She did not consult the King of Hanover because she was angry with him for refusing to give up his apartments in St James's. Nor, though she saw her every day, did she mention the matter to her mother.

Day followed day.

The Queen lost her temporary mood of confidence and grew nervous and irritable.

Lehzen watched anxiously. Melbourne watched sadly. He was as much in evidence as ever, talking a deal of good sense when the Queen had the mind to be attentive, and a good deal of nonsense, too, when she needed distracting. Quietly he was trying to accustom himself to standing in the shade.

Leopold wrote regularly from Belgium. He was gentle and tactful with his niece and bore with her impatience. When Albert wrote to tell her he and his brother could not leave on the proposed date, she was highly indignant. She sent a lofty letter to Brussels complaining of their dilatoriness. 'The *retard* of these young people,' she wrote – being herself younger than one, and a bare month older than the other – 'puts me rather out.' Then, when at last they were able to set sail, Albert was so seasick that he felt unwell for days afterwards, and their luggage being temporarily lost, the two Princes had to arrive at Windsor in travel-stained clothes.

Everything, from the start of the arrangements, seemed to have been set against the visit. At heart no one wanted it except King Leopold and Baron Stockmar. Hardly anyone believed that any good could come from it. The signs were against it. It was bound to fail.

20

King Leopold was proved triumphantly right in his private prediction when at a little past seven o'clock in the evening of October 10th, 1839, Prince Ernest and Prince Albert of Saxe-Coburg strode up the grand staircase at Windsor Castle.

The Queen stood at the top waiting to receive them.

Her hands were trembling with nervousness. For a moment they were still. Then they trembled again, but for a different reason. She smiled at both her cousins and she looked politely from one to the other. But she barely saw the elder, Ernest. Albert drew her eyes and almost all her attention. Even though his clothes were travel-stained they were in the highest mode. His shoulders were wide and strong, his waist small and elegant. His soft hair was brushed forward over his ears and his upper lip was neatly decorated with a thin military moustache. His face was pale, but his blue eyes were as large and deep as Victoria remembered them three years before.

Lehzen standing a little to the rear watched the Queen with all the pain and relief of a woman who has just lost an agonizing tooth. Victoria radiated her feelings. Had that pale young man been a degenerate monster instead of an upright, respectable prince, he could have won the Queen's heart. Not for nothing was she her father's daughter and her uncle's niece. She was all Hanoverian at that moment. All.

Victoria could barely contain her happiness. She danced quadrilles with her cousins, noting 'dearest Albert's' exquisite capacity for dancing, and watched him waltzing and galloping, dances which protocol forbade her from enjoying herself. She rode out with her cousins, being next to 'dearest Albert' and Lord Melbourne. She admired Eos the greyhound who, because he was 'dearest Albert's' greyhound, even had his yawns recorded in her journal.

On the third day of the visit she talked privately and obliquely with her Prime Minister. She thought she was changing her mind about marrying, she said, but did not want to be hurried into a decision. Melbourne knew precisely what this meant; that she had already decided but wanted advice on how soon propriety would allow her to make an offer. He replied in the same way. If the Princes were to stay a week or more, she would find it easier to come to a decision. Her question answered, she dwelt on Albert's merits. Was he not beautiful and amiable and deeply religious, she asked; and Lord Melbourne, his throat tight, had to agree with the first two, though he confessed he did not know the Prince sufficiently well to be sure of the third. However, if he was a strong Protestant he was bound to be popular in the kingdom; that is, he added hastily, if he was not bigoted. With equal haste the Queen assured him that Prince Albert was not.

After dinner that evening Lord Melbourne sat on a chair next to the Queen's sofa. Beside her was Prince Albert. The boy looked as if he wanted to go to sleep. Melbourne wished he could sleep himself. Often he had had the greatest difficulty in keeping awake after dinner at Court, but the Queen had never rebuked him, even when he fell asleep. But now, when he wanted to close his eyes to shut out the picture before him, he could not. He was wide awake. He had to watch.

Victoria could not wait a week. The very next day she sent once more for Melbourne and told him she had made up her mind. He congratulated her. She said she thought the marriage ought to wait for a year – hoping that he would disagree. Dutifully he did. A year was much too long. Parliament would have to be assembled to vote the Prince an income – and until that time it would be wiser to keep the matter quiet. King Leopold would have to know, and King Ernest of Hanover as heir to the English Crown. Otherwise it was better kept a secret for a time. They discussed what should be done for Prince Albert, and Melbourne promised to find out about precedents. Prince George of Denmark, Queen Anne's husband, would be the person to look up.

As he sat there, calmly agreeing that the Prince should be made a Royal Highness and a Field Marshal, and perhaps a Peer of the United Kingdom, Victoria suddenly noticed the lines at the sides of his eyes. He had not been sleeping. For the first time in many weeks she closely studied him, and she was filled with concern. She was so much in love that she wanted to share her happiness, and especially with dear Lord Melbourne, but with a sure instinct she knew that he could not do this. Nor could she expect it.

Not quite knowing how to express herself she stood up and took his hands.

He looked at her in astonishment, and made as if to struggle to his feet. But by the pressure of her fingers she kept him in his seat.

'Lord Melbourne, you have been so kind to me,' she said. 'And I have often been thoughtless and ungrateful.'

'Ma'am,' he said, tears welling to his eyes. 'There is no need ... I am ever your servant ...'

'You have been so careful for me,' she insisted. 'Patient and understanding. I can only guess at the sacrifices you have made on my behalf.'

He resisted the pressure of her fingers and stood up. He kissed her hand.

'You have been so fatherly,' she said. 'So wonderfully fatherly.'

And she left him.

Melbourne looked at the door through which she had passed. He mopped up his tears with a handkerchief and he smiled. With one neat word she had tilted their two-year relationship on to another plane. Clever, astute girl.

Prince Albert loved hunting and sat his horse like an Apollo. Twenty-four hours after the Queen's talk with her Prime Minister, the two Princes returned early from the hunt and put their horses at the hill up to the Windsor Mound. They thundered up, coat tails flying, unaware that the Queen was watching them from a window. She caught her breath. How beautiful he was! Later that same day she wrote in her journal:

At about $\frac{1}{2}$ p 12 I sent for Albert; he came to the Closet where I was alone, and after a few minutes I said to him, that I thought he must be aware *why* I wished them to come here, – and that it would make me *too happy* if he would consent to what I wished (to marry me). We embraced each other, and he was *so* kind, *so* affectionate.

21

Prince Ernest was as jovial as Albert was serious. He congratulated him on his engagement as though he had hooked a fine salmon. Albert thanked his brother and was not in the

245

least put out by his manner. He had been brought up for Victoria just as Ernest had been brought up for the ducal throne of Saxe-Coburg, and there had always been a chance that, in the end, she might not ask for his hand. Now she had, and he was suitably gratified.

He told Ernest that he had been agreeably surprised at Victoria's fervour and that it was touching and a little frightening to be the target of so much devotion. He thought it would not be difficult to love her in return. In order to get to know her better he had consented to stay on in England for a few weeks. If the rumours of her flightiness and obstinacy were true he would then have the chance to correct these faults. The former could be eradicated by a steady application to serious matters, the latter most easily broken by teaching her obedience.

'Don't play your fish too fancifully,' warned his brother, 'or you might not land her.'

It was friendly advice but unnecessary. Victoria was already Albert's, body and soul. She saw a great deal of him and made no protests that she was bored or muddled when he strove to toughen her character with chess and lessons in diplomacy. Moreover as long as he was beside her, it seldom occurred to her to question his authority or the quality of his advice. On two matters, though, she maintained her independence. She would not allow him to enter the discussions with regard to his honours and income after their marriage because in theory at any rate, these gifts were from her. Nor would she permit him to include her mother in those few persons who knew of the engagement before it was made public. He remarked that it was peculiar to say the least. Her mother ought to have been the first person to know. But she was adamant. Her mother, she said, was a great blabber and might make use of the secret for her own malicious ends.

It followed that, when towards the end of November Victoria announced her engagement to her Council, the Duchess of Kent was in tears and full of bitter reproaches.

Without seeking an audience she tried to enter the Queen's apartments and was barred. The disgraceful noise she made reached Lehzen's ears and she begged the Queen to receive her mother. Reluctantly Victoria agreed. Albert who was with her bowed to take his leave. 'No,' she said. 'Remain; please.'

The Duchess was unaccompanied. Her dress was dishevelled, her cheeks scored with tear-stains.

'Mamma,' said Victoria coldly. 'What are your ladies doing to let you wander the Castle by yourself?'

The Duchess paid no attention to the rebuke. Instead she rebuked her daughter and, for good measure, her nephew Albert. Like a prophetess she pointed to them both and swore they deserved to be as wretched as they had made her.

The Queen was frankly terrified. When the Duchess had gone she threw herself into Lehzen's arms declaring they were cursed. Lehzen pooh-poohed the whole thing, and called upon Prince Albert to reassure Victoria. To her dismay he refused. Instead he changed the subject.

He was assiduous in his attention to Victoria and charming as ever to her closest friend the Baroness; but he did not forget the picture of his aunt, her finger outstretched, wishing unhappiness upon them. He was a rationalist. He was a scientist and a philosopher. Yet he came from the German uplands where an overzealous Protestantism made the people superstitious and credulous believers in sorcery and vampirism. He could not bring himself to believe that the Duchess of Kent had cursed them both, yet later he acknowledged that from that moment their happiness was limited and they were harassed by a series of unfortunate happenings.

He wrote a gloomy letter to his stepmother on the announcement of the engagement:

My future position will have its dark sides and the sky will not always be blue and unclouded.

At the same time he wrote to a close friend:

My future lot is high and brilliant, but also plentifully strewn with thorns.

22

King Leopold was in a frenzy of excitement.

'They have precedents,' he told Stockmar. 'Why do they not keep to them?'

Stockmar made every effort to calm his master. He had brought the unwelcome news that Prince Albert had been voted £20,000 less a year than Melbourne had asked for. George of Denmark, consort to Queen Anne, had been given £50,000 a year in 1683. Prince Albert was to receive £30,000.

'It is a slap in the face,' said Leopold, striding up and down the room. 'Worse than denying him precedence, though Victoria asked for it above her uncles and even above herself. It is designed to keep him to his place.'

'The Queen is herself an exceedingly rich woman by inheritance,' the Baron pointed out. 'They will always have sufficient.'

It was not often that Leopold was critical of his mentor, but now he told him there was a world of difference between an ordinary married pair and the Queen of England and her consort. There should be no question of having sufficient and managing. In their position they should have far more than enough.

'It is that King of Hanover,' he burst out. 'Victoria's heir with the large moustaches. He and his Tory followers have taken every opportunity to make difficulties.' He stopped, sat at his desk, and sorted through a packet of letters. 'There was Albert's religion,' he shouted, throwing a letter down. 'Doubting his Protestantism simply because my brother and I have become Catholics ... then the flat refusal to make him King-Consort, or even a peer.' He threw the whole packet down. 'All, all they will give him is naturalization, and £30,000 a year. It is monstrous.'

Stockmar decided it was prudent to let him run on. At the

back of Leopold's anger was pique at Victoria's neglect. Beyond thanking him for Albert – as though the Prince had been sold in a market – she had been writing less and less. Stockmar had no doubt he would regain part of his influence, and would always be a valued adviser to Victoria, but she was too busy at present, preparing for her wedding and doing battle with Parliament on Albert's behalf, to give much attention to her uncle.

23

Albert was solemnly attending to the death and burial of his youth and freedom. That, at the age of twenty, was how he regarded marriage in a foreign land. He made sentimental journeys to places which once had had a special importance for him; to the stork nests at Rosenau, to the picnic clearings in the woods where the family had breakfasted in summertime, to his old schoolroom and nursery, to secret hiding places in the table lofts and kennels at Coburg Castle.

Deliberately, it seemed, he was heightening his natural tendency to be despondent. Then he was cast down by the news from England. He became gloomier and gloomier as the days passed and the posts brought little but bad news. Victoria's subjects were clearly unsympathetic to the match. She herself was strangely insensitive to his hurt male vanity. When they had been together at Windsor she had not questioned his authority. Now she and Melbourne were making the decisions and few were to his liking. He felt keenly his humiliating position as a professional husband, but he generally held his tongue and his pen. It was only when Victoria suggested Lord Melbourne's secretary should be his own confidential secretary that he made a protest.

I give you to consider, dearest love, if my taking the secretary of the Prime Minister as Treasurer would not from the beginning make me a partisan in the eyes of many.

He added that all the gentlemen of his household should be

either of very high rank, or very rich, or very clever, or persons who have performed important services for England.

In the event he was given Melbourne's secretary, willy nilly. The Queen adored him but was not averse from rapping his knuckles.

I am distressed to tell you what I fear you do not like, but it is necessary, my dearest, most excellent Albert.

She was biting when he suggested they spend longer than two or three days on their honeymoon at Windsor.

You forget, my dearest Love, that I am the Sovereign and that business can stop and wait for nothing.

Albert sought the advice of their mutual grandmother, the old Duchess who had planned the match twenty years before. He said he was willing to accept an inferior position as consort to a reigning queen, but was he to tolerate these constant humiliations? Could he speak out? Ought he to?

Wisely the old lady flattered him. Victoria needed him, she said. His sound judgement, his learning, his grasp of affairs most of all his high moral code would be of inestimable use in England where the old ruling classes were blaspheming foxchasers and port-swillers. When he could bring his good influence to bear on Victoria she would be less intractable and less inclined to be domineering. Until then he had to be patient, and understand that to her also this was a trying time. She was having to face a hostile political party and press whipped up by her wicked uncle, Ernest of Hanover.

Albert accepted her advice to be patient and let things ride for the present. He realized he had to. He was in a vice from which there was no escape. He tried to make the best of things, but it seemed as if an avenging shade was bent on destroying his peace of mind. Often he thought of his aunt the Duchess of Kent, and as a precaution, an insurance against fate, rather than out of affection, he opened a correspondence with her. He wrote her reassuring letters which implied that after February 11th, on which happy day he would become her son-in-law, all would be well between her and Victoria. He sent her keepsakes too. And she responded with surprise and with affection. But his low spirits did not lift. He took pleasure in less and less, disliking the Court balls arranged for him by his father and the military reviews and night tattoos given in his honour. Things went wrong again and again. Even when Victoria sent him the Order of the Garter by two of her gentlemen, it came so late that malicious neighbours had already started the rumour that he was not to be honoured with the blue ribbon at all. Finally, at a banquet, when his father called a toast to the Queen of England and 101 cannons saluted from outside, a muslin curtain, billowing above the banqueting table, caught alight from a candle sconce and alarmed everyone present. It was regarded as a singularly ill omen.

The Dowager Duchess of Saxe-Coburg had not overestimated the difficulties Victoria had to face in the weeks before her marriage.

Parliament behaved boorishly in denying the Prince an income set by precedent. And the Tory press went out of its way to express the people's dislike of foreigners in general and petty German princelings in particular. King Ernest was reported to have called Prince Albert 'a paper Royal Highness', a phrase which was seized on by political pamphleteers and cartoonists.

Melbourne did his best for Victoria. He hid from her the worst excesses of the campaign against her, the distribution of ribald ballads throughout the kingdom which described in obscene detail her liking for venery and ridiculed her love for Albert. To soften Parliament's insult he suggested that perhaps it was unwise for the Prince to be given a large income when lean times were ahead for the people. His own view that the Reform Bill would be a panacea for no one except the industrial nabobs and trading middle-classes had proved sadly accurate. There was unemployment and real want amongst the poor. For this reason he said it might be as well to accept a reduction in

Prince Albert's income. The Queen was unpersuaded. She saw only what she wished to see, and, so far as she was concerned, the 'mob' was now to receive £20,000 a year which by right belonged to her beloved Albert. This, she told Melbourne, made her loathe the mob as much as she loathed the Tory party.

He persevered. Because he loved her he went on trying to reason with Victoria until the day she told him she had decided the wedding should be held in a room at the palace so that Wellington and every single hated Tory could be excluded from the ceremony. She had also decided not to appear at church on the Sunday before her wedding because she did not like being stared at. And she had made up her mind that Albert should stay at the palace before the wedding because the English custom of separating bride and groom was foolish nonsense.

Melbourne was dumbfounded, and when he found his tongue and was opening his mouth to protest, the Queen cut in again. Albert, she said, had proposed that no one should be invited to act as bridesmaid who had a dubious past. Finally she peppered all this by scolding him for not looking after her interests with sufficient energy, and demanding for the tenth or eleventh time that Albert be made King Consort.

The normally placid, easy-going Melbourne was at last out of patience. He reminded the Queen of their positions, of hers as a constitutional sovereign with very limited rights and a great number of duties, of his as her adviser and the holder of real power. She could, of course, choose her bridesmaids in any fashion she liked, but it was cant and un-English to exclude girls for the reason she had given. It was also inadvisable for the Queen of England to scorn publicly the time-honoured customs of the English. If she wished she could hide herself away from the gaze of her people but this would neither increase her dignity nor recoup the popularity she had already lost. Furthermore, if she considered him unenergetic and idle in his duties he hoped she would dismiss him without delay, but as long as he was her First Minister it was his duty to advise her that excluding all Tories from her wedding, and in particular the hero of Waterloo and great friend to her family, would be a disastrous thing to do.

'As for this King-Consort idea, Ma'am,' he finished strenuously. 'For God's sake, let's hear no more of it. No more of it, Ma'am. For once you get the English people into the way of making kings, you will get them into the way of unmaking them.'

She was white-faced and looked, as he thought, exceedingly angry. He prepared to be stern and hold his ground. But in fact she was aghast at having driven her amiable Prime Minister to such straits. She accused herself to him, and afterwards to Lehzen, of giving way to her moods and fancies and hating the people she loved. It was a habit, she explained bitterly, which she had learnt too well in her childhood.

He would accept no apology, realizing, he said, that she was living under some strain at present. 'It was my duty to advise, Ma'am, a duty I shall carry out as long as you wish me to serve the throne.'

Victoria had a wise head on her young shoulders. She hurried past this difficult emotional moment by returning at once to business. She accepted his advice on all points except two. She really would prefer, she said, to stay indoors on the Sunday before her marriage, and she wanted Albert to go direct to Buckingham Palace. As he had won the important points Melbourne at once gave way. Then, together, they discussed the perennial problem: the Duchess of Kent. She was refusing to dine at the Queen's table for two reasons: because she was not to be given precedence over George III's daughters at the wedding, and because she had been ordered to move into a separate establishment after the Queen's return from her honeymoon.

24

The Tory press's hostility to the Queen's match and her continued unpopularity with the governing classes did not prevent the majority of her people using the royal wedding as an excuse for a junket.

There were jollifications at Dover where Prince Albert arrived accompanied by his father and brother. His face was biscuit-coloured and he was so dizzy after the rough crossing that he neither knew nor cared where he was or what he was doing; but he much improved while the cavalcade was being put together, four travelling-carriages, two britzkas and a pair of fourgons. There was no denying the warmth of the people's welcome and they had taken the trouble to come out in the cold and rain. It was a demonstration which much relieved him. He had expected worse.

There was jollification at places on the route to London despite the fact that it began to pour with rain, and in the capital cheering crowds lined the streets to Buckingham Palace.

There was jollification at Windsor where Lehzen had gone to make arrangements for the honeymoon. But there were also jollifications in other parts of the kingdom where up to that time little interest had been shown in the sovereign. A brand new device, called the penny post, which used a stamp of the Queen's profile, ensured that her portrait was spread rapidly all over the British Isles. Those who associated royalty with the bloated Hanoverians and who, from all they'd heard of the goings-on at Court, had come to the conclusion Victoria was much the same, were surprised and delighted to see that they had a queen who was a robust and fresh-looking young girl. She appealed to the romantics and won their hearts from the penny stamp. They loved the idea of her marrying a handsome young prince even though he was a foreigner.

Almost at the last moment Victoria panicked. Worry, late hours, picking at her food rather than eating, and then a sudden feverish head cold which put her to bed for two days all cast her down. In her agitation she wondered if she was doing the right thing. Was Albert the right husband for a queen of England? Could she not stay unmarried as Queen Elizabeth had done?

Lehzen gave her a soothing draught and sent for the Prime Minister. 'Lord Melbourne,' she said. 'The Queen is kicking against it. Her nerves are ragged. She is brittle. Only you, I think, my lord, can persuade her that she is taking the right course.'

Melbourne bowed to the Baroness. He promised to do all he could.

Victoria relaxed a little when she saw him. But she insisted that, since Albert's arrival at the palace, he had been distrait and agitated. It was a bad, sad portent.

Melbourne would not hear of it. What was more natural, he asked, than for a young man in a foreign country to be nervous before his marriage? 'I think, Ma'am, that you'll wish to be patient with the Prince and help him all you can. He will feel strange amongst us otherwise. As to marriage itself ...' He spread his hands. 'Why, it's in human nature. It's natural to marry.'

Softly, skilfully he moved her out of her jaded low spirits – aware all the time that he was giving himself his own *congé* – until she was calm again and could talk unexcitably of the wedding which lay ahead.

Prince Albert received a letter from the Queen on the morning of their marriage. She merely commented on the rain which was sleeting against the palace windows, and said she hoped he had slept well. She concluded:

*Send one word when you, my most dearly loved bridegroom,
will be ready.*

Thy ever-faithful
Victoria R

It was not a particularly encouraging document. Albert's depression was acute. He visited Ernest, who was more interested in a mangy spot on their greyhound's fur than in his brother's pre-marital anxieties. Therefore Albert took the unusual step of consulting his father, and instantly regretted it. The swash-buckling Duke Ernest shouted with laughter and made a remark so bawdy and offensive to Albert's modesty that he flushed red to the lobes of his ears. He returned to his apartments and stood moodily beside a window.

Outside in the pouring rain the Londoners were gathering. Some were perched in the trees, others were sitting astride the fences. Most were huddled under umbrellas. A few were already drunk. One was singing a popular ballad at the top of his voice:

> 'She's all my Lehzen painted her,
> She's lovely, she is rich,
> But they tell me when I marry her
> That she will wear the britsch.'

With a sharp exclamation of annoyance the Prince left the window and went to his desk. There he wrote to the one person he believed understood the difficulties of his position, his grandmother in Coburg:

> In less than three hours I shall stand in front of the altar with my dear bride! In these solemn moments I must once more ask your blessing, which I am sure I shall receive, and which will be my safeguard and my future joy! I must end. God help me!

25

Those with tickets of admission to the Chapel Royal in St James's were hardly representative of the English people. No one who had seriously crossed the Queen at any point in her reign was present. Critics of the Prince were rigorously excluded. Of the whole Tory party only the Duke and Lord Liverpool were there — a situation which Wellington remarked reflected more disgrace on the Queen than on his party. Nevertheless his heart warmed towards her in the solemnity of the occasion. The Duke loved royal ceremonies, the more exaggerated the better, and he alone in the congregation did not doubt the taste of 'See the Conquering Hero Comes' being played as Prince Albert walked up the aisle. Resplendent in the scarlet uniform of a British Field Marshal and supported by his father and brother, the Prince looked handsomer than ever. With his strong historic sense Wellington could see that this marriage was a very important event.

Stockmar was there. He had come at the Queen's express invitation, not only to represent her Uncle Leopold who was now back in high favour, but also as her own mentor and Albert's in the peculiarly difficult art of ruling. Unlike the majority of guests he was dressed in unrelieved black.

The English royal family was almost complete. The King of Hanover, refusing to give precedence to Prince Albert, had stayed away. His sisters the Princesses Augusta, Sophia and Mary were by the altar rail to weep as women will at weddings and allow the guests to make the strong contrast between their massive maturity and the Queen's fresh youth. The Duke of Cambridge was burbling to himself, unaware because of the eclipse of his hearing that he was at all audible. His Duchess plucked at his sleeve occasionally to remind him, but he lived in the ghostly world of deaf people, and made loud remarks throughout the ceremony. Fortunately they were cheerful and not scurrilous. The Duke of Sussex was also in high spirits. In return for giving Prince Albert precedence over him, the Queen had recognized Lady Cecilia — not of course as his official wife but as his morganatic wife and Duchess of Inverness in her own right. He thought Albert the handsomest of bucks and said so, and was delighted to give Victoria away. Despite the fact that he was in full military uniform and they were in a consecrated building he wore his black skullcap in case of draughts.

The guests were gratified to see the Queen's mother in tears because that was as it should be. But they were not a mother's ordinary tears on such an occasion. The Duchess wept because her punishment was still continuing. That morning Victoria had kissed her aunts but not her mother. They had exchanged gifts as was customary, but without a word. After today the Duchess would have to live apart. Her only hope was that Albert would soften the girl's heart. She believed and hoped and prayed fervently that he would. Otherwise her unhappiness would go on and on and never end.

Lehzen kept her eyes down through the ceremony. Finding it so difficult to dwell on the present, she took refuge in the past and dreamed of the time when her beloved Victoria had

257

been at the centre of her existence. What pains change brought, how much was wrecked and remedied by time; the dainty Feodore now a fat German Duchess, old Späth exiled, Mr Davys now a bishop, Conroy away in exile, Flora Hastings in her tomb at Loudon. She looked up once or twice but then down again quickly. She would not show her eyes swimming with tears. It was a point of pride with her. Quite unnecessary. A self-inflicted punishment. No one anyway, she thought, would take notice of old Madame Caraway. She bruised herself with this hateful name from the past and kept her eyes down.

She was mistaken. More than once Melbourne regarded her. He had a great well of pity for the Baroness. From what he suffered himself he guessed at her pain. He, too, found it difficult to look at what was happening at the altar rail and he practised every sort of device to concentrate on other things. He was carrying the sword of state as he had done at Victoria's coronation. Now he studied it minutely, its cutting edge and its decoration, the pommel and cross-guard. That done he deliberately turned his mind to Brocket, to the plum trees his gardener had marked for grafting, and a set of books sent down from London to be read there when he had the leisure. He thought of affairs of state – of his brother-in-law's Opium War against the Chinese Emperor and the corruption in Hong Kong, of Louis Napoleon's threats to the security of France, of the beginnings of a British Empire in Canada and New Zealand. He thought of Mrs Norton, his dearest Caroline who he knew would prepare his supper that evening, choosing his favourite foods and wine, prepared and happy to soothe and console. He thought of everything he could to take his mind from the altar rail where the love of his old age was being given to another man.

Victoria said her replies in a clear voice and so did Albert.

Hardly anyone there knew that few couples have gone to the altar with so strong and uneasy a suspicion that they were making a mistake. But few couples have left an altar, cemented together for better or worse, with so complete a conviction that all would be well.

And their conviction was right.

The immediate and continued success of the marriage was a sign to Victoria the romantic that the best alliances are heaven-made. To Albert the realist it was proof of the value of discipline in marriage. To Stockmar it demonstrated the importance of thorough and careful selection and preparation. To Melbourne the cynic it was an object lesson in relying on luck.

As they walked from the chapel to cheers and the fanfares of trumpets the Queen of England had already shed all connection with her past – with her dingy girlhood at Kensington and the success and mistakes of her first years as Queen.

Now and for ever she was Albert's Victoria.

Elizabeth Longford

VICTORIA R.I.   £1

'A wonderfully vivid portrait built up with skill from massive research and presented with a beguiling artistry' – LIFE

'Easily the best life of Victoria that has yet appeared' – NEW YORK TIMES

'It is hard to imagine how Elizabeth Longford's detailed and vivid volume could have been bettered . . . Her book is scholarly yet racily readable, witty yet wise' – SUNDAY TIMES

'Nearly two generations have elapsed since Queen Victoria died, and yet this is the first complete and authoritative biography . . . She has done a first-class piece of work . . . A most admirable biography' Sir Charles Petrie, ILLUSTRATED LONDON NEWS

Andrew Duncan

THE REALITY OF MONARCHY   45p

'I often thought they were the most dreary family in British public life. Not so at all. In their private life, closely observed, they are amazing – this book has you roaring in the aisles, as they say, having to hold yourself together. It is so funny and unbelievable and has never been told to us before ... Monarchy can never be the same again.

'It's lack of gooey indulgence will be welcomed by some and enjoyed by many' – EVENING NEWS

'A serious work but enlivened with the most touching human and humorous stories' – THE TIMES

Susan Howatch

Susan Howatch 'knows how to spin a colourful story' – WOMAN'S JOURNAL

PENMARRIC   50p

The magnificent bestseller of the passionate loves and hatreds of a Cornish family.

'Grippingly readable' – SUNDAY TIMES

'A fascinating saga . . . has all the right dramatic and romantic ingredients' – WOMAN'S JOURNAL

Susan Howatch wrote six compulsive stories before she wrote *Penmarric*. Here are four of them and the other two will be published in due course.

CALL IN THE NIGHT   30p
THE WAITING SANDS   30p
THE SHROUDED WALLS   30p
THE DARK SHORE   30p